Unspe

CW00525027

Dear ...,

HAPPY BIRTHDAY !

Wishing you everything that Brings Joy in life.

Best Wishes

Christopher Fordham.

Unspeakable Things

When the past comes back to bite you.

By Christopher Fordham

For Charlotte

Cinderella, dressed in yella
Went upstairs to kiss a fella
Made a mistake
Kissed a snake
How many doctors did it take?

Friday, 9th June 1979

Prologue

Savannah, Georgia. USA

A tall, heavy-set man in dirty overalls poured himself a stale coffee and sat down on the worn customer bench outside *Grand Ignitions Automotive Repairs*. It was set about half-a-mile out beyond the 7-Eleven at Needle Brook and was one of those small, road-side repair shops that was good for oil changes and exhaust repairs, adjustments to brakes or a bit of spot-welding to a leaky floorplan. In the garage was a lone hydraulic car-lift with an old Ford pick-up raised up high; out front was a stack of slow-rotting tyres. The shop windows were brown with dirt and everywhere was covered with a thin film of grease. As the man drank his coffee, he thumbed through a well-fingered copy of *Playboy* magazine.

The mechanic worked alone, mostly - Scott Hardie, the owner of *Grand Ignitions,* would stop by occasionally to check the register and to take the cash but had not worked in the yard since throwing his back out over a year ago - and that suited Vance just fine. He didn't like anyone checking over his shoulder or calling his time, he worked best when left to his own devices – besides, he worked hard, never complained and rarely thieved: as such, he was seldom out of work.

He sucked in the heat of the afternoon and took another swig of coffee. There were no paying customers today and the pick-up on the car-lift was his own. He had spent the morning tinkering with the suspension –Vance kept it purring along just as fine as the day it had rolled off the production line. Its sit-up-high cabin and sweep-over front wheel arches gave it a purposeful and muscled look; there was enough chrome to mean business and a cargo area big enough to carry a cow. He loved this lime-green monster as much as he did his girls, and if he were to tot up the hours that he spent cleaning, polishing and tweaking it, the pick-up could argue that it saw more love and attention than the twins did.

Another slug of coffee and he leaned back against the hard wood of the bench, stretching his long legs out in front of him. He glanced at his watch: 4.15pm. Yep, that pick-up sure had its uses.

His days usually ran with little routine - work started at 7.30am and he kept on going until all the jobs were done, or the sun set – whichever came sooner. But in the last couple of weeks he had taken to giving himself a break at just this time of the afternoon. He had very few pleasures in life; he did not drink, nor did he gamble. He did not blow his money away on women or indulge himself on anything except spares for the Ford. He looked after his two little girls (as best he could), and sometimes – well, occasionally - took them to church on Sunday. He worked every day of the week and didn't bitch about it. He reckoned he owed himself this little pleasure and didn't beat himself up about it too much – far as he was concerned it was one he deserved. Besides, this regular afternoon break was a relatively new thing and he saw it as payback for the toil he put in day in, day out. He put his hand inside his overalls and began to jerk off.

In the heat of the afternoon there was no one around to see this - and should anyone drive by they wouldn't see anything but a greased-up mechanic with his hand in his pants anyhow. He was hardly making a show of it, he justified. And besides, it felt good, and that was all that really mattered. His eyes were closed but his ears were open; he entertained himself whilst he waited for the show to begin.

You could pretty much set your clock to the bus and it came around the corner just after quarter-past the hour. This far out of town was the last stop – and the big yellow coach would trundle off to the depot once the last couple of students were off. Vance opened his eyes as soon as he heard the distinctive growl of the engine, (a fleeting thought sprung into his mind as to how he could make that engine purr like a pussycat, given a day or two…) Then his attention was back again, he was getting close to the business end of his work-out and everything was in the timing. He tightened his grip and quickened his pace.

The bus stopped just up the road from *Grand Ignitions.* Where he was sat in the shade of the lean-to Vance was pretty much obscured from sight, his dark skin and overalls provided perfect camouflage against the dusty tyres and junk of the yard. Shit, what a perfect time he had had of it these past few weeks! Any moment now and one of the prettiest girls would come off that bus, *wigglin' and a-gigglin',* and finish Vance off in an explosion so big he'd near blow a hole through his goddam demins.

He remembered back to the first time he had spotted her. A school bus had pulled up, and from it came one of the most delightful girls he had ever seen. She was high school, he figured; old enough, just about. And damn, she was pretty – young and fresh and just his type. He watched her walk a full forty yards from the bus-stop, across the yard, and out of sight down the road towards home – wherever that might be…

From then on, and so long as Hardie was doubled-up with his crooked back somewhere else, 4.15pm was break time for Vance. Wack time. Slap-the-salami, choke-the-chicken - all awhile watching that pretty girl walk on by.

This afternoon Vance was building up a right sweat. It was a real hot one, the mercury was probably touching a hundred degrees. He heard the clatter of the bus door open and felt himself ready to burst – he waited expectantly, on the edge, for his girl to step off… and then there she came!

She *was* a pretty kid, possessing an easy beauty that was at once fresh and honest and care-free. In a few short years she would blossom into an attractive woman - but now, she tripped along with the last ebbs of childhood slung over her shoulder along with her bookbag and pencil cases. She waved to the driver - who waved back, then threw the bus into gear and pulled away. Within a moment, Vance and the girl were the only two people within a square quarter mile.

Vance was hit by an intensity that gripped him by the throat, almost choking him with pleasure. *Fuck she was beautiful!* He had waited all day for this moment – these briefest of seconds – and today she was utterly radiant. She was dressed in the tightest of shorts and a sleeveless tee so thin that it made Vance shudder. He watched her walk; watched her long, tanned legs; watched her swing her hips and flick her dark hair off her shoulders.

Suddenly he was done. He exhaled hard and a touch too loud, releasing his grip and twitching uncontrollably as the girl walked past barely fifteen feet across the yard from him.

She heard something, a gasp she thought, and stopped mid step and looked over.

Vance froze; this was a first. This was not what usually happened. She was meant to carry on walking past, walk on home and not see him - leave him to clean himself up in the restroom out the back. Not turn around. Never turn around!

'What are you doing there, mister?' she called out, innocently.

Vance managed a scant *wassat?* in reply. He felt like he was a boy again, like the time his mom had caught him gazing over the underwear pages in the Sears catalogue. *You Dirty Boy! Whatchu doin? You Dirty Filthy Boy!* He felt his cheeks flush, and anger and resentment rise uncontrollably inside.

'I said, what are you doing there?' she asked again.

He heard the same accusatory tone that his mother had had. She took a few steps towards him, not sensing the danger she was in.

Vance staggered to his feet. The next few seconds happened in a whirlwind.

As it dawned on her what he had been playing at, her hand went straight to her mouth in shock - then uncontrollably she let out a slight scream. Vance rushed forward, reaching out first to try and gesture, *shut-up girl!* then to try and stop her – *stop the damn noise!* She turned swiftly to run but slipped on the dusty forecourt and fell. Vance grabbed her by the ankle, pulled her towards him and lifted her up - cupping his massive hand over her mouth. She struggled hard; desperate to scream through his fingers, trying to catch her breath. He dragged her into the garage, one massive arm wrapped around her tiny torso. She bit, and scratched, and pulled, all the while trying to yell into his hand – a hand that felt so big it seemed to grip her entire life. She kicked his shins with her heels and elbowed his ribs.

As he dragged her, kicking and writhing, Vance couldn't help but think how small she felt, like he was wrestling with a wriggling puppy. She had managed to draw blood when she bit his hand, but the rest of it he had hardly felt. Now in the garage and out of sight of the highway he felt safer and in control; he loosened his grip, not to let her go, but to see if she would calm a touch and stop her struggling. And momentarily she did, enough for Vance to catch his first up-close look into her beautiful, stubborn eyes. For a moment they looked at each other – and Vance believed she was going to behave. He took his hand from her mouth, but she screamed, and he had to punch her hard to shut her the fuck up.

Wednesday, 8th July 2015

Chapter 1

Early Evening.

In summer, the heat builds in Savannah Georgia like a grill set to slow burn. When the sky is clear it is sometimes a dry heat, but when the clouds roll in you may as well be sat in a vegetable steamer. That evening, when Kristen Engelmaier heard her husband's car pull onto the driveway, the heat of the day had cooked up a storm over the Atlantic that drew in like a lumbering hippo. Deep, heavy clouds rose into the stratosphere and thunder rumbled beyond the Savannah River in low groans; purple lightning licked the darkness and the air hung sticky and thick.

Kristen sat out on the rear deck of 23 Wellyvan Street, the beaten-up suburban place she shared with her husband Bradley for the past two-and-a-bit decades. Somehow, she looked too thin and fragile for her fifty-something years – all pale skin, and greying hair falling limp to her shoulders. Maybe it was the drugs, or, perhaps, the alcohol that had ravaged her looks and demeanour so unkindly. Even her eyes were dull.

She had a decision to make.

She paid little regard to the thunder or to the few heavy drops of rain that were now starting to fall. Her mind was full – racing uncontrollably with a thousand dark thoughts - and her heart felt empty and hollow; she had no control over the emotions that swept through her body. Hate and desperation, self-pity and self-loathing – an endless wash of numb pain. She had a gun in her right hand that she nursed in her lap. It felt heavy and solid. It was her husband's – but she had learned how to fire it; Bradley had taken her down the range to teach her – just in-case she ever disturbed an intruder or got caught in a convenience store robbery. She sniffed, then sighed involuntarily, gazing at the weapon – she knew it gave her one definitive way out; a way to turn the light off for good, to wipe away her scars and blow away in a splatter of brains her shit life – it was as much as she deserved, she knew that for sure. A bullet to the head would also be much quicker and final than her go-to mix of red wine and oxycontin.

She gazed momentarily around the yard then raised the gun and placed it in her mouth – her tongue zinged with its familiar sharp and metallic taste. She took the pressure of the trigger under her index finger. She thought of the boys – *how many had there been in total? Half a dozen? A couple more maybe? All those unspeakable things.* Her trigger-finger began to squeeze – any moment would come a dazzling, incandescent flash of brilliant light – followed by darkness, and deathly peace.

She drew breathe to calm her quickening pulse.

But then - typically - she thought of Bradley, and her confidence drained away and anger suddenly bubbled to the fore. *The fucking asshole* she thought. She took the gun from her mouth and shook her head with a slight sense of disappointment that she had allowed him once again to invade her thoughts and stop her from finishing the job. She sat silent for a moment then pulled an oxycontin from her back pocket and popped one of those instead. Once, these had been prescription – but now her dealer provided a regular supply. She stood up, then walked out into the yard where the rain was now fall in heavy, leaden drops. She had made her peace with dying years ago; it held no fear for her – and it would come soon enough. *This was not the right decision. She could not pull the trigger on herself yet.*

As the thunder cracked again, she heard his car pull up onto the driveway. She tucked the gun into the waistband of her jeans and headed back into the kitchen.

Chapter 2

Bradley was a big guy pushing into his fifties: he weighed over 200lbs, carried a spare-tyre good enough for a heart-attack and was the sort of man who could step out of a shower and still smell greasy. He was short on words, less on education, and today suffered a hangover that made his head pound, and his hands shake. He thumped his battered chevy onto the concrete driveway then slicked back his thinning hair; he knew for sure that Kristen was going to make this a fucking evening and a half.

Throughout the day he had rehearsed what he was going to say. He was pig-headed but knew he was in the wrong; fuck, it didn't take a genius to realise that you do some dumb shit when you're completely tanked. But in fairness, he reasoned, Kristen was as much to blame for last night as he was. He knew too that she was bat-shit crazy, but she'd be reasonable - *right?* Bradley hoped that the next hour or two would follow their usual pattern: *Row. Fight. Forgive. Forget.*

He parked up, pulled his clip-on tie from his collar, and strode up the short, steep driveway. He crashed the flyscreen door and disappeared upstairs without a word to his wife, or the latest kid. *Christ, first I need a shower* he thought.

Chapter 3

Kristen was in the kitchen – the oxycontin had not yet kicked in, and she felt a sickening wash of dread at her husband's arrival. 'Hey kid,' she said, 'do you hear that? It's time to scram.'

The little girl was not Kristen and Bradley's. She was probably about five years old but might have been as young as four, or as old as six – it was hard to tell. It was a foster kid; and as Bradley strode through the hallway, she looked up with a jolt that made her cornrow braids dance. She had been glued to a re-run of *Sesame Street* for at least an hour - and if she could have spoken - she might have argued her case for more TV, but she was a mute. Instead, she pleaded with her eyes.

'I said scram!'

The kid stomped off, sulkily, and moments later slammed her bedroom door behind her. For the first time in the weeks since she had arrived, Kristen regarded the child as nothing more than an encumbrance. The maternal instincts which the girl had initially roused within her were artificial, borrowed from a time past. This girl wasn't hers; once tonight was out of the way she would need to speak to Officer Grandig at Savannah Child Protective and get her gone. Bradley had said something once – that she had been playing happy fucking families and it was a goddam sham – and on that one occasion, she realised, he had been right.

'Quit slamming doors!' Kristen yelled, then turned back to the kitchen and took the opportunity to fill her glass. Bradley would be down in a few minutes and no doubt start his usual climbdown. His usual denial. His usual 'let's forget all about it.' But whatever. She was done with that. She reckoned she had time to get dinner sorted before it all kicked off.

Chapter 4

When Bradley finally entered the kitchen, showered and clean, Kristen was stood at the countertop spearing diced chicken, eggplant, okra and red onion onto long, steel kebab skewers. Bradley contemplated planting a kiss on her cheek but thought better of it. He sniffed instead, took a beer from the fridge and a bag of potato chips from the store cupboard, and sat himself down at the table behind where Kristen was working. 'We should call Officer Grandig,' he began. 'This foster placement needs to end. We can't always be fighting like this.'

'Yeah, whatever,' Kristen said, dismissively.

'You've nothing to say to that?' Bradley asked.

Kristen shook her head and continued with the kebabs.

There was a moment of silence, then Bradley began drumming his fingers on the table. 'Nothing to say at all?' he asked.

Kristen, still skewering meat contemplated this, then asked pointedly, 'Where were you at last night?'

'Huh?'

'Where were you? You didn't come home,' she asked again.

Bradley thought for a second. He couldn't see her face or read the tone of her voice, not exactly. He took a mouthful of chips.

'Yeah, sorry about that babes. Rough night.'

'Yeah, how rough?' she asked. As she spoke, she breathed deeply, trying to calm her nerves. She pressed her waist to the countertop to reassure herself that the gun remained where she had tucked it. She felt it push into her hip. Though she had her back to him, she made a mental picture of how he was sat, how he held his beer. She listened to him munching chips and visualised his fat, feeding face. Kristen put the skewer down, and with her back still towards her husband, she lifted the hem of her tee and grasped the butt of the gun. Her heart hammered in her chest and she felt breathless – her head spinning; she was going to kill her husband – here and now, once and for all – in the kitchen. *Screw the mess. Screw the noise. Fuck him.*

Bradley could not see the gun, but the tone of his wife's voice made him bristle, and he stood up, ready to start the fight: 'Don't you take that fucking tone…'

But it was Kristen was who acted first, gun in hand, turning and screaming wildly at her husband: 'No! Don't *you* take that fucking tone *with me*!' Almost blindly, she pointed the gun at her husband's chest and squeezed the trigger three times in quick succession - thirty years of hate coursing through her.

Bradley froze dumbly. He saw panic flash across her eyes as she looked down at the gun in her hand – the trigger mechanism steadfastly refusing to engage. He shook his head in disbelief.

'You've left the safety catch on – you dumb bitch,' Bradley said, incredulously, before bellowing: 'You were going to shoot me!'

Then he launched at her. Swinging the back of his hand under her chin with such force that she spun on her feet, collapsing onto the countertop, her face falling into the cut vegetables and half-prepared kebabs. Kristen's world went blank momentarily, then came back into sharp focus as Bradley swung her round by the shoulder and grabbed her face with his sweaty hand. Blood trickled from the corner of her mouth. He had snatched the gun and this time he held it to her head, pressing it home, hard – safety catch off.

'How does that feel, huh!? You psycho! You're fucking insane! How does *that* feel!?"

Kristen tried to wrestle free, but Bradley had her pinned. She scrabbled her hands behind her on the kitchen surface, desperately grabbing for something – anything she could use to beat him off.

'Oh, this time you're dead bitch! Don't you ever! *Ever!* pull a gun on me – you hear!?' He was shrieking, his face was in hers, and droplets of his saliva sprayed her face.

Then Kristen's hand fell on something hard, and she grasped at it, trying to secure a grip on its handle. She continued to struggle against her husband, juggling it in her hand until she had it firmly in her grasp.

Like the gun moments before, Bradley did not see the kebab skewer. He did not see Kristen steady herself, nor register as she swung it wildly towards his head in one final act of desperation and hate. This time, she nailed it.

With his face inches from hers, she shrieked brutally – the steel kebab skewer burying deeply into the side of his temple: 'Fuck you!'

Bradley fell instantly silent, his mouth hanging open, and dropped the gun. He looked like a fish just clobbered with a mallet. He staggered slightly on his feet. As he did, Kristen screamed again, pushing the skewer harder, forcing it deeper through his skull and across the frontal lobe of his brain. A reflex fired and Bradley raised his arms up for protection just as the skewer passed out the other side of his skull and exited between his right eye and his ear. Then he fell. To his knees, firstly, then backwards onto his back, twitching; his bowels released, and he pissed himself on the floor.

Kristen exhaled, the tension releasing like a pressure cooker. She looked down at her husband laying at her feet.

'Mahmahmahmahmah,' he gibbered as blood trickled from the two small puncture wounds where the skewer pierced his head.

'You asshole!' yelled Kristen, standing over him – sweat beading across her forehead and her whole body trembling. 'That's as good as you fucking deserve!'

Bradley's eye's watered: optic nerves and a billion synapses short-circuited through his body, the only sound - *mahmahmah* - but slower now, just like his fading heartbeat.

Kristen stood, transfixed, and watched his empty eyes, blood pooling around his lower lids: she wanted her face to be the last thing he saw before death.

'Mah…mah…mah… …'

She knelt over him; rage was beginning to bubble uncontrollably. 'I hope you can see me Bradley; I really want you to see how much I hate you! I despise you and everything you stand for!' She was leaning in now: 'But most of all I hate you for what you've done to me – now, last night, last year, in those first few months and years… This is payback. You never helped me – you just made everything worse!'

She grabbed the handle of the skewer, pulling it back, withdrawing it slowly from his head, her eyes shining brightly as she inflicted revenge on her husband.

'Can you feel this?' she asked, twisting and pulling in one slow, protracted motion. 'Or are your nerves shot now?'

Again: 'Mahmahmaahmah.' His eyes bulged, almost seeming to burst from their sockets whilst the rest of his body spasmed.

'Good,' she said, 'I hope so.' Then: 'This is for Aimee.'

With that she pushed the skewer back into his head – hard - up to the wooden handle and out the other side once more.

'Maaaaaaahmmmmmmm…!'

Bradley's head fell back, his mouth open and still.

Kristen watched him for thirty minutes or more, watched him bleed a little, and watched the colour drain from his face. Every so often there had been a slight gurgle or sigh – the body slowly shutting down, she supposed. Lying there, skewered, he looked so pathetic, particularly with the wide piss stain spread across his pants. She wondered how it had been possible for this man to so comprehensively stifle her life. Someone ultimately so fragile, it amazed her - now she had finally killed him - that he had every wielded such power.

A month earlier. Wednesday, 10th June 2015

Chapter 5

Officer Grandig – big, forty-something, with her heart of gold hardened from nearly twenty years working cases in the Savannah Child Protective Service - flipped her old but perfectly functional Rolodex round to 'E' and leafed through to the well-worn card of Kristen and Bradley Engelmaier. It was late Friday afternoon, and this was her last roll of the dice. If she could place this little kid before she left, well that would be sweet - something would have been achieved in this steaming afternoon full of social workers, paperwork and meeting rooms with busted air-con. She sighed, partly because the Engelmaier's were far from her favourite foster carers – *there was something about the two of them she just didn't like, something she couldn't put her finger on* - but mainly that in red ink across the Engelmaier's index card she had once scrawled BOYS ONLY and drawn a cartoon pigtailed girl with a frowny face next to it. She knew this was going to be a long shot. Grandig believed Kristen had her reasons but figured she might reconsider knowing Hale County Children's Home was the alternative. She punched the numbers into her desk phone and counted the pips, half-expecting the answerphone to kick in.

Pick up!

'Hey, Kristen, is that you honey?'

'Uh-huh, who's this?'

'This is Officer Grandig over at Child Protective. I'm sorry to catch you so late in the afternoon: how're you Kristen?'

'Yeah, I'm good. You?'

'Oh, Kristen, I've got myself a problem over here and I don't know whether to scratch my watch or wind my butt… I'll cut to the chase: I've got this sweet little thing one of the officers picked up earlier today - wandering lost over Montgomery Street, damn near got itself run over…'

'Uh-huh?'

'…I've got no missing children matching the description, I've run the computer State wide, and nothing's coming up – not a single match. It's so late in the day the kid's either gonna stay here in my office under a sack of unending court orders or get dropped off down at Hale County – you get my drift? Any chance you can you help me out with an emergency placement, honey?'

There was a pause on the line, then: 'How long are we talking Grandig?'

'Oh, just a couple of days, three at the most. You know the score. Just long enough to get the papers organized and get a short-term placement lined up. I wouldn't usually bother you with one like this, but all my Shorts are either vacationing or out of town, and I ain't got any other ideas tonight.'

Another pause, then: 'Hale County, you say? Can you give me thirty minutes?'

'As I said, it's you or the children's home, Kristen. I'll give y'all an hour if you can help.'

'No, half an hour is just fine. I gotta get the room ready.'

'Kristen, I owe you girl.'

'Don't I know it,' she said. 'What did you say the kid's name was?'

'No idea – I'm hoping you might be able to get through and help piece this one together for us. I'll see you in thirty – you're a doll!'

'Yeah. Sure.'

Chapter 6

It was as if the sun stubbornly refused to sink any lower than a hand's width from the horizon. The air was thick and the temperature gauge on Officer Grandig's dashboard had steadfastly refused to dip below 98 degrees for the past five days; her windows were down not to cool the car but to ensure they didn't pass out. The little kid in the back, still silent, rested her head against the open sill and let the air rush across her face and through her hair. Grandig tilted her rear-view mirror so she could watch her as she drove; *hell, this was an odd one.* She flicked the radio on and tuned in to WLFS for its easy mix of classic country, gospel and local advertisements.

'Would you like some music, honey?' Grandig asked over the thundering air from open windows.

The kid didn't respond - or didn't hear. Whichever it was she kept her gaze outwards, watching the sidewalks rush past. The car smelt of feet and fast food and the back seat seemed to be upholstered in old magazines, newspapers, manila folders and french-fries. As they drove on, the suburbs emerged from downtown's muggy fug. Magnolia trees and Spanish moss replaced the projects and the air seemed to clear as a slight coolness began to creep into the car. The hum of the tyres as they crossed the Talmadge Memorial Bridge was soporific and in the rear-view the kid looked stupefied, hypnotized almost - but her glassy eyes stubbornly refused to close.

By the time Grandig pulled into Welyvan Street, with its Phillips 66 gas station and IHOP restaurant on the corner, she thought the kid was finally asleep. She pulled the car across the street and bumped the curb outside number 2310. Kristen was already at the porch, waiting.

Grandig got out and strode up the path to greet Kristen: 'Honey – like I said, I owe you big time!'

Kristen looked over to Grandig's car then drew a deep breath. 'It's a girl,' she said.

'It's just an emergency placement,' Grandig interjected quickly. 'Just a day. Two max, promise.'

Kristen looked unsure. 'We don't do girls, Grandig. You know that.'

'Uh-huh, uh-huh – I know that, Kristen. But look, it's you guys or Hale – and look how little she is – you can't do that to her, can you?'

Kristen scratched her nose: 'Just an emergency placement, right? Short term?'

'Sure – sure!' Grandig replied. 'Definitely a short – just while I figure out who the little mite is, and who she belongs too.'

Kristen nodded. 'Okay – but just a day or two.'

Grandig was relieved. 'Thank you, Kristen – and say thanks to Bradley too – you're just wonderful – both of you!'

'Sure, sure,' Kristen said. 'No need to sugar coat it.'

Grandig noted a look in Kristen's eyes – she seemed somehow - spaced. 'Are you okay honey?'

'Yeah, I'm fine, Grandig,' she looked away. 'Sorry – I've had a migraine all day – it's lifting, but I'm good. It's just my tablets.'

'Well you take care of yourself. And be sure to call if you need anything. I'll be in touch as soon as I have any news, okay?'

Kristen frowned – she looked neither happy nor convinced.

'I'll bring her in then,' Grandig said. 'She's a dot!'

Kristen nodded, reluctantly.

Chapter 7

Within an hour of arriving the kid had eaten three-quarters of a Papa John's then collapsed on the bed in the newly repurposed spare room, dead to the world. Kristen watched her from around the doorframe. She watched the girl's tiny chest rising and falling slowly. *How old was this girl - four? Five? Six maybe? So fragile.*

Kristen felt a low dread rising within her that she had not felt for many years. She cursed herself for agreeing to this. *And Christ - what would Bradley say about it?*

She stared at the girl for some time – watching her sleep. But at a little after eight Bradley's beaten-up blue chevy clanked noisily up the drive - the exhaust catching the rise of the storm drain and sending a shower of sparks across the concrete – and she left her alone. With his heavy shirt yanked open Bradley slammed the driver's-door, grabbed the crate of cheap beer from the back seat and made his way inside to where Kristen was waiting.

'Is that you, Bradley?' Kristen said. 'How's your day been?'

'Yeah, usual crap,' he replied. 'Game's about to start – I got to get out of this shirt. Can you put this beer in the cooler for me?' He dumped the crate in her arms, squeezed her butt and made upstairs to change. 'Are you going to watch?'

'No, I don't think so. Think I'll just sit and read - if that's okay?'

'Go nuts, girl. Hell, you smell sweet – shame for you it's game night.'

'I know my place…'

Bradley laughed. Tonight, it was all about the game and so long as nothing detracted from it, he'd be happy.

The last couple of hours had gone past in a whirl; she had fed and settled the kid, cleaned the TV room, put out the nachos and chips, left the sports pages on the arm of the recliner, laid out some pants and a clean shirt on the bed, then showered and got dinner ready. It was a routine she was used to, and one that was easier and less painful to fulfil than to break.

'Have we got some chips!?' Bradley yelled from upstairs.

'It's all taken care of.'

'Thanks babe.'

The TV was already on and Kristen opened a can of beer and dropped it in the recliner's cup-holder. She flicked on ESPN and by the time the Tigers were running out onto the pitch Bradley was in his chair.

'Would you unplug the phone, Kristen?' he said, as he drained the first can and hammered the volume button.

'Of course, honey. Are you good for beer?'

He nodded. Bradley was already engrossed in the pre-game stats that blinked across the bottom of the screen as some blonde screeched out the stars-and-stripes. Kristen retreated and pulled the door behind her – he'd be good until at least midnight.

Kristen checked on the kid. The house was hot; the air-con hadn't worked in years but the new addition to the household was still fast asleep. Kristen leant on the doorframe and took in the room; it didn't look too bad. Back in the nineties, when Bradley and Kristen had first sought approval to foster, they had spent nearly five-hundred bucks redecorating this small room and kitting it out to be boy-friendly. A Buzz Lightyear bed, funky wallpaper, a bed, desk and storage – all those things. Today, though, the shine had faded. Kristen had found some flowers from out the back and put them in a vase by the bed, dug out a pot of colouring pencils and paper and left them on the desk, and found an old floral rug from the cellar that went someway to making the room seem more appealing for a little girl. Tomorrow she might even switch the cowboy-themed curtains for something prettier.

She sighed. Who was she kidding? This couldn't last more than forty-eight hours - she knew she could not do this, this mothering bullshit. Besides, Officer Grandig had said herself it was only until a regular short-term foster family could be found. This time, Bradley and she were only an emergency placement. She closed the door. *Time for wine.*

In the upstairs bedroom, Kristen sat on the bed, with a bottle of red and her scrapbook from the side drawer. She and Bradley had fostered off and on for well over a decade now – and a lifetime ago since what had happened to Aimee.

She leafed through the scrapbook. Dozens of kids had passed through their home since then – and she'd kept a record of them all. Some stayed only a matter of hours – others for several months. The longest placement - a freckled red-headed boy called Mitch - Bradley had wanted to adopt, but after just shy of a year Grandig had placed him out of county with a distant relative who had come forward at the last. Those were the hardest, she thought; those with which you had time to make a bond.

Kristen drank and continued to flick through her scrapbook. Ragged pictures of the kids who had passed through her life smiled out of the well-worn pages. There had been a few girls – in the early days - but not many, they were too hard. So, the boys came, and the boys went. Joe, with the abusive, sex offending father; Samuel, with the drug-addicted mom; Raymond, whose mom who just couldn't cut it; Charlie whose entire family had been wiped out when their pick-up collided with an 18-wheeler... All the stories, similar; all of them tragic. Memories stirred: she'd liked some of these kids – at the time. But if truth were told, she had been indifferent to quite a few of them. And a handful – *well, you can't like them all*, she thought.

By the time she closed the book the bottle was drained; she glanced at the clock: 11.26pm. Bradley would be up soon. Then she'd have to tell him. Still – she reasoned – it was likely to only be the weekend. She'd take the kid out, keep her busy. He wouldn't even get a look-in before Grandig was back to take her away again. That would be Saturday, or Sunday maybe; Monday at the latest. They would cope.

Chapter 8

Two days became three, three became four. Four became a short-term placement. Officer Grandig had called on the Monday morning to check Kristen's migraine had lifted, and to say she hoped to have the placement solved by that afternoon. She called early evening to say she was still having difficulty and again Tuesday to say the same. On Wednesday morning Kristen and Bradley agreed to keep the kid until a suitable foster family could be arranged – and who knew when that would be.

Wednesday, 1st July 2015

Chapter 9

Morning.

A slow fortnight had passed. Kristen sat in the swing seat on the back veranda whilst the kid played in the garden under the shady boughs of the Candler oak. Kristen put down the book she was re-familiarising herself with: *Savannah Child Protective Department's Guide for Foster Families.* She watched the girl. Kristen knew these kids well - kids the guide referred to as '*troubled children*', or '*displaced individuals*', or '*victims of abuse*'. And she knew they came with their own demons, that at some point always crept out.

'You okay, kiddo?' called Kristen.

The girl looked up from the dusty spot where she played, then returned to the doll.

'Say, do you wanna come draw?' Kristen asked.

The kid looked up, quizzically at first as if no one had ever asked to draw with her before, and then jumped to her feet discarding Barbie in the dirt. She nearly tripped up the steps in her effort to get to Kristen and she threw herself into the swing-chair with such a leap as to set it swinging almost back into the window behind.

'Well jeez!' exclaimed Kristen, 'I guess drawing's just about the most fun thing around, huh?'

They sat on the veranda for an hour or more, Kristen flicking through the pages of her book as the kid wore down the Crayola to little nubs of wax.

Finally, Kristen looked up from her book, her mind swimming with nightmarish images conjured up from the horrific details she had just read. It was a sobering read for anyone, and Kristen was through with refreshing her knowledge. She knew that for all the author's good intentions there was nothing anyone could really learn from it; *children like this kid couldn't be cured with advice from child psychologists, therapists or family liaison officers – she knew that first-hand. No amount of delving or prying into a child's state of mind is going to undo the horrors of abuse so clearly detailed within this guide.* It made Kristen mad. She flicked to the front of the book and checked the publication date: *six years out of date. May as well be a hundred* she thought. She stood up and sighed. She knew things didn't change. That people didn't change. That kids like the one at the end of the garden would keep on coming, despite the best efforts of Grandig and her team. To Kristen, the system was just a mop that sloshed around scummy water – it never actually cleaned anything up. These kids: the Joes, Samuels, Raymonds, kept coming and coming like dripping water into an overflowing, cruddy bucket. *This shit's gonna keep on flowing... until someone turns off the faucet,* she thought.

Inside the house the telephone rang, jolting Kristen from her thoughts. 'You okay, honey?' she called to the kid, 'I gotta get the phone!'

The kid looked up, briefly, affirming that all was good. Kristen returned a wave and dashed into the house grabbing the phone from its cradle on the kitchen wall.

'Hello, this is Kristen Engelmaier.'

'Oh, hello there, Mrs Engelmaier, I'm glad to have caught you at home. This is Andrew, from St Mary's Church – I'm the manager of the pastoral team.'

'Oh hi!' she exclaimed. 'Yes, I remember.'

'Oh, please don't be put out,' he continued, 'I just wanted a few words. I've not seen you in a while, but I understand from some of our parishioners that you have taken in another little orphan. I just wanted to say that if there is anything I can do to assist, just go ahead and ask.'

Kristen felt her chest flush. Had it been another time – another lifetime, perhaps - she would have admitted to having a crush on this man. She had met him perhaps half a dozen times – and he looked young even for his youthful years; a dark head of hair and a deep southern tan; chestnut eyes offset by titanium-rimmed glasses. She hadn't realised he had ever noticed her before. 'Oh, that's very kind. Yes, that's right. Child Protective dropped her over last week. I've been meaning to bring her to church to introduce her, but things have been so hectic these last few days…'

'You know we've missed you at church, Kristen, you two come on by whenever you're ready, okay?'

'I'll be sure to.'

'Well, that sure would be nice. Give the kid a chance to play with the other children. I'm sure she'd have a ball. How's she settling in?'

'Settling in well… I guess,' and here Kristen paused, 'Kinda, anyhow… She's a quiet one – not said a word yet since she arrived.'

'Is that normal?'

'Not to this extent – no, not really.'

'Is she mute?'

'Seems to be; selective, at least. Before you called, I had just been catching up on my Child Protective training but figured there ain't nothing new anyone can teach me.'

'Uh-huh.'

'But you know, you read this book, you read that book. You take in this kid, that kid. It doesn't get any better, you know. Understanding what's going on inside a kid's head ain't solving the problem; hell, no one even seems to know what the problem is! These kids are messed up – as far as I can see there ain't no point in any psycho-analysing nonsense. You know what Child Protective says?'

At the other end of the phone line Andrew shook his head.

'…. Child Protective talk about putting the child in the middle of a professional Circle of Care,' she laughed. 'Do you get that? This little kid with a juvie psychologist on this side, a paediatrician on that side, a Community Welfare officer over there - next to *them* - Child Protective and a Social Inclusion team, Family Support and let's not forget the Community idiots… Put that bunch in a room and you won't even see the kid for all the freakin' good these professionals try and do.'

'I hear you, Kristen. I surely do.'

She laughed again, 'You know what the real problem is?'

'Go ahead…'

'…And Lord forgive me for saying so, but it's the parents who get away with dumping a kid in the middle of a street for suckers like me to come along and put back together.'

Her words hung down the line for a moment.

'You're right on the money, of course…' Andrew said.

Kristen continued. 'How do they continue to get away with it? You know, most of the time, they're the ones that get the most help! Did you know that? They whine and they moan, and they abuse their kids and we pay for their benefits, give them their housing, and pick up the pieces of their goddam mistakes.'

Andrew laughed. 'Kristen, you're right… But don't cut yourself up about it. Look at the good you do and take comfort from that. God sees you, and he loves you for the good you do. Take the world off your shoulders for a minute…'

She had got herself worked up, and she didn't like that. She exhaled, shaking her head and looking at the kid still playing under the tree. 'So, what's new at St. Mary's then?'

'Oh, you know,' he started, 'It's all sex, drugs and rock'n'roll at St Mary's...'

Kristen smiled at the expression; relaxed again, her rant over.

'You know, I going to leave you be,' he said, 'I only called to say 'hi' and here I am taking up your afternoon.'

'Oh, by all means you're quite welcome,' replied Kristen.

'No, no. I really must – I've got lots going on at the moment. But Kristen please, keep in touch – I'm here if you need me, if you need to talk. About anything. And as I said, we all miss you – I'm here as a friend if you need me.'

'Thanks, I appreciate that,' Kirsten said. 'I'll keep in touch, promise.'

'You do that,' Andrew replied. Then before hanging up, said, 'And speak soon.'

The call left Kristen with a mix of emotions. She was a good fifteen years older than Andrew but if she was honest with herself, he stirred some long, distant feeling. Like – she pondered – like when she was a kid. Back before *it* happened, and everything went wrong. Before her childhood ended suddenly and so irrevocably. Andrew seemed so youthful and clean-cut – so appealing. She yearned for the simplicity of life he seemed to exude. *If only* she thought. But she couldn't see that happening – they sat at different ends of the religious spectrum, for one. She wore her Christianity like borrowed clothes. God meant nothing to her, He had abandoned her years ago. The scars up her arm were proof enough of that. *And 'as a friend',* she thought. She had no friends – she couldn't remember the last time she had held down a friendship or had trusted herself to let anyone close enough to form that kind of relationship. *No, the thought was nonsense.*

Tuesday, 7th July 2015

Chapter 10

Early evening.

Lazy days had ticked on. Kristen had the kid in the tub when Bradley's busted-up chevy hit the driveway at just after eight that night. She listened out for the slam of the car door, the muffled cursing and the yank on the rusty front flyscreen that signalled him home. Bradley wrestled for respectability but struggled to hide the fact that he worked in containerized freight – he might not drive a crane or forklift but he still clocked-in with a card, wore a cheap shirt and answered to a foreman ten years his junior. Within the next dozen of years he'd likely be dead from a heart-attack or an industrial accident. Either way, Bradley Engelmaier had achieved little of which he, or Kristen, were proud.

'That you, Bradley?' Kristen called from the bathroom; she moved the large glass of red around the side of the sink, out of sight of the open bathroom door. He stuck his head in, surveyed the scene and remembered instantly there was a kid in the house.

'Y'huh. How goes happy families?' There was a hint of sarcasm in his voice, barely discernible, but Kristen clocked it. He was drunk and so was she.

'Yeah, we're good; ain't we munchkin?' she tousled the kid's wet head with a soapy hand.

'Are you talking yet, kiddo?' Bradley asked.

The kid looked up momentarily, then turned back to the plastic toy she was playing with in the bubbles.

'I'll take that as a no,' he said. 'You know, honey-pie, you're going to have to start communicating with us sooner or later, yeah? We can't have a cat-gotcha-tongue here. Start talking or start walking.'

'Bradley, give it a rest, will you? Don't talk to her like that.'

She turned back to the kid and took her chin in her hand, 'Don't you listen to him. He's just crabby because he's been working all day.'

'I'm just saying Kristen, we got to *positively reinforce*,' he stressed these words like he knew what he was talking about, like he was sober. 'You know, the necessity of... You know, talking?'

'Beat it, Bradley. You're half cut. Go get yourself showered.'

Bradley cocked his head, sucked his bottom lip and raised his eyebrows in a way that said *you know I'm right*; but he couldn't really give a hoot about the kid. He thought it was a monstrously bad idea having a girl in the house. He knew it would not work and he had decided to tell Kristen the same. It would wait though. She was clearly having one of her mother moments and he could happily sit on it for an hour or two.

'Playing at fucking mom, what a crock of shit - I know your true colours.' He pulled the door to, just a little bit harder than necessary to shut it.

'Fucking asshole,' Kristen said, under her breathe, then turned her attention straight back to the kid: 'Are you alright here if I go make him some dinner?'

The kid looked up from the tub and nodded.

The kitchen was a tired place that had been promised much but never seen anything delivered. All the cupboard doors were dark, and the linoleum was a muddy brown. All the white-goods were a decade old and even the small kitchen table with its aluminium chairs seemed an after-thought. Kristen poured herself another large glass of wine, probably fuller than was necessary considering the bottle was already over half empty. She looked in the refrigerator and pulled out some chicken, slamming it in the oven. *More than he deserves.*

A few minutes later Bradley strutted into the kitchen commando in his sweatpants. 'What's for dinner?' he asked, nodding towards the oven.

'You know Bradley - you can be a colossal prick, sometimes - do you know that?'

'Huh?' he responded, then: 'Well, what's got into you?'

He pulled a beer from the fridge and his mind flickered into gear; he didn't think she had it in her tonight – what with the kid an' all.

'And it wouldn't hurt you to get in a little earlier, once in a while. Give the bar a miss once or twice a week.'

'Hey, don't get cute on me. Someone's got to earn the money.'

'Oh, spare me the clichés Bradley, we're not on the breadline. Everyone works; everyone's got a job to do; spare me your hand-to-mouth sob story.'

'Jeez, what's your problem tonight!?'

''You,' she said. 'You're the problem. Are you aware we have another kid in the house? Do you get the responsibility that comes with that?'

'Oh yeah babe, I see what's going on here. Don't you fret about that.'

'And what's that supposed to mean? This is supposed to be something we do together – when are you going to start pulling your weight?'

He paused, then: 'We had a rule.'

'Uh-huh? And what was that?'

Another pause, 'You know damn well what.'

'You tell me Bradley.'

He shifted on his feet, then looked her straight in the eye. Her face was tight with anger; red wine was arguing with American beer.

'No fucking girls…'

'Oh, screw your rules, Bradley, I am so tired of listening to your bullshit.'

'I ain't gonna have this row again with you Kristen. It ain't me that can't cope. It ain't my fucking pariah. You're the one, Kristen. You're the one with the issue, not me!'

'You're so full of shit it frightens me, Bradley. I see it in your eyes every time.'

His chest swelled and Kristen braced herself: *here it comes,* she thought. She grabbed the bottle and filled her glass. *Fuck you!*

'I was gonna talk this through calmly with you but seeing as we're having a fucked-up night of it, I'll cut to the chase. You call Grandig in the morning and tell her to come over and get that kid out of here, you hear? Do the fucking right thing for once and get her placed somewhere else. This is too fucked-up to believe.'

'You know what Bradley, get out,' Kristen said. 'Fuck off and leave me to do it myself.'

'Is that what you want, Kristen? Well that's fine with me. Hell, I tell you what, how about I give Grandig a call? Tell her you're babysitting one of her casefiles, drunk as a skunk. See where that gets you.'

'Oh sure. Give that a try, Bradley. Pull shit like that and see where it gets you.'

'Are you threatening me?'

'Fucking do the math.'

Bradley paused momentarily, his frustration was burning through his chest and up his throat. He did not have the words to argue with Kristen or control the temper that was beginning to flame deep within his belly. He leapt at her, exploding, knocking one of the aluminium kitchen chairs clattering to the floor as he flew across the kitchen. He grabbed Kristen by the tails of her shirt, ripping it up the seam as she pulled away. He grappled with the shred of her top to get a firmer grip, as she simultaneously reached out, scrabbling for anything within reach to pull herself away from his grip.

'You bitch,' he hollered. 'Why won't you just keep that fucking mouth of yours shut?'

She struggled, but Bradley managed to grab her right arm at the wrist. He yanked it up between her shoulder blades. The agony was instantaneous, and Kristen screamed as if her whole arm had been wrenched from her shoulder. She froze, instantly, to try and reduce the pain. Any movement now and Kristen thought she would pass out. Bradley, though, did not stop, but gripped her around the neck in the crook of his other elbow. 'Shut the fuck up,' he hissed in her ear. 'The kid will hear.'

Kristen wriggled against Bradley's weight, but she was paralysed with pain. 'Let me go, asshole!'

Bradley dragged her across the kitchen, another chair upturning and spinning across the floor as he did. He still held one arm tight behind her back, but he released her from his stranglehold, grabbing her by the back of the neck instead. He pushed her face forcibly against the table.

He was panting, enraged. 'Why the fuck do you always make me do this, Kristen? You always have to poke me, don't you?'

Kristen gasped for breath. Her head spun and every part of her body strained against Bradley's hold. She managed a *fuck you*, but her words were lost through her own clenched teeth.

Bradley continued to grind her face against the table. 'You know, you need to be a little nicer to me, Kristen.' He leaned in close to her face, 'You talk to me like I'm retarded, but I'm better than you. You think you've got the dirt on me? Well that goes two ways, don't ever forget that.'

Kristen heaved, trying to pull away from Bradley's grip. Every muscle, through her burning shoulder, back and neck blazed hot and frigid. She couldn't break away; Bradley was too strong for her attempts to free herself. He blew in her ear. 'Right, girl?'

'Let. Me. Go!'

Bradley squeezed her arm a couple more centimetres up her back, sending a new burst of electric-like pain through her arm and shoulder.

Beads of sweat broke from every pore across Kristen's skin. She willed herself not to break, not to give in, *but Christ!* She breathed heavily, 'Quit it Bradley, I'm sorry, let me go. Please!'

'I ain't the only one with secrets, am I?' His grip tightened further, and Kristen felt her vision blur in a dizzying wash; she was about to pass out.

'No,' she said, 'You're not! I'm sorry. Sorry, Bradley!'

She continued to struggle, and this time Bradley released his hold on her slowly and deliberately, the way you might release an aggressive, snapping dog. The pain abated in a wash. Kristen's face was pumped with blood, and now she spun to face her husband. 'One day I'll fucking kill you!' she screamed. 'Fucking asshole!'

Bradley laughed, wiping his mouth with the back of his hand. 'Yeah, right,' he said. 'Good luck with that.' He took a quick step forward, then with speed too swift for Kristen to react, punched her hard in the stomach. She fell to the floor like a doll.

Bradley watched her, then snorted. Kristen writhed on the linoleum, gasping, choking, and coughing for breath. She spat to see blood, but there was none; not this time.

Finally, Bradley stepped forward and kicked her sharply in the back of the ribs for good measure. 'You ever threaten me again, babes,' he said, 'and we'll see who ends up dead. You catch my drift?'

He turned and left, leaving her trembling in shock on the floor.

She lay motionless for a minute, waiting to hear Bradley fire up his car and depart. Soon enough, the familiar growl of his engine burst into life and the screech of his tyres faded into the hot, evening air. She had the sudden urge to run upstairs, grab Bradley's gun, and blow her fucking head off – make this shit stop once and for all. Christ – how hard could it be? She had tried it many times before - one quick squeeze of the trigger then darkness. Death could come quickly – she knew that. But slowly she calmed, she sat up, butt on floor, hugging her knees. She took a few deep breaths to calm her winded lungs. She breathed deeper still; experience told her a sharp pain in her chest might mean a cracked rib, but luckily, no – just bruising today. The shock - adrenalin she supposed - was slowly leaving her system and the involuntary trembles began to dissipate. Gingerly she got to her feet.

She rolled her shoulders and rocked her head to and fro, side to side. *No lasting damage* she thought. She righted the upturned chairs. Then reached for the wine. She emptied the bottle and drank it like cordial, then downed a couple of oxycontin for good measure.

She did not cry. Not then while it happened, nor now. Tears, she had learned, achieve nothing. In the early days, yes, she would sob every time she took a kicking. But no longer. Tears were just a call-sign to the perpetrator, another way to show weakness. Kristen had learnt well enough that Bradley was not moved by tears, and she had promised herself years ago not to waste the emotion or energy.

Kristen pulled another bottle of red from the store-cupboard and sat at the counter and drank until the drugs and alcohol made her numb. She knew this routine as well as any other in her life. Bradley would not be home tonight; he'd crash on someone's couch or sleep in his car – go to work and joke about the wife kicking him out; laugh it off with the fucking hicks and losers that spent their dollars on beer, fast-food and ball-games. But he'd be back again tomorrow evening. They wouldn't talk for a day or two, side-stepping each other around the house, the bedroom; but then they'd gradually slip back into the old routine… How she hated it. How she hated herself for being the victim. And how she hated him: Bradley who never quite made it; Bradley who never quite delivered the goods; Bradley who would never stop hitting even when she begged.

Bradley had taken his advantage and broken her years ago; he was the goofy teen with the aggressive temper who would never take no for an answer. She'd been cute then too.

He'd been gone over an hour when she finally remembered the kid was still in the tub.

Chapter 11

Later.

'Oh, shit baby, I'm so sorry!' She grabbed the shivering girl up in her arms and wrapped her in a towel – cuddling her in her lap. Her shoulder twinged painfully. 'Oh God, I'm sorry, are you okay sweetie?'

The kid looked up at her with frightened eyes. Though the evening was still warm, the water was now stone cold and her blue lips trembled.

'Oh, honey - why didn't you get out? I was just down the corridor; why didn't you come and find me!?' but Kristen's words were hollow. What they both knew she was really saying was, 'I'm sorry honey, I'm drunk. I rowed with my husband - I was wrapped up in my own business and forgot all about you. I left you here to freeze on your own whilst all you could hear was f-this, and f-that… You'd probably be safer back wherever you came from.'

Kristen felt anger boil up inside her – a fine fucking mother she proved herself once more to be. She looked at the kid, who sniffed, dropping her head as if acknowledging Kristen's flaws.

Kristen prickled. 'Are you judging me – you fuck!?'

The kid blinked; a look of shock flitted across her face.

'You little brat – don't test me, okay? You don't know what you're dealing with here – you think life's hard now, do you? Well trust me – there's a whole lot worse to come.'

She dumped the kid back in the cold bath. The kid edged back – big tears welling in her eyes.

Kristen leant forward – she could feel her mood swinging dangerously but couldn't stop herself – she grabbed the kid by the bare arm and yanked her. 'What did your daddy do, huh? Did he rip out your tongue?'

Then Kristen squeezed the kid's cheeks, forcing her lips open. 'Nope – didn't rip your tongue out – I see it in there. You're just too goddam rude to use it – that's your fucking problem.'

Kristen let go and splashed cold bathwater into the kid's face.

'You watch it, kid,' Kristen said as she stood to leave the bathroom. 'You better begin to show some gratitude or God help me; you'll see just how I deal with shits like you.'

She left the kid in the tub and walked out.

'Get yourself dry and get into bed; you fucking pain in the ass.'

Chapter 12

Evening.

Twenty minutes after beating Kristen, Bradley pulled into the parking lot of his favourite sports bar and jammed his chevy between a white Porsche - parked bravely here - and a Pontiac Firebird so scraped and mangled that it looked as if it had crashed to its spot from the interstate above. He had not been expecting a row with Kristen tonight, and in many ways, it was a bonus that presented him with a night on the beers.

Inside, noises mingled: country rock with a split rack of pool balls; fizz from a frosted beer tap and the wood-on-wood scrape from bar stools on the deck; burbling sports commentary from a dozen TV screens with the low grumbles of agreements and contradictions from the night's punters. It was perhaps half-full and for every group of work-weary lunch-bucket workers crowding the pool tables there was a loner at the bar. The place was buzzing yet socially derelict all at once: it was a shithole and Bradley loved it.

Tonight, unable to pull a familiar face from the crowd, Bradley sat himself on one of the high stools at the bar. The first beer was quick to come courtesy of a young, attractive barmaid and he drank it, huddled over the bottle as if he was hiding a secret. He watched the girl closely – she looked like a sophomore, probably paying her way through college - and she worked like a pro; flashed a smile here, a wink there. And all the time she kept the tips coming, tucking them away between the waistband of her short denim skirt and the tattoo of an animal paw that decorated her midriff.

Bradley watched her as she knelt down to pull the bottles from the cooler – *hell, if that skirt rides up any higher it's gonna make my night.* Bradley handed her over five bucks and caught her eye, holding it long enough to tell the girl he was interested in whatever she had to offer. The girl held his stare – then broke it off with a wink and got on with her business. He smiled: he took his mobile from his back pocket and texted Kristen.

You need 2 get things in fucking perspective. I'll b home tomorrow.

He sat and drank for three hours or more, watching punters come and go, and commenting to no one in particular about the various sports results drifting in across the glowing screens, all the while drinking himself as drunk as he could be without falling flat on his ass. By eleven, it was only the barmaid and him left in the place. And as the place had quietened down, she had turned to her studies, engrossed in a book by Nathaniel Hawthorne. Finally, she looked up: 'Do you want one more before I lock up for the night?'

Bradley thought she was gorgeous, and she'd been putting it out most of the evening. Fuck crazy Kristen, this girl had the moves that inspired Bradley tonight.

'A Maker's Mark would be good,' he said. Then: 'What's your name, honey?

'Sandii,' she said, breezily, 'With Two 'i's.' Then, 'Bourbon straight – coming right up.'

She put her book down, checked her watch then grabbed the waxed-topped bottle from the shelf. 'You got about thirty minutes before closing, so better make the most of it.'

Despite the hour, she was still cheerful, and she filled the glass to the brim. 'I hope you're not driving home – I seen the state trooper cruise past a couple of times already. He takes down licence plates then jumps on you half a mile down Garrard. You watch yourself.'

'Thanks for the tip-off, kid. I was gonna leave the car in the lot overnight. If that's okay?'

'Sure thing.' She turned to go back to her book, but Bradley was not going to let her off the hook now.

'Whatcha reading?'

'This? This is just a college book, 'The Scarlet Letter'. Have you read it?' she asked with interest.

'No. I don't read much. Is it good?'

'Well, huh, yeah – kinda, I guess. It's on my reading list so I just plough my way through them.'

'You wanna read me some?'

She looked at him, briefly scanning his face and eyes for any tell-tale sign that he was fooling with her.

'Are you kiddin' me?'

'I ain't kidding you. I wanna hear somathis…' he grabbed the book and examined the front cover.

'You're sure?'

'Yeah, I'm sure. Come sit round here, next to me.'

She wasn't sure – but thought he was probably harmless enough. He was also way too drunk – she figured it would be okay.

She perched herself next to Bradley and read. The words were lost on him and they washed over his dumb and unengaged mind; but the view she spoiled him with was not lost. Long, bare legs tanned from weekends on the beach and that blouse open one button too many. He watched her full lips too - and her soft tongue, and his mind raced until his crotch bulged.

Sandii was caught in the text, a momentary drop in her guard long enough for Bradley to slip his clumsy drunken hand between her thighs. She fell back as if electrocuted, almost stumbling flat to the floor, the stool clattered sideways. Bradley instantly held his hands up to say, *hey, what did I do!?*

She scrambled backwards ungainly; her face instantly flushed with rage: 'Fuck! What the fuck is your problem!? Get the fuck out, you creep!'

'Jeez, easy kid! No harm done. Sorry, yeah?'

'Sorry?! You fuckin' freak!'

Bradley shrugged his shoulders. In this one slight gesture he told Sandii exactly who he was, and who he thought she was too: *Fuck you, bitch.*

She had raced round and put the bar between herself and Bradley, and now grabbed the telephone in her right hand: 'Get out. Now. Before I call 911!'

Bradley didn't bother hanging around; even though he fancied telling her exactly what he'd like to do to her given the chance; to tell her what a fucking prick-tease like her deserved. He grabbed his jacket and flicked her the middle finger and stumbled out in the night. He was wretchedly drunk; his feet and legs moved independently of one another and his brain couldn't quite fathom where everything had just gone wrong. *The girl was begging for it.* But fuck her, he thought; *fuck the miserable little jumped-up college-whore. Fuck'em-all.*

Back in the bar Sandii cooled herself down. She locked the doors as soon as the man had left, flicked all but the bar lights off, then texted her mom to say she'd be home in twenty. She poured herself an orange juice then grabbed a clean cloth to wipe the bar and tabletops. What an asshole that man was; she felt dirty where his hands had groped her and wanted a shower, she wished she'd had the courage to punch him in the face too.

Then as she wiped the bar down her luck really did change and she knew instantly that on this occasion she might get the last laugh. Had she not been returning to college so imminently, and this her last shift before then, she might not have been so brave. But she guessed the passcode to the phone that the man had left on the bar *(0000-dickhead!)* and she could not resist.

Sandii texted in that excessively quick way that only young people can then clicked the send button. Next, with a cocky self-satisfied grin she tossed the phone in the trash, grabbed her bag, locked up and walked out.

Wednesday, 8th July 2015

Chapter 13

Morning.

As the breaking morning sun crept over the Candler oak, throwing heat and an amber glow across the dusty lawn, the kid and Kristen ate a breakfast of *Poptarts* and *Apple Jacks* on the deck. Kristen drank coffee and wondered where Bradley was. She did not care as such; just wondered. The kid drank juice – and watched Kristen cautiously.

'Sweetie-pie, I'm sorry, okay? I was nasty last night – but I didn't mean anything by it. Am I forgiven?'

The kid looked up and shrugged.

'I say we throw our kit in the car then give Andrew a call. You can have a play in the church playground, if you like – you'll like it there. Are you up for that?'

The kid paused, then nodded, reluctant, pastry hanging from the corner of her mouth.

'Well go get your pencils and paper together then; and stop giving me such a hard time.'

The kid zipped inside.

Kristen felt low. Despite the caffeine rush, oxycontin, and a hit of vitamin D from the morning sun, her comedown from last night was still harsh. She felt jittery and on-edge; there was guilt too – rumbling for the way she had behaved towards the kid, and bitterness and resentment towards Bradley. How she hated him. Her emotions were brewing, and she felt out of control. *Today might be bad*, she thought. *Today, I might do something stupid.*

Chapter 14

Mid-morning.

Kristen and the kid got the run-around trying to track down Andrew. The church was open, but he was nowhere to be seen. She tried the office out back, which was locked. She and the kid were about to give up when she caught sight of a *Post-it* taped to a side door of one of the ancillary meeting rooms. As luck would have it, it was a 'be-back-soon' meant for someone else but had Andrew's number penned at the bottom: she called.

They chatted briefly and arranged to meet downtown at an address Kristen did not know. They drove into the city then ditched the car and followed his directions on foot to a turning off the main street, down a side alley arriving at a large, steel door. A battered intercom was almost hidden behind a large green waste-dumper, and she pressed a button labelled Refuge. If you didn't know this entrance was here, you could walk past its location for a lifetime and never seen it.

As it turned out, that was the point. Kristen and the kid were buzzed in, made their way down two flights of stairs to a large open-spaced cellar lit by strip-lighting and high, narrow windows that gazed out onto the street above. Air-con pipes and a network of ventilation ducts snaked the grey walls and ceilings, and boxes and packing crates lay strewn about the floor. Half a dozen people, volunteers Kristen guessed correctly, were busying about unpacking, slapping on white emulsion, and generally trying to turn this musty hot cellar into something more presentable.

'Hey, Kristen, good to see you! How are you and the kid getting along!?' He was bright and cheerful, and dressed in jeans and tee. He looked young and fit.

'So, this looks exciting,' said Kristen: 'What's going on?'

Andrew put down the paint roller he was holding: 'Come along, let me give you the guided tour.'

The kid had already found herself a large empty packing box and was sat in the middle of it. She had her crayons out and looked expectantly from Kristen to Andrew.

'Hey kid, go nuts! You draw and play in those all you want. They're only for the trash,' said Andrew.

Massive Grin.

'Can I fix you a coffee, Kristen?' he asked.

'Sure. Coffee would be great. Thanks.'

'No problem,' he beamed.

Around the central open-plan space there were a number of storerooms, big enough to house large racks that were currently being dismantled and moved out. One of these was already clear – and a makeshift kitchen had been set up.

'Sugar?' asked Andrew.

'Sweet enough,' Kristen replied, then cringed a little.

Andrew laughed: 'Sure.'

'So, are you gonna tell me what's going on here?' Kristen asked.

'Well, this is my new project,' he said. 'This old cellar is soon going to become my own little refuge centre. City Hall have provided the space – free of charge – and given me a free hand to do with it what I will.'

'And what are you gonna do with it? A refuge centre for who?'

'Single moms. Pregnant teens. The usual desperados, you know. All those folks who got nowhere to go, no one to help. They'll come down here.'

Kristen raised her eyebrows.

'I know. It's kind of crazy huh?'

Kristen nodded. *That was pretty much it.*

'So, what do you think?'

'I think it's amazing.'

'Good! I'm glad you approve!'

'Sure, I approve – who in their right mind wouldn't?'

Andrew smiled. 'You'd be surprised.'

Kristen nodded: she knew the score.

'And let me show you what we're going to provide,' he was excited. 'We've got this central area for meeting and recreational; a small honesty café over there; a couple of break-out rooms for the community nurse and a guidance councillor, a couple of restrooms, and a play area for the kiddies. It's gonna rock.'

'How are you funding it?' she asked.

'Well, the set-up costs are minimal. Then going forward we'll rely on donations, volunteers and goodwill; the usual Christian stuff.'

Kristen was intrigued.

'You wanna catch some rays?' he asked, 'before it gets too hot? Kid's cool playing down here.'

'Sure, that would be nice.'

On the way out, Andrew introduced Kristen to some of the volunteers: Dave, a hippy-type, thirties, born-again, beard braided into a single line of beads. A couple of youngsters, Lisa and Dizzy, students probably, bright eyes and nearly every part of their ears, noses and lips pierced with hoops, studs and bars. And Marcie – middle-aged, overweight and sweaty but along with Andrew, seemingly the heart of this organized chaos.

They made their way up to the shady square on Bull Street. Andrew bought a couple more coffees along and they found themselves a bench to sit on and watch the blue-collars, mums, dopers and homeless mingle under the shadows and relative cool shade of the oaks.

'Y'know, the thing I love about this city is the curious mix of folk you get kicking about these squares, don't you think?' he said, 'I don't believe there's anywhere else in the whole US where that happens: not that I've seen, anyway.'

'You're probably right: not that I've seen much else other than Savannah: pretty much Georgia born and bred.'

'Is that so?'

'Yep; home-girl me. Never taken the plunge. Don't even have a passport.'

'Are you serious? Wow; you surprise me – I wouldn't have guessed that.'

'Straight up.'

Kristen suddenly felt small, that her years glued to Bradley made her inferior in Andrew's eyes. The feeling of inadequacy was uncomfortable but one she knew well, and she swiftly batted it away with an uncompromising excuse. 'Well, actually I do have a passport…' she paused, 'but only because I needed one to register to foster. Bradley and I have never used them to travel; passports by default, you know. What about you?'

'Oh, I've been lucky,' he said. 'I've seen a lot of this world. Not that that makes me special or anything.'

'You *are* lucky.'

'Yeah. But you know, for me – travelling was the opportunity to find myself – if you'll excuse the cliché… I came out of school with no real comprehension of who I was or what I was going to do with my life.'

He spent the next thirty minutes talking in the shade of the trees and hypnotizing Kristen with tales of trips to the Far East and Africa, the Middle East, Europe and Asia. There had been nearly a decade of missionaries and self-discovery, he said, which all sounded mystical and alien to Kristen.

Kristen shook her head but smiled at the same time. 'You've lived a hundred lives compared to me,' she said.

'Well, whatever. It's no great shakes. Friends are what are important, right?' he said.

Kristen laughed. *That word 'friends' again.* There was literally no one in her life she could honestly call a friend. The very premise was incomprehensible. 'I guess.'

She wondered what friendship with Andrew could actually bring her; what empty hole it could fill. *What would it look like? What would it feel like? What would it cost?* She wondered whether she could trust him; or herself.

'Can I show you something, Andrew. I think this might give you some perspective on my situation.' She reached in her bag for her phone, then continued: 'Just take a look at this text.'

Hi Girls. Im txting this 2 all females in BRADLEYS (?) address book. Fucker just put his hand up my skirt n gave me big come-on, SKUMBAG!! Soz if TMI but pls sum1 bring this pedo in2 line! XX

'Oh my,' said Andrew. 'You got this when?'

'Last night… I know it real; that's typical Bradley behaviour. We'd rowed.'

'Have you spoken to him about this?' he asked.

'No. He didn't come home last night. But we're finished.'

'Kristen, this could be a prank. He might have had his cell stolen, or something. You don't know.'

'Yeah, I do,' she said. 'That's just Bradley's style. I don't need answers, Andrew – I'm just showing you. Just so you can see.'

'I'm so sorry Kristen. I can't imagine what you need to hear right now.'

Kristen looked up into the oaks and to the Spanish moss in the branches. She could feel tears welling in her eyes – that tell-tale desperation and sorrow washed through her again. She waited until she could speak without her voice cracking: 'It's okay, I don't need to hear anything, thanks,' she said. 'I've just got a choice to make – that's all. I've known for years but I've been too scared to act. This text – it's giving me the perspective I need. I've just got to make my mind up, that's all.'

Andrew nodded but said nothing.

Chapter 15

Midnight.

Kristen drove off the driveway with Bradley's body bundled in the boot, a picnic blanket thrown over him. She had made the right choice in killing her husband – not herself - and had no regrets.

She was hot. Not least from the huge effort it had taken to manhandle his limp body out into the car. She had left the skewer in place – she liked him that way – and now drove down quiet streets and out to the interstate. If she could manage the next few hours without being pulled over, she knew she was home and dry.

There was little traffic at this time of night, and she took the Talmadge Memorial Bridge out of town towards South Carolina. The Savannah River meandered and spread, and behind the roads swamps and oxbows sprawled out across the low country. The roads became increasingly treacherous in the dark and the Chevy bore every bump and hole under the heavy load in the boot.

Kristen knew the area well. She took the Tulepo trail, then hooked off down an unmarked track pushing through about a mile of swamp backlands. Finally, just before a barred and bolted gate blocked the way, Kristen pulled a sharp right down a narrow path lined with water hickory and bullweeds. This path narrowed to a tight single track and petered out at the shore of a minor oxbow lake of the Savannah River. She got out; it was still eighty degrees or more, and she began to sweat.

A short walk up the shore led to a rarely used lock-up, down the side of which were stored a couple of old but perfectly functional flat-bottomed boats, one of which had a fuelled-up outboard; most likely belonging to one of the many fishermen who angled for bass, bream or catfish. In the past, Bradley and she had taken the boat for an afternoon outing down the river: tonight, she dragged it to the shore then floated it down to the car to dispose of his body.

Chapter 16

At 2310 Welyvan Street screaming echoed unanswered through the house. The kid was bolt upright in bed, delirious, with a temperature raging through her terrified body. She trembled uncontrollably: her eyes were glazed but her mind saw horror. Her ears too heard unimaginable suffering, the like of which she had never experienced before – yet the house was silent save for her screams. She yelled again, sobbing through the tears, but still no one came to sooth her nightmare.

The kid was alone in the house and the scent of blood filled her nostrils. She could smell it clearly.

Chapter 17

With effort Kristen managed to tip Bradley into the boat and then under the black night sky she set of with her husband for one final trip up the river.

She weaved the boat slowly through the tidal flows, the motor creeping barely above idle. Twenty, then thirty minutes passed. Finally, beneath the bough of an ancient, towering black gum tree she pulled a sharp left, leaving the relatively wide stream for a narrow, tight channel: it appeared to lead nowhere. Roots and weed scraped the bottom of the boat and from the gloom ahead a rundown wooden structure slowly came into view: a boathouse, and beyond that a small lake probably fifty yards across. This little stream was the only way in and out.

You couldn't guess at the boathouse's age - It sat in the grounds of a large, plantation - though that itself had been razed to the ground decades before. The boathouse, however, had survived the fire and though was part-collapsed, and rot was slowly destroying what was left, it remained intact. A jetty also remained, though the end protruding outwards into the lake was mostly submerged, and many of the wooden shingles had fallen away. Kristen steered the boat along the jetty and inside the boathouse itself. She cut the engine.

The place was silent save for the occasional drip-drip of water from the roof above. Along one side was a walkway, still solid, and at the far end a narrow platform running the width of the structure – part of which had slipped away leaving a natural ramp into the water. And it was here that Kristen guided the boat to a stop.

Almost immediately there was an enormous clattering and splash as something massive, dark, broad and flat sprang from its resting place and disappeared startled into the murky water. Kristen jumped, and as her weight shifted the entire craft nearly capsized.

It was obvious to Kristen what it was - though if she had been in any doubt, the tell-tale zig-zagging breakwater disappearing out of the boathouse confirmed it: an alligator – and a big one. Her heart raced; she knew that gators could easily kill you when startled. She glanced around: she couldn't see any more but that wasn't to say they didn't lurk beneath the surface. She would need to be quick.

Kristen scrambled out of the boat and pulled it as far as she could up the partly submerged platform. Her feet skittered out beneath her on the slimy wood and mosquitoes buzzed in her ears. She wrestled with the deadweight of her husband, though rolling Bradley out was easier than getting him in – and he splashed out onto the deck. He was sprawled on his back, feet in the water, head - and skewer - caught at an awkward angle, half peering up at the roof. Kristen hoped his corpse wouldn't last long – the gators and other carnivorous creatures - turtles, salamanders and the like - would soon do their work.

And that was her plan – to leave Bradley in this long-abandoned boathouse, away from any passing fisherman or boaters, and let the gators dispose of the evidence. She didn't say goodbye; there were no last words that hadn't been said already. She simply revved the engine and got the fuck out.

Thursday 9th July 2015

Chapter 18

By the time Kristen had navigated the backstreams, found her car and driven back to Welyvan Street, first light was breaking. The events of last night seemed ethereal and she could barely comprehend that it had happened. The mud on her boots confirmed it though - that and the spots of blood dotted through the hallway.

She crept into the house and into the kitchen. The remainder of last night's kebabs lay out, and the bowl of chips that Bradley had been munching. She made coffee.

She sat at the table where just a few hours earlier Bradley had drunk his last beer; she could see the ring mark left by his bottle. She placed her mug directly upon it, rotating it slightly to hide the mark. She had some work to do today - and likely over the next few days too - to make sure all signs of Bradley were totally eradicated from her life. She did not want any reminders of that asshole left in her house, or her life. She would also need to clean the kitchen and hallway thoroughly; she had seen enough episodes of CSI to know that a careless murder would soon unravel if it wasn't properly cleaned up. That said, she had little reason to believe Bradley's disappearance would be classed as anything other than a missing person; and she could sure help paint a convincing story around that possibility.

She picked up her cell phone and flicked aimlessly through her messages. They would prove useful in building a smoke screen; she knew they pointed to an unhappy marriage and a man who was sleeping around. She imagined herself talking to the Savannah PD: *'And then these texts, officer… And when he came in drunk there was this huge row and he threatened to hit me again, and I was frightened for the kid, and we fought… [a few tears here, for effect] And that was the last time I saw him. Gosh, I hope he hasn't gone and done something stupid.' Easy-peasy-lemon-squeezy.*

The sun was now full up over the horizon and golden rays streamed in through the window. This was indeed a bright new day and it was time to get on with it. She'd get the kid up, then clean, then head out and find Andrew around mid-morning. She'd call Grandig later this afternoon when Bradley's work would finally call to check up on where he was…

Out in the hall she surveyed the floor closely: there were only a few spots of blood she could see, and most of them were on the runner, which she could just trash and replace. There were a couple on the wooden floor too, which would take a while longer to sort out but nothing that would cause her any major work. She felt confident.

She knocked quietly on the kid's bedroom door, entering quietly as she did: 'Wakey-wakey, sunshine!'

There was no answer. The sheets were piled high on the bed and the pillow lay discarded on the floor: the kid was nowhere to be seen.

'Honey, where are you at?'

Kristen felt that chill, the one parents know: the moment they realise their kid is not where they thought they were. She checked the closet, then under the bed. Sickness began to swell in Kristen's stomach.

'Hey kid, this ain't funny! Where are you hiding…!' She raced upstairs to her bedroom, but the bed was still made up: the closet empty too, and likewise the bathroom and walk-in wardrobe…

Panic.

Kristen raced downstairs and into the den: 'Hey!! Where are you, kid? I'm serious, stop messing with me!'

The kid was gone. Kristen raced into the back yard. But again, the kid was nowhere to be seen. She tried down the end of the garden too, hoping to hell that she was playing in the old Candler oak – but no.

Over the next fifteen minutes Kristen turned the place upside down, but every room was empty, every closet, every wardrobe, every space under every bed…

Finally, Kristen stopped. This was bad. Her story up to this point looked good but now it turned sour. A missing adulterous husband was fine; that was easy to explain away. It would even get rid of the kid back into the system and leave her to get on with her life. But a missing husband *and* a missing foster kid? That was going to throw up one hell of a mess – and one that was going to put Bradley and the kid on every front page of every newspaper from here to New York City. And Kristen really didn't want that sort of attention.

'Fuck!'

Chapter 19

One of Bradley's eyes flicked open – weepy and bloodshot. The lower lid was crusted with crud from the river and dirt swam across his eyeball within gloopy brown milky tears. Fragments of leaf, miniscule flakes of dirt and mud - bacteria and micro-organisms from the stagnant water all danced in the minute twitching from his puffed eyelid. His brain now functioned like an ancient stalling computer – hopelessly begging every axon, dendrite and nerve-ending to interpret the neurological pulses that stuttered like flickering candlelight down his optic nerve to his pierced brain into vision – into sight. This was not life – Bradley was not alive. But yet – the electric waves that flashed like torchlight through the fog was not death, either. He was languishing in a state that the majority of us only experience for the briefest and most joyous of milliseconds – that occasion before life snuffs out completely. People have survived much worse: earlier that summer whilst on a spring-break fishing trip a sixteen-year-old boy had lived having been harpooned through the head by his best buddy. Admittedly, the kid had received the best medical provision Miami had to offer, but he had lived – and his story and the horrific images of his x-rayed skull punctured by that heavy spear had been wired to every newsroom around the globe. Bradley though would die, completely – eventually. But for now, a few hundred nerves jangled, and a few scant million synapses pinged and pop inside his skewered head. And his life flashed before his itching, bleeding eyes like a misfiring TV set searching for reception.

His skin crawled with biting insects and blood-sucking parasites – yet his brain no longer interpreted physical pain or discomfort – this semi-conscious swamp that he now swam in like soup countered reality like a heavy anaesthetic. His one open vein-clotted eye flicked this way and that yet saw nothing; mucus gurgled in his throat. Then that sticky swollen lid squeezed out a mucky tear and it closed, and his memory swam again as the gators nuzzled up to his feet in the mud.

Saturday, 23rd June 1979

Savannah suburbs.

The first xeroxed 'missing' posters appeared on the evening of May 24th, 1979. They were taped to streetlamps and fire hydrants and tacked to telegraph masts and tree trunks – they fluttered in the summer night haze all over Cotton Hill.

For a month now, ten-year-old Eric DesMoiles had been pasting the neighbourhood – pedalling the sidewalks on his chopper, weaving precariously - a heavy shoulder-sack laden with the posters unbalancing him awkwardly to one side. This was not what he would class as a top Friday night – *that* would consist of a couple of Kroger corndogs, a bowl of chips and the Dukes of Hazzard on TV. Every moment or so he would leap off, sending his bike crashing to the tarmac, to stick up another poster to a mailbox or fence – sweat soaking his fringe of copper hair and beading his forehead. This routine had been repeating itself over and over since about four in the afternoon and was only punctuated by the occasional wiping of his face as he jumped back on his bike – each time two or three posters still scrunched up in his hand against the worn grips of his bullhorn handlebars.

He took off again, heading up to the corner of Fletcher Blvd and Bush – his mind focused on his simple task: '*This is what you can do to help,'* his exhausted mom had told him with desperation. *'You can jump on your bike and spread the word.'*

He pedalled like a lunatic.

He took the turn wide – sweeping out blind around the bend and did not see the older kid coming the other way until it was way too late.

Eric's chopper broadsided him, knocking him to the sidewalk and sending his Lucky Strike cigarette flying into the gutter. Struggling to control his bike, Eric pulled what seemed a gravity-defying side-to-side wobble, tipping to-and-fro like a quarter spinning out on the table. Within five yards though he lost it and crashed to the concrete, bloody and grazed. Both boys lay momentarily stunned on the sidewalk, but it was the bigger of the two kids who got to his feet first.

He was much bigger than Eric - all-hair-and-muscle – and aggressive: 'You complete retardation!' he yelled, rubbing his grazed palms on his jeans. 'You little cocksucker! You nearly fucking killed me!'

Eric stood up dazed, legs wobbling – red scrapes peppered with blood shorn over his knees and elbows. His face was pulled tight in a mix of shock and pain and fear, and he desperately fought back tears in front of this hulk of a boy who he guessed weighed twice as much as he did. His posters had spilled from his sack and now blew lazily down the street; Eric's lower lip trembled. He managed to blurt, 'I'm sorry,' before the first big tear leaked from his eyes and washed a salty path down to the corner of his mouth.

The bigger kid, in tight Levi's and a faded red t-shirt that read 'Enjoy Cocaine' rather than 'Enjoy Coca-Cola' was, despite his ungainly knock to the sidewalk, pretty cool. Eric, through his tears, looked at him with just a wayward hint of envious admiration.

Enjoy Cocaine was perhaps six or seven years older than the scrawny kid now grubbing in front of him in the dirt. Being unceremoniously dumped to the floor by a ten-year-old had left him not just with the wind knocked out of him, but with his ego and carefully prepped coolness looking more than a hint shabby. He looked around for witnesses but no one else had seen the accident, there wasn't anyone on the street except him and this little turd. He momentarily considered his options either to flatten the runt or walk away.

He took a step towards Eric who was now making a desperate attempt to gather up his posters. Blood trickled down his shins and *Enjoy Cocaine* could see the boy would be digging grit from his grated knees for a week: 'What have you got there?' he asked.

Eric thrust a poster forward, his lips pursed tight as he snorted teary snot from his nose – pain and frustration aside, crying in front of *Enjoy Cocaine* was not cool.

'Is this your sister?' *Enjoy Cocaine* asked, looking at the grainy black and white photo of a girl - thirteen, maybe fourteen years old – whose image filled the page. He could see some resemblance between this little shitbag stood in front of him now and the admittedly fairly hot chick smiling up from the poster.

'Uh-huh,' Eric snivelled.

'No shit… Lost, huh?'

A million thoughts raced through Eric's head. A month ago, 'lost' was such a little word – it described his *Boba Fett* action figure - who he suspected Pete Jacks had swiped from his school bag on the last day of term - or *Stretch Armstrong* who he had not seen since that yard-sale mom held shortly before they moved house. 'Lost' was disappointment, an annoyance, and if he was brutally honest – an opportunity for compensation-in-kind if he just managed to play mom effectively enough, and it had to be said he was pretty good at that trick... But now, in these past few weeks, 'lost' had taken on a whole new meaning altogether. Now it meant emptiness, hollowness – *a feeling like someone cut off one of your legs but left the feeling of it behind* - it meant crying in your room at night with your head stuffed into your pillow so mom doesn't hear – so it doesn't set her off again too. 'Lost' brings cops to your house to drink coffee and shrug their shoulders, and neighbours with homemade meatloaf to see if there's any news. And it meant in an odd way that he was pretty much invisible to mom: and he didn't really understand why. *Aren't I even more important to you now she's 'lost'?* It didn't feel like that: not one bit…

'Yeah, lost,' Eric replied.

Enjoy Cocaine looked again at the poster. *Nope, never seen her,* then: 'I should break your fucking face – you ride that bike like a motherfucker.'

Eric nodded. Had he not been so tangled up in posters, mangled bike and blood he would have run. His mind swirled.

Enjoy Cocaine sniffed: 'Hey, a-hole - you owe me a smoke. You got one?'

Eric shook his head.

Enjoy Cocaine looked at him; he had a desperate urge to twat this little fucker. He took a step forward, then: 'Do you know who I am?"

'No. uh-huh.'

'Good,' then briefly checking the sidewalk for looky-loos, *Enjoy Cocaine* slugged Eric hard in the guts: 'Hope you find your sister, dickhead.'

Eric fell to the ground spluttering and gasping, and *Enjoy Cocaine* felt instantly better. Shit, he'd been beaten upon himself since he was a crawler – and he was none the worse for it – it'd probably do the little spasmoid some good, you can't just ride the sidewalks like a waster all your life. *Enjoy Cocaine* screwed the kid's posted into a ball and stuffed it into his pocket and walked off without a look back – tugging another smoke from hipster pocket as he went.

***

A storm half the size of the state rumbled and crackled around the dark horizon and as day turned to dusk the air was hot enough to poach a turtle. It was hard to tell if the sky was clear or whether the deep magenta-purple hue was a thick storm blanket of heavy cloud. Lightning split the skyline and left its cordite waft on the still, evening air and from a barely discernible growling whisper came thunder loud enough to rent wood.

This summer had been a particularly hot one and as Bradley Engelmaier put it – *school was out - and he was free as the wind that cuts the cheese.*

Earlier that afternoon, he had dumped his bike underneath the footbridge that crossed Needle Brook - a low and stagnant mosquito-ridden, trash-filled stream that meandered behind the trailer-parks and abandoned commercial outlets that littered the outskirts of Cotton Hill. This town was dead, dry and overgrown – stuck out on the periphery north of Savannah and was pretty much regarded as the city's landfill. Bradley had lived there since birth.

He pulled his BMX from the undergrowth and headed out to the 7-Eleven on the slip road to the I-53. It was only a short ride and within five minutes he pulled a long and flamboyant skid into the dirt out front. At this time of night trade was brisk – Bradley, though only just seventeen had the frame of a twenty-two-year-old and he sauntered into the store with a bravado that enabled him to disappear within the throng of other shoppers. He sauntered to the beer cooler and lifted out a case of Eagle Red, cheap but drinkable – then walked straight out without paying. An old boy, standing in line for a quart of milk and a bottle of *Pepto Bismol* yelled at him to haul his *ass back in and pay for that beer* but Bradley just flipped him his middle finger. The cashier, a short round Mexican woman with gold earrings and two similar teeth to match, sucked her teeth and watched him leave - she was not interested in picking a fight with that one.

Bradley stashed his beer in a canvas holdall and peddled back across Needle Brook, down the Torbut Path and out into the fields. Cotton Hill sat like wasted flotsam between the creeping urbanization of Savannah's industrial region and Georgia's historical farming communities that had been in the death-throws themselves for decades. That meant Bradley - chewing a *Juicy Fruit* and humming *Hot Stuff*, with the dust kicking up from his tyres and eddies of cotton fibres dancing in his wake - could be away from the dirty urban-scape and cloaked within the shade of the pines and cypress trees, kicking his feet in the cool waters of Tosser's Rock with his best buds Col and Archie within minutes.

The three boys rubbed along well – though they would not grow old together and read eulogies at their funerals, what they did have was good and afforded them some fun in the summer recess. Col was a regular country kid who beat up on his younger brother, played football with no particular talent or style and spied on the girl across the street when she forgot to close her curtains - he was as average as the next kid. He was no great thinker – he bummed reluctantly through school with the closed look of a loner who had washed his sweaty palms of education, and whose mom and dad had pretty much done the same of him. If Col was going anywhere, he would do it under his own volition – but there were few who would wager he would end up anywhere other than working minimum wage.

Archie was similar, a little rough around the edges and not the sharpest tool but largely a good kid – though when he was thirteen, he had had an accident that had damned near killed him. Playing decks on the curb-side outside his house, pretty much minding his own business, a car had swerved off the road and near-sided him from behind. The driver was neither drunk nor speeding and was traveling at less than twenty miles per hour - but she had been juggling with the stereo and a Marty Robbins tape and had momentarily taken her eyes off the road. Anywhere else along the street she would have mounted the sidewalk and wiped out a mailbox and had it not been for particular poor luck Archie would have come off with just bumps, bruises and a mighty fine tale to brag about in the school yard. But as the fender had nicked his shoulder it hooked into his camo-jacket sleeve and pulled Archie out into the road, dragging his left arm under the front wheel. By the time the woman had pumped her brakes, Archie's arm - or what was left of it - was streaked in a thirty-yard bloody stripe along the road. To add insult to injury, when the woman got out and saw what she had done, shock hit her stomach like a balled fist and she instantaneously puked all over him. Archie lost his arm between the elbow and shoulder and was frequently told he was the luckiest sonofabitch alive.

That evening, with Bradley's stolen beer and nearly two packets of smokes between them, the three boys hooked up at Tosser's Rock - a huge mound of out-of-place granite part buried in the sandy shore of a shallow, elbowed crook of a larger tributary that meandered through the forest south-west of Cotton Hill. It was perfect for jumping, bombing, throwing, pissing and spitting from - and as generations of schoolboys would declare it - a perfectly sublime place too from which to stand and knock one off. It was also far from the nearest road – somewhere to disappear – a retreat to goof around in without getting under the feet of anyone who might be tempted to rag them to the town authorities.

'Now this is living,' said Col, relaxing back on the sand with his rucksack as a pillow, stretched out like a lizard in the heat.

'Sure is,' said Archie, making with the smokes – he had a dumb habit of lighting three in his mouth at once, something he couldn't do very well.

'Don't bum the end of my smoke, bandit,' said Bradley. 'Why do you always do that? It makes you look like an asshole.'

Archie tossed his head, a mop of shaggy blonde hair flicked from his eyes: 'You wannit or not?'

Bradley reached over and took it, passing the second to Col, who cocked his fingers like a pistol back at Archie in appreciation.

For a few moments the three boys sat and smoked on the sand – Col puffed on his cigarette and nodded slowly and wisely as if to acknowledge that this Lucky Strike was good shit indeed. Archie, holding his cigarette cupped inwards and shaking his hand to and fro – as if weighing up this exceedingly fine tobacco, reciprocated the look. Thunder rumbled.

It was not lost on Bradley that Archie and Col had their own friendship thing going on between them. Not that Bradley cared – *shit, if those gay-boys wanna get it on who am I to give a fuck?* 'You two are a pair of cocksuckers,' said Bradley: 'You smoke like my grandmother.'

'Yes, we do,' answered Archie, slowly. 'Twenty-a-day, after sex…'

Col nearly fell in the river – guffawing and laughing, rolling on the bank clutching his sides, 'After sex! Archie, you are Cotton Hill's very own Steve Martin!'

Bradley flicked back a *screw you* with his middle finger but even he saw the funny side of it, 'Yeah, nice one, bandit. You're sweet as…'

Bandit was Bradley's nickname for Archie - after the one-armed slot-machines that filled the bars and amusement parks down by the beaches. Archie didn't really get it, but he didn't really care anyway. That was Archie all over.

Col was still chuckling on his back at the shoreline as Bradley ring-pulled a can of Eagle Red, sucking off the froth that fizzed from the top of the aluminium can: 'You wanna beer, fucknut?'

Col exhaled loudly, that wrapped up his significant delight in Archie's humour: 'Oh yes, bring it on…'

Bradley grabbed a can, shook it hard, yanked the ring-pull and tossed it fizzing and frothing into Col's lap. It landed right on his privates and as he knee-jerked into a foetal ball, grabbing his privates, beer spewed and fushed into his crotch, soaking his jeans. This time it was Archie who nearly pissed his pants – high-fiving Bradley as Col writhed in the sand.

The three boys were jerks, but jerks together and the loose, jock-humoured relationship they shared together was strong enough, just about, to withstand the not-insignificant trials they all endured individually.

Col stood up, the blow to his manhood had taken his breath away and he flung the now empty can back at Bradley: 'Give me a full one, asshole.'

Bradley dummy-punched a throw with another can at Col's crotch - effectively enough to make him flinch again - then tossed the beer lightly into his buddy's hands: 'Good catch, numbnuts.'

'Numbnuts – love it!' hooted Archie.

'Why the hell would you go and do a dumb-ass thing like that!' said Col, pulling his wet pants off and standing there in his underwear. 'I'm gonna have to spend the night with my cock out!'

'No change there – once a fag, always a fag,' said Archie.

'Takes one to know one. I bet your boyfriend loves that tight rubber grip of yours…'

Archie flicked him the middle finger: 'Suck on that.'

'Is that what you said to your boyfriend?' replied Col, before wading out into the tributary and dunking his pants in the water, washing out the beer.

'Girls,' said Bradley, 'You sound like a pair of pussies – give it up.' He tossed Archie a can, then stood up and stretched. The storm continued to shell the horizon and the sky bled magentas and cyan - lightning licked the horizon beyond the trees of the tributary - then angry thunder booming and banging so massively the boys could feel it in their chests. Raindrops as big as peanuts began to fall from the sky, intermittently at first, sploshing off the boy's arms and pocking small round divots in the sand, then more lightning – more thunder. Col, Archie and Bradley scrabbled for cover under the line of trees that edged the river.

'Getting dark,' said Col, pulling his sandy legs back into his still wet pants. 'What are we going to do now?'

'Drink more beer?' suggested Bradley, the idea of doing anything more than that seemed ridiculous.

'You know – if you girls want to just sit around here all night – we've plenty of beer and smokes, but I know something we could do that's *much more fun*.' He punctuated these last three words with a sense of conspiracy – a knowing tell-tale rise of his eyebrows and a slight nod that said he had a secret to share that was nearly fucking killing him.

The rain was beating off the leafy canopy and the sun had succumbed to the dirty half-light that precedes darkness. 'What have you got in mind, Bandit?'

Archie took a long draw on his smoke and looked Col straight in the eye, then Bradley too. 'How'd you pair of girls like to see a live sex-show?!'

Bradley looked at Col, quizzically, then back to Archie who held his mouth in a tight hole trying best he could to blow smoke rings, to keep up the tension he had suddenly created amidst the group of testosterone teens. 'You are so full of shit,' said Bradley. 'Don't even pretend you're for real.'

Archie smiled a broad and satisfying grin: 'Yeah, I'm for real,' he replied. 'Are you in?'

'You ain't talking about *Teddy's Bar* are you?' asked Col. '*Teddy's* ain't never got a live sex-show going on – just a bunch of sad old hounds shaking their titties for tips.'

'Like you've ever been in *Teddy's*,' said Bradley.

'No, I ain't, but I heard a couple of guys talking outside there once, saying a couple of those girls were all over each other, up on stage. And I mean, *all over* each other…'

'That's a crock,' said Bradley. 'There ain't no live sex-show going down at Teddy's. Besides, you two boys would never get in Teddy's in a million years.'

'Neither would you, Bradley,' replied Col. 'They check IDs before you go in – your fake driver's licence ain't gonna fool the grunts on the door at Teddy's…'

'If you two would just shut up for a minute,' said Archie, 'I ain't talking about Teddy's. I'm talking about a real-life sex-show. Not on a stage. Not between two butt-ugly old whores in a bar. Not for an audience. Real… proper… sex…'

The three of them burst out laughing – Archie spoke those three words like they were the most important and profound he had ever uttered in his life.

'Where is this *sex-show* anyway?' asked Col.

'Wait and see,' said Archie, then: 'Come on pussies – are you coming, or what?'

That was of course a ridiculous a question: 'You better not be shitting me, Bandit,' said Bradley.

***

Bradley and Col crashed through the trees and shrubs, pounding after Archie who flew like the wind. They chased him for what seemed an age, their lungs burning and their shins bleeding from knocks, and bangs and stumbles. They raced away from Tosser's Rock, through the woods that screened the tributaries and back-waters then out into farming country and cotton-fields. It was dark now and they eventually slowed to a brisk walk – Archie all the time taking the lead, batting back their questions with an arbitrary, 'You'll see soon enough.'

They walked across an open field where cotton balls grew from papery bushes. The forest once more tinged the edge of the surrounding field and just as Col and Bradley began to doubt, Archie pointed and said, 'over there.'

Over there was a bank of trees the trunks of which were knitted with thick gorse that looked impenetrable. But as the other two boys spat their disgust in heavy flobs to the floor, desperately trying to hack the pain from their stinging lungs, Archie disappeared into the undergrowth, crawling down an otherwise indiscernible passageway most likely created by some form of dog-sized wildlife.

They scrabbled on their knees, feeling their way in the darkness, twigs and thin branches scratching at their faces. 'This better be worth it, Bandit,' remarked Bradley. 'Or I'm gonna rip you another asshole.'

Archie ignored him, scurrying on like a fox.

Finally, he stopped, and with a rough heave pulled himself upright. The three of them emerged from the bush and stood in the shelter of the pine trees looking down at an old, disused barn seemingly forgotten in the gulley amongst the trees.

'There you go,' said Archie, triumphant. He was panting still and looked at the barn expectantly.

'There you go?' said Col. 'You bring us on a wild-goose chase to the middle of nowhere to a fricking barn and say, 'there you go'?'

'You are shitting me, right?' said Bradley.

Archie looked crestfallen, then his face sparked like a light and he was off again, racing down the slope. 'Come on! You ain't gonna believe what's inside!'

The three boys scrabbled down into the clearing in which the barn sat. It was timber-framed and clad in old, splintered panels. It was big though – about quarter the size of a football pitch – large enough to lose a couple of tractors or combines in. It was also deserted but the tyre-truck marks that led up to the old barn doors showed that someone was up here on a regular basis.

'Come on,' Archie beckoned. 'Come inside. We need to get hid.'

'Hid from what?' asked Bradley.

'Hid from *who*?' said Col.

'You'll see.'

Inside, the barn smelt damp and rotten. Looking up, they could see the storm clouds through holes in the roof and underfoot the dirt was moist and muddy. Whilst the panels and shingles were decaying and rotten, the huge heavy posts and beams that comprised the barn's inner structure were strong. The outer shell might not last another year, but its oak frame looked like it would last a century or more.

They gazed around for a few moments taking in this largely forgotten building. It was empty save for a bundle of old farming tools, some rusted bailing equipment, and an assortment of diesel cans. 'This place is a shithole,' remarked Col.

'Yep,' agreed Bradley. 'Let's torch it.'

'No,' snapped Archie. 'We ain't gonna torch it, Bradley. If you start acting like a jerk you can just forget it, okay? I ain't brought you up here so you can start any of your shit – get that straight. I told you, there's something you two got to see.'

'Yeah, we get it, Bandit,' replied Bradley, 'A live sex-show apparently. But I ain't seeing anything like that going down here. Not unless it's the Beverley Hillbillies…'

For the first time since he had brought the subject up, Archie looked distinctly unsure, 'Yeah, well it's something like that anyway.'

Bradley laughed, 'The Beverley Hillbillies – are you shitting me, Archie?'

'Look, I dunno how to explain okay? You'll just have to judge for yourselves, it's weird shit, that's for sure.'

'I thought we came here to see sex,' asked Col. 'But now it's *weird shit*?'

'It's all of that. It's sex and it's weird shit. I dunno, yes – both. It's nuts,' Archie replied.

'Right then,' said Bradley. 'Let's get to it. Do we have to hang around in this barn all night or is something gonna happen? Because if it ain't happening I'm out of here and you two dickwads can toss each other off all night, for all I care…'

As Bradley spoke, the dull sound of an engine rumbled from somewhere outside, then headlights shone through the gaps in the boards sending yellow light fanning out across the floor.

'Jesus!' yelled Archie. 'Quick - this way!'

***

The three boys bolted into the dark recess of the barn. Archie led, leading them to the rear where a ladder provided access to the hayloft above. As headlights stole the darkness, the boys disappeared upwards and out of sight. Their hiding place gave them full view of the barn below and they scurried on their bellies to peer over the ledge above where now the vehicle, a pick-up, had parked.

'What the hell are we doing here, Bandit!' asked Bradley, under his breath, 'If you get me killed, I swear I'm gonna come back as a ghost and rip your cock from your balls.'

'Relax, Bradley,' he replied. 'He can't see us up here – trust me, we're completely hidden – it's like totally abandoned.'

'So, who's this guy, then?' asked Bradley.

'I don't know. He showed up about a month ago. I was hid up here and saw it all – he does her on the back of his pick-up.'

'He's fucking massive,' said Col.

The three of them peered down – they were pretty much directly above, and it dawned on both Col and Bradley they were in for one hell of a view. 'That's gonna bruise her butt…' Bradley quipped.

Col sniggered: 'How often does he, you know, come up here then?' he asked, 'Have you been spying on them nightly?'

'Hell, no!' he replied. 'I ain't no perv - I've seen it two or three times – four, max. But you can tell by the amount of tyre tracks that he's up here most nights.'

They looked and all agreed – this was clearly a regular hang-out for the guy in the pick-up, who as they peered, opened the driver's door to the F100 and climbed out.

'Where's the girl?' asked Bradley.

Archie pointed to the offside of the truck, to where the man now walked and opened the passenger door. In the glare of the headlights it was difficult to see clearly into the cab and he swung the door open to release his passenger.

But instead of one girl climbing out; two did. And instead of a woman, it was two young girls – no more than five or six years old. The man put a hand on one of the girls' shoulders and bent down to whisper something, handing them a jump-rope as he did so: both girls nodded. Whilst none of the boys could hear exactly what was said, his meaning was clear: *clear off out of here, and don't get up to any trouble.*

The two of them - in dirty old dungarees and matching *Grand Ignitions Automotive Repairs* baseball caps - trotted off with the rope out of the barn into the darkness. No right parent of sane mind would send their kids off like that, but the man had other things on his mind right now.

'Archie, what the hell is going down here – who are the kids?'

'Bradley, I swear to God I have no idea.'

'And where's the girl, Archie? If you're shitting us I swear I won't be responsible for what I do to you.'

Col chipped in: 'Jeez, you two – keep the noise down. That guy's got to weigh 250 pounds – if he sees us up here spying on him we're going to end up buried in the woods!'

'Keep your knickers on, pussy – he ain't hearing us up here. And where's the fucking girl!?'

As Bradley whispered these words the man moved away from his truck into the darkness. In the silence the boys became aware of the sound of singing from outside the barn; the two girls were playing jump-rope, oblivious to what was about to happen inside.

'Cinderella, dressed in yella…!'

For a few moments the man was completely enveloped in the shadows, but the boys could still hear him; the distinctive sound of a lock clicking open and an old wooden door being yanked open.

'Went upstairs to kiss a fella…'

The barn fell still again, just the sound of the jump-rope song cutting the air, then more indiscernible noises from the darkness, then the sound of a female voice, muffled. Somewhere off to the side of the barn there was clearly another room – and in it the man had a woman.

'Made a mistake…'

Momentarily he pulled her out into the glare of the headlights, where she stood trembling in a large filthy sweat-top, her wrists bound behind her back and tape across her mouth.

'And kissed a snake…'

'Fuck me, Bandit,' whispered Col, panicked, 'He's got someone prisoner down there! You didn't think to mention that!? He's a goddam kidnapper!'

'How many doctors did it take?'

Archie didn't say a word. 'I swear – I had no idea; I never knew she was locked up – I had no idea!'

'You're a fucking creep, Bandit,' Col went on. 'You knew – you knew and never said a word! You said you've seen him three or four times, shithead! You knew he had her locked up down there, and you did nothing!'

Bradley was silent – then rolled off his belly and punched Col hard on the arm, 'Shut it, moron. Keep your voice down, you're gonna give us away.'

The three of them shut up. Shut up and watched. Watching above whilst the man carried the girl around his truck and placed her onto the back of the pick-up. She had lost pounds since the afternoon he had abducted her – and whilst he had fed her and watered her, the weight had fallen off her delicate frame and now she appeared pale and bony against his massive body. That song again cut the stillness.

'Cinderella, dressed in yella
Went upstairs to kiss a fella
Made a mistake
And kissed a snake
How many doctors did it take?'

As the man assaulted her the boys stared on, their eyes glued to the crime. He raped her for thirty minutes or so, and they watched it all, unblinkingly.

When it was over, he rolled off the girl and she turned away onto her side, hiding against the threadbare blankets and rugs that were scattered across the bed of the truck. The boys didn't see her face, or her tears, or the fear and terror that were wrought across her entire being. The man sat up, and wiping the sweat from his face and torso, fumbled for a heavy roll of tape that was stashed in the back of the pick-up. He threw her the sweat-top she had been wearing and told her to put it on. She turned slowly and pulled herself up and did as she was told. He bound her arms behind her once more and secured tape across her mouth. He did it all without saying a word to her - she may as well have been a doll. Then, he lifted her up in his arms where she hung limp and lifeless – he carried her back into the darkness and out of sight.

From the hayloft above, the three boys lay in stony silence for a moment, watching him carry the girl away.

'Holy fuck,' said Col, splitting the silence. 'Do you know what we just saw? You know, *do you get it*, Archie?'

The three boys slowly, quietly, pulled themselves up and away from the ledge above the pick-up.

'Yeah, I get it,' Archie replied. Until thirty minutes ago, the whole episode had been fantasy – grubby boy gratification like the thrill of sneaking a look in the female locker-room or spying through the drapes on the girl across the street. Now, however, they realized the shame in goggling pretty much the worse crime there was.

'What do we do now Bradley?' asked Archie.

Bradley was lying on his back, his mind swirling and gushing with an emotional overload that his immature and feeble conscience could not decipher nor manage. *Fuck - how he had enjoyed that show! How he imagined himself rolling on top of that girl, rather than him! Oh, what he would have done to have exchanged places and enjoyed her for himself…* But then he knew something more; all the time he had watched and grinded his pathetic groin on the boards, he knew this girl – knew her name, where she came from, and just who was looking for her. *And I watched…* he thought. Finally, though: 'We're going to rescue her.'

With new purpose Bradley scrabbled in his pockets for a ball of paper. He pulled it out, uncrumpled it, and showed it to Col and Archie – they studied it in the soft moonlight that shone through the barn roof.

'Where'd you get this?' asked Col.

'This morning,' Bradley answered. 'Some runt in the street rode his bike into me: he was handing these out – had a bundle of them in a bag.'

'Shit,' remarked Archie. 'She's like, a missing person.'

'You twat, Archie – of course she's a missing person. She's a kid – just like us. Please don't tell me you thought they were boyfriend-girlfriend?'

'I told you – I didn't know!'

'Yeah, well now you do. And how long have you known about this? How many times have you been up here watching this shit going on and not thinking to tell anyone? You really are an asshole, Archie – you know that?'

'Shut it Col,' interrupted Bradley. 'This little wankathon of Bandit's ends now. You guys ain't gonna pussy out on me, right? I reckon I could pretty much have him on my own; the three of us shouldn't have any trouble at all. We bang this fucker up and the three of us'll be heroes – follow me.'

The man was still off somewhere to the side of the barn as Bradley, Archie and Col scrambled down the ladder from the hayloft. For three teenagers they were surprisingly quiet and in the semi-darkness their stealth ensured they would have the upper hand when the man appeared again. Bradley had grabbed a hayfork, Col and Archie two pieces of timber that had once been perhaps axe-handles: they waited offside of the pick-up, their hearts beating like madmen.

'Are you sure this is a good idea?' asked Archie, the colour had drained from his cheeks and he looked like he might just pass out.

'Shut up,' said Bradley, under his breath. 'When the time comes, just hit the crap out if him.'

Cinderella, dressed in yella
Went upstairs to kiss a fella

At that moment he reappeared, stepping out of the darkness and wiping his nose on the back of his hand. His mind was now back in reality and his next task, now fully satisfied, was to find his girls and get off home. He walked along the driver's side of the pick-up towards the barn doors, and as he did Bradley crept around the front of the truck behind him. Col and Archie followed.

Just as the man passed the end of the pick-up, he heard something – and turned back. Bradley swung the hayfork and its two iron prongs clattered against the side of Vance's head. He managed a very surprised sounding 'what the fff…!', before he fell unconscious to the deck liked a floored rhinoceros. Upon which, the three boys pounced with their weapons and battered him relentlessly, near hysterically – not out of real aggression, more from fear that he might just well stand up and beat the living crap out of them if they didn't. Seconds later though, Bradley stopped, and Archie and Col followed suit – they looked at the motionless heap: 'He ain't going nowhere,' said Bradley.

Made a mistake

They were panting like wild animals and their heads spun dizzily from the adrenalin that now surged through their blood. Vance was out cold – but he was not dead, and a man that size would not remain unconscious for long. Archie steadied himself with his good arm against the pick-up: 'I think I'm gonna puke. Can you drive this thing, Bradley?'

Kissed a snake

'Sure. Come on; let's get him tied up. I ain't hanging around here any longer than I have to.'

Using the tape the man had used to bind the girl, the three boys tied his feet and secured his arms behind his back - for good measure they also taped up his eyes so that he could see either. It took all three of them to drag him to the side of the barn and tie him with the remaining tape to one of the supporting beams. They then switched attention to the girl.

How many doctors will it take?

The room in which she was hid was a side storage unit integral to the barn's western side. The door - which Bradley levered open with the hayfork - slid open sideways and it was not immediately clear where she was. The air inside this tiny room - barely big enough for Bradley, Archie and Col to crowd into, was musty and damp. For a moment the three were dumbstruck – *where the fuck is she?* There was nowhere to hide anyone in here. It was Col whose eyes fell to the floor first, and almost immediately as they did, he stamped on the boarded floor – a hollow *thunk* resounded: 'She's under here,' Col said.

The three fell to their knees, brushing away the dust and dirt with their hands. Frantically they clawed at the boards, scraping away with their fingers to reveal the outline of a trapdoor – none of them spoke, each one was choked with adrenalin and desperation; they made their fingernails bleed. 'Pass me the hayfork,' Bradley finally yelled. 'Pass me the fucking fork!'

Archie passed it over, sweat dripping from his forehead into the dust. His ears rang with the rush of blood coursing through his head as Bradley levered up the board. Though no one said so, each three were expecting to find her dead. Col had earlier said they were dealing with a killer... *and shouldn't she be making some sort of noise now? Screaming? Shouting? Banging on the boards?*

Archie would later swear that when they finally lifted the trapdoor he only puked because he thought she *was* dead. Col - though he never did admit this - had his eyes shut as Bradley opened the cell in the floor – he didn't want to see a dead girl looking up from the grave. And Bradley – tough guy Bradley – who for all his bravado was just a second away from blubbing like the kid he had slugged early today - a lifetime ago. The little kid whose sister was in this hole - whom he *just knew was gonna be dead with her neck broke... Just knew it!* The air felt like it was going to going to explode.

She was not dead. And as Archie puked and Col listened for any tell-tale sign that it was safe to look, Bradley lifted the girl out of the shit-stinking hole. She was alive, and as Bradley pulled away the tape that bound her wrists and covered her mouth, she began to cry uncontrollably. Sobbing and wailing – her eyes darting around, frantically searching the darkness for signs of her captor - she was hysterical and gibbering incomprehensibly, so utterly full was she of indescribable fear. The boys did not know what to do – the way she was clawing at Bradley's shirt she seemed somehow feral, not at all the pretty girl they had seen on the poster. Then Bradley reacted in a way that surprised both himself, and Col and Archie: a gesture that was both in polarity to the gawky teenage meathead that he was. He grabbed her, firmly and supportively, and hugged her to his chest, like he was holding a kitten: 'Ain't no one gonna hurt you, you're safe now.'

The girl snivelled and nodded, snot ran from her nose and mingled with tears in a salty mess on her dry, cracked lips; she looked out at her unlikely rescuers. Though her eyes were puffy and bloodshot, the boys could not help but see the petrified creature behind them. And the rawness of her fear that seemed to bleed through every cut, graze and sore on her abused body frightened them much more than the monster that was stirring a few feet away in the barn. And then she spoke, so quietly that each boy missed what she said. She swallowed hard and said it again: 'Water.'

***

DI Osemon leant back in his chair and surveyed the cocky kid in the *Enjoy Cocaine* t-shirt. In front of the inspector on the interview table were three manila files – the first held the hastily typed-up transcript of Bradley's first interview of the evening, detailing his version of the events in and around the barn. The second thicker file were his police records, and whilst largely petty they were not insubstantial in volume – and the final file held the testimonies of Col and Archie, and a few scribbled notes gathered from the officer who had spoken briefly with the DesMoiles girl, who was now sedated in Savannah General. Osemon lit a cigarette and took his time to flick through the first file once more: the thick tick-tock of the wall clock beat a loud monotony through the otherwise silent and stifling interview room. It was 3.21am, and Vance had been in custody for approximately four and a half hours.

Vern Wessell, the duty attorney, was sat next to Bradley and he shifted in his uncomfortable plastic chair. He was tired; he was old, and his time was cheap, and he was bored of this nonsense. But he knew how these things worked, and he was confident that this affair was not going to cause him much more than perhaps a little form-filling. He certainly was not of the opinion that this was going to get hardball. He scratched his greying, thin hair and pushed his glasses up his nose.

Osemon looked up from the papers, drew hard on his cigarette then exhaled the smoke from the side of his mouth away from the pair sat opposite him. He sat up straight again in his chair as if to speak. Then didn't.

Osemon did not like Bradley. He did not like boys that caused him trouble. And he knew that the chances were that Bradley would indeed *cause him trouble.* Osemon did not care about the how and whys – he just knew that one day he would be looking over this table at Bradley Engelmaier and it would not be about an event like this evening's episode; nor would it be about petty shoplifting, vandalism or fighting in the street, or any of those many low-level offenses that currently filled his burgeoning police file. No – as far as Osemon cared, this teenage scumbag would be one of tomorrow's drug-dealers or car-jackers, or the asshole who pops a bullet in the face of some have-a-go-hero shopkeeper over the contents of the till and a display case of cigarettes. *Low-lifes like Engelmaier don't come to anything but a sack of shit* thought Oseman, pulling on his cigarette once again.

And yet the asshole's story stacked up. Osemon had interviewed the three of them: Bradley, Archie Brodit and Col Dewy. Even the notes from DesMoiles corroborated the boys' stories. There was barely a needle he could drive between the four of them. And what grated him the most - and what Osemon really wanted to avoid - was the fact that they would soon walk out of the station to a herd of reporters who would ensure they would be heroes by the end of tomorrow. And he would be the asshole cop who hadn't done his job.

Osemon started at last: 'So, let's run this through one last time, okay? Just to be sure. Anything I missed, or you don't agree with – just shout.'

Wessell nodded and yepped before Bradley could open his mouth.

Osemon went on: 'To state for the record, the time is 3.23am on Sunday, 24th June, 1979. Present are Bradley Engelmaier, DOB 21.4.62 (age seventeen years and one month, parents invited but not present) of 1543 Sequoia Avenue, Cotton Hill; and duty attorney Mr. Vern Wessell… To proceed then, you arrived at the barn at approximately 9.30pm to 9.45pm.' He looked up; Bradley nodded.

'You stated that the barn was known to Archie Brodit, but until last evening you had never been there before. Archie Brodit, Col Dewy and yourself all state that you were in attendance at the barn to, and I quote, 'smoke some tabs and drink some beer.''

Bradley nodded.

'At the time of your arrival, the property - now identified as being a disused storage facility of the ownership of Carl Hapseed, *Hapseed Cotton farms* – and located on the outskirts of his farming acreage and approximately three-quarters of a mile from the nearest road, the Osprey Hill Pass - you state, was empty.'

'I'm sorry – can you run that pass me again, Officer?' Bradley was slouched in his chair, and as far as he was concerned this was all now a waste of time. He had concerns, real fear in fact that he could be looking at a potential charge – even jail time, but he was knackered: a physical and emotional tiredness so deep that Osemon's words seemed to wash over him like warm water. Had Vern not kicked him under the table he could quite easily be asleep. And how wonderful that would feel now.

Osemon looked up: 'That's Inspector, not Officer.'

'Gotcha.'

'Thank you, Bradley... I stated that the barn appeared empty when you arrived – is that correct?'

'Uh-huh.'

Then Osemon was back to his notes: 'You state that approximately five minutes after arriving at the barn you heard the sound of an approaching vehicle - now identified as a Ford F100 Ranger pick-up and driven by the now positively identified Mr Reginald Vance - and that he parked up inside the barn, below where yourselves were situated in the, and I quote, 'hayloft.' Is that correct?'

'Yes.'

'And the pick-up pulled up directly below you?'

'Yes.'

'Would you say you had the perfect view of the events that then unfolded in the barn below?'

'That's what I said. Absolutely,' remarked Bradley.

'And there is no way you could have misinterpreted what you saw?' asked Osemon.

'No way. We all saw what he did. The man's a fucking crim.'

'Okay,' Osemon continued. 'We'll get to that in a moment. You state that from the vehicle - and after the man had got out of the vehicle - he was immediately followed by two young children – girls – and that the man said something to them, before ushering them out of the barn.'

'Uh-huh.'

'Did you hear what he said to the two children?'

Bradley paused. He hadn't heard a thing – Christ, he was too excited about the promise of a sex-show to pick up details like that: 'No, sorry – as I said earlier, I heard nothing.'

'Okay Bradley, we'll move on. So, the attack – after the children had left the barn the man disappeared from sight and returned moments later with the girl – now identified as Miss DesMoiles.'

'Yes.'

'And again, I use your words here, 'he took her to the back of the pick-up where he started to *fuck her up real bad*.'

'He did.'

'By which you meant he had intercourse with her?'

'Intercourse?' asked Bradley.

'Yeah, *intercourse*. He had sex with her. He *fucked* her,' said Osemon.

'Yes.'

'And just to be clear,' continued Osemon. 'It was evident that this was not consensual?'

'Con-*what*?' asked Bradley.

Jesus, what are they teaching these kids in school, thought Osemon: 'The girl was not a willing participant '*in the fucking*,' is what I mean.'

'No. Definitely not.'

'Okay. You stated that the attack lasted approximately two or three minutes,' Osemon looked up and Bradley nodded. 'And that immediately following the attack he led her back to 'wherever it was he had been keeping her.'

'That's what happened,' said Bradley.

'Two or three minutes – you're sure the attack lasted no longer than that?'

'Max.'

'Okay,' continued Oseman, moving on again, 'When he disappeared, that's when the three of you hatched the plan to rescue the girl?'

'Yes.'

'You came down from the hayloft and armed yourselves with the nearest weapons you could find - you had a hayfork, and Col and Archie had…' he rifled through his files, 'sticks… You hid on the far side of the pick-up and when the man reappeared you approached him from behind and hit him with the fork. Correct?'

'Yes. I hit him with the fork, then Col and Archie laid into him with the sticks too. We gave him a battering – okay? I don't think that's unreasonable, do you?'

Wissell chipped in: 'Inspector, can I ask here that you are not intending on bringing a battery charge against my client? It is more than evident that under the circumstances he was acting in self-defence for the girl.'

Osemon sighed, *these things would always be so much easier without the fucking lawyers.*

'Rest easy, I just want to be clear about the facts.'

'Then go ahead,' replied Wessell.

Osemon went on: 'And after the beating, and when you had tied him up, that's when you found the girl?'

'That's when we found the girl.'

'Okay, I'm good with the next bit – we're nearly done here, Bradley,' said Osemon.

'Great.'

'So, after you got the girl, the three of you bundle into the pick-up, leaving Mr Vance tied to the post, and you make your escape. Are you a good driver, Bradley?'

Wessell: 'Again; and under the circumstances I don't see the relevance of your question. My client was in a pressure scenario where he had good reason to believe his life, and those of others, were in immediate threat.'

'In threat from a *semi-conscious* man, tied to a post?'

'That is correct. And you know that is exactly how a judge and jury would see it too. I'm sorry, Inspector – I ask for assurance that you are not in the process of *building a case* against my client. I assure you, any failings on behalf of yourself or of your police department in rescuing the DesMoiles girl are only going to be magnified, and the repercussions significantly exaggerated, if you force me to defend the *heroic actions* of my client – actions that evidently came about through your own ineptitude and inability to solve this case first.'

Bradley smiled.

Osemon eyeballed him; *shit, what a crock this day had become.* He knew he was on a hiding to nothing. 'Let me ask the questions, Mr Wessell – if you don't mind?'

Wessell nodded. 'But steer clear of the insinuations please.'

'Bradley, tell me about how you killed the kid then.'

Wessell sighed. 'Inspector, your line of questioning is antagonistic. I ask that you treat my client with the respect that he deserves. We both know he's going to be a hero in tomorrow's news – you may even be lucky enough to have your picture next to his in the evening papers - though I'm not sure your headlines will be as exultant as my client's.'

Oseman was growing tired of this bullshit but he wanted to hear it one more time. He didn't think he had missed anything; he didn't think in fairness that Bradley had omitted anything – but he wanted him in the spotlight once more, just in case. Just one moment more of pressure - one more opportunity to find anything that might detract from those headlines.

'It's okay,' said Bradley. 'I'll say it once more for the inspector.'

This time Osemon nodded, and Wessell knew it was a gesture of weakness. This was in the bag.

'No Inspector, you're right. I'm not a great driver. I'm seventeen years old and don't have a whole lot of experience. As I said earlier, when we jumped in the pick-up, we were all shitting ourselves – fuck, Bandit had even chucked his guts up, we were all *that scared.* The guy was definitely coming round, and he was big – we'd tied him up with tape, but none of us thought it would hold him for long. None of us were gonna stick around to see what was coming next.

'So, we jumped in the car and I floored it – fast as I could. The pick-up keys were in the ignition and it just flew – took off like a rocket. We was all in the front, squished up, and I was struggling for the gas pedal, the brakes, I was all over the place. The pick-up lurched out of the barn then we picked up speed. I remember veering left, struggling with the steering to pull it back – I couldn't see much either, then this tree was coming right at me. I remember hitting the gas instead of the brakes, and it was so fast. I couldn't hold it steady – that's when I saw them…'

'The two girls?'

'Yeah, they were stood like right next to the tree – I just caught them in the headlights. I heard Archie, or maybe it was Col shout something, someone definitely shouted 'look out!' or 'watch it!' but way too late – and as I said, I was struggling to control the pick-up – it was all so fast, Inspector – and we was shitting ourselves, and I just ploughed into her – I missed one girl, but hit the other. I saw the other one - the one I missed - through my side window. But the other girl, the one I hit – I don't know where she went. I don't know if she went under or over, I didn't see… It was an accident. I'm sorry – really sorry I killed her. It was an accident – but it wasn't my fault. Vance, he's the one you should be blaming.'

And there it was – same as the last time. Osemon knew it was case closed.

Wessell smiled: 'There you have it, Inspector; I think we're all clear on the matter, don't you? No inconsistencies. My client has made it very clear that he is remorseful, and that the hugely regrettable death of the minor, was an accident under a quite extraordinary set of unimaginatively stressful conditions - particularly for someone of my client's young age. There are no grounds at all for any charges here Inspector, and you know it all too well. Bradley, we're done – I advise you that you answer no more questions this evening.'

Osemon tapped out one more cigarette, and closing off the interview, turned off the tape player: 'I do have one more question though, if you don't mind. Call it my own personal curiosity, if you like.'

Bradley looked at Wessell, who shrugged – *the tape's off, why would I give a boot?* So Osemon went on: 'There's only one part of your story that doesn't stack up – and I'm a little curious…'

'Yeah?' said Bradley.

'You stated that your vantage point from the hayloft gave you the perfect view of the attack in the pick-up.'

'Uh-huh.'

'And that the attack lasted no more than two or three minutes?'

'That's right,' said Bradley.

'But Miss DesMoiles said that this last attack was the longest of the many, many attacks that she had suffered at the hands of Vance. And that she believed it lasted for at least half an hour – probably longer.'

Bradley was silent, and before Wessell could interrupt, Osemon continued, 'I put it to you Bradley, that while she was being raped,' he let those words hang in the air a moment, 'you and your little scumbag mates were jerking off and watching it happen…'

'Do not answer that question, Bradley,' said Wessell.

Osemon continued and called out as they made their exit from the room: 'You're a big man, Bradley. You could have stopped him at any time! But you were up in the hayloft getting off, weren't you?'

The door shut and the room was silent again: Osemon smoked his cigarette, satisfied at least that he had made his point, however irrelevant and ultimately pointless it was.

Thursday, 9th July 2015

Chapter 20

Morning.

Grandig arrived at her workstation and sank low into her well-worn office chair. Her desk was a heap of paper and coffee mugs and her PC hummed at her like an expectant puppy might wag its tail. A red light on her telephone flashed 'new messages' and though it was only a quarter past nine in the morning, there were already a handful of *Post-Its* stuck to her screen with barely legible names and numbers scrawled across them – Grandig picked them off, screwed them into a loose ball and flicked them unread into her wastebasket. Filing was always her first job of the day.

Before she had time to retrieve her chocolate muffin from her purse, her office phone rang. She toyed with letting it ring, but finally reached over and answered it.

'Grandig – shit – I'm really sorry, I've got some bad news.'

Grandig sat up in her chair: 'Kristen, what is it girl? What's happened? Are you okay?'

'Yes, I'm fine. It's the kid – Jeez, Grandig, I don't know how – but she got out last night.'

'Got out – what do you mean, Kristen? Where is she now?' Grandig felt the cold sweats run through her veins.

'I don't know Grandig – that's what I'm trying to tell you. I got up this morning, and when I went to her room she was gone. I've searched the place but there's absolutely no sign of her.'

'Christ, Kristen! Have you called the police yet?'

'No, not yet. I wanted to call you first.'

Grandig paused. Usually, there was nothing particularly unusual about a foster kid running away – it happened pretty much all of the time. But this kid was *little*. Foster homes were meant to be safe places – with carers taking steps to stop this thing from happening. Sure – you could never keep a teenager under lock-and-key, they'd always find a way to get out if they really wanted to – but a little kid? That sounded careless: neglectful. 'Was your place secure last night – how'd she get out?'

'I don't know Grandig. As I said, she was gone when I got up this morning?'

'And what about Bradley?' Grandig asked. 'Where was he?'

There was a momentary silence on the line, then: 'He'd left for work already.'

'Have you called him?'

Kristen was in danger of tying herself up in knots. 'No, as I said – I called you first, Grandig.'

Grandig drew breath. This was bad. Her day had just begun and now it was fucked up beyond belief. 'Well, you call him straight away and call me back, okay?'

'Sure – right away.'

'Ask if he saw her before he left for work - and in the meantime, I'll ring this through to Savannah PD.'

There was another pause on the line, then Kirsten said: 'Is that strictly necessary?'

'Yes! It's necessary, Kristen! She's a little kid wandering the streets of Savannah – who knows what kind of danger she's in right now! Chrissake!'

'Yeah – of course – sorry, this is just kinda stressful Grandig.'

'Kristen – don't take this the wrong way of anything – but,' she paused. 'Were you guys drunk last night – or, high?'

'Jesus Grandig – no! Where did that come from!?'

'Just gotta ask, I'm afraid. I need to be sure you guys were doing your jobs properly.'

Kristen bristled. 'No, Grandig. Bradley and I were fine. We were not drunk, and we were not high. Okay?'

'Okay, Kristen,' Grandig replied, not wholly convinced. 'Don't worry too much just yet. She'll turn up. These things happen.'

***

She hung up, then immediately tapped the speed-dial for an all-points bulletin to the duty officer on the front desk at Savannah PD. It was a bizarre conversation; these things are usually formal and by-the-book, but when there's no name, no date-of-birth, no next-of-kin, no discerning features or description beyond *a little female kid*, the duty officer came back with *and you seriously want me to ring this through?*

'Yes, *asshole*,' Grandig punched back, 'I want you to ring this through. Now.'

'Fine,' came the terse reply. 'But, don't expect any come-back for at least twelve hours. At the earliest.'

***

Next, Grandig flicked her mouse and her monitor pinged into life; a dozen emails dropped into her inbox, each message part of a long chain of communications linking some poor fucked-up kid to Savannah's Child Protective Service - but these kids were now the least of Grandig's problems. *At least these kids are identifiable in the system – at least I can do something with them,* she thought. *Fuck.*

Grandig did not have the first clue what to do with the kid. She grabbed the painfully thin case file for the child and opened it up. Inside there were the notes from the officers who had picked her up that first day, a brief report from the district nurse who had given her the once over ('no apparent signs of violence / injury / or abuse present'), then Grandig's own subsequent details regarding the emergency placement with the Engelmaiers. Apart from that, there was zilch. No names, next of kin, social security number… nothing.

Grandig felt shit; in fact, sick to her stomach. Her gut always told her that there was something not right about Kristen and Bradley. They were always the last couple she called – literally, when she had no one else to step in. Now, there would be investigations, interviews, suspicions and accusations… both from Child Protective and the Police Department. *How the fuck could the Engelmaier's just let a little kid walk out of their house?*

Chapter 21

It seemed pretty much every winged creature that inhabited the marshes floated and danced on the hot, thick air that hung in the boathouse. They were soporific on the sticky sweet fermentation that caked Bradley's congealed and blood-clogged orifices: bugs crawled in his ears and up his nose, mosquito larvae flicked and wriggled in the tiny pools that welled in his eyes, and snails slooped a mucousy trail from the corner of his mouth to under his jellying tongue. Yet still his heart flicked a desperate beat, faint and faltering, keeping his near-decomposing body just the right side of life.

Consciousness ebbed for Bradley like horrific drunkenness. His mind fell about as it did when fuelled by a night of beer and bourbon; his stomach attempted an empty wretch, his eyes soft-focussed again then the lights went out once more. If only he were dead…

Chapter 22

Early evening.

Grandig drove in autopilot, thumping down Crespolina Blvd out of downtown. It was not late, but she was tired – her conversation with Kristen buzzed in her head like an annoying fly. There had been no word on the kid – Kristen had called back to say Bradley hadn't noticed whether she was in her bed when he left – and the Savannah PD had not found any sign of her out on the streets. The day had burnt out in a flash and the kid had up and vanished. Round and round the conversation swirled again – *why hadn't Kristen called the PD? That's the first thing you do if you get a runaway – it's right there in the Child Protective manual! And why the reluctance to ring it through? 'Is that strictly necessary?' Isn't that what Kristen said?* Usually, Grandig was adept at flicking that little button in her head that switched her mind back and forth between work and home, a nifty trick that stopped the realities of her day-job sending her completely insane. But tonight, she could not find that button and that brief but troubling conversation replayed itself over and over in her head to the sound of beach houses drumming past her open car window.

She clicked a speed-dial on her phone and called the one person she could rely upon to help put her mind straight.

***

The old woman's gait, on decayed hips that should have been replaced decades ago, rolled an awkward shimmy as she hobbled down the path to meet her most precious ward: 'Oh my special girl – look at you!' Her smile was broad and bright, and her hands stretched out in front of her ready to hold and cherish Grandig's face in the way that only old people do: If she could have lifted Grandig off her feet with her warmth and passion she surely would have done so.

In turn - as she bound enthusiastically up the path - Grandig did not see the wrinkles, nor the arthritic limbs that now crippled Momo - her rock for many years – but saw a friend, glowing and loving, who seemed to dance down the path to greet her. 'Oh Momo, how are you, I miss you!' They fell into each other's arms with squeals and kisses, and it was Grandig who bear-hugged and lifted the woman from her feet.

Momo exhaled loudly, half from joy of seeing Grandig, and half from having the wind squeezed out of her: 'Gee, you can't be treating me like that – you damn near broke my ribs!' but she chuckled, and Grandig knew her too well to think she might have hurt her.

It was full dark, and as they made their way inside the bugs and crickets were singing in the grass. Momo lived out of the city amidst the low country that sprawled out from the Savannah River. Her house was old and smelt of damp books, wood floors and a dying hint of beeswax – and in a way she and her home were quite similar, in that once they had been fine and well-cared for but were now both scuffed and getting a little dog-eared. But that was good, because this was a house that had been lived in – and whilst it was now pretty much an empty shell in which the old Momo rattled around like a dry wrinkled pea, Grandig knew it had once been full to the brim of noise and fun.

Momo made tea as Grandig cleared the sofa of books and magazines and dumped herself down. A couple of candles burned, and their dull flickering light made shadows dance: 'You need help in there?' she called out, but Momo called back that she was fine and dandy. Grandig looked around: the house had grown a middle-aged spread of clutter and junk, and dust had crept in and made itself at home. It was clearly a long while, years most likely, since the place had been spring-cleaned - Momo was too old for a house this big Grandig thought - but for all the paraphernalia that burgeoned from its seams, the echoes of Grandig's past still rang true and bright in her ears. God it was good to be back.

Momentarily Momo appeared, wobbling still and with two glasses that Grandig spotted were only three-quarters full – most likely so she would not spill any carrying them through.

'I ain't so quick on these feet nowadays, Gee – takes me a goddam age to mix two drinks,' she said. 'Good job it ain't lunchtime either, you'd probably starve to death waiting.'

Grandig smiled: Momo hadn't changed a bit – her arms were always open. 'I reckon I'd survive Momo.'

'Good for you.' There was a pause, then a grin: 'Ain't it just lovely to see you!'

And then Grandig and Momo talked for an hour or more, about nothing and everything, catching up on things they had missed and news that had passed them by. Grandig leant back and spread out, her butt sinking low and her thick thighs tipping inwards – she pretty much took up the whole sofa. Momo watched her as she herself sipped her tea and looked how Gee had grown upwards and outwards over the years. There was no judgment there, just tacit observation of how the little kid she had once known – back then a bag of skin and bone - had changed over the years to become her own unique woman.

'You see your picture over there,' she said, waggling her finger towards her sideboard. 'I look at you every day just to keep my eye on you.'

Grandig looked to where she pointed, where dozens of picture frames encased photos of kids who had since grown up or were now growing old. Some of the pictures were black and white, others faded yellow and auburn – a few, the last, fairing the aging process a little better and remained still quite clear. Scattered amongst the frames were candles - some burning, some burnt out – and those that flickered glowed a warm blanket over the faces. 'I bet you say that to everyone,' Grandig replied.

'Sure, I do,' she replied.

Grandig pulled herself out of the chair and stepped over to Momo's collection of memories for a closer look – she had seen the one of herself before, but not for some years, and she looked for that old picture with the gawky kid grinning inanely back: 'Here you go, here's the angel,' she said.

'Damn right she's an angel,' Momo replied. 'Still is, too. You pass her over here an let me take another look.'

Grandig passed her the frame and sat back down.

Momo looked at her picture of Grandig. She remembered, back then, that there wasn't nothing to the girl. She told her often back then that she was all knees and elbows, with an ass so bony she could scratch her own initials on a bench just by sitting on it. Momo chuckled silently to herself – that was certainly not the case now.

'You arrived with that photo the evening they dropped you off here, did you know that?' Momo asked.

'No – I don't remember,' Grandig said.

'It was one of your only possessions,' Momo replied. 'That and the clothes you arrived in. That picture was tucked into the pocket of your dungarees.'

Grandig had arrived perhaps a week before that – Momo remembered. Late in May, and the hot summer had already set in for the season. She remembered how Gee sat silently amongst the branches of the magnolia seeming to want to be hidden, but still just in sight – all at the same time. She spent hours there, silent and motionless, watching intently as the hours passed. She minded her own business – and moved deeper into the branches if anyone came close or attempted to strike up conversations. But she was always there, in the background, amidst the wilting blooms of pinks and creams.

Despite the many anxious visitors this bony little kid seemed to attract back then, all wanting her to spill the beans, Momo was the only one that Grandig would talk to – and the thought of those first few words still brought her a smile even now. Her new guest had been with her for perhaps a little less than a week and as of yet had not uttered a single word - not uncommon, she had been told. Her habit of not-quite-hiding in the magnolia tree was established, as too was the other kids disinterest in the newbie. Momo's house was broad and rambling, a single storey home with a veranda that swept around looking out towards the tributaries of the Savannah River. Though it was too far inland to see the beach, it lay less than a mile from the shore – and most days a warm easterly breeze blew the smell of the ocean right up to where Momo sat with her morning coffee.

'I was thinking about eggplants,' Momo said, breaking the silence as she turned the photograph between her fingers: 'Did I ever tell you that?'

Grandig shook her head. She remembered nothing of back then.

'I was sat out there,' she gestured with a finger waving at the porch door. 'Just minding my own business. Well, the sun was barely up over the ocean and the place was quiet. For all I thought, you was still all tucked up in bed fast asleep. That was my hour – just for me and my coffee, no one ever going to be disturbing me because no one was ever up, just me and my thoughts. Anyhow, there I was, when all merry-hell breaks loose... 'Momo, come quick – she's dying!' that's you, hollering like a banshee, tearing round the side of the deck like a lunatic, 'Come quick, she's DYING!'

'Well Jesus and God almighty if I didn't nearly drop dead from shock right there and then – my peace was shattered like someone let a firecracker off in my ear – damn near drowned myself in coffee. You was all red, and a sweat was breaking out across your forehead: 'Come quick, she's dying – she's dying!' you kept yelling and screaming, and by this time I'm shouting *who's dying, who's dying?* My coffee mug is spinning off down the deck with a clatter, and you're dragging me by the arm off round the veranda from where you come from, tears welling in your eyes and a lump about to break in your throat - and it's all I can do not to trip over my damned feet in the panic.'

Momo smiled: 'Do you remember who it was dying?'

Grandig shook her head.

'That damned magnolia tree – that's who was dying. Except it weren't dying of course – just its spring petals dropping, that's all. But you were carrying on like it were blue murder. My heart was beating so fast I thought it was going to bust right out of my chest - damned near went into cardiac arrest right then and there. You sure were a case.'

'Still, I figured if you've never had a magnolia tree before then why the hell would you not think it weren't dead? The way it drops all those petals – sure looks dead, we figured that together when you calmed down a bit. Crazy kid, you were a nut back then – and man alive, you loved that magnolia.

'You know what?' Grandig said. 'I don't know what the hell you're talking about. I don't remember *any* of that nonsense, not one bit of it.' But she smiled because she knew that whilst she could not remember it, it did not mean it had not happened. And the fact that she did not remember, did not surprise Momo one bit either. She knew Grandig had put her memories of that time in a box, taped it up with the strongest tape, and buried in her mind somewhere so deep she would never find it again. Fingers crossed.

It was just shy of nine, and one of the candles fizzed and snuffed out on the sideboard. And it was then that Momo realized that it was she who had been guzzling all the tonic, and that Grandig had called her this evening because Grandig wanted to talk… *wasn't she the old girl hogging the chat?*

'So, Gee, did you come out here for a reason besides letting me yak-yak-yak in your ear for an hour? Because if you did, let's get onto to it, else I'm to bed and you can bag the sofa.'

Grandig pulled herself up and drew a mighty big breath: she was not sure she had the energy to talk about it now – but she came with a reason, and she felt in the end that she might feel better for sharing her thoughts and concerns: so Grandig talked. She told Momo all about the little mute kid, how she had been brought in and how despite some pretty hard effort she could find neither hide-nor-hare about who she was or where she'd come from. She told Momo about Kristen and

Bradley, *the last carers on her list.* She told Momo about how the kid had disappeared and about the subsequent conversation she had had with Kristen who seemed so reluctant to follow the rules. She told Momo that she could barely think straight for the headache pounding in her head.

Momo kept quiet. She understood Grandig's work and knew the stress and anxiety that came with working for Savannah Child Protective – she also appreciated that Grandig did not have a safety valve to let off steam, and that tonight was as much about that as it was anything else. When Grandig finally stopped, Momo reached forward and took Grandig's hand in her own; she stroked her comfortingly: 'You know what, Gee?'

'What's that then?' said Grandig.

'You're a good girl. Always have been. Always thinking of others – you've a heart of gold and I love you so much.'

Grandig smiled. 'What would I do without you, Momo?'

Momo patted her hand. 'Grandig – go home. You're tired. I'm tired! Get some rest – go through your files – and figure out what's biting your ass about those two foster parents of yours. I'm always here for you – you know that, right?'

'I do indeed – Momo. I love you too.'

Friday, 10th July 2015

Chapter 23

Evening

Andrew had called Kristen to say they were holding a pre-launch party by way of a thank-you to everyone who had chipped in these past few weeks to help get the refuge up and running. Despite the late invite, he persuaded her to head along - and not withstanding Kristen's protestations that she had not done anything to warrant an invite - in the end she had not taken much convincing. She had spent the most part of the day cleaning the house of any memories of Bradley, and a chance for a beer or two and to let her hair down for a while was an inviting proposition. Besides, with Bradley out of the way – and without the hassle of the kid anymore, *why the hell shouldn't she try and party a little?*

She spent an age trying to figure what to wear – and ended up with the classic Levi's and a white tee. She looked at herself in the full-length mirror in her bedroom. The warm glow from the early evening sun shone burnished amber shafts of light through the slats of her window blinds; this golden hour was as flattering as sunlight could ever be, but Kristen sighed with disapproving bitterness. *When did I turn into this ageing sack of shit?* she thought. She could not recall one particular moment when it happened, a time when the clock said *Hey Kristen, you've had your time, you've missed your fun – now I'm gonna start wearing that tight little body of yours down, start pulling at its seams and wearing you out a bit…* Nor incidentally, could she remember a time when she looked in the mirror and saw some beautiful, fresh youth looking back at her. Had that ever happened – and if so, had she ever appreciated at the time? She knew she had been robbed of those days, and that the glorious youthful beauty she so longed for now, had never made it out of that hole all those years ago. She brushed the thought from her mind

– Bradley had finally paid his dues, and God knows Vance had - she did at least take comfort from that.

When she arrived at the party a little past nine, her stomach was in knots. She couldn't remember the last time she had been out, let alone to a party. She knew she had no social skills, and the prospect of making small talk with a bunch of hipsters filled her with a sickening fear. But – Andrew would be here; and she took comfort from the fact that he wanted her to come. Before she went in, she popped a couple of pills, just to take the edge off.

Kristen was surprised to see the place so full. Whilst the first time she had visited there was perhaps a dozen or so people involved, now there were pushing a hundred or more; it seemed like everyone had brought a friend except her. And hell – she was clearly the eldest one here; this had been a mistake, she thought.

The music was banging – she was not a prude, but fuck, it was loud! Someone had wheeled in a set of decks and amps and the place was pounding and vibrating with noise. Beer flowed, ambient lighting glowed and pulsed, and for a few minutes Kristen thought the easiest option would be to sneak home and turn her cell phone off. All around there were hip young things, drinking beer and putting about their stuff. Exposed skin was everywhere; midriffs were bronzed and jewelled, smalls of backs on show to reveal ornate, Celtic tattoos and there wasn't an ankle or toe that wasn't wrapped by some itsy-bitsy ring or silver chain… Kristen could not feel more out of place – she felt like she was at a party for some new band or teen movie, not a fucking woman's refuge.

But before she had a chance to disappear Andrew spotted her. He was looking very cool and was enjoying being the centre of attention. He flashed her a quick grin but was caught in conversation with two twenty-somethings; a fairly attractive brunette, whom for all her gesticulating and non-stop motor-mouthing seemed to be pretty opinionated, and a guy who stood hunched with his hands in his pockets nodding like an idiot. Every now and again she would stop to guzzle her beer, then look at Andrew and wait for him to agree with whatever crap she was yacking, then carry on talking again. The guy with her just yapped *yup, yup, yup* like some well-trained lapdog that had fallen out of her purse. This annoyed Kristen, mostly because they were stopping Andrew talking to her, and she was stood like an idiot all on her own. Having gone to the effort of getting herself out, she wanted some time with the host himself.

She was sat to one side in a big, old armchair that seemed to swallow her up. A great deal of hard work and effort had gone into the place to make it look old and a little rundown, and yet hugely accessible. It was brand new – but distressed, Kristen thought it no different to all those trendy bars and cafes that were springing up all over downtown Savannah – was this really a refuge, or somewhere to order a European beer?

She glanced at her watch and realized she had been at the party for nearly an hour and had not said so much as *hi* to anyone – was this what it was like being old, or just having no friends? Whichever it was, Kristen's butterflies had subsided, and she was beginning to feel pissed off – and captive, too, that she couldn't yet walk out without looking like a sad desperado, and angry that she didn't know how to cut it with this crowd of assholes. She popped another pill – her head beginning to spin.

There was a small bar set up in the little annex where Andrew had served the coffee from earlier in the week – and she could see beer and a small, mixed array of liquor bottles. She fought her way through the crowd of sweaty people and wedged herself into a scrum pushing for drinks. Was she the only one on her own? She gave it her best shot to raise a conversation with a guy stood in front of her in the line, but he looked at her like she was his mother. Kristen could feel her pulse beginning to race and a rage starting to burn inside herself – she was being trampled on and ignored, barged this way and that by people twenty-five years younger than her, who were then looking down their pimply noses at her and judging her for being there. And where was Andrew now!?

When she got to the front of the line a tall, guy in a vest with short, dreadlocked hair and muscled arms shiny with sweat raised his eyebrows which Kristen took to mean *What can I get you to drink, ma'am?* He had a tattoo of the sun scorched onto his shoulder.

'Do you have anything stronger than beer?' Kristen yelled.

The dude cupped his hand to his ear.

Fucking boom boom boom music - am I the only one who can't hear shit? 'I said, *do you have anything stronger than beer?*'

The guy didn't answer, ignorantly Kristen thought, but then mixed her something with coke and passed her a tall tumbler filled three-quarters full.

'What's this?' Kristen yelled, snatching the glass from him and drinking it straight down – but he didn't answer. The girl behind her in the line tutted in disapproval and raised her eyes, *very uncool.* Kristen caught her glance: 'Don't fucking judge me, bitch,' she said, but for the *boom boom boom* of the music she did not or chose not to hear her.

'Another one... Please,' Kristen said to the barman.

Kristen took the second cocktail then grabbed a bottle of beer that someone had left on a table. Had her anger not been growing steadily she would have left – but fuck it, why should she go? She didn't give two shits for all the do-gooders, hippies and simpering community-lovers that were swelling this place beyond capacity – she was only here because Andrew had invited her. 'You lot can go fuck yourselves,' she said, slightly too loud to go unheard. A few heads turned.

She caught sight of Andrew again; this time he had the captive audience of a blonde girl who looked half his age. Kristen recognised her; she had been introduced that first day she had visited the refuge: *Dizzy. How appropriate.* However, she was beautiful, Kristen thought, and she guessed the girl would rely on those good looks to get whatever she wants. Kristen detested her for it. Kristen watched from a distance, taking in her body language and watching his closer still. There was a subtle nuance in the pair's relationship; the merest of signs that this was not a purely platonic set up.

Her temper boiled but she had no release valve to vent her anger – no one to row or fight with. How dare he - how dare he drag her all the way into the city then ignore her! That's the sort of thing Bradley would have done.

What hurt the most – what stung more than anything, as she drank more, was that not one solitary person had said a word to her all evening. She felt she deserved attention – the effort she had made to come and be supportive warranted that, at least. Forget the fact that the fucking host had *invited her* anyway. Did that not seem to suggest he might at least want one stand-alone conversation? Ignorant asshole. All that *friends* bollocks he had spouted – underneath he was just like Bradley.

She looked around at all the other people enjoying the party, she was the only single person here. Not single in a relationship sense, she assumed there were many individuals out there looking to go home with someone new tonight. But single in the *alone* sense – and that was a feeling that she did not like. She had been alone for a lifetime, ever since she was in that pit, the captive plaything of Vance - Kristen rocked on drunk feet and felt her stomach heave.

She dashed for the restroom and was horrified to find several women waiting patiently for a solitary cubical: 'I'm gonna puke!' she yelled. It is amazing how quickly three swift words clear a line.

Her head was spinning from drugs and alcohol. She locked the door to the tiny cubicle and looked in the mirror; she took a moment to reacquaint herself with the dishevelled, pale, old and grotesquely angry woman who looked back at her. *When did I turn into you?*

'Yo lady, how long does it take to take a crap?' A loud, aggravated voice pierced the cubicle from the other side of the restroom door, followed by titters of childish laughter.

Kristen smiled; there it was. She had been here all evening and not a single word had been uttered to her face. How beautiful it sounded: *not 'it's lovely to see you,' or 'thank you for coming,' or 'I'm so glad you made it, I've been dying to see you…' but, 'Yo lady, how long does it take to take a crap?'*

Kristen did not answer. She looked at herself in the mirror once more. She *was* strong. She *was* capable. And God dammit she was going to leave this place with people finally taking notice of her. She felt her head rush – she was drunk, and she was high, and she knew the feeling well and liked it. But she was also determined, and she was angry.

She took her bundle of keys from her purse and holding them tight in an open fist she slammed them hard into the mirror. Shards of glass fell into the sink below; a few slivers dug into her palm and drew blood. She exhaled shakily but with control and put her keys back in her bag. She looked back one last time into what remained of the shattered mirror; her hair fell lank into her face, stuck to the sweat that she hadn't noticed beaded on her forehead. Her eyes looked hollow.

'Yo, bitch, seriously! – there's a fucking line out here!'

'Screw you,' Kristen answered. 'And all your little whore mates.'

She picked the largest shard of glass from the sink and held it like a switchblade. Then, with a coolness and composure of a surgeon she slashed the glass across her eyebrow – only stopping when the razor-like pain took her breath away with a cold, sharp gasp. Her skin split open and hot blood spewed from the gash like water from a faucet; instinctively she dropped the glass and grasped the wound with her hand, heavy red blood oozed from between her fingers. She felt a cold, nauseous wave flush through her body, and she had to fight an impossible urge to pass out.

She managed to slide the lock of the restroom and fell out, ungainly, into the line that waited outside. There were screams, yells and swearing as her blood splashed and smeared onto new dresses and outfits, and Kristen remembered the world tipping sideways and falling upwards and away from beneath her feet. Then blackness enveloped her, and silence came at last.

Saturday, 11th July 2015

Chapter 24

First light.

A dull, warm light flashed on and off, on and off, on and off through her sore, aching eyelids. A droning filled her ears and her head pounded with what felt like the death-throes of the heavy music of the night before. Kristen open her eyes.

The world recoiled horrifically into focus and her eyes, struggling momentarily to understand her current reality, were unable to make sense of her surroundings. But slowly, and with a horrific dawning of recollection, Kristen realized she was in the back of a taxi thundering across the Talmadge Memorial Bridge, tyres drumming across the steel roadway and the sun flashing through the many uprights that supported the suspension cables above: on and off, on and off, on and off… She clutched paperwork in her hands, and she noticed a plastic band with her name and date-of-birth fastened around her wrist. Both papers and ID bracelet held the logo of the Savannah General Hospital. She reached for her forehead and felt bandages, a stinging pain greeted her slight touch; she winced aloud, and it drew the attention of the driver in front.

'Did you trip down the stoop or did your man smack you one?' the driver said, peering in the rear-view mirror. 'You've been out cold since I picked you up – reckon I was gonna have to take you home and call the paramedics all over again.' He sniffed, like he had seen all this before, and Kristen smiled wanly. 'If you're fella's beating up on you, you need to call the cops on his ass; ain't nothing right in beating a woman.'

'It wasn't my husband,' Kristen said, her words drifting off to nothing.

'You got someone waiting for you?' he persisted. 'You don't wanna be on your own looking like that. How many stiches you got under there?'

Kristen didn't have a clue. She suspected the paperwork she had crumpled in her right hand would have the answers, but with her head thumping the way it was, it was going to be hours before she was able to read her hospital dispatch notes.

'I'll be fine,' she said. 'Do you know where you're going?'

'I got a home address of 2310 Welyvan Street. Is that where you live?'

She had to think about it momentarily, but then nodded in agreement.

'You sure you're gonna be okay?' he said, looking again in the rear-view. 'You don't look so good.'

Kristen's head was swimming: 'My husband works shifts; he'll be home around nine. I'll be fine till then.'

'Well as long as you're sure,' he replied. 'I'd hate to think something bad might happen to you all on your own.'

Kristen closed her eyes and she snuffed out of consciousness again.

Though it was not yet eight, the morning sun was hot. All she wanted was bed and sleep. There were no recollections: not of the party, the anger, nor the trip to the emergency room. Only dreamy, hazy images occasionally punctured her dreamy unconscious state.

The taxi-driver did her the service of keeping his mouth shut for the rest of the journey and she dozed in her dull, foggy state for the remainder of the ride. It wasn't until he pulled into Welyvan Street that he piped up again: '2310, you say?'

Kristen nodded in her muggy sleep.

'You've got visitors, lady. You sure it wasn't your man beating on you last night? Savannah PD are parked on your driveway. You want me to call someone for you?'

Chapter 25

Morning

Kristen's head felt clogged with hangover and concussion. Beneath the dressing, her wound from the night before throbbed with a blistering incandescence: inside her skull, her brain smouldered as the SPD officer, now sat opposite her, fumbled for his notebook and pen. She wondered whether she had it in her to talk her way out of the mess she now found herself in. From within her fug she peered around the utterly spotless kitchen, but soupy images of splattered blood dotted her drifting thoughts. Her eyes fell to the drainer on the sink where the dishes were piled high - *there's Bradley's Last Supper dish* - *Pfooph*! an image of his punctured head, the dripping skewer still protruding through, suddenly drained through her thoughts. Nausea rose in a thick heat and she swallowed to suppress it back to her stomach.

She looked at the cop; a blonde-haired brute with a blotchy, acne-pocked face - who for his muscles and brawn looked so less comfortable brandishing a pen than he must a gun. Her eyes fell to that little indentation on the side of his temple set back from his eyes. She thought how delicate that spot was, how thin and fragile, but ultimately so utterly vulnerable too - an image of her infant's fontanel, warm and sweet to her lips, briefly dipped into Kristen's mind. She had to refocus her mind and suppressed the urge to reach out and touch him there.

The cop had wrestled his pad and pen from his breast pocket and looked up. Kristen drew a deep, silent breath: 'Can I get you a coffee?' she asked: '*get you*' slurred into *gair-yoo.*

'Oh, yes ma'am. That would be good,' he indicated with his pen to the heavy ring of bandage and dressing around Kristen's head. 'But are you sure you're okay to do this now, though? Looks like you've taken a pretty ugly knock to the head?'

'Sure, I'm fine. I imagine it looks worse than it is,' she spoke slow enough to ensure she pronounced the words clearly and yet she heard her words coming back to her as if uttered by someone else.

'How did you do that?' he asked.

Do what? She thought. Then flicked the coffee machine on. *One thing at a time, please.* Every action was a monstrous effort - as if she had to think twice before doing anything: 'I… I tripped on the sidewalk last night. It was my own stupid fault, not looking where I was going. I was out looking for the kid – it was dark. No great shakes though, I'm fine.'

'Looks nasty,' he said, but dismissively. He was now scrabbling with his pen to get it to work. Kristen made a mental note that she might need to remember this first lie she had told. *Write that lie on a Post-it Note.*

'Your coffee? How do you like it?'

'Oh. Black – with one please, ma'am.'

'Right, coming right along – my mind's a little fuddled.'

Kristen passed the cop his drink then poured one for her – the cop watched her as an orderly might watch a psychiatric patient. She sat and joined him, and as she set her coffee down her shaking hand made the mug rattle coarsely as it met the tabletop.

The cop looked up: 'You sure you good to do this now?' he asked again.

'Yessir, absolutely. It's been a tough couple of days and my nerves are shot to bits. Once we're done, I'll try and get some rest. My husband will be home soon from nightshift.' *Lie number two…*

'Sure, okay. Well, I'll try not to keep you long; I've got most of the details from Grandig at Child Protective anyway. This is just formality, okay?'

'Okay,' Kristen replied.

The cop shifted in his seat and took a mouth of coffee. 'Geez; that's good – thank you.'

'You're welcome.'

'Right, okay. Let's crack on.'

Let's.

'So, this kid. Did she have a name?'

'No. Well, not that we ever knew. She was a mute.'

'"Mute?"' He asked.

'You know, didn't say a word. The entire time she was here. She didn't speak. Only kid I ever known like that – we mostly called her… *Kiddo*.'

'Mute,' he said slowly.

'What?'

"*Mute,*" you said.'

'Mute?' Kristen struggled again to remain alert, 'Right. She was mute and we called her 'Kiddo''. Kristen watched as the cop evidently struggled to spell the word in his little notebook and went on to repeat the word again to commit it to his disastrously small word-bank.

'Okay. And how old was the kid?'

Keep in the game, Kristen: 'Well, as I said, she never spoke a word. But I would say she was perhaps five, maybe six years old.' *Do you need me to help you with the spelling?*

Again, painfully slowly, the cop wrote this in his book.

'And when did the kid go missing?' he continued, not looking up from his pad.

Kristen took another mouthful of coffee and cradled the mug in her hands: 'It was the night before last. We checked on her before we went to bed – she was fine, she must have crept out some time after that.' *Post-it Note. Lie number three.*

'What time was that?' he asked.

'We were in bed sometime after 11pm. We read, watched some TV. It can't have been this side of midnight.' *Lie. Post-it.*

'And before she disappeared, how was the kid?'

'Well, as I said, she was mute – so it was really hard to know exactly. But she seemed happy enough.'

'And everything's good in the house, you and…' he flicked through his book, 'Bradley – your husband. All good there?'

'His head's a little messed up but he's good.'

'Yeah, I bet. Stressful time for everyone, I guess.'

'Absolutely.'

And so the conversation chugged along. The lies kept flowing - as many little inaccuracies littering Kristen's account of events as liberal misspellings scattered the cop's notes. She lied about what she did the night the kid disappeared, where Bradley was and what he did (or didn't) do, and she lied about how she was so sick with worry. She lied some more about where she was last night, and how she ended up in hospital, and lied and lied again about Bradley and nightshifts and how he worked so hard she barely saw him. And how her head spun!

Finally, the cop let out a big sigh. 'I'll level with you Mrs Engel…' then stopped mid-word and studied his little book again. Kristen waited through the awkward silence as the cop struggled to disentangle the pronunciation of her surname.

'It's *EnGelMayer. With* a hard G,' she said.

'Sure. *Engelmayer.* Apologies. Is that Australian?'

'German. Or so I was led to believe.'

'Right. Anyway – I'll level with you. There ain't much here to go on, you know?' he said. 'We've had the details from Child Protective and we've put out an APB but based on this, there ain't a great deal we're going to be able to do. I reckon the best chance we got of finding her is if someone brings here in – or if she wanders on back here.' His radio crackled and he drained his coffee and stood up. 'When's your husband home? I feel bad leaving you here alone...'

'Thank you, officer, but I'm fine. Bradley will be back anytime now.' *Liar, Liar Pants on Fire.*

Kristen saw the cop to the door and waved him off from the porch. The sun was full up now and its heat was warm and comforting; a dull breeze shimmied the leaves in the trees and the gentle murmurs of Saturday morning drifted aimlessly without flounce or fanfare. The squad-car rolled out of view and left the empty street with nothing but the faintest hum of exhaust. A bird chirruped somewhere as a lawnmower started up, and across the neighbourhood the lazy broad *parp* of a cargo ship's horn drifted out as the vessel navigated the Savannah River.

Kristen went back into the house. The lurching panic she had felt when she first pulled up in the taxi this morning had gone, and the uncontrollable shakes she had managed to calm. But she could still feel the dull bursting sensation of raised blood pressure and anxiety, and a heavy angst that made her clench her fists and turn her knuckles white. Her hand moved instinctively to her own wound, and she winced. *There* was the root of her brooding anger: last night's party and her own careless behaviour. The way she had behaved now reminded her of a Gary Larson cartoon – a small child sat at the back of the class clutching a strange contraption covered in an assortment of buttons and levers; the caption simply stated *Terry activates his attention-seeking device.* She was angry because she had shown weakness last night, demonstrated to the sycophantic hoards that not only was she on the periphery of their sad little group, but inexplicably that she wanted to be in it. *Stupid, sad, desperate, attention-seeking girl.* The acknowledgement brought a wave of nausea and Kristen made for the bathroom, swallowing hard to avoid retching on her empty stomach. She leaned over the porcelain rim of the toilet but managed to control the urge to puke. She breathed deeply and exhaled slowly and repeated again. A cold sweat broke across her forehead and her mouth ran dry but the nausea subsided. It occurred to Kristen that she was also still very hung-over.

Once calm again she stood up. The bathroom was cool and as she leant on the cold, white basin, breathing deeply still, fragments of the night before flashed back to her. With hands still trembling, she slowly unwrapped the bandage that was bound around her head. Beneath, from the corner of her eye to the front of her ear was a large piece of padded gauze held in place with steri-strips, which Kristen carefully removed. Underneath, her skin yellowy-orange from iodine, was a neat two-inch laceration; carefully glued stiches bonded the fresh, blood-crusted wound closed. She admired the handiwork of the duty doctor who had cleaned her up and felt an odd satisfaction at her *own* work – she touched the cut lightly with her finger and accustomed herself to the ensuing stinging pain. Biting hard on her lower lip she continued to stroke her finger along the cut. The nerve-endings zinged in a hot, electric flash and she felt a brief yet gratifyingly tight, squirm of excitement flush her reddened cheeks every time her finger snagged against the raised skin.

She rested more that day, drifting through passing hours. Later she bathed and soaked out the dirt, iodine and alcohol, exfoliating her pores in warm, soapy water. The party now seemed a strange memory or an imagined dream: not real to Kristen at all. She liked it that way and pretended that that was the reality. By the time she came downstairs again it was early evening and the amber shards of sunlight stretched through the leaves of the Candler oak and dusty air of the garden. She was at peace - rested but vaguely skittish from her comedown. She could live with that for the time being, it would soon pass, no doubt.

She poured herself a large glass of wine and sat curled in the easy chair in the den overlooking the garden. Her mind wandered from this to that, there was no real direction to her thoughts – then without warning, probably because life was slowly returning into focus, she thought of her cell phone and retrieved it from her bag. The battery was flat but when she plugged it in it pinged into life: nine missed calls and three messages.

She called her voicemail: *'Kristen, hi, it's Andrew. Jeepers, I hope you're okay? Can you call me as soon as you pick this up, please? I just need to know you're okay. I called by your place earlier and there was no one home. I'm guessing you're with friends. Please, just call to say you're fine, okay? See you soon, yeah?'*

Kristen took a mouthful of red; *'friends', right.* She figured she must have been comatose when he called round earlier. The second was also from Andrew, in the background she could hear echoed voices and clean-up noises at the end of the party: *'Kristen, hi, it's me, Andrew. Fuck – I hope you're okay... Look, I would have come to the hospital with you but there was no one here who can set the alarms – I can't leave the place unalarmed, I'm sorry. Fuck! Please call me, I don't care what time it is – I'll wait up for your call… Sorry about tonight. Call me. Please.'*

Kristen was fairly sure she was at that time unconscious in the recovery ward. The words rang in her head: *Sorry about tonight.* I should fucking hope so, she thought.

The last message was Grandig: '*Honey-bunch, it's Grandig. Hey sweetie, you gotta give me a call okay, right now – soon as you pick this message up. You'll be getting a visit from Savannah PD soon. Hope that doesn't take you by surprise – fuckadoodle I wish you'd answer your damn cell! Anyway – call me when you get this okay?'*

By the looks of her call-log it appeared that Grandig and Andrew had called at least two or three times each since leaving their messages. She was glad she had spent the afternoon asleep, the last thing she wanted to do now was catch up with either of those two assholes. She pulled the drapes across the windows and relaxed back into the chair.

The empty house had a stillness that Kristen found deeply satisfying. She realized that she had never had the house entirely to herself before; that while she had been married to Bradley, and with first Aimee and then with the constant stream of foster children, that the place had never truly been her home. But now with Bradley gone - and presumably the last of the foster children disposed of - Kristen felt she could feel her home breathe, and who knows, maybe it could sometime become a refuge for her.

A bleep from her cell phone brought her thoughts back in line, and she gulped another heavy mouthful of merlot. Her head really was awash today, she thought.

Kristen, please call me. I'm worried sick about you. Even just a text 2 say that UROK. Andrew.

She thought for a moment, wondering whether to give him the satisfaction that she was okay and off his hands – or to leave him wondering for another night. The way he had treated her she felt like leaving him in limbo, but she felt there was a good chance he might just turn up at the house again – and she did not want that. She typed a quick response:

You have my blood on your hands.

But she did not send it. Instead she deleted the message and merely responded:

All good but got a sore head. You need to get the floor tiles in that bathroom checked! Silly me. Need sleep now - catch up soon. K

That should keep him off my back for a while, she thought, and tossed her cell onto the coffee table, powered down once more. Her limbs felt heavy and her head felt as if it had been lifted from her shoulders, given a heavy shake, and then set back in its place again. She decided to go to bed and draw a close to the day.

Sleep came easily to Kristen once again. Shrouded dreams emerged like gators from the silted mud of riverbeds. Images and recollections – some real, and some fabricated by the paintbrushes of her unchained imagination. She tossed restlessly in bed.

She saw a baby, newly born, naked and screaming, its tongue stuttering and gibbering, sprawling and wriggling on the floor of the bathroom. Its face was contorted, but more horrifically, its body was vandalized in rough, scribbled colours – limbs scrawled and muddy-brown from the frantic colouring-in of a childish hand, as if it were a picture in a drawing book. The kid was in the tub watching – holding her crayons as if to say, 'look what I drew!' – but of course she said nothing. Then Kristen heard the words *Aimee - Amen. Aimee - Amen.* Backwards and forwards, *Aimee-Amen. Aimee-Amen…* It sounded stretched and thin, a nightmarish amalgamation of her voice and Bradley's. The name though, her daughter's, had a strange, unfamiliar tone. Then the dream was gone, gurgling away like water down a plughole.

From her reedy bed of dreams came a new sensation: a bursting, ripping pain from deep within her belly. She looks down at her distended abdomen and sees a huge, swollen lump. She knows in her dream it's a tumour, its fat and poisonous and growing and eating her alive. Then she's aware of Vance: he's there now, pounding away on top of her. And then she realizes, *of course! It's not a tumour after all; I'm pregnant.* Emotion floods through her like hot liquid through pipes. Euphoria that she's not dying from her tumour, but full to the brim with motherhood instead! Then instantly she realizes, like a sickening douse of putrid water, that her motherhood *is* cancer; impregnated into her by Vance. She feels vomit rising in her throat, then darkness sweeps in again.

These ghosts fade. Light appears like a sharp knife and Kristen is aware she is laid up in a maternity room. Kristen feels like cattle, helpless and terrified, splayed on all fours like a cow. She sweats and moans; wishing to God in heaven that someone would reach up inside her and pull the cancer out. And finally, it ends with a gushing relief, and a bloodied purple *mass*, a giant heaving clot is handed to her wrapped in a rotting blanket. It's not a baby – she is sure of that – and senses a gator now lying heavy on her chest. She hears the midwife barking at her to feed the baby, but it won't take, and instead *the thing* roots its tongue into the air and screws its face tight like an ungrateful gibbon. Kristen feels the choking of a dark, stagnant cocktail of bleeding panic and loathing…

Her mind empties into black again and Kristen's dream lurches forward. She passes a bedroom - is it Aimee's, or the other kid's? Or that of the countless other children that had visited it in the past - and looks in. The room feels empty and lifeless – the air is still, and Kristen detects a faint smell that she cannot quite place. It is a memory-smell, not a scent left by an unmade bed or dirty laundry but one that is of a time and a place distant from now. She breathes deeper; *What is that?* Then suddenly it crashed into her head like a derailing train, invading her mind, her vision and the thin aching unreality of her sub-conscious. The room decays in front of her: paint and wallpaper peeling from the walls; furniture tugging and clawing at the floor and shifting position like some horror movie; time spins backwards as the room resets itself to some twenty years hence. In the dream, Kristen's head pounds; she staggers against the doorframe, her mind lurching like a lost ship on stormy seas. Swinging chairs, beds, table and lamps, replacing themselves to positions from time past.

Kristen's dream locks on a room from twenty years ago - Aimee's bedroom. Bradley has painted this room a peachy orange – and it glows warmly in this afternoon from 1985. It has everything a little girl could wish for – cuddly-toys and dolls stuffed into overflowing drawers, picture books and cartoon creatures adorning shelves. *Teddy Ruxpin* bedsheets and pillowcases... Every girl's favourite bedroom. But then there is that smell again – dour and rotten. And it emanates from the bed. And Kristen finally knows what that smell is, and it is as vivid as the taste of vomit in her mouth is real. She looked towards the *Teddy Ruxpin* sheets and sees Aimee – *corpse Aimee* - her skin pallid and dry, her blue, hard lips pulled in a desperate toothy grin, and eyes half-open but lifeless. Her arms are raised, and her hands and fingers are clawing desperately against some invisible force, curling, flexing and tightening. And the smell! That death-sweet whiff is rich and sickly in the air and it dances in Kristen's nostrils in gloating antagonism: '*Daddy! Daddy!*' the corpse gargles through its sticky throat: *'Help me! I can't breathe Daddy – Daddy! Daddy! Help!'*

Kristen woke to the sound of her own sudden scream. She did not know what time it was, but it was dark outside, and sick was caked to the side of her face and matted in her hair. A broken wine glass lay in shattered pieces nearby and a puddle of wine was drying darkly crimson to the hardwood floor. Kristen focused her eyes and began to weep quietly – the bedroom lay in front of her. But it was the real bedroom – not the one from her nightmare, the one from decades past; the one in which her daughter lay dead on the bed.

Chapter 26

Bradley looked. No more than that. An isolated blink that burst light across his retinas and seared his brain like it had been tossed on the grill. They closed, then opened again. White light came first; laser-bright and painful. Then another blink... Green light now – duller - and hues of browns and distant blues. A muscular reflex at the back of his throat attempted to swallow but there was no liquid there to facilitate any downward passage of the congealed blood and mucus that clogged his mouth.

His eyes opened again and this time his pupils contracted, tightening in aperture and limiting the unbearable flow of light… As they did, focus came; the minute muscles in his eyes working correctly - effectively - the first time any part of Bradley's *body had worked properly since being skewered. Inside his brain, barely discernible pulses of life flickered. The tiny processes that convert light on the retina into vision flashed briefly. Bradley saw.*

Then he uttered a glottal noise, a word-like sound that drifting away in an exhalation of breath:

'Aimee!'

Monday, 13th July 2015

Chapter 27

Morning.

Halfway between Bull and 14th a young woman stood at the corner of an access alley behind a row of cheap restaurants and gift-shops. She had chestnut eyes and a dose of matching freckles, but any prettiness she had was hidden beneath the dirt of the streets. She leant against the grimy bricks; her body hung limp like a dirty overcoat slung on a nail. At her feet was a plastic BiLo supermarket shopping basket; it was wrapped in silver duct tape and polythene that blocking the holes from the elements. She was trying to light a damp cigarette she had picked off the sidewalk, hair in face, cupping a trembling hand around her disposable lighter. She drew hard on the cigarette and tilted her head away from those who walked past.

A guy in a suit, talking on his cell phone, crossed the street in front of her and did a double take, stalling his conversation momentarily as he caught glimpse of her basket, then dismissed what he saw and carried on back to his office. The girl caught his glance and scooched the BiLo basket with her wet foot, tucking it behind her as best she could and away from any more curious eyes. She drew on the smouldering butt again sending oily smoke creaming around her face.

As the basket grated across the ground a murmur rose out. What suit-man had seen was wrapped in a jumble of old sweaters - It cooed again, this time tiny hands drawing up to claw away the grubby sleeve that had fallen across its face. It was a few months old, crusty-eyed and snot-nosed. It looked healthy despite the dirt, and though suit-man took it initially for a doll, it was very real.

She could easily still be a girl had her fortunes been different. However, she had recently spent her sweet sixteenth knocked up and without a dollar to her name. She nudged the basket with her foot as another mom might rock a cradle.

She was watching a doorway across the alley. The drizzle was growing steadier now and she and the baby were getting damp; a quick glance to the blackening sky told her it was not going to improve. She pulled a crumpled flyer from her denim pockets and checked she was in the right place – she had been stood here twenty minutes and not seen anyone go in or out. She wanted to be sure before committing herself to pressing the buzzer: she wanted to see who worked here, and who stopped by. She was not going to rush into anything. She sunk to her haunches and sat on the floor, dangling her smoky hand into the basket to comfort the baby: she could wait a little while longer if needs be.

She was suddenly aware that someone was stood over her. She looked up and saw suit-man silhouetted against the daylight. He held out a hand and proffered up a brown paper-bag: 'Here. Are you hungry?'

She looked at him: immediately fearful. She wished she were stood up and not sat on the floor, hot vulnerability flushed her cheeks. She could not run.

He said it again: 'Are you hungry? It's a burger.'

His face looked genuine, but she was wise to nice men who stopped to talk to young girls.

'No.' she lied. 'Fuck off.'

He looked surprised: 'Take it… For the baby, if not for you.' It was a ridiculous suggestion, but suit-man knew as much about babies as he did about teen moms. 'It's a *Five Guys…*'

She stared up at him and said nothing. She knew as much about *Five Guys* as she did about men who wore suits.

He looked around. He was suddenly feeling nervous – somehow threatened, uncomfortable that his random act of self-gratifying generosity was being shunned firmly back in his face. He looked over his shoulder to make sure no one was looking: he felt like anyone seeing this act might misconstrue it as being *something else.* Then he looked back down at the girl - went to say something else but chose not to - and placed the bag at her side. 'Whatever. Have it anyway.'

He walked off and did not turn back.

She watched him go then looked at the bag. A small patch of grease stained the bottom of the sack. She looked at him again, watched him walk away then took the bag in her hands: it felt warm and heavy. She opened it.

The burger tasted good – in fact, the best food she could remember eating for a long while. The drizzle was now steady rain, but she did not care – the *Five Guys* tasted great. She broke a bit of bun off and held it to her child's lips – it was not used to solids and it rolled it around its mouth between wet toothless gums. She was lucky it did not choke.

She took the decision to come back tomorrow. Someone at the gynaecology clinic had given her the flyer - they had known nothing about it, except that it was 'new', and meant for 'girls like her' - so she could afford to be cautious. No one was expecting her: she would bide her time. She walked away in the rain, damp butt and wet feet, dragging the baby behind in its shopping basket.

Chapter 28

Afternoon.

Grandig and Kristen met over coffee at a diner called the Green Banana: Kristen ate granola whilst Grandig had two eggs and bacon on biscuits with a side of grits. Kristen felt it was an unnecessary meeting but Grandig was keen. Over food Kristen understood that Grandig had dismissed the possibility of the kid coming back at all; she had said that was '*about as likely as seeing the pope in speedos…*' Kristen lied about her injury, spinning the same yarn she gave to the police officer. Grandig said there had been no updates from Savannah PD over the weekend either; *zilch sign of the kid.* They talked off-subject a bit too, which Kristen felt less comfortable with: Grandig was usually so totally work focused that it felt like she was being interviewed. Kristen guessed that Grandig was just not adept at making small talk, but contrived questions about her friendship circles and whom her *girlfriends* were, were just odd.

When the discussion came to an end, stilted somewhat but with all bases covered, Grandig was about to up and leave when Kristen asked: 'Hey Grandig, where do we go from here? I mean, with the department and all?'

Grandig sat herself back down again and pushed her plate to the side: 'How'd you mean, girl?'

Kristen leant back in her chair: 'Look – I know this situation is gonna have caused you a whole heap of shit at CPS: Christ, I ain't never lost a kid before, not permanent anyways, certainly not one so little…' she paused, then: 'Are you gonna take me off the books?'

Grandig surveyed her closely and caught her gaze with hers: 'It ain't good, Kristen – I'll level with you that much. Losing a kid – particularly one so little – there's going to be a lot of questions to answer when the dust settles. You know that, right.'

Kristen nodded.

'And what about Bradley. How is he?'

'Oh, Bradley's fine – working too hard, as usual - I barely see him.' Kristen paused, then: 'You know, Grandig – you've always been good to us – but this puts you in a real predicament, I get that. I appreciate all you've done over the years – I know we've never been that model foster family, but you've always stuck with us. But this kid was a toughie – for many reasons. It was hard. Not just because she was a girl, and I'll be honest, that wasn't as bad as I thought it would be, but because where Bradley and I are at the moment – personally. You know?'

'You and Bradley having some trouble, Kristen?'

Now Kristen's mind ticked: *How much to give away?* 'Yeah, a little. I'm mean, nothing serious, nothing - you know - that won't be sorted out. But I think a little *us-time* will be a good thing.'

'Kristen, I am genuinely sorry to hear that. Anything I can do?'

'No. But thanks, Grandig – that means a lot. As I said – it's nothing serious. Bradley needs to get his head straight a little and I need time to figure things out, that's all.'

'Girl, you got it. And you just give me a call if I can help any?' Grandig stood to leave: 'We'll have to keep in close contact too, Kristen. Just until this is all wrapped up, okay?'

Kristen said: 'And any news our end I'll be on the phone in a beat…'

'You got it.' Grandig flipped Kristen a wink and a smile and pushed her way out of the café. Her mind was racing so much, so full of thought, that Grandig didn't notice she nearly knocked one beret-wearing young poet-type to the floor, spilling his kale, pine nut and ginger smoothie all over his tweed jacket.

Chapter 29

Kristen watched Grandig leave. She followed her with her eyes as she walked out of the *Green Banana* onto the street.

Kristen held her coffee mug up for the waitress to see, *refill please*. As she waited for her to return with the jug, Kristen looked out without great purpose across the café, at the cacophony of people gathered there: socializing, working, talking and just passing time. Her gaze fell on woman tucked away in a quiet corner, a black cloth draping broad across her chest - it was clear she was breastfeeding her baby. Watching this sight, Kristen felt a surge of jealousy. Kristen gasped slightly as she struggled to control this pang of emptiness. It punched her like that final suffocating grip of utter desolation and loneliness hits the person who steps out in front of an oncoming subway train or walks off the top floor of a car park. Watching, Kristen recalled a distant bleak memory from her own past. She saw *young Kristen*, holding Aimee too tight in a frustrated grip, shrieking at her, yelling, sobbing through tears, demanding, begging her to take her own nipple into her mouth. But Aimee would not: she squirmed and wriggled, bleating tears of her own, stubbornly refusing to feed. *That* was Kristen, and her recollection of motherhood.

She sat there in the *Green Banana*, suddenly feeling that insane angry wave of absolute failure again – an act so simple and natural that all women could do it, even sat in a busy café in downtown Savannah with the world watching – all except her. The pain was as real and as painful now as it was back then. She looked away.

Then, most unlike her, she began to cry – slow, steady, and increasingly uncontrollably. The tears flowed oil-like and the more she fought to stop them the greater the pain began to boil. Her face contorted to a dark grimace, and her fists and jaw clenched tight. She shook, and she spilled her coffee.

The *Green Banana* was busy and full, a loud bubbling melee of chatter and noise. But as Kristen's muted cries became louder, this background noise sidled away to uneasy silence. People turned and looked – some out of concern, most out of embarrassment.

Kristen caught herself, suddenly aware that she was unexpectedly centre of attention in a crowd of strangers. She looked up; her face puffy and blotched, and her hair matted to her skin in salty tears. Reddened eyes peered out across the *Green Banana*. She snorted snot from her nose: 'Whatareyall looking at?' she slurred.

Someone giggled a confident rebuke. Eyebrows were raised and people turned away. Hands covered mouths to mask judging whispers to friends.

Kristen exhaled a shaky breath to calm her tears: she wiped her eyes on the sleeve of her shirt leaving a mascara stain on the white cotton.

The waitress suddenly appeared at her shoulders: 'Are you alright ma'am?' she asked. 'Do you want me to call someone for you?'

Kristen blew out another breath that was more controlled this time. She pulled her hands through her hair, fixing it behind her ears – straggly but no longer falling dishevelled across her face. 'Who the fuck would you call?'

She stood up, ignoring the gaze of eyes that fell upon her, and grabbed her bag. *You cunts can go fuck yourselves* she thought as she left, but only after her green eyes fell enviously on the mother and child one last time.

Chapter 30

Fumbling for her phone, Grandig slipped on the wet sidewalk, turned her ankle and nearly broke the heel of her shoe. She exclaimed a loud *damnation!* and stumbling forward, just managed to stop herself falling flat on her face. *Goddam it!*

She recovered enough to sit down on a bench in Chippewa Square and did her best to rub the pain away – her heavy cleavage making it difficult to reach her foot. She tapped the speed-dial and momentarily got connected to her office:

'Hey Hun. It's Grandig … yeah, fine, though just near ripped my god-darn ankle in two slipping on the sidewalk … yeah, you better believe it, girl … Yep, I'd a probably cracked the friggin' concrete! Anyways, can you do me a quick favour … shimmy over to my desk and grab me a number from my rolodex … you're a hun.

'Okay, flick around to E, wouldya … Uhuh. Now, find the card for Engelmaier and let me know when you got it … … You do? Gra-and! Now, there's a bunch of numbers on there, and I need the work number for Bradley Engelmaier … … that's the one … Yep, I got a pen, fire away …'

Grandig scribbled the number on the palm of her hand and thanked the person on the end of the line. Then she dialled.

It rang out for a moment, then a man answered: 'Oh hi there, sir, I wonder if you could help me. I am trying to locate a Mr Bradley Engelmaier and have this as his main work contact number, would you be able to put me through? … Oh sure, you ask away; my name's Officer Grandig from the Savannah Child Protective Service … … No, this is not a police matter. Mr Engelmaier is a registered foster-carer with the CPS … Oh you know that. Yes sir, he is indeed; very noble … Is Mr Engelmaier available? … … … Uhuh, I understand … … Uhuh … Well I'm sorry to hear that… … Yessir, I believe it's going around … …Can you tell me the last time he was in work? … … Last

Wednesday? … Oh gee, well okay, I guess I'll try to get him at home … … Yes sir, I know, the flu can be particularly nasty … I will. Yessir, I will. … You've been very helpful, yessir, thank you … Can I just grab your name, if it wouldn't too much trouble, just so as I can let Bradley know I've talked to you … … … Uhuh, Uhuh, no, I've got that … … Thank you, Archie, you've been very helpful … … I gotcha. Mm-hmm? … … Oh sure, it's Officer Grandig … that's right, from CPS … … … and thank *you* sir.'

Click.

Grandig sat awhile and thought. Busted - that just didn't make sense – if Bradley was ill with the flu – why didn't Kristen just tell her that? It was no skin off Grandig's nose if Bradley had the flu or not – so why lie? She wondered whether the guy at the dock, Archie, was pulling her chain, but Grandig couldn't figure a reason why he would – and he seemed helpful enough – again there seemed no reason for him to spin her a yarn.

She stuffed her cell phone into her bag and headed back to the office, a nagging suspicion itching her ass.

Chapter 31

Despite being mid-afternoon, the boathouse was masked in a thick gloom. The overhang from the live oaks and the thick fairy-tale overgrowth of knotted shrubs, thorn-bushes and ivy kept all but the thinnest shreds of sunshine from penetrating – what scant light there was twinkled and sparkled from the reflecting surface of the pool that lay beyond the collapsed boathouse doors.

Bradley still lay where Kristen had dumped him. His heartbeat faint but regular.

Across his lap, lying like an obedient dog, was an alligator. It was a huge male, monstrous, at least fifteen feet from snout to tail and weighing in at over half a tonne. It was muddy-brown, with hues of olive green flashed across its spiny back. Its belly was sallow but full, and its head and jaws pinned Bradley to the deck. He guarded Bradley like a possessive child guards his French fries.

Bradley let out an almighty gasp, spluttering blood and gunk from his mouth and lungs. His muscles reflexed, trying to move, but he found he could not; he heaved his head up and saw the creature – his brain processed the image, with only vague success, and suddenly Bradley imagined Barnie the Dinosaur – purple and bright, with a curious song ringing in his ears: I love you, you love me, we're a happy family, with a great big hug and a kiss from me to you, won't you say you love me too! The gator thumped his tail from left to right but did not release the weight of his head from Bradley's lap.

Bradley groaned as his mind chugged: Barnie. Dinosaur. Gator. Dinosaur. Gator. Gator. Ga-tor!

Muscle spasms twitched and lurched again – with almost an urgent panic Bradley tried to move his limbs – but he could not; too much like Frankenstein's monster was his dilapidated body and malfunctioning brain. The gator opened his jaws ajar: he let out a hiss to tell his dinner to be still, don't move. Bradley heard, felt fear, but relaxed; his head fell to one side and he looked out across the boathouse.

Bradley was still just alive. His brain was mostly dead, but there was function – better now than last night even. As he lay there, his pet warm in his lap, his brain played around like a computer trying to reboot from an old back-up. His fingers twitched; his eyes moved left to right; he wiggled his nose – but all directed by the automatic capabilities of his brain, not consciously by Bradley whose control over his own faculties was nil.

That tune again: I love you, you love me, we're a happy family… And as it sung in his head, he became aware of movement from the corner of his eye. His brain flashed a hot spark of energy as if someone had hit the command key in his head: look now Bradley! Immediately he moved his head to the right and saw, imagined…

A girl.

Yes, a girl. His brain kicked in more successfully this time. Young and pretty. Balancing precariously on the rotting boards of the boathouse. Beware the dinosaur! he thought. His mouth made a 'beh, beh, beh!' sound.

She stepped tentatively on the deck so as not to fall, careful to avoid the wet slime that slicked the surface of the wooden floor: one wrong step and she would undoubtedly slip into the water and drown. She was little too; her hair braided in neat little rows.

I know you. 'Neh, neh, neh….'

As she walked, calm yet stealthily, a dozen eyes seemed to appear from the darkness. Gators. Dozens of them, females – obedient and subservient, a slithering mass of a thousand awful teeth. But the girl did not seem to notice – not a care in the world.

She picked her way through the rotted boards. Her little dress was dirty – not surprising considering the mud she must have waded through to get into the boathouse.

Bradley saw her. Watched her. His brain clicked and processed. I know you… I know you!

She cocked her head; cute little dimples pinpricked her cheeks. Her eyes were bright, real and alive. Then her little voice, round and sweet, infantile, pure and clean: 'Bradley! I've come to visit you!'

Bradley blanked out and the world went black.

Chapter 32

Mid-afternoon.

Back at the office, Grandig now realised what was biting her ass about Kristen and Bradley - it boiled down to the simple fact: *They didn't seem to like kids.* That sounded crazy – put so bluntly, but she squared it in her mind. Sure – it was a job; people got paid to foster. And hell, it was hard work. But – for most foster carers, there was usually a sense of joy, of achievement, having provided a spell of stability for some of the most vulnerable children in Georgia. She didn't get any of that from Kristen and Bradley – everything seemed a chore – every placement an arm forced up the back. She didn't get a sense of what motivated them to do it. Kristen didn't seem to give a hoot about the kid when they met earlier at the *Green Banana – just so odd.*

Also – there was something else. The day she dropped the kid off at the Engelmaier's she could have sworn that Kristen was high, or something. Kristen said she had a headache, but Grandig worried all the way back to the office that she shouldn't have been in such a hurry to dump the kid and run, that she should have hung around a bit longer and risk assessed. Her pupils had looked so damned big; was she convinced Kristen wasn't a dope-head? Not entirely. Or something worse? She hoped not.

Anyway, what Grandig was onto now was a proper case-review of the kid, and of Kristen and Bradley. Should the little girl not turn up safe and sound - and Grandig knew that was a sad possibility - this would be deemed correct procedure anyway; check through the paperwork and make sure everything was right and proper with all the 'i's dotted, and 't's crossed. *Should* it get to that point, all the kid's Child Protective paperwork would get transferred to 'missing persons' with Savannah

PD… Grandig couldn't help think that if it got that far, the kid really would disappear right off the system for good. 'Missing Persons' meant a few weeks of faces on milk cartons, grainy pictures in the back pages of local newspapers, then - particularly for kids like this one - consigned to police files that never got opened again.

The kid's folder remained mercifully small and took Grandig just a few moments to look through. With no known background information to the child there was nothing to do here but put them back and file them away again.

Kristen and Bradley's story was different; they went back a long way with the CPS and had been fostering for an age – in fact, they were one of the first couples Grandig had recruited – right back when she was fresh out of college and still wet behind the ears. She pulled their original registration file from the cupboard aside her desk and flicked through those earliest of records. The CPS process was thorough - numerous interviews were carried out, references and character statements taken, and Kristen and Bradley were finally welcomed into the fostering team in the late nineties. Everything was in order. Nevertheless, Grandig had a pang that she might have missed something all those years ago. Something that made Kristen and Bradley far from responsible individuals. *Why did she feel she had somehow fucked up? Yes, she had her faults – she was messy as hell and she had the filing skills of a five-year-old, but she was always competent at making the right decisions and getting the job done effectively.* All the paperwork was in place, the cross-checks, the interviews, the sign-offs; It looked like she was worrying about nothing.

The last thing Grandig wanted to check to put her mind at rest was the Engelmaier's references; everything else was good, despite her nagging doubts. She could not remember who the Engelmaier's had selected as referees, but they would have submitted both a supporting statement, and had an interview. Grandig did remember though one of them had a prosthetic arm, *you remember things like that.*

Grandig waited until the office fell quiet – around a quarter to six by the time most had had enough of the day, then pulled together a few of her reference files and notebooks and headed for CPS1 where the archived files were kept. She waited until the place was quiet for two reasons – firstly, it was easier to get her head around the job without the constant interruptions of day-to-day business, but secondly because she did not want anyone to see her questioning her own work - she still had that nagging feeling she had somehow screwed up on the Engelmaier case. That tingle of fear had shot down her spine again when Archie Black had told her Bradley was off with the flu when Kristen had said not twenty minutes before that he was fine. *Why would she lie?* Yes – she said they were having a few issues, but there were now more than a few alarm bells ringing in Grandig's head. CPS1 would hold the answers, she was sure. At least in calming her nerves and proving to herself she had done nothing wrong.

Grandig was going to review the background checks and referees, then do a quick scout through the early placements the Engelmaier's took on and see if everything looked in order. Cross those off the list then she was good. Deep down Grandig knew she had her faults – sometimes, just a little bit too disorganized for her own good. Better at it now of course, a few years' experience under her belt, but all the same – *propensity to be a dunderhead.*

Back then, references were recorded on carbon-inked sheets that produced tear-off copies in triplicate. One was for CPS, one for the police department to run a criminal background check, and one for the applicant. The wording of the reference itself was largely irrelevant (rarely did a self-nominated referee foul up the process) but they were there to confirm that there was nothing nasty in your past – a kind of promise from a close friend or colleague to confirm *you were who you said you were.* The police background check was vital. Fuck this up and you were out. Grandig pulled down a couple of files and started sifting through the Es.

There were a lot of them. Earls, Earlhams, Ebsons, Ebbonets… it took her a while, but she finally fell on Engelmaier. She lifted the lever arch arm and removed the documents.

It took a moment to refamiliarize herself with the form - Grandig hadn't used one of these old-style records for years. The paper was thin, almost like tissue, and the stamp at the top dating the document was smudged and unreadable. This one had to be nearly twenty years old. It contained all the information you could pull together on any one married couple. Names (married and previous) home address (now and for the last five years), dates of birth, occupations, places of work, next of kin, schooling, passport number, national security numbers – everything, all carefully handwritten into tiny boxes on an over-complicated form. It may have been twenty years ago, but the system was thorough. She leafed through the pages, eyes casting down the faded print looking for anything out of order – anything that might indicate a foul-up – but there was nothing.

The little collection of papers ran to four pages in total - carbon copy on the top. Behind this coversheet was the PD criminal record check generated by the background sheet, and all was clear, not so much as a DUI for either of them. It would have been impossible for Kristen to cheat the system – *and hell, what was she really looking for anyway?*

Grandig moved on to the contents of the reference itself. It was a very generic statement that Grandig had typed herself as she took the interview with the nominated participant: *Bradley's one-armed friend – she remembered that correctly, didn't she?* She read it through, and it revealed nothing out of the ordinary – the process followed a scripted questionnaire that the department had been using for years. All was in good order. So, what was his name, again? She struggled to read the scrawled signature at the bottom, but her typed script was as clear now as it was then: Archie Black. *Well go figure*, thought Grandig, *the one and the same…*

She toyed with picking up the phone there-and-then and calling him back. They had only made their introductions a few hours back: *hey there Archie, it's Officer Grandig, we talked earlier today? I was calling about Bradley Engelmaier…* But then – what did she have to ask? There was nothing here that caused her any concern. She was wasting her time – all along, that silly little alarm-bell was ringing for no good cause at all.

She glanced at her watch – her stomach had let off a low little grumble saying it was time to feed it again. The files were scattered out in front of her and she was inclined to leave them there until tomorrow. But to what end? Wasn't she happy now that there was nothing wrong? She kicked back in her chair and thought it through one last time.

Where did this begin Grandig – you worry-guts? What kicked you off on this self-questioning panic-bus you've been riding? She could not answer the question… Well, not with anything concrete, her big worry came from her gut. And it rumbled again.

Okay, okay, she said out loud, *I hear you. Let's go eat.* She took one last flick through the papers, replaced them in their respective folders and switched the light as she left CPS1.

Chapter 33

Evening.

The heat had not yet dropped out of the day and kids were still playing in the fountain on Ellis Square even though it was heading towards 7pm. There was a little bistro, tucked away from the prying eyes of the tourists heaped on the orange tour buses. It was called *Boodles* and Grandig headed there for a late sub and cold beer.

It was cool inside, and a ball game was playing on the big screen behind the bar: bare bricks and aluminium ceiling fans – the place was far from original, but the food was good, and that's what mattered to Grandig.

As she waited, she checked her phone for missed calls - there were none - and she thought momentarily she should call Momo. She flicked through her address book and was about to hit the call button when she stopped: hell, she knew in her heart it would make the old girl's day, *but could she really be bothered? No, she could not.* She would be on the phone for an age and her sub would be here any moment. She dumped the phone back in her purse.

The commentary from the game drifted over the tables and Grandig's mind was suddenly empty – finally switched off from the whole damn Engelmaier affair. She yawned: mouth open, big and wide - Momo would have said *good job I's wearing boots; I'd a fallen right in!* Someone hit a home run and she didn't even register.

'Meatball sub and fries,' said the waiter.

Grandig was out for the count.

'Meatball sub and fries,' he repeated, placing the food in front of her.

Her head snapped forward in the way it does when you doze off momentarily on a subway train, jarring forward and waking her rudely. The short moment of intense restfulness sent her brain immediately into overdrive; it flicked everything into gear computing who she was, where she was, what she was doing, and who she was doing it with… Perfect clarity.

'Meatball sub and…' but before he could finish the sentence for the third time, Grandig was up and on her feet.

'Holy shit!' she cried, then: 'Put it on the hot-plate, will you? I'll be back in a bit!'

The waiter was impressed with how fast the chick could run: 'Crazy.'

She ran fast and she did not stop. Sweat was beading her face and her lungs were burning like she had inhaled flaming gasoline. It was probably a third of a mile back to the office and she did not stop to catch her breath until she was stood waiting for the lift. CPS was deserted except for one or two working the late shift. The doors opened with a bright *ping!* and Grandig took the elevator.

Back in CPS1, the pain in her lungs refusing to die away, she grabbed the same files she had been looking through earlier. Her fingers were sweaty enough to leave damp marks on the pages and she rubbed them on her skirt to try and dry them off. Her lungs were barking from within her chest. She flicked through the E's again: Emmerson, Embrook, Enderley, Engelmaier…. She ripped it from the file without lifting the release arm, then collapsed in the chair and drew breath.

She looked down the form once again. Her eyes frantically searching out where she suddenly realized it had all gone horribly wrong: *let me be wrong, let me be wrong. Sweet Jesus and Holy-assed Mary, let me be wrong.*

But there it was. Her heart sank and she could not stop the tears from swelling, and even though sweat was still pouring from every pore in her body, she suddenly felt very cold.

'Oh no… Oh good God, no,' she said, shaking her head in denial.

She flicked through the PD background check to try and prove herself wrong, but her worse fears were right. Tears fell now in big drops, splashing onto the laminate surface of the table as she realized finally her gut had been right all along: something *was* amiss: 'No, no, no, no, no!'

Grandig took a tissue from her purse and blew her nose. Her hands were shaking. There on the form, clear as day, Kristen had entered her married name as her maiden name, and vice-versa. They sat next to each other in neat boxes and at the time Grandig had not spotted this simple reversal of fact.

But worse, her first name was entered in the box above as Christine – not Kristen. Grandig had to assume that back then she had not noticed: not noticed, or assumed Kristen was a nickname or full name – just too plausible.

However, the problem so evident now - why Grandig was fighting back the tears - was that the criminal record check had been carried out on someone called Christine DesMoiles – not Kristen Engelmaier. Grandig knew that name and scoured the page to find it: she saw it confirmed under *next of kin*. Christine DesMoiles was Kristen's mom. Names all switched, addresses and dates of births too – all the information there, just in the wrong boxes. A badly designed form and a rookie CPS Officer – too careless to take proper care with all the damned paperwork. And it was mom, and not the daughter, who was the one with the clean background check.

And if that was the case, Grandig realized, if she had indeed been duped by Kristen to check the background of her mom, it led her to only one question: *who the holy fuck are you, Kristen DesMoiles, and what have you got to hide?* Grandig leant forward on the table, resting her head into her arms and sobbed.

Chapter 34

That evening Kristen's stomach felt shitty. She did not know whether she had eaten something that disagreed with her, had drunk too much coffee in the afternoon, or was coming down with some sort of bug. Whichever, she decided alcohol was just as good as Pepto-Bismol and that a bottle of merlot and a shit-or-bust strategy was as likely to sort her out as anything.

She had come home and got changed and she now sat on her bed with her scrapbook in her lap. She had taken some time to light a few candles, pull the drapes to, and tidy away the clothes she had left dumped on the floor earlier. She was on to the second large glass of red and she could feel the effects of the alcohol just beginning to nudge the senses a touch. It was a good start to the evening. She stroked the front cover of her scrapbook. On initial inspection it could be mistaken for an old photograph album – it had a hard, reinforced paisley cover and was a little *oversize*. But inside, it had many pages of low-grade sugar paper, worn and in some places torn too, and filled with photographs and keepsakes of all those children.

There was Mitch – a sweet boy, orphaned, all alone in this world – quite the little chap. Davy too; just a bit too angry and messed up though. Brendon, Simon, Alex – all very short placements – probably less than a week: they were easily forgotten. She turned the page: Joe, with the rapist father who beat him with a belt and turned his fists to his wife. She reflected momentarily: she remembered she did not care much for Joe. Turned the page again: Charlie – he was fine. Turned again: Curtis – *the little bastard son of a serial sex offender* she caught herself saying aloud. *That was harsh but true* she thought: she did not care for him much either. Shawn neither – he was as bad. Likewise, Tim *the nasty little shit.*

Page after page, face after face. I liked *you*: but I didn't care for *you. You* were okay, but *you*, I did not like. Slowly counting the boys on her slender fingers and washing each down with mouthfuls of merlot.

She was vaguely aware that she had counted seven – *seven steps in turning off the water supply* - when someone hammered abruptly on the front door. She slammed the book shut, then hid it away in her bedside drawer – glancing at her alarm clock she saw it was still early – not yet nine. *Who the fuck?*

She sat on her bed and listened, waiting to see if it was a cold-caller who might simply go away – or someone who really wanted to see her. A moment passed and then they hammered again – insistent. A mild panic swept over her and her stomach lurched. The wine, up until this point, had done a good job of settling her, *but who the hell was this*?

Knock! Knock! Knock! once more.

She grabbed a sweater and pulled it on; her heart was beating fast. *Maybe it was a delivery? Yes, that was it – an order she had forgotten she had placed. A delivery guy – yes that fits.*

She got downstairs, took a deep breath, and then swung the door open.

'Oh!' she exclaimed, it was not the delivery guy, but Andrew, and he stood on the porch with a bottle of wine in his hand.

'Hi! I hope you don't mind,' he said, smiling, holding up the bottle of wine, 'but I was kinda bored, and sat at home on my own, and I thought – *well, I wonder what Kristen's up to…'* he smiled, less confidently this time, more like he was *fishing,* speculatively: 'I hope you don't think me too presumptuous, but wondered whether you might like to help me drink this?'

She was blindsided and must have looked it too because Andrew very quickly continued: 'Oh, hey, I'm sorry. I've caught you at a bad time,' he thumped his hand to his temple, 'I don't know *what* I was thinking – I *wasn't* thinking, clearly. I'm sorry – this is really impertinent of me – I'll leave you to it. I'm sorry.'

She laughed, *'impertinent'!* 'No – that's okay. Please. Come on in.'

'Are you sure,' he looked genuinely uncertain. 'It's not too late?'

'No,' she relied, now almost composed. 'It's not too late at all. Please.'

Kristen led Andrew into her home. She found herself feeling distinctly odd: excited and flushed but jittery – it was pleasant, and not a sensation she was used to. 'Would you like to sit inside, or on the deck?' she asked. 'The mosquitoes aren't bad – we could spray, if you like?'

'The deck would be lovely,' he responded. 'And I never find the bugs a pain. Let's sit out, that will be nice.'

'Deck it is,' she replied. 'I'll just go grab a couple of glasses, go on through.'

Andrew walked through the lounge – it was not big, but was very clean and tidy, almost sterile, Andrew thought, for the absence of the usual paraphernalia that clutters a family home. He made a snap judgment: *the husband doesn't do clutter.*

'Where's Bradley?' he called back, 'I don't want him thinking I'm imposing, or anything. He's welcome to join us.'

Kristen was just taking another wine glass out of the kitchen cabinet - *shit, Bradley!* 'No, don't worry, Bradley's away on business,' she called back. 'He's away for the week. Some 'port' business – I forget. I'm never really sure what he does anyway.' She laughed, joining him from the kitchen, 'Please, go on through.'

'Sure thing. It's funny how that happens, isn't it? You spend your life married to someone but then don't have the first clue what they spend the vast majority of their time doing.'

'Beat's the hell out of me,' she said.

Out on the deck they settled into a pair of rocking-chairs.

'It's a screw-top,' he said. 'I'm afraid it's Californian – I can't pretend to imagine it's any good either, I took it from the church store – it's the Blood of Christ, if you get my drift.'

'Stolen from the vestry?'

'Yeah, something like that.'

He poured the wine: it glugged pleasingly into the glasses.

'That is a mighty fine tree,' he said, pointing at the Candler oak at the end of the garden. 'Quite the garden feature. You sure are lucky to have that out here.'

'Yep,' Kristen replied. 'Of course – it stops anything else growing – lawn's a dust bowl. It drinks all the water before anything else gets a look-in. Good for swinging in though.'

They small-talked for half an hour of so but discussed nothing. They drank wine (Kristen more than Andrew) and talked about the garden, the church, and this, and that. Had Kristen been sober, she might have been anxious in anticipation of the what his real agenda was, but she felt the loitering warmness of nearby drunkenness and any anxiety was comforted by it.

Eventually though the natural conversation died away, and as the indigo darkness of night began to bleed like an ink-stain from the eastern sky, Kristen moved the conversation on.

'So, down to the chase then. To what do I owe this pleasure? I can't really believe you came over tonight just to talk blindly for an hour,' she asked. 'Is it business? Or is there another agenda?'

He smiled. 'No. No agenda. Just social,' then he paused. 'Where did you say Bradley was?'

'Away.' Then: 'Do you often arrive on peoples' doorsteps with a bottle of wine in your hand?'

'More regularly than you think,' he replied. 'My work calls for a lot of socializing. It's in the job description. Admittedly, it's usually with young lovers who think they want to get married, or old people who think they're about to die, or relatives of people who *have* just died - but yeah, socialising is right up there on the pastoral job spec, and a bottle of wine always seems to help the conversation flow.'

'Uh-huh,' she said, meaning *you learn something new*…

'Yes – a lot of talk about love… But much more about dying.'

'So… what brings you here tonight then?'

He raised his glance and for a moment said nothing – stalling to find the right words. It was a perfect evening. The sun had dipped down behind the tree and the deck was shrouded in the evening shadows. It was beautifully warm, but the air had now lost the heavy humidity that can make summer in Savannah so desperately hard work. There was a slight perfume on the air that might have been honeysuckle or jasmine, or honeysuckle *and* jasmine. 'I have a favour to ask,' he said, 'but first,' and here he leant forward clasping his hands, fingers interlocked, 'how are things, Mrs Engelmaier?'

'How are *things*?'

'Yes. How are you doing?' He punctuated each word clearly and slowly.

'You're serious?'

He shrugged: 'Sure. Kinda.'

'Kinda how?'

'Kinda I know you're going through a period of,' he paused to find the right word, '*roughness*.'

Here we go she thought. And like that, her mood swung. It was as if the equilibrium pitched just off centre for a moment, sending the whole scales tumbling over.

'Look, I've not come over to pry - '

'Good.'

'But I'm just a little bit worried about you. I understand that the little girl, the kid you were caring for, has run off and - '

'You heard about that?'

'Yeah, course. Well, I saw it on the news – and then heard the description then put two and two together.'

Kristen put her glass down: 'That's quite a leap you've taken there.'

Andrew inhaled deeply: 'Yes, well, call it intuition. Then with the party and all, and you getting a little, well – out of your head. And you're… injury. I realized it all made sense. Hey, look, I'm not judging you.'

Kristen smiled. 'I hope not. That wouldn't be very Christian.'

'Of course not. I'm not. If it weren't for people like you, where would these kids end up? But I get it, that it hurts. And seeing how you've suffered – I wanted to check you were really okay. Okay?'

'Yeah,' she replied, 'I get it.'

'So…' he passed Kristen her wine glass again. 'Relax, okay? In a *good, caring way*: how are you?'

Relax? she thought, *are you serious? The last person who told me to relax is fucking dead.*

But as Kristen swallowed those words she paused and reflected: how tempting it was to blurt it all out... *Okay – so you want a dialogue – well here it is: How has it been? Well, seeing as you asked, Mr Care-for-the-fucking-community, I'll tell you: it feels like a goddam fucking relief if you want the truth. This little 'fostering gig' has been a means to an end – if you must know. It pays well – particularly these last-minute emergency placements – pays top-dollar, actually. But Jeez, I'll share this with you – it's a fucking pain in the ass. It was Bradley's idea to get into this shit – did I ever tell you that? Once Aimee was dead, (I told you about Aimee right? – No? – Well she's my dead kid, but that's a whole other story,) he figured it would 'fill a hole'. Can you believe that!? Fill a fucking hole! I fucking ask you!? And believe this, if you will, he had me convinced for a while too – told me that's what we should do – that it would help 'heal the wounds.' You get the irony there, do you? Replace your own dead child with someone else's cast-off… Genius, don't you think? But you know what, Andrew? Bradley knew shit about that. Knew shit-all about the wounds and what they were. I was bleeding well before Aimee died. Real blood – real fucking blood. Like the blood I splashed across the restroom floor the other night… But let's jump forward, shall we – are you with me so far? When CPS came around with that little girl – knowing full well that we don't do little girls – I was like, you're kidding me, right? A girl – A girl!? We don't do girls!! Bradley – yes, Bradley would do girls – he fucking doted on Aimee – and I don't mean normal, like. He* FUCKING DOTED ON HER *– not me, his wife, there was no fucking look-in for me. No, once Aimee came along Bradley was not interested in me one bit. The one person in my damned life who had once showed just the slightest bit of interest in me – worshipping at the feet of someone else! And don't ask about those seven boys – the fucking sons of* *murderers and rapists and wife-beaters and child-molesters – under my own fucking roof… So, ask me again how I am, and I'll tell you,*

'I'm fine. Really. I'm all good.'

Andrew sighed: 'You know, you come across a bit of a closed book – but that's okay. I respect that.'

'Well, sometimes there's just nothing to talk about. Sometimes, we invent these little sub-plots to life that just don't exist.'

'I get that. No sub-plot.'

'No sub-plot. Not to me, anyway.' She leant back in her rocker and raised her glass as if to raise a toast. 'Sorry if I came off a little *abrupt*.'

Andrew could not fathom out this creature. He knew there was a connection there – but he could not break the ice. Either it was the wrong time, or the wrong place, or she herself was hot-or-cold. He wanted to go there – but could not make it happen. *Maybe that's a good thing - she's one fucking misnomer* he thought.

Kristen yawned loudly. The red wine was casting its mellowing effect on her, and despite her latent bubbling anger her stomach-ache was practically gone. 'So, what's this favour you have to ask? It's getting late.'

Andrew shifted in his chair: 'Well, I've been thinking.'

'Uh-huh?'

'Seeing as there's no sub-plot here, and you're all fine and good, with presumably some time on your hands…'

"Yeah?'

'How would you like a job?'

'Are you serious?' she asked.

'Absolutely.'

'What kind of a job?'

'Well,' he said, 'I need someone to help man the ship down at the refuge. Help out a little. You know, be a little pro-active, see what needs to be done…'

'Go on,' she said.

'I was thinking of asking one of the girls, but you know what they're like. They're great and all, but not so worldly wise. I need someone who can spot the issues and solve the problems before they happen.'

'You mean a General Manager?'

'Well, not exactly. Nothing quite so grand as that. To be honest, I don't have the budget for a General Manager. But someone who doesn't mind putting a few hours in and making sure the place becomes the success it can be – that's what I'm really after. How does that sound to you?'

'Hmmm. Working for peanuts, I take it?'

'Pretty much: you know where we're at with this thing, right? There's no business plan or financial model – just an idea to help people out. It's a social enterprise – and I just need someone who can make it all move along. A 'suck-it-and-see' approach really. Are you in?'

'Can I think about it?' she asked.

'Sure you can,' he said. Then: 'Have you thought about it yet? Are you in?!'

She laughed. Andrew certainly had a cheeky perseverance. *Some other time, or place perhaps – who knew what could happen between them,* she thought. 'Yeah, I'm in.'

'Great. Can you start tomorrow? Is minimum wage okay?'

'Yeah. I'll be there.'

He visibly relaxed, his shoulders loosened, and his face brightened a little: 'I'm really pleased. I think you'll find it very rewarding too. To me it seems a great fit – I'm really excited about introducing you to some of our new drop-ins. You'll bring a lot of value to them – I figure you'll have a natural empathy with some of those struggling moms.'

'I'm sure I will.'

This time it was Andrew who took a mouthful of wine. Up until now he had drunk very little, but it was as if he needed a little Dutch-courage: 'Can I be honest with you Kristen, just for a minute?'

'Yeah, of course. What is it?'

'I think you deciding to give your time for these girls is one of those decisions that is going to define you. Shape how you're seen by other people. I think, if I may be so bold, that people are going to see a *new you.*'

Kristen internalized this for a moment; did she like the sound of that? It was as if he had somehow shaped her; played her like she was malleable clay: 'Do you really think so?'

'Yeah, I do,' he drank some more. 'I think you're going to be surprised by what you can learn about yourself. About who you can really be.'

'Oh. Okay,' she strung that last word out some, then shrugged: 'I'm not really sure what to make of that.'

'I mean – you might discover who you really are, who lays within that fragile outer shell. It's going be a great experience.'

Kristen replied: 'I don't really think I'm looking for that, to be honest.'

'Sure you are. And you might make some friends. Trust me. It's a good thing.'

Those words swam in Kristen's head: *trust me… Good thing.* She did not trust him – not really. And a *good thing*? She thought probably not. But it sounded like it might be fun; that there might be a game to play. For that reason alone, she had agreed.

He put his hands on his knees then smiled a very broad smile that seemed almost unnatural. 'And on that note – I guess, it's probably time I bid you good evening.'

It *was* getting late. The sky had scorched out through burning reds and ambers, the tiny dots of starlight dusting the blackness. The air had a freshness to it – not cold, never cold, but certainly less *baked* and intense. A few fireflies zipped and fizzed, and the trees sang with the constant churring of insects. Kristen stood first: 'Thank you for coming over this evening,' she said. 'It's been nice.'

'I enjoyed it too,' he replied. 'And thank you for agreeing to my request. I'm excited to have you on board.'

'Me too,' Kristen said.

Once he had left, Kristen finished his cheap bottle of wine, and downed the remainder of the good bottle she had left in her bedroom. Her head was spinning drunk and her thoughts and emotions churned. She collapsed back on her bed, and as she focused on the loft-fan the room began to spin around it.

Something coursed through her body: like adrenalin maybe, or some other chemical that told her Andrew had touched and grated some nerves this evening. She could feel a physical rushing sensation through her feet, legs, arms, fingers and head. She did not like the way he had snooped on her business: surmised that the missing girl on the TV news was the girl once in her care. She did not like the insinuation, vocalised or not, that she had somehow failed. Nor did she like that he was so fucking righteous - *I think you're going to be surprised by what you can learn about yourself. Who you can really be.* What did he know about who she really was?

There builds the anger again she thought.

Chapter 35

Where Bradley lay, gators looking languidly on through blinkless eyes. He did not know whether he was alive or not: he could not figure whether the little girl sat in front of him was real or imaginary. He felt like he was watching reality through a TV screen. *Are you real?* he asked the little girl.

Of course I isn't real! You really are a big ol Silly Billy!

Honey – do I know you? I'm not sure it's safe to be here, you know. I don't think Barnie's all that friendly…

Silly Billy - Barnie is not going to hurt me – I's a good girl! Barnie only ever eat naughty girls... And boys. You better watch youself Mr Bradley else yous might be next!

You're – you're – you're kiddo!?

Of course I is – you really are stooopid Mr Bradley!

You lived with us in our house, didn't you?

Hmmm. For a little bit – yes.

You're Kiddo!?

Why didn't you talk to us sweetheart?

Kristen was nice but she gets really angry. And you is both always drunk!

You're not real, are you?

Don't be such a Silly Billy! Of course I isn't real!

You're a figment of my imagination – I'm delusional that all – dying. Look at you – you're beautiful – not a hair out of place. You'd have to have swum here; you'd be fucking filthy…!

Mr Bradley. You is a bad man.

No. No. I'm not!

Yes – you is a bad man. Good men don't end up in shitty situations like dis, do they Mr Bradley?

You said a bad word, Kiddo

Uh-huh. But dat is because you is rubbing off on me. Yous is putting these filthy words in my head…

I'm a good man, I'm a GOOD MAN!

No, Mr Bradley, you is the worst kind of man. You fink you is good but really you is bad. Good men are not nasty – and you is nasty Mr Bradley. You have been a very nasty man –You is not nice! You hit and punch and kick…

I don't do that anymore…

Liar Liar Pants on Fire! You do it to Kristen all the time!

No. Not anymore.

Maybe not now: but she has fucked you right up. But you know you had that coming, don't you Mr Bradley?

Maybe.

You has been a very BAD MAN! You still like to think of her in dat hole, don't you Mr Bradley? Think of her all nekkid and dat big man on top of her. I don't think dat's nice. Not nice at all.

I guess not.

Why don't you tell me bout Aimee?

Oh holy shit! You're not real! You a fucking apparition, a vision or something! Leave me alone!

But Mr Bradley if I is in your head – I cannot be gettin out! And your body is all fucked up from dat skewer so it ain't worth getting yourself all cross so why don't you tell me all about your little girl Aimee da one dat is dead …

I loved Aimee.

I know dat, Silly Billy!

She was the most beautiful thing I had ever seen – it was like I became this great fucking teddy bear incapable of anything but loving her. I had never experienced anything like it: the softness of her skin, the sweetness of her breath, she was just so… perfect. She had the most beautiful splash of freckles scattered over her nose, and when her hair was tied back, and she played in those pretty little dresses I can honestly say she was the most beautiful thing in the world. You know what? When she held my hand, my great big fist just swallowed up her tiny paw – she said it was like holding hands with Huxley Bear… God, I loved that – her little warm fingers in my hand – it made my heart flitter, actually flitter, like I was about to have some sort of fucking cardiac episode! Jeez – she was actually perfect…

Ah Mr Bradley it is such a shame that she is ded-as-a-dodo.

Don't say that.

But it is true, isn't it?

Don't say that.

I know she is ded, Mr Bradley. Did you want to tell me about that Mr Bradley?

No.

Aw please, Mr Bradley! Tell me the story about Aimee and Kristen. I LOVE dat story! Dat's what you want to talk about, isn't it? Don't you want to get dat off your chest?

No!
It's not a secret is it, Mr Bradley?
Yes.
But secrets are BAD Mr Bradley. Everyone knows dat!
Leave me alone.
Tell me the story about the dead-girlie and Kristen.
No.
Tell me! Tell me the story!
I will not.
It will help you find da peace if you tell dat story. Tell it please!!
No – stop it. Stop it! Shut up – shut your stupid fucking mouth you stupid fucking bitch!!

'Buh! … buh! … buh! … '

The gator shifted in his lap and a couple of the females slipped silently into the black waters of the boathouse. Bradley's eyes were glazed and opaque and his cheeks were raw and blotchy from insect bites. His head twitched, the most minute of movements, and another bolt of electricity zipped through his brain. It was only small, insignificant to the massive brain trauma he had already suffered, but it was enough to edge him closer to death.

At the moment though, he was still just alive.

Chapter 36

Evening.

For the second time in as many hours Grandig was pouring sweat. She heaved ass from the 5th floor leaving the files and papers scattered across the desk and pounded down the back steps to the carpark beneath the CPS offices. She threw her stuff onto the back seat and gunned the engine of her car, squealing out of the lot and narrowly missing a pedestrian stood on the corner: the old man's newspaper fluttered in the wake of the car and he waved his stick at the crazy driver.

Grandig had not stopped swearing in the fifteen minutes since she found the deception: *shit, damn, crap, fuckaroo.* And now she was bolting as fast as she could to Momo – the one person she had complete faith in to help her navigate out of this damn hole she found herself in.

The traffic out of Savannah was horrific, a thick congestion of commuters jamming every artery of the city: Grandig leant on her horn, swerving and veering from lane to lane, and shrieking profanities from her open window. Eventually though, after dodging and weaving through the cars and lorries - drawing as many middle-fingers from her fellow commuters as she dished out herself - the traffic slowly thinned, and the highway began to flow once more. Her body still pumped with the angry-scared anxiety that had flooded her since spotting the deception on Kristen's form: her mind raced with the possibilities and reasons why she might have done it. *Maybe it's just a mistake* she thought, *nothing more than carelessness on a form that's just too complicated. Maybe there's nothing to be worrying about at all, you silly goose!* Then her mind spun once more, that sickly wash of paranoia flushing the cold sweats down her spine: *Maybe she has a record, done time for assault and battery, or some kind of firearm offence? Oh shit - that'll be a fucking disaster! Or maybe it's – shoplifting perhaps? Or even a DUI? Christ – that wouldn't be the end of the world – maybe that's it? A fucking Drunk Under the Influence – people worry way too much about little misdemeanours like that. Fuck I hope so. Fuck, please God, make it a DUI – I can handle a DUI.*

Grandig's mind pinged clear for a moment and she glanced down at her speedometer: 85mph. *Easy girl – you don't need to get yourself pulled over now…*

She eased her foot off the gas and took a deep breath, calming her jitteriness and forcing herself to chill. Outside, the freeway had melted away and the concrete expressway either side was now replaced by pine trees and thick brush: the Savannah River meandered only a few hundred yards beyond, and Momo's place was just around the corner.

She pulled onto the driveway that ran up to the house – that familiar and comforting view taking yet more sting out of her tense muscles. She parped the horn three times, a familiar call to the occupant to say *a friend's here.* Momo appeared on the deck before Grandig could hump her ass out of the car.

'Well hello again, my dear Grandig! What a pleasant surprise to see you so soon!' such a genuine greeting, it made Grandig feel like she had come home.

'Oh Momo, I'm so glad you're in!'

'*In*? Where the hell do you think I might I have been going? Jeez-Louise, I can't remember the last time I was *out*, girl!'

Grandig opened the passenger door: 'Jump in Momo,' she said. 'I'm taking you out for some dinner – I've gone and got myself into a right pickle and need food and an ear I can trust. Have you eaten yet?'

'No, no… I ain't eaten yet. Grandig girl, what's the problem?' She asked with concern. 'I don't ever recall hearing you like this before. Are you okay honey? You look as white as a sheet.'

Grandig held her hand, helping her as she sat down gingerly into the car: 'I'll explain when we get there. I'm gonna take you for Chinese food. I'm just about ready to eat my own weight.'

'Promise me you're fine, Grandig – you're scaring me – tell me you're okay then I'll stop worrying.'

Grandig patted her knee: 'I'm fine,' she said. 'But I've screwed up at work. I need to talk a few things through with you – get my head straight on a matter.'

She put her own hand over Grandig's - it felt smooth and warm and comforting: 'Whatever you need girl, I'm right here for you.'

By the time they arrived at the restaurant the evening take-out trade had cleared and the place itself was empty save for a handful of couples catching supper. There were only three waiters working this evening and the kitchen was being run by a skeleton crew. She and Momo sat at a table looking out to the dunes, but neither took in the divine view: their heads were bowed, mouths salivating over the menu – this was all it took to clear Grandig's mind of the stress.

Grandig ordered enough to feed at least six.

Momo looked at it all and wondered who else was joining them: 'This is all for us, sweet-heart?'

'Oh yeah. Well, mostly for me Momo, but feel free to pick,' She goofed a little laugh and grabbed her fork.

Momo did pick – but mostly she let Grandig eat. She knew her well enough to realise that here was a girl in need of her comfort food. There was no point trying to talk about anything of importance until she had come up for breath – at least for the first time. Grandig ate solidly for a good ten minutes.

When she did finally take a break, clearing her mouth with a heavy gulp of beer, she smiled broadly at Momo: 'I needed that, sorry.'

'You go girl – everyone needs a good dinner inside them.'

'Uh-huh. I'm with you on that. Truth is,' she said, dabbing Shanghai sauce from her chin with her napkin, 'I already ordered one dinner tonight and had to leave it sat at the bar. That's the kind of day I've had.'

'You left an uneaten dinner on the bar?' She laughed, but only half-heartedly, she could see that Grandig did not really mean much humour by it. 'So, what's your problem, girl – I should be charging you by the hour for these evening appointments.'

'Ah Jeez,' she started. 'Where to begin? So, you remember last time I got my knickers all in a tizz – well, this is the same case.'

'Kids or carers?' Momo asked. 'Remind me.'

'Carers, sure. I signed them up just after I joined the CPS – so I've been using them for years. Mostly short-term placements.'

'Well, hell – that's a tough job for anyone. So, where's the problem?'

Grandig stuffed another forkful into her mouth: 'Christ – I probably shouldn't be sat here *talking* about it – I should be out there doing *something* about it – but shit, this mistake goes back nearly twenty years, so I figured one more evening shouldn't make a difference… The wife fudged her background check.'

'Oh Grandig! Girl, that's serious.'

'Yeah – that ain't missed on me, Momo.'

'So how did she do it?' Momo asked.

'She switched names and addresses around so we ended up doing a background check on her mom instead of her. Real similar first name too, so I just missed it all on the form. I only spotted it late this afternoon when I was finishing off my case review. The little kid she was looking after has gone MIA, run off – and, well, things didn't quite feel right, you know how it is.'

'Yes, I get it. Gut tells you something's up. But nothing else to go on.'

'Just like that.' Grandig said.

'So, who is this woman, anyway?'

'Her name's Engelmaier, Kristen Engelmaier. But we managed to run her though the check as Christine DesMoiles – her mom. Came through clean as a whistle.'

'Kristen DesMoiles, then,' Momo said, something vague seemed to momentarily register with the name. 'Have you run a new check on her yet.'

'Not yet. That's my next move for tomorrow. The department is all closed up for the evening and I couldn't get it done now without raising it as emergency, or pulling in some pretty big favours… Do that, and I'm shooting myself right in the foot. I'd may as well apply for early retirement…'

'And the kid?' Momo said.

'She's been missing for days. But we had nothing on her anyway – no name, D.O.B, parents, relatives – nothing. Turned up in the middle of the street one day and never spoke a word to anyone. A total mute.'

'And how old was she?'

'Five or six.'

'Oh Grandig, the poor little poppit. Ain't no one picked her up yet?'

'Nope. Not a sign of her.'

Momo paused. Her eyes were heavy and pained – for someone who had worked for the CPS for most of her working life the empathy she felt for the little kids was unending: 'Do you suspect foul play?'

Grandig sighed *honestly I have no idea*: 'Something ain't right. Engelmaier says she and her husband have something to work through, *marriage-on-the-rocks* kinda thing, I guess.'

'And what did he have to say?'

'Mr Engelmaier? I ain't spoken to him directly. I assume the PD have taken a witness statement, but I don't get to see that.' She leant forward, wagging her finger. 'And that was the other thing that got me thinking: I called his place of work who told me he was off sick with the flu – though she told me not an hour before that he was fine. I tell you Momo, I ain't feeling so good about this one.'

Momo took Grandig's hands and squeezed them; she knew there was little she could do to help but offer the comfort that Grandig so desperately craved: 'So girl, whatcha going to do to sort all this stuff out?'

'I was hoping you might be able to tell me,' Grandig replied. 'I'm just so gosh-darn tired I don't know which way to blow wind.'

The old woman smiled. 'Right,' she said. 'Here's what you're going to do; and it's what you would have done regardless of whether you'd swung by this evening and stopped me getting my early night. Not that I mind, Grandig – I ain't been out for God knows how long – and that was one fabulous supper… But this is it. Tomorrow morning you're going to go into work, pull in a favour, and run a brand new background check on that Kristen whatchacaller - '

'DesMoiles,' said Grandig.

That name again Momo thought: 'After that, you're gonna run all her past placements through your computer and check they're all good.'

'Uh-huh, I can do that.'

'Then, you're gonna grab a coffee and get Mrs and Mr Engelmaier on the phone and explain you want a face-to-face to go over a little hiccup you've had with some old paperwork and see what he has to say…'

'Uh-huh…'

'Then,' and she squeezed Grandig's hand again: 'You're gonna stop your worrying – pick up the phone and call me and apologise for being a silly goose!'

Grandig leant over the table and planted a kiss on Momo's head. She loved this woman just like a daughter loves her mom: 'I love you, Momo, you know that, right?'

'Of course,' she said, 'I know that.'

Grandig finished up the food, picked up the check, then took Momo out for a walk along the beach. It was quite dark but there was enough light spilling from the sunset behind them to make out the beach waders chasing the waves, and to watch the rows of pelicans skimming the ocean on their lazy evening fishing trip. Occasionally one would arc upwards and swoop down in an untidy dive, separating itself from the formation that glided ever onwards along the coast. It was idyllic – peaceful and warm, deserted, yet both of them rich in companionship that for each was so precious.

Grandig drove her home. She felt calmer now: more assured and not so panic-stricken. She had a plan. She had talked things through with her Momo and Grandig felt things were probably not as bad as she thought they might have been.

Chapter 37

The spicy food had brought on a bout of mild but uncomfortable heartburn and Momo sat in her easy chair in the clutter of her front room sipping a peppermint tea. It was her own silly fault, she told herself, eating such food so late in the evening; she should have left Grandig to it and had a glass of water instead. She flicked on the TV but despite the dizzying array of channels she could not find anything worth watching so she settled for the crossword and Sudoku in the Savannah Evening News.

An hour later, the puzzles done, her heartburn still smouldered. She toyed with popping a couple of indigestion tablets, but she was not sure whether she had any, and could not be bothered going to look. She was tired *and hell, she might just spend the night in the easy chair.*

As she sat there, her mind wandered onto her poor Grandig and the conversation of the evening. She understood the worries of the CPS all too well, *Christ, enough kids have been through this house to know the strains of Grandig's job…* She sat and remembered all the times she had stressed herself to sleep about *this* kid, or *that* kid – too many times to remember, that was for sure. She knew Grandig would be fine – always had been and always would be: Momo knew the girl had shoulders stronger than a nun's chastity.

What was that name? Desmoines, was it? No. Des something…

She also knew that Grandig was good at what she did. Momo could forgive her for being a little careless with the paperwork – because she knew that the job was not *about* the paperwork: it was about looking after children. Saving vulnerable kids who need someone like Grandig looking out for them. For many of those strays, Momo knew that Grandig was the only one batting for them.

Desulles? Desnoia?

Momo sighed: Christ. She hoped that CPS knew what a good deal they had with her Gee. She knew there was no one better suited to that job

– no one who understood the system better than Grandig herself – born *from* CPS, and now *of* CPS. There was no one more dedicated to the cause than her.

No, it was DesMoiles. Kristen DesMoiles!

And then it hit Momo like a freight train – a wallop so hard in her chest she thought she was having a heart attack. 'Oh my,' she said, a brief exclamation so diminutive it utterly misrepresented the importance of her recollection. 'Oh, dear God, surely not?'

Momo reached for her iPad and tapped *Kristen DesMoiles* into Google; she realized her memory still served her well – albeit it had taken nearly three hours to place the name. The search engine returned over 5000 hits – and nearly all quoting one other name in conjunction with the search: Reginald Vance.

She dropped the iPad and raised herself gingerly from her chair – her legs felt weak beneath her. Slowly, she made her way to the hallway and grabbed her phone. It was past one in the morning, but it did not matter: 'Pick up, Grandig. Pick up, pick up!' It clicked into answerphone.

She dialled again but once more, no answer.

She dialled a third time, hoping the constant ringing might wake her: praying to God that Grandig had not turned her phone to silent.

Click again: '*This is Officer Grandig. I can't take your call right now but if you leave your name and number, I'll get back to you just as soon as I can…*'

Momo spoke, her voice trembling, and full of misgiving: 'Grandig dear, listen, it's Momo. It's really late – I just want to talk to you as soon as you pick this up… Call me right now. I know this sounds ridiculous but please, do me a huge favour and do as I ask? Call me straight away – call me now.'

She hung up. Her heart was beating a thousand beats a minute but she prayed to the Dear Sweet Jesus Lord Above harder than she had ever done in her life before: *Lord, hear my prayer, you get that girl to call me just as soon as she wakes, and I'll never bother your sorry ass again just as long as I live…*

Her chest was tight, and she felt suddenly cold and breathless. She moved slowly back to towards her chair; small, shuffling steps. She stopped, steadying herself against her sideboard as some invisible force seemed to squeeze her chest tighter and tighter – she gasped, and called out – pain now ripping through her body. Her legs began to buckle beneath her. Pain and fear made her head spin uncontrollably and as she fell, she instinctively grabbed for one of the photo frames – sending all the others crashing as she collapsed.

She lay on the hardwood floor among the broken frames and shattered glass. She clutched the picture of her dearest Gee close to her chest as the light on her world stuttered to darkness.

Monday, 18th February 1985

Chapter 38

'Death House', Georgia Diagnostic and Classification Prison, Georgia.

The guard was called Howie – it was a jolly name for someone who played an admittedly small part in a macabre production. He opened the door to the observation room and the people who had been waiting outside - sipping coffee and consuming sandwiches - filed in quietly and without ceremony. The room was small and featureless, three wooden benches had been placed in three rows, and they faced a window that was currently obscured by a curtain from the other side. Howie rubbed his nose between his index finger and thumb, and he thought briefly as to whether or not he had a handkerchief in his pocket. The door was heavy, and he held it open with his bodyweight as it rested on the back of his boots: he recognized about half of the people coming through the door – the others were nondescripts, *looky-loos.* He noted though that they all shared that dour and sickly look of people attending a funeral.

The first through the door was a press reporter called Peter Consualez, Howie recognised him from previous cook-outs. The next, a couple in their late forties he knew too: Mr and Mrs Penoawicz, parents to Josephine Penoawicz who was the first girl murdered. Then a couple more Howie did not recognize - *more victim's parents,* he guessed. Then it was the Owin's – he remembered them from the news, and they were the parents of Lisa Owin - *found buried in a shallow grave out on the shore of St Augustine Creek, her feet and hands were still hog-tied.* And lastly it was that girl, Kristen DesMoiles - *the only one found alive* - and her boyfriend Bradley, who along with a couple of buddies, Howie recalled, had managed to beat Reginald Vance into semi-conscious and call the cops – *quite the local hero.* Next came the lawyers - Howie could spot them a mile off - they always looked sweaty and nervous at these events, as if they were the hosts of a badly catered party.

Yep, quite a crowd for tonight's barbeque Howie thought.

There were not enough seats for all the guests – and the guard found himself with Kristen DesMoiles stood next to him, with Bradley Engelmaier next along. *A rose between two thorns* Howie thought – *she's grown into quite the pretty young woman these last years*: he found himself breathing in deeply to see whether he could smell her perfume.

With everyone now in, Howie let the door swing shut. The room fell quite dark with just a little light peeking in from the room beyond the drawn curtains. Howie leant in close to Kristen and though completely against protocol whispered to her: 'Sonofabitch gonna get what's coming to him now, sweet-heart.' He then reached in front of her and took Bradley's hand, 'Good work on bring him in, son.'

Bradley nodded in appreciation and gave him a cocky grin back: 'Damn straight.'

As Bradley spoke, the curtain was pulled open by a guard in the next room and the observers got their first view of the condemned man and the execution chamber.

It too was a small room: though instead of a dozen seats, one solitarily imposing oak chair dominated. Three guards were stood a few feet from the chair and they looked forward stonily.

There were a few muffled gasps from the observation room and a woman nearer the front began to sob quietly. Reginald Vance was already strapped in - facing the window - his eyes peering into the blackness of hate beyond the pane.

The woman stood up: 'I'm sorry, I've changed my mind, I want to leave now,' her voice broke with tears, and a little commotion bubbled in the tiny room as she grabbed her purse and coat. The man next to her - *in his best suit* Howie noted - stood up with her and they shuffled their way to the back of the room. 'I'm so sorry – do excuse me.'

The guard squeezed up next to Kristen so he could open the door to let them out: 'Are you quite sure ma'am?'

'Quite sure,' she snivelled into her handkerchief. 'I'm really quite sure, I don't want to watch.'

He let them out without a fuss. The door closed firmly behind them and swift silence followed – everyone quiet in nervous expectation. Then a crackle from the speaker of an intercom system filled the room. The observers sat silently watching the condemned, as the voice, clear and resolute spoke out from beyond the window: 'Reginald Vance, the sentence of death passed down on you by the State of Georgia is now set to take place. Do you have any last words?'

The room was hushed. Vance's eyes were wet with fear and he searched for strength to speak without crying: 'Ayuh…' he swallowed hard, 'Ayuh, want my girl to know I love her…'

He paused, as if he was going to say more, then nodded resolutely. He held his gaze firmly on the dark window infront of him and drummed his bound hands on the oak arms of the chair.

There were more murmurs from within the observation room: there were to be no apologies tonight.

One of the prison team then stepped forward – and the countdown to the execution began. He placed a small, damp sponge on Vance's head. With the assistance of his colleague they then attached the skullcap to his shaven head, strapping it securely in place behind his head and under his chin. Vance began to shake uncontrollably: 'Oh Jesus, oh Jesus, oh Jesus. Help me Jesus…'

There were no pauses now: just swift actions to get the job done. They placed a black hood over his face, then returned to their positions. The third guard flicked a switch which turned on a green light, a signal to the unseen executioner to turn the power on…

'Ain't no fucker gonna help you now, asshole,' Bradley whispered to Kristen, squeezing her hand.

As the power began to surge through Vance, Kristen gazed at the crucifix above the window. She could hear her abductor and rapist dying (*fry you monster!* someone from within the room yelled) but she herself was not watching. Not that she felt pity for the man – far from it – and not because she was afraid. Just at that very specific time she found herself captivated by Jesus' own execution. She had no faith of her own, no belief and no understanding of God: *and yet… and yet.* Her life and her own moral compass had been shaped and moulded by the actions of others, and as she listened to Vance cooking in the room beyond, his death made utter sense to her. Killing him was right, it was proper. Jesus died for the sins of mankind – Vance died for his sins. It was meant to be, and it was good, and it was simple. And it was, after all, very final. In that moment, listening to three-thousand volts ripping through Vance whilst seeing Jesus nailed to his cross, Kristen realised that death was a beautifully cleansing act. Call it murder or execution if like, the result to her was the same: everything clean, washed away like shit tipped from an over-filled cruddy pale - everything was forgiven, and order was returned. She only wished she had been able to flick the switch on Vance herself.

Had she been looking for reason or justification? she thought not, but she had found it just the same. And it was so simple, this act of killing and of dying. She looked around her and saw those mothers sobbing and crying out in pain – she felt like shouting out, asking them what they had wanted to achieve this evening, why they had chosen to come? *They had come to watch him die, hadn't they*? Come to see the man who had murdered their children give his life for theirs? *So why the tears – why the drama now?* This was the payback. This was justice. And it was so very easy. In fact, as justice was played out, she thought it was all really such a fuss. *Why not just have taken him out the back of the prison yard that evening he had finally been captured and shoot him? That would have been easy.*

She looked up – and as she did, Vance's body fell limp as the power supply was turned off. Smoke puffed out in thick wisps from beneath his hood and from his trousered thighs. A man in a white coat appeared from a door at the back of the chamber and Howie leaned into Kristen again: 'That's the doctor,' he said. 'Gonna check to see if the he's dead…'

He took a stethoscope from his pocket and pressed it to the chest of the man in the chair. He listened closely for a few moments and then shook his head, retreating back through the door from which he had come. The power was turned on again. And this time Kristen watched - for the additional thirty seconds it took to finally kill Vance.

Tuesday, 14th July 2015

Chapter 39

Morning

The girl with the BiLo basket at her feet watched Kristen unlock the door to the refuge and make her way inside. She had been spying from her usual spot since 8am and it was now just gone ten - unless someone had made a particularly early start, she knew that no one else was there. She had been staking this place for days like a starved fox, skulking around to see whether there might be free food to nip at or donations to pick over – and today she thought she might be brave enough to creep inside and take a cautious look.

She was nervous, and her distrust of people was strong. She was what was defined officially as an *unaccompanied youth*: in real terms that meant she was homeless, broke and without prospects. Stick a baby in a BiLo basket and the girl had the full package.

She had drifted from children's homes into transitional housing for adults, largely on account of her newly acquired status as single mom – she and her baby knew from recent experience the best places to sleep rough in Savannah. She was not an adult though, *not really* - she had never finished school, could barely read, and could hardly look after herself let alone the baby. What she had learned from her grim, nomadic life around the streets of Savannah - and learned well - was that help was very hard to find. This place, the refuge, she had decided over the last few days might be worth a look. And despite *The Christian Thing* so evident by the bible quotes on the flyer, a free lunch was a free lunch.

A voice called out from across the alley: 'Hey there sweet-heart, do you want something to eat?'

The girl looked up. Whoever it was had broken her daydreaming and her natural reaction any other time would have been *head down and move on quick*. But she was sat on the ground, the baby asleep in the basket and the woman from the refuge was now striding over to her – there was no time to go anywhere.

'Why don't you come on inside,' the woman said. 'There ain't no one around except me – we're all good.'

The girl looked at Kristen dumbly: she had no words to speak and, in her chest, she could feel her heart thumping as if she had been caught doing something wrong. She chewed gum incessantly.

'You look hungry,' Kristen said.

Again – no words came, and she found herself mumbling an awkward apology; *what for, she had no idea.*

Kristen smiled. 'You ain't got nothing to apologise for girl – come on. Come inside. I won't bite – I promise – let's find you something to eat.'

The panic the girl felt subsided a little bit – this woman seemed nice enough. And shit, what had she come here for anyway? Hand-outs and free food - that's what – and she ain't gonna get those sat on the sidewalk. She stood up and took hold of the basket. They crossed the alleyway together, the girl a few steps behind Kristen watching her walk and weighing up her own final options: she figured she could run, if needs be, *if it turns out to be some kind of religious nut-house or loony asylum for freakos…*

'My name's Kristen,' Kristen said, turning back momentarily. 'I can help you with your baby. I'm a foster carer but I work here voluntarily some days.'

The girl nodded, not knowing what to respond for the best, then warily offered an introduction of her own: 'Um… I'm Samantha. I don't really know what I'm doing here; someone said I should just come along? Are you some kind of social worker?'

'Me?' replied Kristen. 'Social? No – as I said, I just volunteer here. I do it for fun.'

'What happened to your eye?'

'This,' Kristen held a hand to her self-inflicted cut. 'I fell. It's nothing serious – looks worse than it is.'

'It looks nasty,' she replied.

They were stood at the alley door now and the girl still appeared hesitant.

'Are you going to come in? There's no harm in getting something to eat, you know.'

The girl took a beat to make up her mind, a moment of uncertainty then in with both feet. 'You're not gonna try and… convert me or anything are you? I ain't into that kinda stuff, just so we're clear.'

'No – I ain't into that kind of stuff either, trust me,' said Kristen. 'This is organized by the church – but God is not a part of the package. We're just here to help - now why don't you let me help carry your baby downstairs and get some breakfast? Have you eaten yet today?'

Samantha shook her head: the prospect of some decent free food sounded good. 'His name's Billy,' she said, the baby's name's Billy.'

'Well, I'm real pleased to meet you both,' said Kristen, 'come on in.'

'I don't like carrying him around in a shopping basket, you know,' she said defensively. 'It's just, well, I don't have anything else.'

Kristen put her hand on the girl's shoulder and smiled. 'I get it. I'm not judging you. I just want to help.'

The girl spat out her gum and they went downstairs. Once inside, she settled herself on one of the large sofas and pulled Billy from his BiLo basket. He was a scrap of a child, dirty and smelly, bagged up in a grubby yellow babygro several sizes too big for him. His diaper was full and heavy, and the sweaters he had been wrapped in stank of stale pee. 'Do you have anywhere I can change him?' she asked.

'Sure,' Kristen replied. 'There's a mother and baby room in the far corner. Help yourself to whatever you need in there: there're diapers, wipes, everything you should need… Do you like breakfast burritos?'

'Dunno,' the girl said, getting up and taking the baby to get him changed, holding him like he was a leaky milk cartoon.

'You want a hand?' asked Kristen.

'No. I can manage.' But not giving the impression that she really could.

Kristen left her to it and went to the kitchenette. She fumbled with the microwave and breakfast burritos, stumbling over buttons in an attempt to fire the damn thing up. Eventually, the tell-tale whirring began and the little plate inside began to turn around and around. The little plastic sack containing the burrito puffed up and a faint whiff of processed bacon drifted out on the steam from the vent. Watching the plate turn slowly Kristen was suddenly full of the recollections from the Refuge launch party. This little room was where the bar was, with that arrogant tosser barman with the tattoo. Over there stood those haughty jumped up bitches with their high opinions and judgmental glances. Kristen felt herself tense at the thought – and behind her was the restroom. That was the place where she had splashed her blood with the broken glass.

The microwave pinged, waking Kristen from her thoughts - the burrito was heated. She opened the door and sickly-sweet steam phoofed out in a cloud – she juggled the wrap out of its hot packet and onto a plate, then made a couple of instant coffees. Back out in the main area she took a seat on one of the sofas and waited for the girl to return with the baby, stirring her coffee absently.

She looked at the heap that represented Samantha's belongings. She had told the girl she was not judgmental – but who couldn't be, faced with this? There was the BiLo basket, of course, and that spoke volumes. The bedding too, old sweaters that looked like they had never seen washing detergent – they reminded Kristen of the clothes you see third-world refugees wearing on those sob-story TV appeal ads. And lastly, a small canvas rucksack, also filthy – Kristen had not noticed that bag before and glancing back to check the girl was still occupied in the mother and baby room, she opened it and took a look inside.

There was not much there: some gum and a couple of dollar bills, a few cents, a crumpled cigarette pack containing a couple of tabs and a disposable lighter tucked inside, and a knife – an old kitchen paring blade with a wooden handle that Kristen guessed she kept for personal safety - Christ-knows the trouble a kid like that could get herself into.

Then she heard the lock slide open on the mother and baby room. 'Did you find everything you needed in there, girl?'

'Yeah, thanks,' she said, still carrying the baby at arm's length, though he did now at least look a little bit cleaner. 'Can you help me with this, please?'

'Sure, hon – pass him over,' Kristen said. 'There's breakfast for you. Enjoy.'

Samantha tucked into the microwave food – she did not care that it tasted like old tyres, and she ate it like someone was about to take it off her. She too was dirty, hands like she had been digging the garden and clothes that suggested she worked in a carwash. She wore a general waft of baby-puke and not one part of her appeared in anyway *looked after.*

Baby Billy wriggled in Kristen's lap. He now smelled of cheap baby-wipes – Samantha had done a half-hearted attempt at cleaning him up but he, like his mom, was in need of soap and a bath.

As Samantha finished off the burrito and reached for her drink Kristen asked her where she lived.

'Around,' she said, purposely not giving anything away, then: 'I don't suppose you have juice, do you? I don't really like coffee.'

'Sorry, sweetheart – coffee's all we got today. We're not really on top of the house-keeping stuff, not just yet, anyway.'

'Uh-huh,' she replied. 'No worries.'

'So, what does *around* mean?' Kristen went on. 'That sounds a little evasive – it doesn't look like you've got yourself anything sorted. Have you been kicked out of somewhere?'

Samantha looked up, and for the first time Kristen saw *a kid,* hiding in plain sight beneath the weary baggage of an adult world of which by rights she did not deserve to belong. She looked *old*: not like an adult seems old with greying hair and wrinkles, but in an *experience* old, as if too much life had already been poured out of her immature and delicate body: she looked like a teabag, squeezed and twice used. And her eyes - that should have shone bright and clear - looked cloudy and dull like the empty eyes of a fish frozen on ice in the window of the deli-mart. Kristen saw nothing of the sweet-sixteener that should have been there. And Christ – the kid she saw reminded her of herself – that night she had been pulled out of the hole.

'You know how it is.'

And Kristen, for a moment, realized *she did know how it is.* It was an uncomfortable sensation, and it rocked her momentarily like someone had knocked her off balance. She looked at the girl again, at this dirty disgusting child, and imagined how much they probably had in common.

'So, what can I do to help, Samantha? What is it that you need?' She was still cradling Billy in her arms, and he was still and silent.

'Are you fine with Billy?'

'Yeah, sure. He ain't so much bother, is he?'

'Not *now,*' she said, sulkily. 'But he's got me kicked out of more accommodations than I can count because of his bellyaching, though.'

'We can help you get that organized. Fo you have anywhere permanent sorted?'

She paused, brushing her hair off her face: 'No – nothing long-term. There are a few places I go, but nowhere I can stay for more than a few nights. There ain't many places in Savannah if you've got a kid.'

'And no family?'

'No.'

'Not anyone?'

She shook her head – almost insolently – as if the suggestion itself was crazy. 'Ain't no one only Billy and me. No one else gives a shit. You know that.'

'And how old are you? Fifteen. Sixteen?' Kristen asked.

'Sixteen. Old enough.'

'Sure. So, you're adopted right?' Kristen asked.

'Nope. Never adopted. Fostered, off and on. I've been in children's homes mainly – but I got kicked out of the last one on account of being pregnant. That's how much *they* care.'

'Jeez – that's rough. But if it helps at all, I do understand, you know.'

Samantha looked up: 'Yeah, course you do,' she said sarcastically, 'Can I have my baby back now?'

Kristen looked startled: the girl's voice sounded accusatory – as if Kristen had forcibly taken the kid, not just held him so she could eat some breakfast. 'Yeah – sure you can. I'm sorry – here you go.' She passed the bundle over to Samantha who tucked him back in his basket. She was getting ready to leave.

'You don't understand,' Samantha said, sullenly, matter-of-factly, wrapping the stained sweaters round her boy. 'No one does. People say they do – but they don't. You *think* you get it, because you see people like me all the time. I do understand that - ' she said, with sarcasm. 'And I know I'm not special – there's nothing unique about me. But *you* see people like me, and you talk to us, and you make yourself feel better by working in places like this, and then at the end of the day you go home to watch TV or sit in your pool or do whatever it is that helps you forget. And whoopy-fuckin-do, you *do* forget: about your shitty day and about the shitty people like me – and that's why you *don't* get it: *get it?*'

Kristen smiled. It was quite the rant. In fact, Kristen admired her drama and contempt: it was impressive, she thought. 'Wow – you're welcome,' she said. 'But you think whatever you like. Though take my advice: I don't really give a fuck. I'm sorry your life's messed up, I truly am. But don't begin to assume you know what *I do* or *do not* know. Not on the basis of this five-minute chat over a breakfast burrito, anyhow. My advice is, take all the free stuff you need: we've got plenty. Yeah, we're out of juice, but I'll send you on your way with all the diapers, baby-clothes, and formula you can carry. And when you're over feeling sorry for yourself – come on back and apologise for your dumbass attitude.'

Samantha crossed her arms and pouted: 'I was only saying…'

'You know, Samantha, don't bother.' Kristen stood up: 'Whether I get it, or don't get it – it doesn't really matter, does it? Because it isn't me having to deal with it. And I'm sure you're smart enough to have figured out whether I go home to the TV, or the pool, or whatever – *I go home*. And you,' she smiled, 'and Baby Billy; put up with your shit.'

'Fine.' Samantha said.

'Yeah. But listen to me before you go. I will help you. I will do for you whatever I can. But don't jerk me around with your self-pity – I can't change what's happened to you – but I can help you going forward.'

Samantha listened: she got the feeling Kristen probably knew more about stuff than she gave her credit for. But Samantha was still a teenager, and aside from the knife in her bag, attitude was her only weapon: 'You're not going to say *keep it real*, are you?'

Kristen laughed. She had not dealt with a sixteen-year-old for a long time – and never a girl. 'How about you take my number and give me a call if you need anything? In the meantime, I'll get you a bag of stuff to take away with you, huh?'

'If you like.'

'Yeah – *it would make me feel better*... What do you need?'

After Samantha had left, with Kristen's number scrawled on a scrap of paper, Kristen reflected. The girl was sullen, that was sure, but she had a least plucked up the courage to come in and get some food. She had also willingly taken a goody bag of baby stuff, and Kristen had told her in no uncertain terms to come back again. Whether she would or not would remain to be seen – but Kristen had felt a connection with her, and though she did not like it, it had been there all the same.

The refuge was now empty – and this last few minutes, Kristen's first morning working the place, was as busy as it was going to get all day. She made herself more coffee and sat herself back on the sofa. Andrew had left her a list of jobs to be getting on with, but those things could wait.

Kristen wondered where Samantha was hanging out. Ordinarily, she could call Grandig and do some digging – but that was out of the question now. She wanted to get to know her more – she was part repulsed and part fascinated by the girl and her baby. The repulsion part was easy to identify – she reminded her of herself: her Vance half, at least, the part of her that still lingered in that barn, with him. Samantha was dirty in that way too – worse perhaps, because she still had a living reminder of whatever sordid or sinful escapades led to the baby Billy. This repulsion part made her want to scrub it all clean – to bathe, soak and rub away the muck and filth and make it all better. The fascination was different though, and as she sat and thought about it, she realized her interest did not really lie with the girl at all. Samantha was obvious: screwed over, abused, washed-up and finished. Samantha was going nowhere – a written book, spent. But what was little Billy's story - what was in *his* backwaters? There lay her fascination: Baby Billy.

As she had sat there watching Samantha eat, the little baby had lay still in her arms. He had felt warm and alive, a bundle of flesh so new as to be free of any personality of his own. Kristen did not believe in nurture – but she believed wholeheartedly in nature and gene-pools and family traits – Christ, she knew *all* about those. The boy was the product of the father and that was that. As she had held him in her arms, she wanted to know all about Daddy, and Daddy's dirty little secrets. He was no good – no respectful man got a teenager pregnant. At best he was a high school football jock – egged on by peer pressure to dip his wick. But Kristen did not think that scenario likely: Samantha did not strike her as a girl who hung around football jocks. Careless boyfriend? Possibly – that would fit. Druggy boyfriend? – yes, that too. Druggy boyfriend-dealer whom she owes some money – yes, that seems more likely – fucked her up for meth money. Or maybe just a scumbag dealer who likes a bit of teen ass and just took from some messed-up, homeless girl or a sicko wino who pounced on her while she slept in the park or another homeless junky who raped her in her hostel bedroom…

Kristen snapped out of her thoughts and looked down. As her imagination had flowed with those angry images, she had, without thought, broken the coffee stirrer and pushed it hard down the length of her forearm. The skin had caught and broken, beads of blood rising from her torn flesh and dribbling round her arm. *Jesus!*

She jumped up: *thank God this time it's not bad enough for a hospital visit.* She dashed to the kitchenette and ran her arm under the faucet – it stung, but the pain this time was bearable.

Chapter 40

Grandig licked her fingers: her desk phone receiver was sticky with maple glaze and she had it clamped to her ear, talking with her mouth full. She had a missed call from Momo too, but the pen pusher over at Savannah PD that Grandig was now haranguing, *virtually begging with*, had taken it upon himself to give her a hard time. Momo would have to wait.

Grandig continued to plead with the officer. Her request was simple enough, *he knew that, but CPS just did not have the authority to call through a no-notice background check – you do understand that, don't you Officer Grandig? That privilege is reserved for arresting officers…* or cops more senior than he was, and certainly not some antsy fricking social worker.

Grandig begged.

Finally, getting the clear understanding that this annoying bitch was not going to let it go, Penpusher relented: 'Okay Officer, listen. Get me your paperwork over here, and I'll run it through for you this morning. Not because I must, you understand; but because I'm going to be helpful.'

'Hun, I get that. I'm real appreciative. You're clearly a really busy man.'

'I drew duty desk – so yes. Real busy. Officer Grandig, is it?'

'Uh-huh.'

'Grandig, my name's Officer Alec. You owe me a favour.'

'You betcha,' *Asshole.* 'When can I expect a turnaround on this?'

'I'll get it over to you by close-of-play.'

'Would lunchtime be too much to ask?'

'Yes, Grandig, it would. Duty desk sucks – I've got a list as long as my arm.'

Click.

What a dickhead, Grandig thought. She considered CPS and the Savannah PD to be one-and-the-same. All on the same team if you will, but with different responsibilities: batters, pitchers, fielders… But Officers like Alec, jobsworth Alec who took it upon himself to make life as fuckeroo awkward as possible just went to show how wrong she was. She kicked back in her chair and demolished the last of her pastry.

Chapter 41

Forty minutes had passed since Samantha had left, though Kristen was confident it would not be long before she was back. She may well have been a sullen and moody teenager, too proud to let anyone close, but Kristen knew that she was also desperate and would soon be hungry again; she would definitely call.

Alone in the refuge, Kristen took the time to flick through the visitor's book and take a glance down the list of drop-ins. Registration was not obligatory, but anyone who was happy to give their details had a record written up and stored in a card index at the main desk where Kristen now sat. Though the place had only been open a few days there was a healthy bank of cards already neatly filed – she flicked through them, randomly pulling cards out and inspecting the names. Without great purpose and largely because she was nosy, she fired up the donated laptop and launched Google. Into it she typed these names, curious to see what she could find about the refuge drop-ins.

Most names brought search results but nothing of any great interest. A few brought up the Central Courthouse of Savannah's register and detailed minor felonies, fines, court orders and the occasional jail-term. Kristen enjoyed a curious salaciousness in uncovering these fine details of people's private lives, turning over stones and revealing the toads beneath; for this alone Google was a beautiful bank of dirty secrets. She tapped in Samantha's name but was disappointed in the results – a few high school sports fixtures and results that might or might not have been the girl who had just been visiting, but nothing more. She then tapped in her own name: Kristen Engelmaier.

Google chugged momentarily.

Nothing.

She then tapped in Kristen DesMoiles.

Bingo. There came back thousands of hits – articles from every newspaper from across the southern states. Pictures too: of herself as a teen – the one used on the missing posters her brother had pedalled across the neighbourhood, press pictures of Bradley, Archie and Col the morning after her rescue from the pit, and images of Vance himself, filthy dirty Vance – her skin flushed.

She reached for the *esc* key in an almost instinctive reflex action, to clear the scream of memories that the search result returned. Her finger hovered over the key, but then, then: her eyes fell on those two girls… It was a dusty, blurred image – thrown up from a small newspaper article following Vance's guilty verdict and subsequent death sentence. It was a victim piece, focusing not just on Kristen and the other girls, all raped – some murdered, but on Vance's girls too: the twins. Kristen found herself mesmerized by the image; she could not remember having seen it before.

It was a long process – unlocking and releasing such emotional trauma was a tragically difficult process. And now, looking on those twin girls in their dungarees, she remembered those days in exquisite detail. Her finger trembled over the *esc* key still, but she did not press.

She had grown to hate those girls, whose singing had infiltrated her own nightmares in the barn. She felt she knew them well, almost intimately, playing jump-rope outside the barn as she was raped inside. They sounded so happy and innocent as they played: Kristen often wondered *did they know what was happening inside?* As Vance grunted on top of her, and being too sleight to fight him off, she tried to blank him out – close her mind to her physical ordeal and find a respite in a different, imaginary mental plain. But she could not. For every time she closed her mind to the pain of her attack, there came the song again, seemingly *mocking her* Kristen believed, *resenting her, hating her, and willing her to die.*

Cinderella, dressed in yella
Went upstairs to kiss a fella
Made a mistake
Kissed a snake
How many doctors did it take?

Kristen looked closer still at that grainy image. Those scrawny girls reminded her of someone, but she could not place who.

Then a rush of warmth came across her as she recalled their final comeuppance; she had the last laugh, she knew that. She remembered her rescue by Bradley and his mates – she remembered the sound of them pounding Vance, the ensuing moments of silence followed by their muffled voices through the boards that hid her beneath the floor of the barn, then their faces as they lifted the lid and saw her beneath: they looked frightened.

Then it was a blur. Panic, running, leaping in the truck, all four of them screaming and yelling as Bradley grappled with the lurching Ford pick-up. She remembered how terrified they seemed – how just like kids they all were – tears streaming from their eyes as they blindly skidded along the dirt track away from the barn.

She remembered she was sandwiched between Col and Archie, Bradley in the driving-seat next to Col. He grappled with the steering-wheel, wrestling it as if in a fight, struggling to keep the wheels on the dirt. Then one of them yelled out louder, she recalled it was Archie pointing madly to the track up ahead: at the two girls now stood dumbly in their path. Bradley yanked at the wheel, desperate to avoid them.

Almost immediately as Archie pointed and yelled, Kristen's heard the girls sing: *Cinderella dressed in yella.* Rage poured in torrents, and Kristen shrieked uncontrollably, clawing maddeningly at the Ford's dash seemingly trying to rip her way out of the car to get to the girls.

The boys panicked. Archie and Col grabbed at her, pulling her back into her seat as Bradley fought for control of the truck as it loomed down on the two girls who stood like deer caught in spotlights. At that moment, as adrenalin instantaneously pumped through them all, Kristen threw herself towards Bradley and grabbed the steering wheel, heaving it towards her and pulling the Ford into a broadside skid towards the girls. The tyres lost traction, spitting dirt and mud as nearly a ton of steel careered out of control.

For a fraction of a second there seemed to be silence; everyone frozen in time. Then, a sickening thud as the rear of the truck, wheels still spewing up dirt from the track, spun out and hit one of the kids.

She slammed the screen of the laptop down and held it shut with both hands; she knew the memories of Vance were not buried deep and it only took an old photo or the chant of a jump-rope song to disturb the dirt that covered them over. But that image was a real blast-from-the-past, she had not thought of those two girls for such a long time, her only regret was that she only killed one of them.

Wednesday, 23rd October 2002

Chapter 42

Savannah Juvenile Detention Centre

Kristen leant against the trunk of her car as the early morning traffic cruised past; she gazed across the highway to the juvenile detention centre from where Joe was about to be released. It was a sprawling place, all dark grey buildings and razor-wired fences, and looked, Kristen thought, every bit as formidable as Savannah's Coastal State Prison - *for fully fledged offenders* - over at Garden City. She sniffed - she didn't envy Joe his time here. *Not that he didn't deserve it, of course* – but it will have been hell, all the same. Kids or not – this placed housed the worst under-18s Savannah could muster, and it will have been over two years of fighting, intimidation, dirty tricks, and pissing the bed in fear.

She looked at her watch. The sun was breaking over towards the ocean and the air was still and cool – pretty much a perfect, autumnal morning - and it had just passed 6am. She had called Joe perhaps half a dozen times during his sixteen months in Juvie – he had no family contact – and his friends were not the sort of people to keep in touch during a stretch inside. His social worker may well have called, maybe even visited, but no one who would really have been looking out for him. Kristen had offered to pick him up and take him for breakfast, and the boy had jumped at the offer.

Then, right on time, Joe Mayes appeared from the front of the detention centre. He looked pretty much as Kristen remembered him – back in the day when Bradley and she had fostered him; he was now seventeen and had filled out a little, particularly across the chest and a touch in the face – and there was a whisper of a moustache but he still looked more boy than man.

He blinked as he walked out into the sunshine, rucksack over his shoulder and dark hair shaggy in the morning air. He looked around for his ride – and saw Kristen waving from beyond the fence. He waved back and jogged keenly down the path to the electronic pedestrian gate – his final barrier between rehabilitation and freedom. He took a deep breath – waited for the harsh electronic bleep to signal the gate was unlocked – then pulled it towards him and stepped out.

'Joe, hi!' yelled Kristen from across the highway.

Joe waved again and dodging traffic crossed over – he jumped in the passenger seat as Kristen fired the engine. 'Hey, thanks for this. I appreciate the ride.'

'No problem, kid,' she replied, signalling her turn and pulling out onto the highway. 'There's a coffee there for you – it might be a little cold though. Half-an-half, with two sugars – just how you liked it.'

Joe took the takeaway mug from the cupholder and took a mouthful. 'Fuck,' he said. 'That's the best coffee I've had since I can remember. Everything in that place tastes of piss – no matter what you have.'

Kristen nodded. 'Well, enjoy. And get used to it. That's the last you're going to see of that place – right?'

Joe smiled. *I hope so.*

Kristen headed out east onto the interstate while Joe drank the rest of his coffee. They didn't talk much – he told her the address of where he would be staying, a place his parole officer and social worker had arranged for him – and Kristen said she would drop him off once they had eaten. She told him to relax, and that it would take half an hour or so to drive back downtown for breakfast.

Joe was grateful to Kristen. He hadn't seen her – or Bradley - in the years subsequent to leaving their care, but she had reached out to him while he was in prison – she said she knew when someone was in need of a friend. She was right. She had heard about his conviction on the local news networks – and told him she wanted to be there for him; that she would do her best to help him out, and that she'd be there the day he was released. She had been true to her word. The warm sun was still low on the horizon and it felt great on his face – he realised he hadn't properly relaxed since being locked up. 'Thanks Kristen,' he said, reclining his seat. He closed his eyes - the thrum of the road was hypnotic; he could feel himself succumbing to sleep – it was washing through his body like a drug.

'No problem,' she replied, looking over at the boy. She saw his eyelids sink and watched Joe fight against their weight, like they weighed a hundred pound each. By the time she had looked back at the road, then back again to her passenger, he was asleep. She pulled off the interstate and headed out towards the Savannah River.

Joe didn't wake when the car peeled off the interstate onto the highway, nor minutes later when Kristen pulled away onto the quiet backroad that meandered almost aimlessly aside the river. He didn't stir either when the car bumped along the Tupelo trail – forgotten by all except the occasional fisherman – that twisted and turned down to the sandy banks of the oxbow lake. He didn't even come-to when she cut the engine, got out, opened his door and reached over to release his seatbelt. He only opened his groggy eyes when Kristen yanked him from his seat by the lapels of his jacket, and his head cracked hard on the baked earth by the shore.

'Get up,' Kristen demanded.

The sun seemed to spin in the sky. Joe floundered on his back trying to make sense of the situation he found himself in; his eyes wouldn't focus, and he felt drunk, *no – high, extremely – dangerously high.* Something was pulling his feet and he became aware he was sliding along the ground on his back. He scrabbled with his hands but grabbed only dust and sand. 'Wha-at the fuck!?'

Suddenly, he felt cold running up his back – *water*, enveloping him – it was instantly all around him, soaking him through. Then whatever – *whoever* – had been dragging him, released him – and he instinctively turned onto his front and tried to stand – but he couldn't. He was – *off his face.* His stomach lurched, then he stumbled, face-first, back into the shallows of the river. Water filled his mouth, muddied his eyes, and muffled his ears. He tried to lift his head – tried to breathe – but couldn't.

As he foundered, Kristen leapt astride his back and used all her force to hold his head beneath the water. He wasn't a big teenager – and she probably weighed the same as him pound-for-pound. Additionally, she'd spiked his coffee with enough oxycontin to floor a buffalo. She was enraged – her mood and demeanour had seemingly switching on a dime.

'I thought you liked it rough!?' she shrieked at him, pounding his face into muddy silt that lay less than a foot beneath the water. 'That's what you told her, wasn't it? So, Joe, you like to knock girls around a bit – do you!?'

She yanked his head out of the water, holding him by his soaked, matted mop of hair.

He gurgled and spluttered. He struggled to release himself – to force the weight of Kristen off his back, but he was hopelessly drugged.

'That's fucked up!!' Kristen screamed. 'You little cocksucker, *do you hear me?* She shook him so violently by the hair that a clump came off in her hands: 'it's fucked up! Girls don't like it like that, Joe!'

They thrashed at the water's edge - it was like a gator attacking a deer – the surface splashing violently as Kristen once more held Joe's head beneath the lapping waves of the shoreline. Her anger was explosive.

'You don't deserve to live, Joe,' she barked through gritted teeth. She locked her arms and pinned him beneath the water. 'That poor girl was too terrified to testify against you – that's how you dodged a rape conviction; you're an asshole!'

Joe bucked and heaved but couldn't shift the near dead-weight on his back. He couldn't hear the accusations – just the gushing of the water in his ears, mouth and throat.

'But I found her – you scumbag, and talked to her, and she told me; she told me the truth of what you did! The *extent* of what you subjected her to.'

Joe desperately scrabbled for something to grab but his fingers just sank into soft, silty mud – he writhed and kicked, and his head felt like it might burst – involuntarily he finally inhaled water deep into his lungs and began to drown.

Kristen felt him weaken beneath her – a few more moments he would be dead. 'You're no better than all the others,' she said, then: 'You ain't gonna plea-bargain yourself out of this one.'

She held him under for thirty seconds more then released her grip; he didn't move, just lay face down in the water. She stood up, then sat and watched him for a few minutes from the shoreline. Before she left, maybe another twenty minutes later, she dragged Joe's corpse further out into the depths and watched as the tidal current took him off. He drifted slowly, his head and shoulders barely visible above the water. Soon, the gators would take him – and Joe would never be seen again, just another missing statistic on the parole officer's spreadsheet.

Kristen was soaked through, but happy. 'Scumbag, just like his father,' she said.

Tuesday, 14th July 2015

Chapter 43

The little girl reached over and nudged him. The gator still pinned him to the deck, but Bradley was not aware of *that* particular monster, just the one that infiltrated his mind right now, the little kid with the cornrow braids sat at his side. His vital signs were still slowly blinking out, but his mind stuttered on inside his head, a PowerPoint of hallucinations and memories played out like a dying candle.

Tell me! Tell me the story! said the kid once more.

Bradley managed an outward *mbuh-mbuh-mbum* that was loud enough to make the gator open his jaw just a touch.

I is not going away until you tell me the story Mr Bradley so you may as well get on wiv it and stop your moaning.

Persistent fucking bitch!

Yes, I is persistent Mr Bradley so tell me the story about Aimee and Kristen. I fink you have jus about enough time to get it off that chest of yours before your lights are going to go out once and for all. Don't you fink?

Bradley grunted and a sparkle of images cascaded through his mind: Barnie the dinosaur, Aimee in her pyjamas, and Kristen naked on the flatbed of Vance's trunk. They flashed out like fireworks.

You gonna tell me the story, huh Mr Bradley?

Bradley tilted his head sideways and observed the girl through his gloopy eyes. For just a flick of a second the motion of shifting his head popped Bradley into consciousness and the girl vanished in a blink, fizzling out like a dissolving effervescent pill. In her place Bradley saw the gloomy boathouse, shafts of light teaming through the broken roof from above and he instantly smelt the peaty hum of the still water, steamy and muggy in the air. But then he slowly blinked, gunk oozing from his mucky eyes and he slipped out of reality as quickly as he had entered it: The kid crackled back into his mind again.

Don't be messing around Mr Bradley. You is surely dying here. You ain't got long to be telling me your story before you is ded and gobbled up by the gators. You did see the gators didn't you, Mr Bradley? Der is a really big one sitting on your lap and he is jus about ready to eat you up! You not got long now Mr Bradley!

Bradley gulped a low, guttural swallow.

Okay, kid. I'll tell you it all.

Chapter 44

I really think I loved Kristen back then. And you got to believe that's the truth. But that whole shit with Vance made her one screwed-up crazy bitch – not just a little messed up either, she was pretty much a car-crash from the very beginning.

Right after that episode with Vance the four of us, her, Col, Archie and me were like minor league celebrities – every newspaper and TV station across Georgia wanted interviews and photographs, the whole place went totally batshit for us. I mean, I could hardly walk down the street without someone coming up and patting me on the back or wanting to shake my hand, it felt like I'd gone from villain to hero overnight. I'd never known anything like it - and I have to say I enjoyed it, we all did, well, Col, Archie and me anyway.

Kristen was a little bit more in the background – kinda quiet. Shit, I guess she'd had it pretty rough, so I get that. Anyway, the thing was, the papers and TV people were really keen to get a picture of Kristen and me together. It was pretty weird, but we obliged, and I remember a few times they'd pay us a few dollars which made it feel better, for me anyways. Kristen, like I said, was much quieter about the whole thing, kinda awkward in a way, and shit, she was three years younger than me – so that whole picture they were trying to paint of us, I don't think she liked it much.

I did though. I'd never admit it to anyone, but I had the hots for her. But hell, I just couldn't get that image out of my mind – of Vance banging away on top of her and me watching from the roof of the barn, it makes me hard just thinking of it even now.

So anyways, we obliged with the photos and interviews, played the local hero thing for a few weeks, then pretty much as the summer ended, so too did the interest in Col, Archie Kristen and me – we went back to being just regular kids again. Looking back on it, it was one odd summer, that's for sure.

After that, I didn't see Kristen for about two years, I'd pretty much forgotten about the whole thing, if I'm honest. I guess by this time I'm nineteen, maybe even twenty, and I had this job in the kitchens of a diner out Garden City way – it was nowhere special, just a handful of tables and some shade out front but it was easy money and the guy who ran it never gave me a hard time. I remember this one afternoon, I was stood cleaning a few dishes, and the sink looked out on to the restaurant. The place was pretty empty except for a couple of families – real quiet. But as I stood there, up to my elbows in grimy water, I spotted this one girl with who I guessed was her mom and her baby sister, and she was definitely giving me the eye. She was hot in a plain kinda way, you know? I don't s'pose many men would have noticed her, but I did. I did that double-take thing where I looked over my shoulder, checking that she weren't looking at someone else – it was only me and the cook working the kitchen that afternoon, and he was about sixty. Shit no, it was me she was checking out. Then all of a sudden, she waved at me, real secretly so her mom didn't see, then gave me the cutest of smiles, cuter than anything I'd ever seen before – and shit, if I didn't start getting a boner right then and there at the sink! Cos I suddenly twigged who it was, and she was giving me the definite come-on in that shitty old diner, sat right next to her mom and sister with me washing the fucking dishes!

We carried on eyeing each other for minutes, then she made some sort of excuse, I guess to visit the restroom or something, and she made her way out the back and I slipped out to see her.

I remember the first thing she said, she said, 'Hey Bradley, you've grown.' It seemed an odd thing to say, but you know, I guess I had. Put a final spurt-on in those last teenage years, I guess. I said, 'You too,' in a clumsy sort of way, because she'd kind of filled out a bit, you know. Still, she was no way fat, she still looked lovely in fact, way better than when she was on the back of that pick-up back in the barn. I guess she was sixteen now, maybe seventeen.

Well, it got kind of awkward, from there on. I'm not very good at small talk, and I was sort of rubbing my hands on the apron I was wearing, all greasy. And she was just kind of smiling and not saying much. I remember glancing back at her table where her mom and little sister were sat, and I said something like, 'I didn't know you had a little sister too? I mean, I remember your little bro, he was a bit of a dork, but….' Then she interrupted me, with, 'Oh…' kind of embarrassed, like, like she didn't quite know what to say, 'Oh, that's not my sister,' she said. And at that split moment, I looked at the little kid, who I guess was maybe two years old. I figured it there and then. I mean I'm not stupid, and then it was my turn, and I said, 'Oh.' Then, 'Yeah. Course. I get it.' And she said, 'Her name's Aimee. That's what I call her anyway.'

After that, we started seeing each other, off and on. It wasn't boyfriend-and-girlfriend so much as just hanging out together. Usually, her mom looked after Aimee, and me and Kristen just took off. I think her mom was just glad she had something else to do other than just hang around at home. After the whole Vance thing she stopped going to school. I don't know, but I'm guessing she found out she was pregnant pretty soon that summer it all kicked off. Anyway, having the baby pretty much cut her off from the whole world. So, when I came back into her life, I think I was just about perfect for Kristen.

You is making it all sound like it was all good, Mr Bradley. But you leave out all the bad bits, don't you? Is you ever going to tell me what you did to the little girlie Aimee?

Bradley blinked. The beautiful images bled out of his eyes and the grim, dank musk of the boathouse oozed back around him.

'Mum-muh-muh-muh.'

You is goin to hav to get on wiv it Mr Bradley – you don't want to be stuck here for ever – do you? Do you Mr Bradley?

Chapter 45

Morning.

Andrew's house was in Davis Park Avenue, on the outskirts of the Historic district of the City of Savannah. Here, the streets were pleasant and well-kept. Strips of grass well planted with ferns and small palms separated the sidewalk from the passing traffic. Dappled sunlight glinted lazily through the canopy of trees that over-hung the road. The houses, where stars-and-stripes fluttered proudly from porches, and homeowners kept the small driveways regularly swept and blown, stood nobly back from the road. They were grand without being ostentatious, and prominent without being imposing. Andrew was fortunate to live here. His home was a generous property boasting a beautifully planted, ornate front garden, and an elaborate, wrought-iron veranda at both ground and upper levels. It was owned by the church, of course; a man of Andrew's means could not afford to buy in this street.

Usually he chose to take his morning Americano out on the top veranda. It gave him the perfect view of the street below and a useful vantage from where to watch and listen to the early morning hubbub. He liked the gentle hum of breakfast-table conversations drifting from next door, the chatter of the kids skipping the streets on their cheerful way to school and watching for Miss Chavez's dressing-robe to fall open - as it occasionally did - as she took her trash out each morning. Andrew knew there were simple pleasures to be had for an early riser on Davis Park.

But this morning, Andrew had no time for any of this. Today, he had plans. Sure, he needed to drop in on the refuge and check all was tickety-boo down there. He was pleased how the number of drop-ins was growing day-on-day, and happier still that his pet project took up little of his own time. He was also particularly happy how it was working out with some of his new volunteers. Not just Kristen, but the other girls. He had not anticipated just how well his sex life would be served by his happy bunch of community do-gooders.

He walked briskly to the bus-stop, grabbing a free copy of the local newspaper from the stand just as the bus rumbled in. He gave up his seat to a mum struggling with her wriggling toddler and made amiable chit-chat with an elderly couple vacationing in town.

The bus ambled its way into Savannah and he jumped off at City Market, where shops and stalls spilled out on the sidewalk, and at every corner the homeless sat and weaved dried reeds into baskets and ornamental flowers hoping to sell them on to passing tourists. Andrew picked his way through the traders stopping only briefly for a coffee take-out, sipping his brew as continued his brisk walk through the streets.

Finally, he arrived at *Oma's Jewellery* and the little bell above the door tinkled as Andrew stepped in. A gentle burble from a radio drifted from the workshop and the waft of joss-sticks mingled with the gentle zing of smelted silver. He had not visited before, but the hippy girls who volunteered at the refuge had recommended the place. They told him it was where they bought their piercing jewellery, and their nose, and toe-rings, and that it would definitely have what he was looking for. He browsed for a few minutes, every so often picking up a ring, or inspecting a charm more closely. As Andrew flicked the sales tags over in his fingers, he noted too that the items were not expensive, most fell within the ten to twenty-dollar price range. *Perfect.*

From the back of the shop the owner looked up from her work-desk. She was middle-aged, heavily tanned, and her red-dyed hair tied back in a loose ponytail.

Andrew described what he wanted, and they stood and chatted for a few moments. He was quite specific about the charm, but he said he didn't care whether it was on a ring, bangle or necklace. The charm was the important bit. He took some time in choosing, but finally settled on the perfect piece. The owner wrapped it in tissue paper and popped it into a tiny plastic bag with a little Ziploc; Andrew smiled; it was the exact same kind of bag his weed was delivered in.

Out on the street again, Andrew jumped on the next bus that came along. This would take him west out of town, where he could alight at Bayview and decide where to head to next. It was already steaming outside but the air-con in the bus was cool. Andrew pulled out his cell phone. The number for the refuge was on speed-dial, and he tapped it. It rang twice before someone picked up.

'Hey, Dizzy, is that you? It's Andrew.'

The girl on the other end of the line smiled to herself, 'Yeah, boss, this is Dizzy.'

'I'm just running a few errands downtown, are you on shift all day?'

'Yep, I'm on all day. Where are you at? Are you coming in?'

Andrew gazed out the window. 'I'm on the bus, just heading out of downtown. I'm not sure what my plans are yet, that depends. Is it busy down there?'

'No, not so much. UPS just dropped off the new flyers, and the designer's been on the phone wanting some information for the website. Oh, and the coke man has been in and delivered the vending machines, but apart from that, it's been quiet. You?'

'No, nothing much going on with me today, just the usual stuff, you know.'

'Well,' she said, then: 'It would be nice if you found time to drop in.'

That flirtatious tone was quite subtle, but Andrew heard it clearly in her voice. He had been getting to know her much better recently.

She continued, 'We could, you know, kill some time together?'

'This is a very tempting offer,' he said. 'But I'm actually supposed to be visiting someone in hospital in an hour. Could you wait?'

Dizzy laughed, taken aback. 'Gee, Andrew, you sure are bold, you know that!?' Then, 'Who are you visiting, friend or family?'

'Neither,' he replied. 'One of the parishioners, actually. Her name's Deidre Clarke. She's about three-hundred years old and has been dying for about the last two hundred of them. Her husband called me late yesterday to say he thinks she's about to peg out, and would I go visit? Unfortunately, responding to calls like that is part of my job description.'

There was silence on the line, then Dizzy spoke. 'Andrew, tell me you are not going to blow me out for some dying woman who's not even family?'

'Not so much blow you out, just put you on hold for a while. If you don't mind.'

'Put me on hold!? You really don't have a clue, do you? It's now or never, Bible-Boy.'

Chapter 46

Afternoon.

Samantha had spent the rest of that day in a slow meander around Savannah, shifting from park bench to store-front to street corner, begging wherever she could with her BiLo basket and passenger in tow. Barely had anyone given her a downward glance as she sat, empty cup in hand, asking for spare change or a buck for food. She had even made herself a small cardboard sign, 'spare a dollar for the baby?', but it had had no effect. *Christ, people are so mean.*

Her little package grizzled bad-temperedly from within the basket. The sky was blue overhead and the temperature already in the low eighties. She looked down at Billy's sweaty little face, all blotchy and red: 'Alright little man,' she said, 'I get it, you're getting hot. Me too. Let go find some shade.'

She got up and they trundled off together, a slow walk down the streets and heading in no specific direction. She crossed the sidewalks to keep herself and Billy out of the sun and continued with her line of 'spare any change?' to random strangers.

They meandered a while, back-and-forth, criss-crossing the streets until the two arrived in Forsyth Park, which this morning was relative quiet. Samantha gazed around. There was a walking-tour of tourists passing through, taking in the fountain and the statues. A few more people dotted about stealing a coffee break and chatting on their phones, and another homeless man asleep on one of the benches, an empty beer can hanging loosely from his hand at his side. That was about it.

***

Later still, and hungry now, she tried the missionary, but it was closed. She wasted an hour walking across town to find the doors locked and the windows shuttered. She banged on the doors but there was no reply. The sign on the door said the place should be open, but there was no one in. She sat herself down on the steps and waited an hour, perhaps more, but no one came. The sun peaked in the sky, and she shuffled backwards up the steps to keep in the shade.

At about two in the afternoon she gave up waiting. She traipsed around the city aimlessly, getting hot and tired. Her feet were sore and swollen and she could feel blisters swelling at her heels where they rubbed sockless on her pumps. And she was hungry. *No, she was starving.* She looked up to see where she was, and noticed she was only about five minutes from the refuge. The place with free burritos and coffee. With renewed purpose, she headed off, and within moments was back in the quiet alley where a few days ago she had enjoyed her first *Five Guys* burger.

She stood at the door and pressed the intercom buzzer.

Chapter 47

Andrew and Dizzy had locked themselves in the refuge and took advantage of the seclusion to satisfy themselves fully and exuberantly. Both were completely naked, and were in full, sweaty throes on the couch ordinarily reserved for visitors. They pounded liketeenagers, though technically only Dizzy had this excuse. Andrew did his very best to keep up.

Dizzy had pulled the blinds to the street-level windows that peered down in the converted cellar. *The last thing we want*, she had thought, *is to be to be caught at it. Andrew would lose his job, for one. And me, my reputation.*

Andrew had moved on Dizzy months back and this was not their first time. He convinced himself he was doing nothing wrong and took comfort from the fact that she was nineteen years old and that it had not been an abuse of trust. She was a helper at bible school when they first met, sure, but she was not one of the pupils. *That* would have been wrong, but she had graduated class the year before he arrived. *Nope, nothing wrong here. Just getting down and enjoying myself.*

They continued with sweaty enthusiasm until someone pressed the intercom buzzer from the street above; it rasped gratingly on the reception phone.

'Leave it,' groaned Andrew, 'They can wait… I can't.'

Dizzy laughed. She had no intention of answering. 'Oh, fuck, can you imagine that conversation!' she said over her shoulder. 'Come on, don't stop!'

Chapter 48

She pressed the buzzer again, leaning on it longer this time. Still no one came. 'For fuck's sake,' she said, looking down at her boy. 'Is no one in today? Hello? Hello? Anyone home?' The call-light on the intercom flashed expectantly but no one answered. 'Jesus!'

She picked up her basket and looked both ways up the alleyway. It was empty. No passing stranger with a *Five Guys* this time. 'Hello!? Hello!? Anyone in there!?' She banged the buzzer one last time and gave up. She figured she would be begging for dinner tonight.

No breakfast. The Missionary closed. The Refuge closed. What a shit day.

She turned, but as she walked slowly back up the alleyway her gaze fell to the floor-level windows that looked into the Refuge below. She had not noticed these before, partly because they were greyed-out by the blinds that covered them from within. There were four of them, all in a row. She got down onto her knees to see whether she could see in, to see whether there was someone inside who could not hear the buzzer.

The first glass panel was completed obscured by the blind. So was the second and so too the third. She crept along the alleyway on all fours, trying to catch a glimpse of anyone inside the room below. When she reached the fourth, the shallow angle afforded her a view between the blind into the refuge. The sight of the copulating couple caught her by surprise. The guy had his socks on and wore wire-rimmed glasses. And Samantha was surprised how much younger the girl was than him. 'The dirty fucks, Billy,' she said, aloud.

Chapter 49

Late afternoon.

As so many hot summer days in Savannah end, it had started to rain. It was a heavy downpour that turned the air grey and flooded the downtown storm drains in a moment. Lightning crackled and burst above, and thunder moaned loudly. Torrents of water gurgled and gushed along the narrow troughs between the street and sidewalks, and people huddled under umbrellas and ducked for cover in shopfronts and doorways. Samantha huddled in the trolley park of *Piggly-Wiggly* on East Victory Drive, soaked through, the rain hammering the Perspex cover above. She gently pulled her BiLo basket this way and that, desperate to settle Billy who was shrieking wildly. Though Samantha would not admit it to anyone, she was close to bursting into tears herself.

She watched as a car pulled in, splashing a great sheet of water from the lake-like puddle that submerged much of the carpark. Through the torrential storm and near manic beating of the wiper blades it was impossible to see the driver within, but she peered scrupulously anyway. The vehicle passed her by without slowing.

She had begged the use of a phone from a passing shopper about forty minutes ago. The tattered piece of paper Samantha had stored in the back pocket of her jeans was damp and flimsy, and some of the ink had faded and run, but the number had still been discernible. Fortunately, it did not click to answerphone and the number rang through. The person on the end of the line was sympathetic. *Yes, she knew that store. Yes, she knew where that was. Yes, okay, she'd be there as soon as she could. Just sit tight and wait.*

Another car pulled into the carpark showering a great spray of water again. This time, however, the car slowed, and the driver flashed the headlights, which cut through the rain in a dull yellow glow. It pulled up next to where she sat. The passenger window whirred down just a crack, 'Jump in, kid!' Kristen called.

Samantha was on her feet, instantly. She grabbed Billy in her arms and threw the basket on the backseat of the car. She opened the front passenger door and climbed in quickly, Billy wriggling grumpily on her lap.

'Buckle up,' Kristen said, 'and hold tight to your kid. I don't have a baby-seat.' She dropped the car back into gear and pulled away.

For a moment, both driver and passenger were silent, and Billy was calmed by the swish-swish-swish of the wipers flicking back and forth. Kristen drove carefully in the rain, and concentrated hard on the roads and junction, only relaxing as she reached the interstate out of the city, and when the traffic thinned.

'So, how's it going?' Kristen asked, looking briefly over at Samantha and Billy sat next to her.

'Um, let's just say today's been a pretty shitty day on all counts,' Samantha replied.

Kristen nodded. 'Uh-huh?'

Samantha sniffed back watery snot. 'Yeah. Pretty shitty.'

'Anything I can do to help? Aside from taking you home and getting you both clean and dry? You're completely drenched, by the way.'

Samantha looked down: 'Yep.' Her clothes clung uncomfortably to her body and she was wet through. 'Can you turn the air-con off, please. It's pretty cold in here. Also, I'm really hungry. Do you have food?'

'Have you eaten since this morning?' Kristen asked.

'No.' She paused: 'Thanks, by the way. Thanks for picking me up.'

Kristen looked over again: 'You're welcome.' Then, 'And yes, I've got food at home, plenty. I might need to go out for some stuff for him though, I've not had much call for that recently.'

'Cool.'

Samantha smiled faintly and they fell silent again. Kristen was aware that her passenger's eyes were drooping with sleep, and that little Billy had quickly dozed off on his mom's lap. She would be out for the count in a moment, no doubt. She guessed no-one knew where this kid and her baby were, and that no-one really cared. That was the system, and Kristen knew it well. The girl and her kid were off the radar.

She indicated off the interstate, and turned the corner passed the IHOP into Welyvan Street. 'Hey, Samantha,' she said, 'don't fall asleep yet. We're home.' She humped the car up onto the drive and thumped the break. 'Come on in.'

Once inside, Kristen fixed Samantha a sandwich, which she wolfed, then helped her give Billy a bath. They got him as clean as the little boy had ever been. Samantha had a couple of fresh nappies left and they fixed him up good, putting him down for a sleep in the room last used by the little girl with the cornrows. He rolled a little, so they put two pillows either side so he could not fall out. Once he had settled Kristen fixed Samantha with a robe and showed her where the shower was, *take as long as you want, there's no shortage of hot water.* Whilst Samantha got herself cleaned, Kristen put all their clothes, including the piss-soaked jumpers from the BiLo basket through the washer. After twenty minutes or so, Kristen heard footsteps as Samantha crossed the landing to where her child slept. It fell quiet. She checked a few minutes later, and both mother and son were asleep together in Aimee's old bed.

Back downstairs, Kristen sat at the kitchen table. It was late afternoon, the cut over her eye itched, and she figured she would let them sleep for as long and as deep as their bodies need. She fixed herself a large glass of wine and sat contemplative. Her mind drifted.

The wine was going down well, so she poured herself some more and popped a pill for good measure. She watched as the evening shadows crept in, and the early evening sky began to turn crimson. *Where was this going to end?* She rolled up her sleeve and ran her finger across the train-track scars that ran up her forearm. They tingled like electricity under her touch. She knew, in her heart, that killing Bradley had probably been a step too far, that it was going to be too big to cover up for good. She knew that people went missing all the time and that murders went unnoticed and forgotten. But not people like Bradley. Bradley had an employer, a social security number, a pension plan, medical insurance and a bank account. People would notice, and they would notice soon. And they would call the police and they would come and ask questions. She wondered, briefly, when she would get caught.

She counted the scars that criss-crossed up her arm. She could count sixteen clearly, but others, older ones, merged amongst them. A tally of the years of self-loathing and self-abuse. She stood up and went to the kitchen draw, pulling out a kebab skewer. She sat back down at the table and drew up her sleeve again and began to scratch and gouge until the blood was running down her arm. Kristen continued to count – *seventeen, eighteen, nineteen* – before her light-headedness gave way to unconsciousness.

Chapter 50

Grandig picked up the phone to call Officer Alec one last time. She had called his number every thirty minutes since about four in the afternoon but only got *This is Officer Alec, I'm away from my desk right now but please leave me a message I'll get back to you as soon as I can.* Grandig had already left at least three, each growing increasingly antsy and persistent. She dialled the number again. *This is officer Alec, I'm away from my desk…* She slammed the receiver down, 'Sonofabitch!'

She knew now, having called him first over her breakfast pastry, that Officer Alec had done for the day and gone home. It was a few minutes off six in the evening, and Grandig supposed she should probably do the same. If Penpusher had discovered anything dodgy in Kristen's past, she was going to have to wait one more evening to find out.

She checked her emails then fired down her desktop. She got up, her chair groaning in relief, and stuffed her bag with her keys, purse, and lunchbox. She grabbed her cell phone and remembered the missed call from Momo. *Dangit!*

She grabbed her bag and stomped out of CPS, pressing speed dial for Momo as she left. It rang out – she dialled again, but same thing. She left a message that she loved her and would call back later.

Chapter 51

Evening.

Kristen woke. She was slumped over the kitchen table with her head resting on her left arm. In front of her she could see her empty wine glass, the skewer, and her other arm that was covered in something like black treacle. She had been out of it for no more than a minute or two but in that moment, she had no recollection of where she was or what she had been doing. She lifted her head, bringing her world back into focus. She raised her right arm, peeling it away from the tackiness of the drying blood and the laminate of the tabletop. She had bled a lot.

She went to the bathroom and held her arm under the tap. She grabbed a towel and dabbed at her cuts, managing only to open them up again. Her blood stained the white cotton and dripped into the sink. She rinsed again, and this time, with the towel, applied pressure; she held it a moment then peaked a look. The bleeding was slowing. She rinsed and repeated and this time the blood stopped. She washed and dried one last time, then tentatively dressed her arm with some gauze from the bathroom medical cabinet. She knew how to dress a wound; *of old*. She looked back at the bloody sink and towel as the phone rang. She made a dash.

'Hey, this is Kristen…'

It was Andrew.

'Oh sure, yeah, I'm good. No, not busy. Not really.' she said.

He went on: 'Look, Kristen, this might seem completely out of the blue, but do you fancy joining me for some food tonight? Only if you're free, of course.'

'Oh, well. I'm not sure, Andrew.'

'Nothing weird, I promise. It's just, you know, I've had a really difficult day and I could do with some company and all.'

'Oh?'

'Yeah, it's been a tough one. I've been over at the hospital all day with one of my parishioners and her family. I mean, she was old; so old. But she lost her fight today, Kristen, and it's been really sad for everyone. It takes the emotional toll out me too, trying to support the family at a time like that. Would Bradley mind if you came?'

She thought for a moment *did she really want this?* 'Um, no, Bradley wouldn't care. It's just, I'm hardly in a state to go out right now. And I was kind of getting ready for a night in front of the television.'

He persisted. 'Hey, look, nothing fancy, okay? In fact, I'm just finishing up at the refuge, I'll swing by and pick you up. Would twenty minutes give you enough time?'

Kristen paused. *What is it with this guy?* 'Okay, fine. But look, nothing heavy, okay.'

'Sure. Sure! That's not a problem. Just a glass or two of wine and small talk, I promise. I just need some relaxation to clear my head. Some food, some chat. Nothing heavier than that, I promise.'

Kristen relented, 'Okay then. Twenty minutes, you say?'

'See you shortly,' said Andrew, hanging up.

Kristen checked on her two guests who were still sleeping soundly in the spare room. She toyed with waking Samantha but decided to leave a note instead. She wondered for a moment whether it was wise to leave a total stranger alone in her house, but figured there was nothing incriminating, and nothing worth stealing, so likely no harm there. Besides, she did not get the impression that Samantha was a thief.

She went to her room and changed quickly. She chose a loose, long-sleeved top that she could wear comfortably over her bandaged arm. If she could avoid it, she would prefer to avoid any unnecessary conversations on *that* topic. The cut on her head she had got away with, but fresh wounds on her arm would be more difficult to explain away convincingly. Finally, she put on some lipstick and cheap perfume, *God knows why* – she couldn't remember the last time she'd done such a thing - and went out and stood on the driveway for her lift.

Andrew arrived, and contrary to the impression Kristen had got from their brief conversation on the telephone, they drove to his place for the evening. *You don't mind, do you?* he had asked, and though she felt it a little weird, she said she didn't. Anyway, he told her he would drop her back in a couple of hours, *so no money wasted on taxis.*

'Whoa, nice house,' Kristen said, when they pulled up. 'Is it yours?'

'Well, for the time being,' he said. 'Comes with the job, you know?'

'That's some fringe-benefit,' Kristen replied. 'Kind of big, just for you, don't you think?'

Andrew laughed.

Inside, the house retained all its period features, and Kristen was surprised at how little of a mark Andrew had made on the place. She noticed a couple of buddha statues and some African artwork, but mostly the house felt like someone else lived here. More like a living museum than a home. 'I, uh, love what you've done with the place,' Kristen said.

'Oh, don't say it,' Andrew remarked, leading her down the corridor to the kitchen at the back, 'I'm no home-designer. So long as I've got a bed, shower and somewhere to make coffee, I'm happy.'

'What's with the buddhas?' Kristen asked.

'Them?' Andrew replied, 'Oh nothing. Just memorabilia from my travels. They make me smile, with their little potbellies. They look content, don't you think?'

'Sure,' Kristen said.

In the kitchen Andrew asked, 'White or red. Or beer? I've got a couple of Lites if you'd prefer?'

'Depends; is the red as bad as last time, or is it a good one?'

'No, it's a good one. Italian, if I remember rightly,' he showed her the bottle. '*Barolo Mascarello,*' he said, 'I found it in the cellar.'

'Thanks.'

'Please, take a seat,' he said, 'I'll knock up some pasta to go with the wine. Do you like pasta?'

'Yeah, pasta would be nice.'

Andrew fussed with pots and spaghetti. He fried garlic and chopped chillies, stirring in anchovy fillets, chopped tomatoes and olives. He looked like he knew what he was doing. And as he cooked, they drank and made small talk. He lied some more about his dreadful day, and Kristen lied about Bradley and his flu. She was surprised at how easy she found his company, and how straightforward it was to bullshit him about her husband. They chatted too about the refuge. But again, Kristen decided not to mention her new housemates, Samantha and Billy, and he missed out Dizzy and how well he was getting to know her. Finally, Andrew placed two bowls of pasta on the table and lied that he had got the recipe from an old Italian couple he had lived with in the foothills of the Dolomites.

'Good health,' he said.

'Likewise,' she replied, raising her glass. 'This looks great.'

They ate and drank together, and though their conversations were largely based on lies and fabrications, they were relaxed and good company for each other. Whether it was the drink, or the adrenalin from her earlier self-harming wearing off, Kristen was as relaxed as she could ever remember being. She sensed Andrew's stories were tinged with elaboration, but tonight, she did not mind that. It was nice just to talk with someone for a couple of hours and enjoy getting drunk. She thought, but could not remember, when the last time she had done that with her husband, *or anyone else for that matter?*

For dessert he had bought a couple of *gelatos*. 'Don't force it down if you're full,' he said. 'You won't hurt my feelings.'

'No, thank you. That was delicious. And a lovely evening. You're clearly a very talented cook.'

'Oh, not so. It's actually a really simple dish, just made with good ingredients. It's hard to get it wrong, really.'

'Well, whatever. It tasted really good, thanks. I guess I should be thinking about getting back.'

He did not reply but caught eye contact with Kristen. He held her gaze and leant forward a touch. 'Kristen, do you mind if I ask you a personal question?'

Kristen bristled, she put her wine glass down on the table. 'I thought we agreed no heavy stuff?'

'I know, and you're right, we did. But…'

'But what?' she asked, suddenly finding herself aware of how drunk she was.

He took a visible breath. 'What's the deal with Bradley?'

She felt a shiver of cold prickle her skin. 'How do you mean?' she answered.

'Well, I know it's probably not my place, but you and he don't seem… very close.'

Kristen did not answer. But held his gaze.

'You're right,' she said. 'It's not your place.'

'I know, I know,' he replied. 'But, is everything okay with you guys?'

'Okay how?' she asked.

'Well, I'm worried, that's all. Well, not so much worried, but more concerned. As a friend.' Here, he reached forward as if to take her hand, but she leaned back. She took up her glass and drank, a full mouthful not a sip.

Again, she said nothing.

'I'm not trying to be nosey, Kristen, I promise you. It's just these last few weeks and months… You've had difficulties with your fostering, what with that kid going missing, then whatever that thing was at the refuge party. And,' he paused here: 'Someone said they saw you have a bit of, an episode, at the *Green Banana*.'

A mix of shock and anger bubbled in her voice. 'Who said that,' Kristen asked.

'It doesn't matter who said it, Kristen,' he replied. 'I'm just concerned you're in trouble, and that you've got no one here to lean on.'

'I'm fine,' she said. '*We're* fine. Bradley too. We're both fine.'

He filled their glasses with more red wine.

'What happened to your arm,' he said.

'What about my arm?'

'There's blood on your shirt,' he said.

Kristen looked down, and there on the forearm of her shirt was a fresh stain of blood, about the size of a quarter. She put her hand over it.

'Did you cut your arm, Kristen?'

'Christ, what is this!?' she exclaimed. 'I didn't come here to get cross-examined, Andrew. Leave it the fuck alone, will you?'

'You see? Why wouldn't I be concerned!' he asked, 'It's clear as day that something's up. I only want to help, if I can. That's all.'

Kristen felt tears well up, and it took her by surprise. She had become so skilled at suppressing emotion, that when it crept up on her as it did now, she had to struggle to keep it down.

Andrew stopped talking. He watched Kristen intently but did not spot the tears that sat just behind her eyes.

'No,' she said finally.

'No, what?' he asked.

'No, I'm not okay.'

He shifted his stool around next to her, and this time took her hand. She let him hold it briefly, then pulled it away again.

'Let me help you, Kristen,' he said. 'I can; if you'll let me.'

'Wait up, and let me re-phrase that,' she said, taking a breath, 'I wasn't okay, but I'm okay now. It's complicated, that's all. It's complicated, it's been going on an age, and I'm too drunk to explain it properly.'

'*Is* it Bradley?' he asked.

Kristen sighed in exasperation. *How the fuck can you answer a question like that?* she thought. *How the fuck? Yes, it was Bradley. But it was so much more. It was the beating, the kicking and the hidings he gave her. It was Vance, and that pit. It was Aimee, and the uncontrollable hate, anger and resentment that had never left her. It was the self-harm and it was the foster kids, and it was murder. It was everything, the sum of her whole damn life.*

'He used to beat me,' she said.

Andrew sighed, 'Oh Kristen, I had no idea.'

'Of course, you didn't. No one ever does,' she replied. 'But that's because women like me always work so hard to keep shit like that secret.'

'So, you've never told anyone?' he asked.

'No one. You're the first.'

'When you say, 'beat you', you mean…'

'Kicked, punched… the whole-nine-yards.'

'Shit, Kristen. I'm so sorry,' then: 'Have you called the police?'

She smiled. *How much to say?* 'No, I've not called the police,' she paused. 'They never do a thing. The PD are useless at things like that.'

Andrew nodded.

'Besides,' she continued, 'It's been taken care of.'

The wave of emotion had left her, and somehow, telling Andrew the briefest of truths, brought a vague sense of relief.

'Have you left him?' he asked.

'Something like that,' she said.

'But he's gone. Left the house?'

'Yep,' she replied, 'Bradley's gone, I don't suppose he'll be back this time, either.'

'When did he go?'

'I guess, about a week ago?'

'And you're sure you're quite safe? You can call the police from here, if you like? There are places you can go, Kristen. I can see to that; you just have to ask.'

'You're very sweet,' she said. 'Thank you, it's much appreciated. But as I said, it's sorted. Trust me.'

'Do you have a gun?' he asked.

'What!?'

'In the house? For protection? Just in case…'

'Will you shut the fuck up!' she said. 'You're getting boring. Yes, I have a gun – but no, I have no intention of using it.'

Andrew looked at her. *Would it be wrong to make a pass now?* He thought. 'Let me pour you another wine,' he said. 'You'll stay for one more?'

'I feel I should be going,' Kristen replied. 'But one more, so long as you quit with the questions. Agreed?'

'Agreed.'

He poured two more large glasses.

'Hey,' Andrew said. 'I almost forgot. I have something for you.'

He had not forgotten. Far from it. In fact, he had planned his whole day pretty much around this evening and this gift; he had just been waiting for the right moment. He was a little worried that the whole 'domestic abuse' thing might have put a stop to his plan, but he felt that might just have been side-stepped nicely now; she seemed fine.

'Hold up,' he said. 'Just give me a second.' Then: 'Here; a little gift.'

She took the small plastic bag; 'An eighth of weed, how sweet of you.'

'I don't know what you mean,' he said.

'I'm joking,' she replied, 'What is it?'

'Well, open it and find out.'

Whatever it was, it was wrapped in tissue paper and held fast with tape. She tore it open, carefully, gently, and the tiny trinket fell out on the table. 'Oh,' she said, 'it's pretty.'

'You've not seen it properly,' he said, 'look at it more closely.'

She held it in her fingertips. It was a delicate chain, no thicker than thread, with a small silver charm of interlocking hands. 'Oh,' she said, 'it's lovely – thank you. *Friendship*, right?'

'I saw it by chance,' he lied, 'and I thought you might like it.'

'It's beautiful, I love it, thank you.'

Andrew seized his moment; he leant forward in his chair and kissed her. She recoiled, momentarily, then relaxed. She could not remember the last time she had been kissed so tenderly. It was pleasant, and she enjoyed it briefly, but then she stopped him. 'I'm sorry, Andrew. I'm flattered, but I can't. I'm sorry.'

He asked *why not?*

'Because I'm drunk; you're drunk – and this is the alcohol talking.'

He disagreed. 'Kristen – stop. Let yourself go for a moment; don't shut me out. I see you for who you really are, Kristen – all the good you do. The love you give. You deserve to be happy – stay here tonight. With me. You're a beautiful person.'

Kristen said, 'You're wrong, Andrew. And anyway, this thing with Bradley, it's done. But it's not over. Not fully. And I can't be having a fling. I can't; and neither can you.'

He tried to kiss her again, but she stopped him. 'No, Andrew. We're done here. As I said, I'm flattered, I really am. Maybe next time.'

As the taxi stood waiting at the end of his path, Andrew asked Kristen if he had offended her; with the gift, or with the kiss. She replied no, and that she was flattered that a man as young and handsome as he should find someone like her attractive. He tried to kiss her again and tried one last time to convince her to stay, but she declined. He said nothing more but stood there with his arms open, beckoning her back. In the backseat of the taxi she wondered whether she would have such a chance again.

Wednesday, 15th July 2015

Chapter 52

Morning.

Grandig's alarm went off with a shrill, electronic tone at seven the next morning. She reached over and batted the clock, setting the snooze for another fifteen minutes. Duly, after quarter of an hour had passed, it sounded again.

'Damn you to hell!' Grandig mumbled from under her sheets, 'Leave me alone.'

It ignored her.

'Quit the noise, would you? I'm trying to sleep!'

Still the alarm rang.

Grandig sat up, petulantly. She had the worst case of bedhead imaginable and her face was puffy with sleep. She rubbed her eyes awake. 'Well, fuckeroo, if it isn't morning, already.'

She got up and showered. She dressed and ate toast. She grabbed her keys and bag, and her cell phone from its charging stand. She left her apartment, locking her front door as she left. *Early to bed, early to rise.*

She fired up the car engine, and as she did so her phone bleeped in her bag. She pulled it out and saw the little flashing red light indicating an answerphone message was waiting. She placed the phone in her hands-free car cradle and dialled her messages.

She pulled out of her parking lot, and out onto the ocean road back into Savannah. Momo's answerphone message from two nights ago crackled through the tinny speakers of the hands-free unit.

She pushed the empty food wrappers and discarded soft-drink cups from the little shelf along her dashboard; the LED clock blinked 7.38am. *Way too early to call you Momo, but I'll give you a buzz sometime after my morning pastry. And after I've given Penpusher the what for!*

Chapter 53

Kristen sat on the back porch as the sun rose, her head thick with hangover. In her left hand she nursed a mug of coffee, and in her right hand was Bradley's Browning revolver. Neither currently held her attention. From her swing-seat she watched a robin. It pecked and scraped the hard earth for some breakfast in the still and warm and quiet air.

Kristen raised the revolver, slowly, *ever-so-slowly*, and aimed at the bird. Her hand trembled and the bird danced in her sights. She moved her index finger to flick the gun's safety-catch, then placed it back on the trigger. The bird sensed something, Kristen's movement perhaps, and stopped. Kristen held her breath. Both she and bird were momentarily motionless. Then the bird, seeing no danger, returned to its hunt for breakfast.

Kristen squeezed the trigger.

Click!

It was an empty, hollow sound but bright enough to startle the robin, which flew off into the cover of the Candler oak. Kristen did not react - it was not a misfire - the live rounds were still in her jeans pocket. She rested the gun back down on her thigh and drank some coffee. *Killing is the easiest thing in the world,* Kristen thought, *it's what follows that hurts...* She looked down at her forearm and at the bloody bandage. The physical pain had long subdued, but what remained, *what was always there*, was the deep itch that no amount of scratching would touch.

She dug into her pocket and pulled out three rounds. She loaded them into the gun leaving an empty chamber between each bullet. She gave the cylinder a spin then locked it into place, leaving the safety-catch open. It was such a glorious morning; she knew if it was meant to be, she would have no regrets. She thought first of last night, and of Andrew. *He called me a beautiful person* she recalled. *What little he knows of the unspeakable things I've done.* She thought briefly of Bradley, too – and longer of Vance. A fleeting, dancing image of Aimee drifted through her thoughts. Then back to Vance again. When she closed her eyes and opened her mind, she could smell that pit; the dank, sour earth of the hidden trap. That jump-rope song popped into her head so easily. She fixed her eyes on the Candler oak and held the nuzzle of the gun into her mouth. *Cinderella, dressed in yella, went upstairs to kiss a fella. Made a mistake, kissed a snake. How many doctors did it take?* She would never find freedom because her past always comes back to bite her.

She was not beautiful. She was a monster. She took a deep, steadying breath and pulled the trigger.

Chapter 54

'Hey Grandig, you've got a visitor.'

Grandig had just stepped into reception and was busy trying to dig her security pass out of her bag. She was juggling her cell phone and car keys and managing to tie herself in knots with her ID lanyard. 'Huh?'

'Over there,' replied the receptionist, pointing to the waiting area with its broken chairs and out-of-date magazines. 'The kid in the uniform. He's been waiting for you for the past twenty minutes. He says it's urgent. Are you late again?'

Grandig looked at her watch; it was barely half-eight. 'No, I ain't late. If anything, I'm early,' she said. '*And*, I don't start until nine, so keep your snippy comments to yourself.'

The receptionist sniffed and turned her attention back to her computer screen: 'You're meant to log all visitors with reception first. It's a pain in the ass when people just turn up.'

Grandig waved her hand dismissively then walked over to greet her visitor. The receptionist was right, he was as fresh-faced as they come and looked about twelve. 'I'm sorry,' she said. 'Can I help you? Reception says I've been keeping you waiting...?'

The young man stood up and shook her hand. 'Grandig, pleased to meet you. Sorry for turning up out of the blue, but um,' he was struggling for the right words, so instead he gestured with the large manila folder. It was stuffed full and held closed with a thick rubber band. 'You're going to want to see this.'

'I'm sorry, who are you?' Grandig asked.

'Oh yeah, sorry. I'm Officer Alec,' he said. 'And these are the checks you've asked for.' He paused momentarily, 'Is there somewhere you and I could talk privately? I think I'm about to ruin your day.'

She gave him the once-over. For a white guy he was pretty good looking. Not her type – but, hey, not bad. 'You were quite the jerk on the phone, you know that?'

He smiled sheepishly. 'I have a dreadful telephone manner. And, I'm on duty desk for a month. And that drives me nuts. So, what can I say?'

"Sorry'?' Grandig replied.

He smiled. 'Sure.'

Grandig took Officer Alec up to the first floor and bagged an empty meeting room. Despite the air-con blowing a comfortable twenty-one degrees, her palms were sweating, and her heart was pounding inside her chest. She hated surprises, and this unannounced visit clearly had the making of one nasty shock. She closed the door behind them.

'So, go on,' Grandig said, sitting herself down. 'What have you found?'

Alec placed the folder on the table and carefully removed the rubber band. He opened it and took out what Grandig roughly estimated to be a wad of about a hundred or so xeroxed pages. 'Have you ever heard of Reginald Vance?' he asked, flicking through the papers.

Grandig shook her head.

'Okay,' he said, and sighed. 'Me neither, until yesterday.'

'How bad is this? I'm mean, my heart's pounding like a fuck here.'

Alec looked across the table. *How best to put this?* he thought. Then: 'It's a fucking shitstorm.'

Chapter 55

In person, Officer Alec was not the utter asshole Grandig had taken him for yesterday. He was calm and polite, and judging by the size of the manila folder he had brought, he had been working hard for her. She liked him already.

'So,' he began. 'Reginald Vance was born in 1947, a local guy; he was good with machinery, that's clear from his files. He started out on the farms fixing the bailers and tractors, then picked up an array of work as a mechanic in and about Savannah. So far so good. He was married at some point, the details here are sketchy, and had two kids; twin girls – there's a picture of them here, somewhere. They were aged four when he was arrested in the summer of 1979.'

'Okay,' said Grandig. 'So, what did he do?'

Alec placed his hand on the pile of papers on the desk. 'Give me a minute,' he said, 'there's a lot here; but I'm just going to give you the headline data. You can read this lot at your leisure later.'

'Go ahead,' she said.

'Vance first got picked up in 1972, for aggravated breaking and entering. Picked up, but not charged. On this occasion he managed to provide an alibi, admittedly a shaky one, but it proved good enough for the detective on the case to know he was on a hiding to nothing. That, and the witness wasn't so reliable.'

'How so?' asked Grandig.

'She was a ten-year-old girl,' he replied. 'She was woken in the middle of the night by a man in her room. She said he was big; standing in the corner of her room *playing with himself*, if you catch my meaning. When she was questioned later by the police, she said she recognised him; said she thought he had worked on her daddy's farm. She was able to pick him out from a line-up a few days later. But as I said, he provided an alibi that placed him an hour away near Bluffton and he managed to wriggle of the hook.'

'Scumbag,' Grandig said.

'Anyway, a year later, he does get caught,' Alec continued. 'This time, sexually assaulting a thirteen-year-old girl as she walks home one evening from band practice. Fortunately, on this occasion, a couple of joggers hear a commotion and step in. They're big enough to overpower him, and the girl then manages to flag down a passing patrol car; Vance gets two years for that one and serves eighteen months.'

'Okay,' Grandig said. 'Now what?'

'Hold on, I'm getting to it,' he said. 'So, Vance is put away, and doesn't make a reappearance until 1979. Between 1974 and then, his record goes quiet. But,' he said, 'when he does bob up again, he's progressed to the big league.'

'How so?'

Alec rifled through the pile of paper, pulling out two xeroxed photographs that looked like images from a yearbook, 'This is Josephine Penoawicz,' he said, 'and this is Lisa Owen. Both sixteen back then. Both were missing for over two years before they were found in shallow graves in woods adjacent to farmland over Cotton Hill. Both were severely malnourished at time of death, and the autopsy states they had been physically and sexually abused before being beaten to death with a claw-hammer.'

Grandig winced.

'And these two, here,' Alec produced two more similar photographs, 'are Jayne Holmes and Hattie Savers. Again, both teenagers, both malnourished and abused, and both killed similarly to Josephine and Lisa. These two were found close by in a disused grain silo.'

'How did they link him to the crimes?' Grandig asked.

'They found a fifth girl, alive, on the same property. He'd kept her in a hole beneath the floor of a barn. He was doing to her what he did to the other four. But then, lucky for her, one night a group of boys stumbled upon him raping her and took it upon themselves to rescue her. They battered him unconscious and stole his pick-up, taking the girl with him. The police arrested Vance later that evening, still at the barn. They found the bodies of the other girls in the days after.'

'Fuck,' said Grandig.

Alec passed her one last xeroxed photo. 'And this is what you're going to want to see,' he said.

'Who's this girl?' she asked.

'This is her,' Alec said, the girl who survived. 'Kristen DesMoiles. Or as you know her, Kristen Engelmaier.'

'Oh Christ!' Grandig exclaimed. 'You're shitting me – please tell me you're shitting me, Alec.'

'No, I'm not. And the kid who rescued her? Bradley Engelmaier. In fairness, a quick google now and you can pretty much see it all for yourself,' he said. 'So long as you search the right name, of course.'

Grandig managed a wry smile, 'Oh sure.'

'Anyway,' he went on, 'I'm sorry, but it gets worse. CPS records, *your* files, show no next-of-kin.'

Grandig nodded, she had believed that Kristen and Bradley had never had children. *That's why they fostered.*

'Well that's not strictly the whole truth,' Alec said. 'She did have a kid, a girl called Aimee.'

'You're shitting me,' Grandig said again, shaking her head. 'Why the fuck didn't she tell me that?'

'She's covering it all up. The kid was Vance's – she chose to have it.'

'Or her parents made her,' said Grandig.

'Yeah, possibly,' he said. 'But wait, look at this. This is the kid's death certificate and coroner's report.'

'The kid's dead?'

'Yes,' Alec said. 'She was only seven years old. And look what it says…'

Grandig took the papers, 'the cause of death: unexplained.' She was ashen.

'There are police reports and everything,' Alec said. 'It's worth saying by this point she's married to Bradley. You can read it all, but basically, they said Aimee had some sort of seizure and managed to choke to death in the night. They say they went into her room in the morning and found her dead in her bed.'

'Oh, fuck,' Grandig sighed.

'There were questions asked and a little investigating,' Alec went on. 'But it all looks half-baked, to be honest. Clearly, there was some suspicion, what with the cause of death being unexplained and not natural causes. But Kristen and Bradley stuck to their story. And my guess is, considering what she had been through and that the kid was Vance's; if anyone did suspect foul play, they turned a blind eye.'

'You really think?' Grandig asked.

He paused, 'Sure. Wouldn't you?'

Alec watched Grandig let the information sink in. He knew what this meant. *There was no way on God's clean earth you'd let a couple with Bradley and Kristen's history foster kids.*

'Fuck,' Grandig said. Then with resignation, 'Anything else?'

'No, that's it,' he replied. 'It's all here in the paperwork – you can have it all. Vance was executed in 1985; more than he deserved, if you ask me.'

'And the kids?'

'Whose kids?' replied Alec.

'Vance's. You said he had twins?'

'Oh yeah, that's right. He took them with him each time he went up to the barn. Did I tell you that already?'

'No,' said Grandig.

'Yeah, that's right. Kristen said she could hear them both singing and playing jump-rope outside while Vance raped her. But get this, when Bradley and the others bust her out in Vance's pick-up, they manage to hit one of them as they drove off. Killed her instantly. Poor kid, she was only four. The other, her sister, ended up in care, but I can't find any record of her. There's a xerox of a picture here – somewhere – but it's far from clear. The one twin that survived has been blanked out – to protect her identity I'm guessing.'

Alec rifled through the papers again, found the grainy picture and passed it to Grandig. 'Not much to see.'

Grandig looked at the picture - at the poor mite whose pop was a serial killer. She looked so, *unremarkable* Grandig thought, *poor scrap.*

Alex took the picture back, tidied the papers and passed the file to Grandig. 'Some bedtime reading for you. For what it's worth.'

She took the folder but said nothing. She tried to process everything, but her brain was frazzled. Kristen Engelmaier, the woman who she had known all these years, was a sham; a phony.

'Grandig,' Alec said, breaking the silence. 'Can I ask a question?'

'Go ahead,' she replied.

'What are you going to do?'

'I don't know.'

'No, seriously. What are you going to do now?'

She sniffed. 'Well, I'm going to call them both in and try and get to the bottom of all this.'

'Uh-huh. Then what?'

Her head was spinning, 'I guess I'll get on and run a case-review of all their foster kids – oh shit!'

'What is it?' Alec asked.

Grandig was already on her feet, scrabbling up Alec's paperwork back into his folder. 'Oh shit, oh shit, oh shit!'

'What!?'

'Last week, no, a fortnight ago. One of their placements went missing. A little girl. A mute. She was about six years old. They said she just up and disappeared in the middle of the night. Fuck!'

It was Alec's face that now drained of colour. 'Are you serious?'

'Yes, I'm fucking serious. I called it in as a missing person, but no word of her yet.'

Alec got up too, 'Grandig, can you get me a list of their foster kids? I'll help.'

'You'd do that?' she replied.

'Of course, get me the names over and I'll check them out. I'm only on the fricking duty desk. You get out and track her down. Bring her in. Shit; threaten her with arrest. At the very least wer could have them for providing false information.'

Chapter 56

Click!

Kristen took the gun out of her mouth and took a slug of coffee to wash away the residual taste of gun oil. *Soon* she thought, *this will end differently*.

She caught sight of the robin again, back on the lawn on its relentless mission for breakfast. She raised the gun at it once more and made a popping noise; if she pulled the trigger again, she knew she would blow the fucker away. It ignored her now, brazenly.

'Yeah, fuck you,' Kristen said, getting up. 'Count yourself lucky.'

She tucked the gun into the back of her jeans.

Back inside, she stored the gun in the kitchen drawer. From down the corridor, she heard Billy was awake; cooing from the spare room. She put her head inside the door, 'How are things in here?' she asked.

Samantha looked like another girl. The early morning sun was shining in through the open window and the dirty, dishevelled kid from yesterday had been replaced with a clean, bright teenager. She sat on the bed; her clothes she wore, now freshly laundered, were clean and dry. 'Jeez,' Kristen said. 'Don't you look better for a shower and a good night sleep?'

Samantha smiled; and again, it was bright and crisp and kid-like. 'I feel it too,' she said. 'I, *we*, slept so well. I owe you big-time, Kristen, thanks,' then smirked. 'Not that I've got anything to repay you with.'

'Forget it,' Kristen replied. 'Take what you can get, that's what I always say.'

Billy looked up from his spot on the bed. He was chewing the end of a plastic hairbrush and drooling heavily onto the sheets. He laughed at Kristen, like she had just said something hysterical.

'And what's got into you, soldier?' she said. 'Who gave you the right to eat my hairbrush?'

Billy laughed again.

'He's getting teeth,' said Kristen. 'Have you checked?'

'Checked?' Samantha said. 'How do I check for teeth?'

'Christ kid, has no one taught you anything? Stick your finger in his mouth and poke around. You'll feel the sharp little spikes if he's got any coming through.'

She put her finger in his mouth, awkwardly.

'Hey, easy, not too deep! You're not trying to take his tonsils out. Can you feel anything in there?'

'Nope,' Samantha replied. 'Just slimy. Nothing else.'

'Well, check every day, take it from me, they're on the way.'

Kristen knocked on the doorframe she was leant against signalling the end of the chat. 'How about the three of us go out and get some breakfast? My treat.'

Billy, the hairbrush now jammed back in his mouth looked up like he understood and registered his agreement by flashing a dribbly grin. Samantha agreed too: 'Oh man, yeah! I'm starving,' she said. 'If you're sure that's cool with you?'

'We'll go find some food then figure out what the hell we're going to do with you both. We'll have to find you somewhere to stay, somewhere where you're not getting thrown out every time *that* little pest starts wailing. When those teeth finally cut through, he going to get so much worse. Come on, throw your shit together, let's go eat.'

Instinctively, Kristen drove towards the *Green Banana*, but at the last, remembered her previous visit and what Andrew had told her last night. She diverted towards *Friendly's* and ordered at the drive thru.

With breakfast bought, she swung the car back on to the interstate. One junction down, as the river dog-legged inland, she pulled off again and followed the road into the perimeter of the Savannah national park. It was quiet this morning, and judging from the expanse of available parking, few people were out. They pulled in and Kristen killed the engine. Samantha carried Billy, and Kristen took the food and blanket from the boot to sit on. They strolled down a gravel pathway than meandered off from the carpark and found a good spot to sit and eat. Beyond the grass, the Savannah River stretched magnificently in front of them; a huge ship, a thousand containers stacked on its back, drifted silently past. The sun continued it morning rise into a cloudless sky, the heat tempered by the slightest of breeze from across the expanse of the river.

Kristen threw the blanket on the grass and Samantha sat Billy down. He was just about holding his head up, and she began to spoon oatmeal into his gaping, eager mouth.

'He's one hungry little man,' Kristen said.

Samantha nodded.

After a moment of feeding her son she said: 'You've got blood on your rug.' She pointed at a large, crusted stain on the patchwork next to her knee. 'How do you suppose that happened?'

Kristen felt the prickles run up her spine, and her mind raced. She had a sudden flashback to bundling Bradley into the car. *Had she used the blanket to cover his body? She must have.*

'Jeez, I have no idea,' she replied. 'Are you sure that's blood?'

Samantha picked at it with her nail. 'Looks like it. Gross.'

Kristen shimmied over next to her and rubbed the mark dismissively. 'Well, Bradley used to get nosebleeds, so maybe the last time we picnicked he got one – I don't remember.'

'Oh,' said Samantha, still heaping oatmeal into Billy's face, 'Who's Bradley?'

Jesus fucking H Christ! 'Bradley? He's my husband.'

'Oh,' Samantha said again. 'Are you two divorced?'

For fuck sake. 'Yeah, we're divorced. A long time ago.'

Samantha looked at the brown residue under her fingernail. 'And you've never washed the blanket?' she asked.

'And I've never washed the blanket!' Kristen said with finality. 'But I will now, trust me – now you've pointed it out.'

'Okay,' said Samantha, unaware of the mild panic she had caused Kristen with her questions. 'It's your rug.'

Billy continued with his breakfast and Kristen watched the boat drift past. She made a mental note to dispose of the blanket. She unwrapped her breakfast bun and began to eat.

'So, Samantha, now we've sorted the rug issue, let's talk about you for a minute. How old are you, for starters?'

'Sixteen,' she replied. 'Seventeen next month.'

'Happy birthday for next month,' Kristen said, then: 'Where are your Mom and dad?'

Samantha was still looking off towards the horizon. 'Dad served in the military; he was killed when I was nine.'

'Ah gee, Samantha, I'm sorry.'

She shrugged. 'Shit happens. Then mom died of breast cancer the year after.'

'Christ. Any brothers or sisters?'

'Nope, just me,' Samantha replied.

'Any family? Aunts or uncles?'

She shrugged again. 'I got taken into care when mum died. I stayed with a few foster families, but I was pretty angry then. No one would put up with me for long. And mostly, I couldn't put up with them. I just wanted my family back; back to how it used to be.'

Kristen reached out and put a hand on Samantha's knee, but the girl knocked it back. 'Pity doesn't do any good,' Samantha said.

'No. I know. I'm just trying to be nice,' Kristen said.

Samantha laid the little one down in the shade of the bench. She picked at a muffin.

'And what about him?' Kristen asked.

Samantha responded, matter-of-factly: 'Just some asshole.'

'An ex?' Kristen asked.

'No. Just some jerk.'

Now it was Kristen's turn: 'Oh?'

'Look, it was just some guy, at a party, and we ended up, you know?'

'Yeah, I know how it happens, Samantha. Was it, consensual?' she asked.

Samantha shrugged, 'What do you mean?'

'Did you *want* to sleep with him? Were you okay with it?'

'No,' she was beginning to sound petulant, 'I was out of it, actually, there had been some party at the home I was in. I was drunk. First thing I knew about it he was on top of me.'

'Was it your first time?'

'Uh-huh.'

'Who was he?'

'It doesn't matter.'

'Did you know him?'

'Yeah, I knew him. He was one of the staff.'

'Fuck!' said, Kristen. 'He was an asshole!'

'Uh-huh. That's what I said.'

'Did you report him?'

'What do you think?'

'I think he deserves to go to prison for what he did to you. Christ! You're saddled with a kid, and he's free to do it again! Do you want to report him now? I'll come with you; we can do it together.'

Samantha was looking more bemused the angrier Kristen got. 'No, why the hell would I want to report him? Even if it ends up in court, which it wouldn't because it was a year ago and there's no evidence anyway, he'll get away with it. It'll be his word against mine – what's the point in that?'

'There's satisfaction to be had from retribution, Samantha. Take it from me.'

'Yeah, maybe. But I'm not interested in that.'

Kristen stood up; she walked a few feet forward and gazed out to the river, her back to Samantha and the kid. *What is it with these people?* she thought. *That they can take whatever they want, whenever they want it, and leave kids like her with nothing but shit and baggage and crap. Her life is a train wreck already and she just rolls over and accepts it.*

She turned back around and faced them both, silhouetted in the sun. 'Do you ever stop and think that Billy is going to turn out just like his father?'

Samantha looked surprised: 'What do you mean?'

'It's the truth – isn't it?'

'What is?'

'That he's gonna turn out just like his dad?'

The words hung for a moment, then: 'Why would you say a thing like that?' She picked the boy up and held him close in her arms. 'My boy isn't going grow up *like that.*'

Kristen turned back to face the sun. 'The way I see it kid, there's nothing you can do to stop him turning out like that. Some people are just born bad. Plain and simple.'

'No, that's not true,' Samantha replied. She was flustered, she had never thought of her boy in that way at all. 'I'm going to bring him up to be good, I'll teach him how to be a good boy.'

'Won't do any good,' Kristen said. 'It's in his nature. It's in his blood.'

'Fuck, that's an awful way to think,' Samantha replied. 'I don't know how you could believe that! That's like saying… That… ah, fuck. I don't know. Whatever the words are, that's just screwed up.'

'It's how it is.'

It was silent for a moment. Samantha cuddled her boy and finished her muffin; she knew, resolutely, that she wanted no more to do with this woman. She wanted to leave. 'Can we go now?'

Kristen gazed out at the river. She contemplated all the little shit-bags like Billy that had come through her door. *All those abusers-in-waiting. Hadn't Bradley been a cute little baby once? Vance too, no doubt? Sure, some of those foster kids had been gorgeous, and some had near melted her heart. But she knew that puppies grew up into rottweilers…*

'I said, can we go now?' Samantha asked again, cradling her boy in her lap.

Kristen turned back and sat down again on the rug. She broke off a small piece of muffin and put it in Billy's hand. 'Sure. Where do you want to go?'

Samantha shook her head. 'I don't know. Just take me anywhere. I don't care.'

'And therein lies the problem,' Kristen said. 'Well, we can head back to the refuge. See if Andrew is there; see if he has any bright ideas, or contacts, for anyone that can help you two out longer term.'

Samantha laughed. 'Is he the one with the funny metal glasses?'

'Yeah, that's him.'

'Fuck that,' she said, resolutely.

'What's wrong with that idea?' Kristen asked. 'He's well-connected, I'm sure he could help if he put his mind to it.'

'He's a *douche-bag*!'

'What do you mean?' Kristen said, incredulously. 'He's okay.'

Samantha still had hold of Billy, and she stroked his soft, blonde hair. 'So, you and him aren't, you know…?'

'*You know*?' enquired Kristen.

Samantha sighed, 'Like, an item or anything?'

'No! Of course not! What gave you that idea?'

'Nothing, just checking. I don't want to drop him in it, that's all.'

'Drop him in it?' Kristen asked. A slight bubble of anger rising in her belly.

'Yeah. Right, so…' Samantha was struggling for the right words but there was a growing hint of excitement rising in her voice. 'Yesterday, I went back to the refuge. It was like, sometime in the afternoon, before the storm broke and before you came and picked me up.'

'Uh-huh?'

'And, I was so hungry, and I'd been over to the missionary, and that was closed…'

'Come on, get on with it.' Kristen said.

'Okay, well, I went to the refuge and rang the bell and there was no answer, and I was about to go, but then I noticed the windows that look down into the place, and managed to peak a look in between the blinds…'

'And?' said Kristen.

'He was fucking some girl down there!'

The anger near exploded within Kristen, and her face flushed red. She breathed deeply to control her rage. 'Are you sure it was him?'

'Definitely. He's the hot guy, the one with the glasses, right?'

'Yeah, that's him,' she replied.

'All tanned – really fancies himself – clearly. Yeah, he was screwing some girl. She was waaay younger than him too. I'd say he's definitely batting above his average.'

'Right,' said Kristen.

'Hey, you're not going to say anything are you?' Samantha asked.

Kristen contemplated this for a moment. 'I think I should, don't you?'

'Why? I wouldn't have told you if I thought you were going to get them in trouble.'

'I know who that kid is, Samantha. Well, I can guess, anyway. And she's not much older than you. And he's doing that to her, just what Billy's dad did to you. And you're okay with that?'

'No, I think you've got this wrong, Kristen,' she replied. 'She was okay with it – it was, what did you call it, consensual?'

Kristen laughed. 'The fuck you know! How do you figure that out? That she looked like she was enjoying herself? That she'd *ordinarily* choose a man of his age, *of his position*, to have as a fuck-buddy?'

'Well, whatever,' Samantha said. 'You do what you like, but there's no way I'm going back there. He gives me the creeps.'

He gives me more than the creeps Kristen thought. *He's going to rue the day he fucks with me.* 'Come on, let's go back. We'll figure a plan back at mine.'

They put the leftover muffins and rubbish in the large paper bag that the drive-thru breakfast had come in, and Kristen folded the blood-marked rug neatly in a roll. They walked up along the gravel path to the car park, Billy in Samantha's arms. Kristen deposited the trash in the wastebin, and they climbed again into the car.

Samantha had decided that she would go back with Kristen and make other plans; *if nothing came about, she would just up and leave. There was something weird about Kristen*, she realised, and she had decided she would have no more to do with her or her crazy views about Billy. What a bitch of a thing to say about him.

And Kristen now understood that Samantha was a lost cause, and that her boy was just as bad as all the others had been. She knew there were things she could do to sort that out. More importantly, however, she had discovered Andrew's true colours. That he was little more than a little fuck-machine who would say, do, and be whatever was needed to get his grubby little paws dirty. Here, she was resolute; she knew exactly what had to be done and she would waste no time in doing it.

Chapter 57

Just as Kristen, Samantha and Billy pulled out of the park, Grandig pulled in to 2310 Welyvan Street. She approached the driveway too quick and slammed the underside of her car into the concrete floor, sparks flying. Grandig cut the engine and heaved herself out. She strode up the driveway and hammered on the front door, loud enough the wake to dead. 'Kristen! Bradley! It's Grandig, open the door!'

There was no reply. Grandig hammered again. 'Come on guys – open up!'

She stepped from the door and rapped on the glass window of the front room – she peered in but could see no one. 'Damn you!'

She walked around the side of the house into the backyard. Again, she looked in through the windows, rapping on each and calling for Kristen and Bradley; *no reply*. She banged on the backdoor: 'If you're off sick Bradley, why ain't you replying to me? Hey, it's Grandig here, where're you all at!' She cupped her hand to the glass, trying to get a better view inside. But her view was clear – there was no one home. She sat herself down on the swing-seat and set it in motion with her heels. She dug in her bag for her phone, retrieved it, then scrolled through her recently dialled numbers until she arrived at Kristen's. She pressed the call button; inside the house, she heard the phone ring; *no answer*. She scrolled through more of her recent calls until she recognised the one she had dialled for Bradley's work, for Archie Black. The number rang but no one picked up.

Grandig tried once more, then dropped her phone back into her bag. She paced the garden for a moment, thinking, then rapped on the back windows one last time. *Quit it, Grandig*, she thought, *there's no one home.*

She walked back to the front of the house, and again, hammered the door. Then, giving up, she got back in her car, reversed out, and headed off to the docks.

Chapter 58

When Kristen, Samantha and Billy got back to the house, Grandig had just left. Samantha took her son into the spare room to change his funky diaper. He was beginning to get tired and grizzly; and he wriggled and kicked his disapproval as Samantha wrestled him into a clean one.

Kristen called from the kitchen: 'I'm going to fix me an iced tea, Samantha, can I get you one?'

Samantha was getting more frustrated; both with Billy, and with Kristen. Firstly, she wanted him to stop with his bellyaching, and secondly, she wanted out of this place, *away from the crazy fucking bitch.* 'Sure,' she called back, that would be great.'

Billy kicked again, with both legs.

'Will you quit it!' she said. 'Give mom a break!'

He looked at her disapprovingly, but seemed to sense that she was the boss and he was to do what he was told; she pulled the tabs round his hips and sealed him in. He kicked again, indignantly.

'There. Who's the momma?' she said, 'You wanna sleep, little Billy, do you?'

She lifted him onto the bed, and arranged the pillows down his sides, just like before. He lay on his back and began sucking his fingers rhythmically. She opened the windows then pulled the blinds. 'Yeah, you do want to sleep, don't you?' she said. 'You're my tired little boy.' She kissed his forehead, tenderly.

Just then, Kristen stepped into the room, carrying two glasses chinking with ice. 'Oh, good plan,' she said, 'put the little one down for a nap. Come on, we'll drink these out the back – you can listen for him from the deck.'

Samantha followed her out, and she sat herself on the swing-seat. She took the drink from Kristen and sipped. 'Look,' she said, 'Are you pissed at what I told you about that guy?'

Kristen pulled up another chair and sat down too: 'Am I pissed?' she pondered aloud, then: 'Yeah, I guess I am pissed. But not with you, honey. I'm pissed with him.'

Samantha drank some more. It wasn't the best iced tea she'd had, a little too bitter for her liking – she would have added more sugar. 'If I had known, I wouldn't have told you, okay? I wasn't trying to create any trouble. I was just telling you why I don't want to go back there, that's all.'

Kristen nodded.

Samantha continued: 'I mean, I get it, I get why you're pissed. It's for the same reason I don't want to go back. Sure; I know she's the same age as me and that makes him a total sleaze. It pissed me off: it pissed you off.'

'Yeah, that's it,' Kristen said.

'It's just,' Samantha paused, drinking some more, 'It's just… I've got so few friends in this city; I don't think I need you making things worse for me. Don't get me wrong – *I'm really grateful for all this* - but I'm not planning ever going back there; but you just don't know. One day, I might have to. Diapers don't come cheap.'

Kristen smiled: 'Don't worry, kid,' she replied. 'I won't drag you into this. I promise.'

Samantha finished her drink and the two of them sat and took in the peace and calm of the garden. She wondered how she was going to tell Kristen, that she wanted to go and have no more of her, without actually hurting her feelings. Samantha knew she wanted out, and quickly, but wanted out without poking the bear.

'You know,' Kristen said, 'the last kid we had here sure loved that oak.'

Samantha looked down the garden at the tree with its swooping low bows, and soft lush foliage. 'It is awesome, I suppose.'

'Yeah, she'd sit under that tree and play with her dolls, then she'd come up here and sit and draw in the shade.'

'Where is she now?' Samantha asked.

'She ran away. Fucked off. I have no idea where she went.'

'What?'

'Yeah, that's right. I left her in the bath and forgot about her. When I got back, she was nowhere to be seen.'

Samantha's stomach lurched. A sickly wave washed through her body. She went to stand up, but her legs wobbled beneath her. She sat back down on the swing-seat and the colour drained from her face. She felt like she was going to vomit. 'What did you do?'

'What do you mean, 'what did I do'?', Kristen asked. 'What did I do to the kid, or what did I do to you?'

Samantha could not comprehend. Her forehead broke in a sweat and her head was spinning violently. Her vision was beginning to blur, and the garden swirled sickeningly in front of her. 'I think I'm going to puke,' she said. 'Help, I'm going to pass out.'

'Just relax, okay?' Kristen said. 'It's just the drugs. You're going to be fine. But you're going to sleep for a while.'

Samantha tried to get up again, but her arms and legs were jelly. Her face began to screw up and tears formed in her eyes. She sat forward in the seat, bringing her head towards her knees. 'What have. you. done. to me?' her speech was staccato and fragmented, and her mouth felt fat and bone dry.

Kristen stood up. 'I've drugged you, Samantha. It was in your drink, I'm sorry.'

Samantha's eyes fluttered, then rolled momentarily into the back of her head. She leant back some and fought unconsciousness wildly.

'Look, you can't go telling me what you did about Andrew and expect me to do nothing about it – life doesn't work that way. That man tried to fuck me last night! Actually, tried to get me in bed having just nailed that kid just hours before. How the hell do you think that makes me feel?'

'What are you going to do?' she mumbled.

'Nothing more than he deserves,' she replied. 'You're just too nice, Samantha. You roll over too easily. I've spent my whole life rolling over for men like him – and I'm sick of it.'

Samantha stuttered something indecipherable and her eyes glassed over and rolled upwards again. This time, her eyelids closed fully and did not open. She slumped back into the seat, and her heartbeat slowed.

Kristen watched her whilst the oxycontin knocked her unconscious. She had given her a heavy dose, *but*, she thought, *hopefully not enough to kill her*. She let fifteen minutes pass, then picked up the girl's wrist and checked for a pulse; it was there, but faint. She shook Samantha's shoulders, then slapped her cheek firmly; there was no waking her. *Good.*

Kristen went back into the house and made herself a sandwich. She noticed that there was blood, *her blood*, still on the kitchen table from last night. From her little exercise with the skewer, she remembered. She would clean it up later.

She went to the kitchen drawer and pulled it open. An array of utensils cluttered it up, and Bradley's gun was nestled amongst them all. She toyed briefly with taking a skewer, *she liked the idea of disposing of Andrew in the same manner in which she had dealt with Bradley*, but she figured the gun would be easier. Plus, she thought, it may be useful afterwards.

Finally, Kristen went into the spare room where Billy was asleep on his back in the bed. Shafts of light illuminated dust mites dancing in the air. She reached down and tickled his little fat belly with her index finger. He snuffled but did not wake.

'Hey little puppy,' Kristen said. 'Wake up. We've got things to do.'

Billy pulled his tiny hands into tight fists and rubbed them into his eyes; he grizzled.

'I know, I know,' she said. 'You've just fallen asleep but Mom's not going to be out forever. And if I don't get this done, I'll never forgive myself.'

She reached down and picked him up. 'Now where's that basket of yours?' she asked.

Kristen closed the front door and carried Billy out to the car in his BiLo basket. She flicked the central locking and jammed him in the back. She shut the door, then walked around to the driver's side, and got in, tossing the gun onto the passenger seat next to her - within reaching distance. She looked back; Billy looked up quizzically from his spot behind, still fighting sleep.

'Come on, little man,' she said. 'We've got a date with Andrew; and boy, is he going to be surprised when we show up!'

She turned the car key and pushed the shift-lever into reverse, screeching out onto Welyvan Street in a cloud of dust and exhaust.

Chapter 59

Late morning.

The waiting area at the dock was a converted shipping container that was kitted out with tatty office furniture, a dusty, artificial palm, and a wobbly fan that rattled away in the corner. The stale aroma from a half full ashtray added to the oily grimness.

A vaguely helpful woman – a temp, Grandig assumed, who had not yet developed the pre-requisite skill to be rude and dismissive - apologised for the waiting area. 'It's only a temporary space,' she said, extinguishing another cigarette with her yellow fingers. 'They're sending down a new office on the back of a trailer, but it's been delayed somewhere up the I95. The lorry's broken an axle, or something.' She smiled apologetically, 'Do you want a coffee?'

The fan continued to rattle. Grandig looked over at the dirty mugs and the filter machine - the multiple brown rings that stained the glass jug seemed to mark an anniversary for each time it had been brewed and not cleaned. 'Ah, that's sweet honey, but I'm good, thanks.'

'Really,' she replied, disappointed, as if Grandig was first human contact she had had in a week. 'It's no trouble.'

Grandig smiled earnestly, all she wanted was for Archie to hurry on up doing whatever he was doing, then get over here and answer a few simple questions. Somewhere outside, amidst the hustle of the docks a group of workers started shouting, arguing heatedly about where a crane should, or should not be parked up. There was swearing and name-calling.

'A lot of testosterone flies around here,' Grandig said. 'You have your work cut out.'

The temp laughed, 'Oh yeah,' she said ruefully, grabbing her two-way radio again; 'Boys and their toys, *boys and their toys*.' Then she hollered, 'Hey, Mr Black, are you coming in or what?'

Moments later, Archie banged in through the steel door and threw his hard-hat dismissively onto the temp's desk. 'Christ,' he exclaimed, nodding briefly in acknowledgement of Grandig who waited impassively, 'It's not rocket-science. It says right there,' tapping his clipboard, 'to park the crane up in Bay 2. Why then does Sanchez take it upon himself to put it in Bay 4?'

He threw the clipboard down next to his hard hat. 'I mean, Bay 4? Why the hell would we need a crane in Bay 4!'

Grandig rose to meet him. 'Archie Black, I'm Officer Grandig – thanks for finding time.'

'Yeah,' he said, 'I got the message.'

'Are you happy to talk here?' Grandig asked. 'Or do you want to go somewhere private?' she glanced over at the temp-woman who was taking it upon herself to listen in.

He did not seem to acknowledge Grandig's question, and he continued under his own agenda, pouring himself a mug of muddy coffee. 'You know, we sent off a thousand-foot ship this morning with nearly eight-thousand containers on it. There's a crew of ten onboard, and they're going to steer that ship to China in a matter of weeks. There's another ship and crew waiting to load, and the fucking crane is on the other side of the dock. I'm mean. *Bay 4, really!?*'

Grandig nodded in agreement and raised her hands in solidarity.

'Yeah, okay, whatever,' Archie replied. 'What can I do for you? Sorry to keep you hanging around.'

'No problem,' Grandig replied, 'You're a busy man. I appreciate your time.'

The preceding years had worn Archie poorly. He had given up with prosthetic limbs a decade ago; occasionally, he would wear it with a hook attachment if he really needed to, but most jobs he had now learned effectively one-handed. The sleeve of his work overall was stitched up to the elbow. He looked old beyond his years.

Grandig began. 'It's about Bradley Engelmaier. Have you heard from him recently?'

Archie scratched his head; his hair was flat from beneath his hard-hat. 'Is he in trouble?' he asked.

Grandad pondered this for a minute. 'I don't know,' she said honestly. 'He might be.'

'Well,' Archie replied, 'Kristen says he's got a bad case of the flu, he's not been in for a week or so. I should be reporting him to head office really, he's missing too much time. But, well, I guess you know Bradley and I go back some.'

Grandig nodded. 'Sure, I know that. Have you spoken to him personally?'

'Nope, not in person. Not since he's been off.'

'Uh-huh,' Grandig acknowledged. 'Just out of interest, how much sickness does Bradley take?'

Archie exclaimed. 'Christ. I've not known Bradley take time off *ever.*'

Grandig raised her eyebrows: 'Really?'

'Well, I think he had a couple of weeks off five or six years ago, he had his tonsils out – might have been his appendix – but no, apart from that, I don't recall him ever calling in sick. Hell, thinking about it, he must be pretty poorly.'

Yeah, thought Grandig. *Pretty poorly.*

'The thing is,' Archie went on, 'If you call in sick here too often, you'll come in one day and there'll be no work for you. The company's got no time for shirkers – I better give him a call.'

Grandig went on, 'Well, you can try – but I've called, and I've just been round the house too, but there's no one in. So, unless he's been hospitalised – Kristen didn't say he was in hospital, did she?'

'No, she didn't – nothing like that. Just that he had a really bad chest and was laid up in bed. No one in, you say?'

She shook her head. Archie did not sound like he was lying, he sounded like a busy guy who had not really give his buddy's absence another thought. And the more background to Bradley he gave, the more unlikely it sounded he would ever shirk the day job.

'Archie,' she said, and she lowered her voice because she could see temp-woman was still listening to every word of their conversation, 'I know that Kristen fixed her background check for the fostering gig – you know that too, right?'

Archie contemplated this, then with his hand gestured Grandig to step outside. It was dusty and hot, and the constant clanging-clank of the dock's heartbeat drummed white noise in the background. 'Yeah, of course I do,' he said.

'Any idea why?' she asked, openly.

Archie shuffled momentarily as he considered whether this was going to have repercussions for him. Then, 'That's pretty obvious, don't you think?'

'Why don't you enlighten me, Archie,' she asked.

He thought, *she's going to bust balls.* 'Because of what happened to Kristen when she was a kid, and because of Aimee.'

There it was.

'You provided them a character reference,' she said. 'And you knew they were lying to me. Didn't you?'

He sniffed the foggy exhaust of Bay 2 loading bay. 'Not lying, so much,' he said. 'Just protecting their privacy. They did it knowing that they didn't want the ghosts of her past screwing up any chance they had of finding happiness.'

'Well,' Grandig responded. 'That's one way of looking at it. But it's not really your call, is it? It's down to people like me to make those decisions.'

'Yeah,' he grunted. 'People like you. They're good folk, you know, Officer. Good people.'

'Sure, I know that,' she said, but her agreement sounded hollow. 'But that's all a moot point now, Archie,' she said. 'Did you know that along with Bradley, their last foster kid is missing too?'

'You think Bradley's missing?' he asked.

'Well, he ain't at home, and he ain't picking up the phone,' she said. 'And I can't get hold of Kristen, and his employer can't shed any light on where he is. I'd say we're running out of places to understand where he's at, wouldn't you?'

Archie looked out across Bay 2 momentarily; he wondered whether this had the making of a shitstorm for him, and if he was going to find himself tangled up with the Savannah PD. He hoped not; he did not need that sort of hassle on top of the crap he was dealing with down at the dock on a daily basis. 'So, what next?'

She looked at him straight, and though she knew her judgement had been off in the past, *way off*, she decided she trusted him; that his loyalties lay with his buddy, Bradley, and not with his wife. 'You're telling me you know nothing about where Bradley Engelmaier is,' she asked, finally.

'Swear to God,' he replied.

'Okay then,' she scratched her forehead at the hairline; beads of sweat were already forming from the heat of the midday sun. 'First, I'm going to go back to his home and bust the door off the hinges and make sure he really ain't at home, and then,' she gave it some thought for just a moment, 'I'm going to call him in as a missing person and put out an APB for both him and Kristen Engelmaier. No more than you'd do.'

Chapter 60

Bradley open and closed his eyes, slowly and deliberately; the little girl with the cornrow braids stayed in his vision like a living dream. 'I is just a fragment of your imagination, Mr Bradley, I is not real, you know that.'

Bradley said he knew that and knew and understood that if he was not actually dead, then he was pretty close.

'You have not finishing the story yet, has you Mr Bradley? You has not told me about how Aimee ended up ded.'

'I don't want to talk about that,' Bradley said. 'She's dead and that is all that matters.'

'You is a silly-billy Mr Bradley – I think that when you have told the story that's when you'll finally get some peace; from me and from everything – that's what I think, anyhow.

'We lied to everyone; we lied to the paramedics and we lied to the doctors, too. All different lies to different people. The doctors weren't a hundred percent sure she hadn't had some sort of fit. That was our lucky break. They bought it when Kristen and me told them we found her dead in the morning. It was either a seizure, they reckoned, or she'd managed to choke, or suffocate somehow. Despite some of those medical guys being pretty unconvinced, there was doubt, they weren't sure we were lying. And in that doubt and confusion Kristen and me got away with it. I only think the cops didn't pursue it more was because they figured Kristen had been through hell already – and that they couldn't blame her entirely, even if she had done it, considering who the father was.'

Yes, but murder is really bad, isn't it, Mr Bradley?

'Depends on how you see it, I figure. If you kill a bad person in a war, that's not murder. And if you kill someone who's murdered and tortured lots of other people, that can't be murder either.

Yeah but that's just excuses Mr Bradley coz Aimee wasn't a bad person in a war, and she hadn't even killed or tortured a flea, had she!? She hadn't done anything wrong at all.

Bradley gurgled a bloody clot from his throat, and it oozed down his cheek into the murky water at his side.

But Vance was a dirty, fucking, torturing, paedophile murderer!

But Aimee wasn't, was she, Mr Bradley?

No! No, no, no, no, no, no – she wasn't! But by being alive she made Kristen feel just as bad as Vance had. She couldn't get better, because Kristen never loved Aimee; she tried but she couldn't. She couldn't love her as a baby; and couldn't love her as she got older. And it just kept getting worse and worse and worse. Kristen kept saying that whenever she looked into Aimee's eyes, she saw Vance looking back at her; and that when she got bigger and older, she even began to look like him too.

Ah, that is really sad Mr Bradley – and I think I feel a little bit sad for Kristen now.

You should feel sad for her! She didn't deserve any of this.

Did you kill her or was it Kristen?

Oh Christ Oh Christ Oh Christ Oh Christ!

Ah poor Mr Bradley! I think if you can tell this bit then it will all be surely over for you.

I got in from work one night – I guess it was early springtime. It was warm, not too hot. And the air was still and fresh. I remember walking in from the car, up the drive, and thinking I might have a few beers and catch the ball game on TV. Hell, I even thought Kristen might have made me some food – she makes a mean kebab kid, did I tell you that?

You is too funny Mr Bradley!

When I get in the house, all hell has broken loose. Aimee is shrieking HELP ME DADDY! HELP ME DADDY! and Kristen is nowhere, I can't find her anywhere. So, I go in and sit next to Aimee, and she's still blubbering and there's snot running all down her little face – and I say, 'what's the matter, baby?' I put my arm around her shoulder, and I haul her up onto my knee, and I give her a cuddle, and she's sniffling and trying to catch her breath and that's when I see Kristen, stood behind the door – and she's got a pillow in her hands off Aimee's bed with the cartoon bear on it. And I can see that Kristen's been crying too, and her eyes are all red and puffy – and she's got this real scared look on her face, just like when I rescued her out of the hole – and all I wanted to do was put my arm around Kristen and make it all better again. I'm sure I loved Kristen, even though I know I did bad things to her; deep down I'm sure I did.

Then what happened Mr Bradley?

So, I put Aimee down on the bed, and I stand up and go over to Kristen and ask her what's wrong honey, what's going on? But she just starts shaking and crying and suddenly gets hysterical, she starts just say no, no, no, no, no, no over and over again, through the tears; so I grab her by the shoulders and give her a little shake to calm her down, but nothing works, and I might have hit her a little too – I don't remember, but I think I did – just to make it quiet, just to stop all the screaming and crying. And anyway – that's when Aimee says through her tears, mommy hurt me; mommy put the pillow over my face, and I couldn't breathe…

Friday, 13th September 1987

Chapter 61

Jesus H Christ Kristen, what the fuck would you go and do a thing like that for? You stupid bitch; you could have killed her!'

'What the fuck do you think I was trying to do Bradley!? Either her or me now! It's her or me, Bradley! I can't do this anymore – I can't take anymore of looking in her fucking face and seeing him! It's too fucked up; her eyes, the shape of her mouth, even the damn smell of her breath, her hair! Fucking Vance, Bradley! FUCKING VANCE – and you know what makes it worse? I know how much you fucking LOVE HER! You fucking DOTE ON THAT GIRL! And you have no idea what that does to me, Bradley, do you? I can't bear that you love her, Bradley. That you love VANCE! I thought you'd told me it was over, Bradley, I thought you said it was over.'

'Kristen, stop this – you're sky high! Just stop fucking crying, okay!?'

'I hate this Bradley. I hate her, I hate you, I hate living this stupid fucking lie, Bradley!'

'No wait, Kristen, no wait…'

'I can't wait anymore; I've waited six years Bradley, SIX YEARS! And he's still here; looking at me every time I look into my daughter's face – that's fucked UP! And every time I see that look in her, I'm right back in that FUCKING HOLE!

'Oh Christ, Kristen, put the gun down; put the fucking gun down! I told you never to play with that thing; you'll blow your goddamn head off!'

''She's got to go, Bradley. One way or another, she's got to go!'

Wednesday, 15th July 2015

Chapter 62

Have you ever killed anything so beautiful, kid, so beautiful you really have to find a way to blank the world out to pull the trigger – to shut everything away in your head, and lock it the key – just so you can muster the will to do it? I have.

Ah it was you, Mr Bradley! You killed Aimee!

No, it was both of us! I would never had done it if Kristen hadn't been so crazy! She was the one – she was shrieking, and hollering, and she was waving my gun around like it was some kind of flag! She told me to do, Kiddo, she told me to kill Aimee; she went on and said I was a useless piece of shit, that if I loved her, really loved her, I'd do it for her. She said all sorts of crazy stuff; she said she'd go to the police and tell them I beat her up; that I deliberately killed Vance's daughter that night; and she was all the time shouting, and screaming, and crying, and Aimee was too! She made me so mad, so angry, I couldn't control myself – I grabbed the pillow and did it; and Kristen helped me hold it down until it was over. Killing is easy, it's what follows that hard.

Chapter 63

Early afternoon.

Back in her car, Grandig headed toward downtown, windows full down. The air thundered around as she tapped the steering wheel absentmindedly – candy wrappers and other little flicks of litter lifted in the buffeting cabin. She spotted the exit for Crespolina and put her blinker on.

Grandig tried to ignore the ache of uneasiness that cramped inside her. It had begun with the sickening panic that dropped in her stomach when she discovered the fraudulently completed background forms. But it had not abated, largely because she had too many unanswered questions about Kristen and Bradley. She was worried about the little kid too; the child with no name and no voice. What had Kristen and Bradley done – really? And where *was* Bradley? She hoped she was going to turn up at the Engelmaier's place this afternoon and find him languishing in bed. But she had a nagging doubt that she was being spun a lie so much bigger than just a dodgy background check. Yes, there was no quelling the uneasiness that griped in her guts.

She drove a few minutes more then pulled into Momo's place, a quick pit-stop here and she would be able to get on with her day. She parked up – *can't stay long* she thought.

But when she knocked on the front door Momo didn't answer. That was unusual – Momo rarely went anywhere – a weekly grocery shop, and church on Sunday - that was about it. Grandig knocked again but still nothing. *Strange.* She walked out into the rear garden and called for her – she walked the perimeter, but there was still no sign of Momo anywhere. *Where have you gotten to, Momo?*

Grandig headed up onto the veranda and peered into the kitchen window - nothing. She reached for her cell phone and as she walked back towards the front of the house, she dialled Momo's number. As she passed the front room, Grandig heard the house-phone begin to ring. She looked in and caught a glance of something not quite right – the photo frames knocked out of place on the sideboard, and some broken on the floor. Then, as her mind made sense of the scene, she saw Momo. Still and crumpled were she had fallen.

Chapter 64

Kristen pumped a consistent twenty miles over the speed limit for most of the drive. She did not bother with her seatbelt. The roads and traffic melted in her peripheral vision and the car horns dissolved in a muddy, white noise that enveloped her like fog. She knew where she was heading and drove on autopilot.

'You know, little Billy,' she said, 'You really are the cutest little bundle!? You are. You are! You're the sweetest thing there is, sweet like chocolate and cotton-candy. My-oh-my, yes you are, yes you are!'

She blazed her horn at a trucker who drifted into her lane, 'Motherfucker, get out of my way!'

'And I bet your daddy was just the bonny little lad too – don't you think? Not that you got to meet him, did you? Because he just up and left and fucked off before you got in the world, didn't he!? Yes, he did – yes, he did! He didn't want to know about you at all, did he? Nooo. That nasty man just wanted to get his grubby little paws on your mom, didn't he? Nasty man just wanted to get a piece of that girl, that's right, huh!? What an asshole he was, don't you think!?

Fucker – get off the road!

'And I tell you something else about your daddy too, shall!? Shall I? Do you want to hear about that fucking piece of shit that's your daddy? He's a fucking cocksucker and his blood runs right through your tiny little body too – yes it does, yes it does! You might be a lovely little puppy-dog now, little Billy-Boy, but you are daddy's boy, you know that, right!? You're a little daddy's boy – with daddy's nasty-nasty blood running right through your nasty-nasty body. And I know – yes I do! – that when you grow up, you're going to be just like your daddy – and you're going to like fucking over girls like me, and like you mommy – yes you are, yes you are! And you won't give a damn hoot if they want you or not!'

Shove it up your ass, fucker!

'Well, I know just what to do with nasty boys like you, Billy-Boy – Kristen knows how to swill that bucket, yes I do! You just ask old Bradley! Cocksucker Bradley with the hole-through-the-fucking-head! You ask him, 'who's laughing now,' huh? And he'll tell you – he'll let you into a fucking secret never to mess with me, kiddo. Mess with me and you wind up fucking dead, Billy, Dead as Fuck.'

'Get out of my fucking lane, you blind bitch!'

'And you know what, Billy-Boy? I hate to say it, you being cute-as-a-button and all that, but just as soon as I've dealt with fucking Andrew, do you know who's next? Do you? Do you!? Yes, you, right! Yes, you are! You-are-you-are-you-are-you-are! You're next Billy-Boy. You and your fucking gene-pool are for it! And don't think I won't Cinderella. Dressed in yella. Sneaking upstairs to kiss a fella. You're fucking next, kid.'

Chapter 65

Grandig watched the ambulance disappear up the driveway, blue-lighting and sirens wailing. The paramedics had arrived quickly – they told Grandig that had she arrived an hour later Momo probably would have been dead. They said the old girl was clearly stubborn though. It had been close. They had stabilised her breathing, pumped her full of morphine for the pain – and strapped her to the gurney for the short trip to hospital. The paramedics said Momo was not out of the woods, not by any means; they suspected a shattered hip – at the very least – maybe worse; and she was badly dehydrated. But they had taken Grandig's number and promised to get the hospital to call her with an update, as soon as there was anything to report.

Grandig sat in her car catching her breath, holding the photo frame that Momo had in her hands. She felt fucking awful. *How long had she sat on that message and not called her back – even just to check?* A day, was it – two even? Some friend she was, she thought. She dialled her voicemail and listened to the message – when she had listened to it the first time, she hadn't noticed how late Momo had called. But now - *what was the urgency, Momo? What was so freaking important at one in the morning?*

Grandig turned the photo frame over in her hands – *and why this photo, Momo? It's just me in my dungarees. Why did you have this out again so late at night?*

Then something dawned. Something about the photo that now she realised – that she had never noticed in the many, many times she had looked at this picture in the past. She felt a rush of cold sweep through her body at the dark possibility. In this picture, little Grandig's arm was extending out to the side – she was holding onto something, but the frame mount obliterated her hand. *Yes, I'm holding something; or someone.* This was only half a photograph, she realised.

Still sat in her car, Grandig popped the back off the frame and removed the photo from the glass. It became apparent the photo was folded in half, vertically, and only one side of the picture had been displayed in the frame these last thirty years.

'Fuck.'

Unfolded, the photo showed not just Grandig, but two girls; separated by the deep, course crease where the picture had been folded. Grandig was on the left, the other girl stood next to her on the right. Both were dressed identically; both skinny, all knees and elbows. The young Grandig was faded and dull, but the other girl, the girl hidden from view, folded back and protected behind the glass, was still vibrant and clear.

Everything from the few years prior to her arriving at Momo's was hidden behind a dark curtain of forgotten memories. She had no recollection. She did not remember ever trying to suppress the past – it had just happened.

Grandig sat silently. She could tell that these two girls were sisters; one and the same, but she could not fathom her relationship to either of them. 'I have a twin sister,' she said.

Grandig turned memories over in her head, desperately searching for clues that would help her piece this jigsaw together, but she found none. It was as if her memory had been wiped clean, like a computer, the moment she had arrived at Momo's all those years back. 'I feel like I should feel something; but I don't,' she said to no one. *I feel, if this is true, like I should know, deep down, that I always had a sister. There should be a deep old memory, don't you think? But there's nothing there. I don't remember her.*

Grandig sat looking intently at the picture. She desperately wanted to feel something but these two girls in the dungarees were strangers to her.

Then suddenly her stomach lurched again, and thick dread poured through her veins. *Wait*, Grandig thought, *Wait a minute.*

That conversation with Officer Alec came flooding back to her in a sickening wave. 'Oh Christ! Oh, sweet lord! No – this can't be. No!' She slapped the photo down and grabbed from her bag the folder of evidence Alec had given to her to read.

Tears now broke in Grandig eyes – she knew the truth, and that there would now be no more secrets.

'Reginald Vance,' Grandig said aloud. *We got the background check done on the right person this time – Kristen DesMoiles – her abduction, how Bradley and his buddies managed to rescue her – his two little girls…* Her mind paused, slowed, then she rifled through the folder for the photo of Vance's kids – the one with one of the girls blanked out.

She found it and held the two up next to each other. They were one and the same. Though Momo's framed picture was in its entirety with no one masked out.

'That's the urgency,' she said to herself. *Because Reginald Vance is my Pop. And my sister – she was killed by Bradley and Kristen. Momo knew* – and she needed to tell me.

Grandig had worked in CPS long enough to know that secrets like that were rarely spilled. 'Fuck,' she said. 'Momo, you sure pack a surprise punch.'

A moment passed. She could not begin to process this information or the details about her father that were contained in the fat manila folder that Officer Alec had given her first thing this morning. *He had been executed, that was right, wasn't it?* That he was a serial killer; *four, five, six girls, was it?*

Grandig drew a deep breath, and there, for the first, briefest of moments, she felt emotion rise within her. It might have been grief or the pale shadow of remorse – it may even have been a distant longing for the lost sister who now peered at her from the photo – whichever feeling it was, it did not fall as tears. Grandig looked out across Momo's garden and contemplated this new knowledge and realised it would take her a lifetime to build it into any kind of understanding. Then suddenly a ping of memory like a short sparkle of fireworks flashed through Grandig's mind, burning bright for a moment before disappearing. As it did, the leaves of the magnolia tree at the end of the garden were caught in a wisp of the faintest breeze, they seemed to whisper like secrets. 'Jump-rope,' Grandig said. *I remember playing jumping rope with a girl... And a song about... Cinderella, dressed in yella...'*

She leafed through the manila folder once more. She ignored reports about her father and focused instead on the paperwork regarding Kristen and Bradley. She scanned the coroner's report that failed to provide a cause of death for Aimee Engelmaier and she flicked through the police interview notes taken the night Bradley saved Kristen from the hole. Grandig read, between the lines, that both DI Osemon and the duty coroner had their misgivings – as if there was more to Bradley and Kristen, and their stories – than they could necessarily hang their hats on. And wasn't that a surprise, she thought, that here she was, with a similar sinking feeling; wondering just where the hell Bradley was, and where in God's name was that little kid too, the one with the cornrow braids?

She threw the folder onto the back seat caring not that some of the papers spilled out and fell into her rear footwell, disappearing into discarded chip packets, milkshake cups and empty cartons of fries. Though the jigsaw of her life was still suspended mid-air, and her confidence running just paper-thin, her determination to see this thing through was resolute.

She turned the engine over, banged the air-con unit with her fist in a half-hearted attempted to kick it in to life, and pulled out of the driveway onto the road, heading out for the downtown interstate and back to the Engelmaier's place. And as she did so, a blue chevy roared past her at near fifty miles an hour, swerving out across the centre lines and blasting its horn.

'Jesus Christ!' Grandig exclaimed, 'Slow the fuck down, asshole!'

She did not see, or even hear Kristen Engelmaier call her a bitch and tell her to get out of her fucking lane.

Chapter 66

A dozen miles out to sea a storm was developing that stretched from Sapelo Island in the south to Hilton Head in the north. It was still weak - but its intensity was growing minute on minute. For now, the lightning was occasional - distant cracks licked the air sending the egrets flying across the deepening, magenta skies. As the first of the thunder echoed in the clouds above Savannah, Kristen pulled up on Davis Park Avenue.

She stopped the car twenty yards past Andrew's house, and killed the engine. Billy murmured in the back – the drumming of the drive and Kristen's ranting had sent him back to an uneasy doze. She looked over to check on him, then picked up the gun from the passenger seat – she was always surprised at how heavy a cold, loaded browning felt in her hands. She opened the barrel and inspected the chamber – the three rounds from earlier remained nestled in place. She flicked it shut and spun it, *round and round it goes, where she stops, nobody knows.*

She glanced up the street. Further along, a few kids circled on their bikes and a couple of girls practiced cartwheels and handstands on the sidewalk. She looked back at Billy again: 'Right then, Billy-Boy – let's get this over with.'

She stepped out and tucked the gun into the front of her jeans. She walked around the back of the car and opened the rear passenger door and lifted Billy out of his BiLo basket – he grumbled, but did not fully stir, he rested his hot face in the crook of Kristen's neck. She flicked a glance up the street once more – there was no traffic and the children showed her no interest. A rumble of thunder murmured from far off and she walked briskly up to Andrew's house.

She stopped at the short, wrought-iron gate that led up to his front door. Last night, she remembered, he had tried to kiss her here. As she looked up, the house appeared empty – there was no sign of life downstairs - and upstairs - beyond the veranda, the shutters were closed. She wondered whether he was out. No problem if he was, she thought, she would just sit and wait.

She patted Billy gently on her shoulder and opened the gate. She walked up the path and stood momentarily beneath the porch at the front door, listening. She heard nothing – from here at least, the house was silent. She toyed briefly with banging the ornate, iron knocker but then thought better of it, she supposed surprise was probably the better tactic. She listened again, then tried the door handle, quietly.

The door opened, and a small draft of cooled air wafted out. She smiled – she knew no one left the house with the air-conditioning running. She stepped inside.

She familiarised herself with the lay-out of downstairs. She remembered it well enough and treaded carefully down the parquet-floored entrance hall to the kitchen – her feet soft and silent on the wood. She glanced into the lounge as she passed - no sign of Andrew – the place was tidy and still. At the kitchen door, which was ajar, she listened once more for any signs that someone was in – but again, there was nothing. She put her face to the crack of the door and peered around – the kitchen seemed empty too. As she entered, the door groaned gently on its old hinges and Kristen froze for a second – she could feel her heart beating in her chest. Despite what she had planned, her nerves were alight.

The kitchen *was* empty – but Kristen could now see that someone had been here recently. There were two wine glasses, wet with condensation, stood on the table – right where Andrew and she had shared a meal together. She picked one up – it was still cold, and a mouthful of white wine remained in the bottom. She swilled it around the bowl of the glass and drank it. She picked up the other glass and held it to the dappled light from the kitchen window. She touched the rim where a clear smudge of lipstick had left a greasy residue. She felt her cheeks flush. She wondered whether the girl with the lipstick had been bought a sentimental trinket, whether she had fallen for Andrew's modus operandi. Andrew was just a player like all the other men in her life - just another fucking asshole. She guessed – no, *she knew* - it was the fucking bitch from the refuge – the one Samantha had seen Andrew screwing, and she suddenly wondered whether she had enough rounds in the gun. Billy wriggled on her shoulder, stirring a little in the sweaty nook of her neck.

She put the glass down and took two deep settling breaths to calm her racing pulse. She walked back down along the hall and into the lounge. It was small and smelled of wood and old leather furniture. There was another of Andrew's ornamental Buddhas sat squat next to a carriage clock on the alabaster fire surround – still odd, for a Christian, she thought. Whatever. It was cool here though, the air-con worked well and the dogwood tree in the front garden shaded the window of sunlight. She placed Billy down on the sofa, softly, and let him settle. Silently, she stepped back into the hallway.

The staircase leading upstairs was wood, and its steps covered with a dull carpet runner. She stood at the bottom, one hand on the handrail the other on the butt of the gun and listened again. This time, she heard something, and it made her stop breathing for a second - an unmistakable sound. Somewhere from upstairs drifted a soft female groan. She pulled the gun out, releasing the safety catch, and strode swiftly up the stairs – damn the noise.

At the top of the stairs there was a L-shaped landing, and three doors – two closed, and one ajar. The sound was so much clearer now, and Kristen could see enough through the crack of the middle door to know where Andrew and his guest were. She walked confidently across and pushed the bedroom door open, catching Andrew and Dizzy in the missionary.

She watched for a moment, taking in the curve of his back and buttocks. 'Now ain't that a fucking picture,' she said.

Dizzy let out a scream and pushed Andrew off, grabbing the sheets and covering herself, and he a cushion to do the same. 'Jesus, Kristen! What the fuck are you doing here? What the fuck!?'

The room was dim in the afternoon half-light, the shutters casting amber bands of light across the cotton sheets on the bed – quite romantic before the interruption. Their clothes were scattered across the wooden floor and the wine bottle rested lazily on its side.

'Oh my God, oh my God!' Dizzy exclaimed, the fear rising steadily. 'Andrew, she's got a gun!'

Andrew raised his hands instinctively, still sat on the bed with the cushion covering his lap. 'What's this about Kristen? What's going on? You can't just turn up in someone's house like this!'

'Shut the fuck up, Andrew,' Kristen replied, raising the gun at them both. Dizzy squealed, tears and panic screwing her face.

Kristen leant back on the doorframe. She was confident – almost brash - and brandished the gun with conviction. 'You,' Kristen said, singling out Dizzy with the revolver. 'What the hell do you think you're doing with this piece of shit? How old are you?' Her tone was aggressive and patronising.

Dizzy cowered, the sheet was pulled up to her chin and she refused - or was unable - to look at Kristen, who had now pulled up a chair and sat adjacent to the end of the bed. 'Hey, *fucking bitch*, answer me, I asked you a question.'

Dizzy snivelled. 'I know who you are – you're that crazy lady from the party the other night – the one who locked herself in the bathroom, aren't you?'

'What did you call me?' Kristen said, coolly, aiming the sight of the gun at Dizzy's face. 'You're sat in bed with a guy twice your age, and you call me *crazy*?'

The tears were now streaming down the young girl's face and Andrew made a weak gesture to comfort her. Kristen switched the gun to Andrew: 'Don't you move, or I'll blow your head off your fucking shoulders.'

The pair sat frozen and the sweat from their lovemaking was now ice-cold on their skin.

'Here's the thing,' Kristen went on. 'Earlier this morning I put three rounds in this gun – and I put it to my head and pulled the trigger. Andrew, you were the icing on the cake of my fucked-up life!'

Andrew spoke, his voice flat and unthreatening. 'Whatever's going on here, I can help – it doesn't have to be like this, Kristen, trust me.'

'Trust you!?' Kristen barked. 'Is that some kind of joke – trust you!? After the shit you've pulled on me?'

She pulled the trigger.

Click!

Instantly, Andrew raised his arms to his face and Dizzy buried her head into his chest, wailing uncontrollably as Andrew moved to cling her tight.

'You crazy idiot!' he screamed. 'Don't – don't pull the trigger!'

'Man – you just got lucky, Andrew!' Kristen said. 'Chamber one was empty! Makes the adrenalin pump, doesn't it!?'

'Jesus, Kristen!' Andrew exclaimed again. 'Don't be insane – we can work this out! I'm sorry – I really am – I treated you disrespectfully and that wasn't fair, you're right. But this? This is madness!'

Kristen nodded, 'Yes, you're probably right, Andrew. This is madness, bat-crazy stuff. But,' and she thought momentarily *how the fuck has it actually all come to this?* then, 'But it's real and it's happening, and there's nothing you or I, or this Dizzy bitch can do to stop this.'

Dizzy raised her head, she was shaking, 'Please – please don't hurt him – you'll go to hell!'

'Oh bless,' Kristen said, swinging the gun once more back to Dizzy. 'Shall I tell her, Andrew, or do you want to? Do you think I believe in that nonsense, kid? Do you think for one second that I believe there's such a fucking place as *hell* waiting for me?'

'Dizzy,' Andrew said. 'Don't talk, please – keep your mouth shut and leave this to me.'

Kristen continued, 'If there's such a place as hell, it's here – I'm living in it. Trust me.' She stood up, the gun still pointing directly at the quaking girl. She grabbed the cotton sheet and pulled it, leaving Dizzy curled naked next to Andrew. 'Get up,' she said.

'No!' Dizzy wailed, 'No! – leave me alone – leave us both alone!'

'Get the fuck up,' Kristen said, crossing to the side of the bed and holding the gun to her head, 'and get the fuck out!'

'What?' she replied.

'I said, get the fuck up – and get the fuck out.'

Dizzy looked at Andrew, who nodded reassuringly. 'Do what she says.'

Kristen stepped back and Dizzy gingerly shifted off the bed, her eyes never leaving Kristen or the gun. Kristen trailed her as she gathered her clothes quickly from the bedroom floor.

'Hey, Dizzy,' Kristen said, as the girl crossed in front of her towards the door. 'Don't even think about raising the alarm – I'll kill you – there will be no second chance, no empty chamber next time, I promise.'

Dizzy sobbed; she was incapable of speech. She had her clothes bundled tight and she scampered quickly from the bedroom. As she left, Andrew rose slightly, his arm held out towards his departing girl.

'Make any further move and I'll pull the trigger,' Kristen said.

Kristen and Andrew sat and listened to Dizzy as she escaped down the stairs, and Kristen waited for silence once more. She looked at Andrew, who still sat, almost ridiculously she thought, with the cushion covering his nakedness. She felt completely calm, her racing pulse of a few minutes earlier had settled.

'Kristen, please. Tell me what this is all about? You need help. This isn't going to end well if you carry on.'

She ignored him. 'I've a question for you, Andrew. 'It's a bit random, but I'm just a little curious. Do you actually think there's any benefit in confessing one's sins?'

He looked at her with incredulity: 'What on earth do you mean, Kristen?'

'I'm mean exactly that – is there anything to be gained in speaking out about all those little things that you've done wrong in the past? Does it get you anywhere?'

Andrew looked at the gun. She still held it, finger on trigger. He figured he probably did not have the time to leap up and grab it, before she could raise it and pull the trigger.

'Well,' he began. 'Yes. Some people take comfort from sharing their sins – knowing that they have no secrets from God. But you, Kristen, you don't believe in God, do you? So, sharing your sins will only bring you comfort if the burden of them is too great - if that's the case, then 'yes', again. It might help you.'

She nodded as she reflected on this. 'You're right – I don't believe in God. I can't believe in God – I can't believe that any God would let the things that have happened to me, actually happen,' she paused. 'Do you?'

He shrugged.

'I'll take that as agreement,' she said. 'But I do want to tell you a few things – just to see if it helps – just to see if it makes anything feel any better – are you okay with that?'

He smiled thinly and nodded. 'Do you think I could put my pants back on, first?'

She raised the gun once more. 'No. I think not. Stay right there.'

He sighed. He put his hands flat on the bed and sat up against the headboard.

'So, what I told you about Bradley was true – he used to beat me, all the time. Consistently, punching, kicking, slapping – the full works.'

Andrew nodded, 'I believe you Kristen – and that was so wrong, you deserved so much better than Bradley, and how he treated you.'

'Yeah,' she agreed, ruefully. 'I sure did. But I had the last laugh.'

He paused. 'How so?' he asked.

'Well, a week ago I drove a skewer through his head, dragged him down the Savannah River, and fed him to the gators.'

'You did what!?'

'Yeah,' she said sardonically, 'I'd kind of had my fill of Bradley – if I'm being brutally honest.'

'Oh Christ, Kristen,' he said – both tears and fear rising – 'Kristen, it doesn't have to be like this – I'm not Bradley, I'm not your husband. Yes, okay, I might have – led you on a little – but I'm a good guy, I'd never lay a finger on a girl – I'm not like him. I'd not hurt anyone, not in the way Bradley did. Surely you know that?'

She ignored him. 'And the other thing about Bradley – you won't know this, by the way – is that when I was a kid, I was abducted by this guy – Reginald Vance - who raped me on a daily basis for about – oh, I don't know – a month, maybe – and it was Bradley who rescued me from the pit I was held captive in.'

'What!?'

'But – and before you go and get all sympathetic for Bradley – before he did rescue me, he sat and watched Vance rape me. I saw him – I was on my back on the guy's pick-up, and Vance was on top of me, and Bradley and a couple of his buddies were watching from above. I could see them all. One of Bradley's buddies had snuck in before and just watched away – watched me getting raped and didn't tell anyone.'

Andrew shook his head, 'Kristen – I had no idea – I'm so sorry. You need help – you really do, but what you're doing today is not the way to fix all this – please, let me help you.'

Andrew went to sit up again, but she waved him back with the gun. 'Sit the fuck back,' she said. She continued, 'It's interesting that you say you're not like Bradley – because the way I see it, you're just like him.'

She stood up once more and walked to the window and looked out the slats of the blinds, checking the streets. 'You've a terrific place here, by the way,' she said. 'You're lucky. Do you think you deserve it?'

'I think I bring a lot of peace and joy to the world,' he replied.

Kristen thought on this, 'Do you? Do you really think that?'

'Yes,' he continued, 'I'm not perfect – but I do my best to serve God and his people.'

'Oh, that's funny,' she replied, 'How are you serving Dizzy under that arrangement?'

He paused. 'Dizzy and I love each other,' he replied, unconvincingly.

'You hypocrite,' she said, the anger rising in her voice. 'You're fucking her because she's half your age – and because she's dumb enough to let you! You say you're not like Bradley, when all along you play for what you can get! She drops her panties and you're all over her like a fly on shit. You're just the same as Bradley – you're just as bad!'

Andrew raised his hands to calm Kristen - anger was not good, not good at all in this situation – but as he gestured, something caught his eye in the doorway. He glanced briefly, just as Kristen caught sight of the same thing.

Dizzy stood at the door, still trembling, but now with her clothes back on. Her hair was draggled across her face and she looked like she had just puked. She held a large kitchen knife in her hand, pointing it, quivering, towards Kristen: 'Put the gun down and leave him alone.'

'No Dizzy!' Andrew yelled.

Kristen stood forward and raised the gun at Dizzy. 'Oh, you stupid, dumb, fuck,' she said, pulling the trigger. The noise split the air with a crack so loud it momentarily deafened both Kristen and Andrew. She was blown backwards and fell to the floor on the landing behind her, blood pumping from the cavity ripped in her chest.

'No!' Andrew screamed. He leapt from the bed, naked, and grabbed the wine bottle from the floor. He grasped it by the neck and threw it hard towards Kristen, catching her just below the shoulder. To his disbelief the bottle bounced off her soft flesh and fell to the floor intact.

'Sit down, asshole,' she said, raising the gun at him. 'And cover yourself up.'

'Why the fuck did you do that!' he yelled. 'What the fuck did she do to you!? She was just a kid!'

'Sit down!' she shouted back. 'And don't try and pin that on me – I told her – I told her I'd kill her; she didn't listen to me – I told her!'

'You're insane,' he said, in utter disbelief. 'You're crazy, Kristen, please – *why the fuck did you kill her? Please*, stop this!'

Kristen sat back down on the chair at the end of the bed. Andrew fell back on the bed too. He had his head in his hands and his heart was palpitating from shock. He sobbed.

'Her fault,' Kristen said, emphatically. 'Not mine. I told her.'

She held the gun by the barrel – it felt warm, pleasingly so. Dizzy's corpse, blood still pumping from the wound, gurgled.

'You'll not get away with this Kristen,' Andrew wept. 'This is only going to end one way for you. The noise of that gunshot? In this neighbourhood? Put the gun down, Kristen. The police will be here in moments. Please.'

'Do you think I really care?' The emptiness echoed in Kristen's voice.

Andrew took a few shallow breaths; he could see Dizzy's blood pooling into the room. He contemplated that he had never been so close to death as he was now and rued that it made him feel so acutely alive. He sat silent and watched Kristen as she held the gun in her hand.

From downstairs, stirred from sleep by the gunshot, Billy began to wail. Andrew struggled to place this alien sound in his house. 'Is that? Is that *a baby* downstairs?'

'Uh-huh,' Kristen said.

'Why the fuck have you got a baby?' he asked, incredulously.

'It's a long story,' she replied. 'And I'll get on to it. But first, I've got something else I want to get off my chest.'

Chapter 67

Officer Alec sat at his desk thumping names into his computer. The machine ran slowly but it was methodical and precise. It searched a dozen or more police and social services databases - simultaneously pulling up a raft of information to identify an individual, list their current and previous addresses, all benefits and employment details and history, and – primarily – any criminal background, including arrests, charges, cases dropped, and convictions held. In fact – though it was slow – it was highly efficient.

Alec typed in another name from the list given to him by Grandig. Ordinarily, background checking was a corner-of-the-desk job; any one of a long list of mundane tasks that would end up on the duty desk – but today, he was supporting his new colleague on a hunch that they both hoped would turn out to be unfounded.

Around him, the station was alive with noise and bustle. Across the floor, the charging officer was attempting to file a DUI on an offender who was so out of it he could not stand unaided. Behind that guy, three hookers were bickering with each other, and verbally haranguing their arresting officer. The air was alive with colourful language – all standard, usual stuff for the Savannah PD front desk.

But Alec was in the back office, focused, and the noise in the foreground did not register nor distract him from his task. His cursor flicked momentarily as he tapped the search key again. Then, after a few seconds, the computer regurgitated another long list of information about the twenty-fourth name on the list of foster children to have passed through the Engelmaier's place. Alec scanned it for anything useful – anything out of the ordinary – then drew a line through name twenty-four and moved on to the next one; name twenty-five.

Officer Alec would be lying if he said he had never run a friend's name through the computer – even, more often, the names of some of the boys his sister had brought home – just to check, he would argue to himself, that she was not getting into anyone unacceptable. Jeez – on desk duty, anything to stop the boredom.

Twenty-five. Blank.

Tap-tap-tap. Name twenty-six; he clicked the search button again. To the right of his keyboard was his handwritten list of names; eighteen of them were scratched out. The computer chugged, *thinking about it…* Then chucked out the final tranche of information. Alec scanned his eyes down the blinking computer screen to the last known address – it was recorded as unknown. So too was the dude's employment history. A quick click showed that name twenty-six had not applied for or drawn on any social security benefits either. *Suspicious.* Like the six other names on the list he had not crossed out, it was as if person twenty-six no longer existed.

Alec grabbed a highlighter pen from his top drawer and drew through the seven names in fluorescent yellow. He then grabbed his phone and called Grandig.

'Hey Grandig, is that you?' It sounded like her but there was a howl on the line like she had answered in a gale.

'Sure it's me,' she said. 'I'm hands-free – and the car window's open. Air-con's bust. How are you getting on?'

'Yeah, I'm done,' he said. 'Look, I think we've got a problem. Where are you?'

She checked the signpost on the interstate and adjusted her rear-view mirror. 'I'm about three-miles out of downtown – I'm just heading back to Kristen and Bradley's place. I dropped by Bradley's place of work – but no one's seen him for a week. I need to check the house out again and see if he's home.'

'Okay,' Alec said. 'What's the address – I'll meet you there.'

'Sure – if you like,' she replied. 'Are you going to tell me what you've found, Alec?'

Alec scratched his chin and looked back at his list. 'Well, it could be nothing,' he said. 'But, seven of those names you gave me are nil responses – do you know what that usually indicates?'

Grandig drummed her steering wheel. 'Oh shit – serious? Seven?' then, 'Yeah, I know what means. Seven – you say!?'

Alec nodded at his desk. 'Uh-huh. As I said – I think we've got a problem.'

Grandig neared her exit. 'Shit, okay,' she said, then, 'let me meet you there. The address is 2310, Welyvan Street – you know it?'

'Yes, I know it,' Alec replied. 'I'll meet you at the IHOP on the corner, and Grandig?'

'Yeah?'

'Are you armed?'

Fuckeroo. 'No – I ain't armed, dumb-ass!'

'Okay,' Alec said. 'Meet me at the IHOP then – not at the house, just in case, yeah?'

Chapter 68

Billy continued to belly-ache downstairs, but Kristen ignored him. She held the gun loosely, waving it towards Andrew - her finger ever-present on the trigger. He was back sat on the bed, shivering uncontrollably with shock. Dizzy's corpse lay still.

'This guy Vance,' she continued, 'I'll spare you the details of the story – but let's just say I was the lucky one who got out alive. There were others, girls like me, who didn't survive – they ended up in shallow graves in the woods outside Needle Brook. Of course, you could argue that after what we went through death was the dream ticket – their lives were ruined, but over; my hell went on and on. Vance got caught though, after Bradley rescued me – and he fried for it, eventually. I got to watch the execution and that felt good – to see him suffer for what he did to me. Good old-fashioned retribution. I took some comfort there, to see him pay – it felt right.

The killer for me though wasn't being incarcerated in the hole and being raped, day-in-day-out. No, it's that after it's over, I'm pregnant. Fourteen and pregnant. And no – before you ask – I have to have the kid. Because, and let's scrub any talk about my rights as a victim and a human-fucking-being, I have his kid because my parents say anything else *would be a sin.* Clock that one, Andrew – a sin! Where do you stand on that, Andrew? Abort the runt of a serial killer and I'd be the one who sins – fucking priceless, don't you think?

Don't bother answering. Anyway, you might be surprised here but I can't stand that kid. I try my best – Jesus H Christ I try my best; I swear to God. But every time I look into her face, I see Vance looking back at me – every fucking time. I grow to loathe her; every minute I'm with her I smell him on her breath, on her clothes. I see him in her eyes and in her smile. Christ, I hated her.

Well, long story short and all that, but I couldn't take it any longer. Blah-de-blah, we do the only thing we can do – I'm not going to say it, but you get my drift right? Yeah, right. I think a few people raised their eyebrows when we buried her – but they cut us a break, you know what I mean?'

Andrew nodded. His mouth was dry as sand.

Kristen sighed, then weighed the gun in her hand again. 'I'm not proud of what I did,' she said. 'I hate myself, too. I loathe myself. Ever since Bradley pulled me out of that fucking pit, I've hated Kristen DesMoiles. But I hate people like you more. It's people like you that create crazies like me.'

Andrew tasted death on his lips.

'Look at these scars,' she said, holding her forearms out for him to see the train-tracks running across them. 'You make me do that. You, and Bradley and Vance – you're the ones that cut me. Sorry, Andrew,' she said, raising the gun at his head, 'But I came here to kill you.' She spun the barrel, then: 'One, two….'

'No! No! Please, God – no!'

'Three.'

Click!

She laughed and lowered the gun. 'Lucky break!'

Andrew began to shudder, shaking his head from side to side.

'I play that game because of you. Hold the gun to my head and pull the trigger. It's only right you play a round or two as well.' She waved him up with her gun: 'Put your pants on and comes downstairs. I want you to meet someone.'

Andrew looked, incredulously, then struggled to his feet. Every limb was shaking uncontrollably, and he had an intense urge to pee. He managed to pull his trousers on and follow Kristen out.

She stepped carefully around Dizzy's body and around the pool of blood that had spread from the landing into the bedroom, and she kept the gun on him all the time. He followed, shakily, as she walked slowly down the stairs. As they reached the hall, Billy was screaming his tiny little lungs out. 'Go in there,' she said. 'Pick him up and comfort him.'

They stepped into the lounge. Andrew glanced to the window where the dogwood tree blotted the view to the street. The phone was in the corner, but Kristen stood between him and it; any means of escape or contacting the outside world was blocked. 'I said, pick him up!'

In front of the window there was a leather chesterfield and Kristen sat down on it. Andrew picked up the bleating Billy and tried his best to comfort the infant. He was struggling to control his own breathing. 'Whose is this?' He asked.

'That,' Kristen said, 'is another rapist's little boy.'

'How so?' Andrew asked.

'His mother came into the refuge. Suffice to say I'm going to have to deal with him – when I'm done with you.'

'Killing me isn't going to make things any better, you've got to understand that,' he argued.

'I'm sorry, but I disagree.'

'Okay, but don't point that thing at the child,' Andrew replied. 'He's done nothing to you. Put the gun down, will you – please.'

Billy was howling now.

'Let's be clear here,' Kristen said. 'That child has not done anything wrong. But one day he will. Because he's going to grow up just like his daddy who raped his mommy and got her pregnant. Just like Vance raped me and murdered the others. And just like Bradley beat and kicked and punched. And just like you, Andrew. With all your sleeping around and bedding young girls, you're going to end up fucking over some other kid like Dizzy. You'll manipulate and trick her, use her for your own gratification, and dump her when you're done. You'll wreck her life. Men like you have to be stopped.'

'No, Kristen,' Andrew replied, he bounced Billy to try and quieten him, 'I won't do those things. And neither will this boy. That's not how it works. You don't inherit that sort of behaviour – it's nurture, nurture! Not nature. You must understand that!'

Billy still sobbed in his arms. 'This little lad isn't going to grow up to be a rapist just because his dad was one – so long as his mom teaches him right from wrong and brings him up well – he'll grow up good.'

Kristen leaned back in the sofa. She was tired of arguing with Andrew and listening to him squawk, Christ, he was making more noise than the baby. The gun felt warm in her hand still, and the trigger rested comfortably below her finger. She could shoot him now – *should* shoot him now. Get this shit over with. He looked so awkward with the baby on his lap, so unnatural. 'Give me the baby,' she said.

Andrew held on to Billy who writhed his hips against him. 'No,' he said. 'No, I won't let you have him.'

'Andrew,' she said calmly, 'Give me the baby – you're hurting him.'

Billy pumped his legs against Andrew. His screaming reverberating around the small room.

'If I give you this baby, you're going to kill me, aren't you?'

Kristen nodded her head. 'Andrew, I'm going to kill you whether you give me the baby or not. Please tell me, you're not going to use that kid as a shield?'

Andrew's eyes filled with tears and fresh panic poured through his body. He shook his head from side to side holding Billy to his chest. The boy wrestled against him, shrieking and sobbing.

'Put the kid down, Andrew,' Kristen said. 'I'm not going to ask again.'

'No, no, no!' Andrew cried, 'Please, Kristen, no!'

She raised the gun. 'Three, two…'

Andrew turned his face away and raised Billy up in his arms placing him directly in the line of fire. 'No! Don't shoot, Kristen, don't so this!'

Kristen could sense the adrenalin pumping in her own body. She knew Andrew was going to die. And Billy too. But she did not want it to be like this for the boy – she did not want to kill Billy with a bullet. There was a simpler way to deal with Billy. Something quieter and more peaceful.

Billy wriggled - suspended chest-height like some religious offering. Kristen could not see a headshot and risked hitting Billy if she aimed for Andrew's chest.

But Kristen saw her chance. She wondered whether there was a round in the chamber. She lowered her gun to Andrew's groin and pulled the trigger.

Chapter 69

Afternoon.

Grandig arrived at the IHOP ahead of Officer Alec so did the only sensible thing and bought herself two Belgian waffles with syrup to go. She was parked up and sat in her car and ate them with the little plastic fork, dripping sticky crumbs onto her top. The rain was incessant, and she had to leave her wipers flicking back-and-forth to watch out for Alec. With no air-con, her windows steamed up quickly and she rubbed at the windscreen with the palm of her hand. She managed to smear gloop from her waffle onto the glass.

She did not have to wait too long. Alec pulled up in his squad car just as Grandig finished her first waffle. She used her bag as an umbrella and dashed across the parking lot skipping large puddles as she went. Alec flipped the central locking as she approached, and she jumped in the passenger seat.

'Waffle?' she asked, offering him the Styrofoam carton from under her arm. 'I've not touched it – you can have it.'

Alec raised his hand. 'No, thanks,' he said. 'All good. I ate lunch.'

'Yeah, me too,' she replied. 'But only a salad. And that doesn't count. So...'

'No sweat,' he said. 'Just don't get crumbs on my upholstery.'

'Sure thing,' she replied. *Christ - who knows what he'd think if he saw the state of my vehicle*, she thought. 'So then, tell me what you know.'

Alec pulled the crumpled sheet of paper from his breast pocket. 'There you go,' he said. 'Make of it what you will. There are seven highlighted names on the list – seven nil-responses. Of which, three are confirmed dead and four confirmed missing, I presume dead too.'

Grandig scanned the names. She remembered some of them – others not so much. She read them aloud: *Joe Mayes, Christopher Stevens, Ben Delaney, Joshua Grant, Curtis Arlotte, Shawn McKerry and Timothy Bell.*

'Do they mean anything to you?' Alec asked. 'Is there any kind of connection you can see?'

Grandig thought for a moment. 'No,' she said. 'But some of these were nasty cases. Joe Mayes' dad was a sex offender who used to beat up both him and his mother. That was an emergency case – we ended up rescuing him from school following a tip-off from the principal.'

'Is that so,' Alec replied.

'Uh-huh. And this one,' Grandig continued, taking a forkful of waffle in her mouth, 'Curtis Arlott – his dad was a sex offender. He went down for that, alongside third-degree child cruelty and kidnapping, as far as I remember. In many ways not dissimilar to Reginald Vance. And Timothy Bell…'

'Let me guess,' interrupted Alec, 'No-good dad?'

'That's right,' she said. 'He was a farmer with a history of DV. Killed his wife one night then sat in his car and blew his own head off. Very nasty. The neighbours found Timothy the next morning wandering the fields.' She paused briefly and licked the remnants of waffle off her fingers. 'What are your thoughts, Alec?'

'I don't know,' he said – but, figure this,' he reached over and pointed. 'These three; Joe Mayes, Curtis Arlott, and Shawn McKerry are all dead. Guess how?'

Grandig shrugged.

'They all drowned in the Savannah River. Joe Mayes was first, in 2002 – half-eaten by gators and traces of drugs in his system. Then Curtis in 2005. Then Shawn McKerry's body washes up just beneath the Talmadge Bridge in 2006. There's nothing suspicious on file – they're all recorded as death by misadventure. But put them side by side, and it looks a little suspicious, don't you think?'

'Do you know how many people drown by misadventure in that river every year?' Grandig asked. 'Fuckadoodle - It's like, hundreds…'

'Yep. And how many murder victims get tossed in? To feed the gators?'

Grandig agreed. 'Probably a third of them.'

'So,' Alec went on. 'The Engelmaier's fraudulently complete their application for the Savannah Fostering Service. Three of their past foster kids die tragically under similar circumstances. Four kids remain unaccounted for, probably dead too. Kristen Engelmaier's husband is currently missing – as well as the last foster kid placed with them.'

'Yes sir.'

Alec fired the engine and turned his blue lights on. 'I think she's got a few questions to answer, don't you?'

'Most certainly,' Grandig replied. She sighed heavily. 'You mind if I eat my last waffle?'

'Be my guest.'

It was a straight cruise of about half a mile down Welyvan Street to the Engelmaier's. Grandig sat diligently eating as Alec drove, once or twice sounding his siren to move the slower traffic out of his way. Thunder banged overhead as the storm edged closer and closer inland. Halfway down Welyvan his car radio crackled. He fiddled with the control to adjust the volume and clear the signal of static: '…Park Avenue. Repeat. Double homicide at 1821 Davis Park Avenue. Suspect is a Caucasian female – middle-aged, dark shoulder-length hair. Suspect was seen leaving the property in a dark saloon carrying a Caucasian baby. Suspect is considered armed and dangerous. Repeat. Armed and dangerous. Approach with caution.'

'Jeez,' Alec said, turning the volume back down. 'That's a quiet end of town for a double homicide.'

Grandig wiped her mouth. Gun crime in Savannah was on the rise, she knew that as well as anyone. 'These days, I don't think there's anywhere around here where you can't run into some kind of trouble. And I'm sorry to say that because I love this city, but that's just how it is.'

'I hear you,' Alec replied.

He turned his blue lights off then indicated with his blinkers and pulled up on the Engelmaier's driveway. 'I'm going first,' he said. 'No arguments.'

'My pleasure,' Grandig replied.

Alec unbuttoned his holster but did not draw his gun. They dashed up to the front door, the rain continuing to pour, and knocked. There was no answer, so they knocked again, harder.

Alec stood back and held his hand above his eyes protecting his view from the continuous beating rain. He looked in through the front window and then peered up at the first floor. 'It all looks quiet,' he said.

'Yeah, I was out here earlier,' Grandig replied. 'There was nothing going on then. Can you kick the door in, or something? We're getting soaked out here.'

'Jesus, Grandig,' he replied. 'You can't just go around kicking people's doors down. Come on, we'll go around the back.'

They picked their way through the bins and recycling, the rainwater pouring over the gutters above. They were drenched already. Alec was far more agile than Grandig who was doing a good job of tripping over every loose item that had been left down the side alley. In front of her, Alec disappeared around the back of the house.

'Grandig, get around here!' he called. 'We've got trouble!'

Grandig battled the bins and bottles damn near landing on her ass as she pushed her weight through the narrow passage. She stepped out into the back yard and saw Alec crouched at the swing-seat on which appeared to be a young girl sleeping.

As Grandig heaved herself onto the veranda Alec was barking into his radio for the paramedics. 'I can't wake her,' he said. 'But she's alive, I think she's overdosed.'

He shook the girl firmly by the shoulders – her eyes flickered momentarily then closed again. 'Come on,' he urged her. He squeezed her mouth open to check her airways were clear. 'Come on, wakey, wakey – wakey, wakey kid.'

The eyes opened again, then shut. She was coming to, but it was a slow process. 'Can you see anything through the back windows?' Alec asked Grandig as he continued to try and rouse the girl.

Grandig stood at the rear door and peered into the kitchen. She rubbed the glass with her sleeve. She could see an open drawer, and what looked like the mess someone had made making a sandwich. And something on the kitchen table – it looked like something had been spilt. She subbed the glass again, *is that blood?*

'I think there's blood on the kitchen table,' Grandig said. 'I can't be sure, but it looks like it.'

Alec was pinching the girl's forearm desperately trying to bring her back to the waking world. 'If it's blood – or you think it is, we can break the door down.'

'It's blood. I'm sure of it.'

Alec stood up. 'Okay,' he said. 'She's not going anywhere. Stand back a second.'

He took a couple of steps backwards then launched himself at the door like a wrecking-ball. He weighed a good ninety kilos and the door split off its hinges under his weight, clattering to the floor.

'Impressive,' Grandig commented. 'But nothing I couldn't have done.'

He smiled and gestured inside. 'After you – please.'

They stepped in over the splintered door and Grandig went to the table. 'Christ, almighty. It's definitely blood.'

Alec called for back-up on his radio and drew his gun.

'We'll check the rest of the house – keep behind me.'

They moved silently down the corridor to the first bedroom – the spare room. 'There,' Grandig said. 'The bed's been slept in. And there's a used diaper in the trash. The Engelmaier's don't have a baby.'

'This shit's getting weirder by the minute,' Alec replied.

Down the corridor into the bathroom.

'Ah shit,' Alec exclaimed. 'More blood – there, splattered in the sink. There's no mistaking it. It's not much. But it's definitely blood.'

'Nose-bleed?' Grandig asked hopefully.

Alec ignored her. 'Don't touch anything…'

Before he could finish, there was a crash from somewhere beyond the bathroom. Instinctively, Alec raised his gun and shoved Grandig from the open doorway. Grandig's heart leapt as Alec swept his gun back into the corridor and checked his blind spots.

'Jesus, Grandig! Get here now.'

Alec disappeared out of the bathroom door and ran back to where they had come from the veranda. Grandig followed, her heart pounding like a fuck in her chest.

The girl, whoever she was, had stirred from her blackout. In attempting to stand from her spot on the swing-seat she had collapsed to the deck. 'Grandig!' Alec yelled above the unrelenting noise of the rain hammering the veranda roof above them, 'Get some water from the kitchen!'

They helped the girl to her feet and sat her back on her swing-seat. Grandig helped her drink some water and held her hand as Samantha reacquainted herself with consciousness. Slowly, her eyes came back into focus and she reached up to the large lump that was growing on her forehead.

'I think I'm gonna barf,' she said.

Alec stepped back but Grandig did not move. 'You go ahead kid, if you want to. But drink some more of this, it'll help, I promise.'

Samantha took the glass from Grandig and drank some more. 'Thanks,' she said. 'I feel shit.'

'Hey sweet-heart,' Alec said. 'Who are you? What's your name?'

Samantha thought for a moment. Her world was swimming in a dizzy haze. She fought to clear her mind and wash the influence of the drugs from her body. 'Where am I?' she said. 'And where's Billy?'

Grandig continued to comfort her and hold her hand. 'You're fine – just a little woozy. The paramedics are on their way – they'll sort you out.'

Samantha held Grandig's hand and grasped the arm of the swing-seat with her other. 'No,' she said, a sweat breaking across her forehead, 'I'm definitely gonna barf.'

She leant sideways and vomited violently across the deck. 'Fuck, I'm so sorry,' she said. 'That's gross.'

Alec took another step backwards and turned away. He hated puke. Just a waft of it and it would send him off. He was relieved to hear the familiar sound of the sirens approaching, cutting though the ever-increasing growl of thunder and lightning overhead. 'I'm going to check upstairs,' he said. 'Just to be sure.'

'Go ahead,' Grandig replied.

Samantha drank some more water. 'Where's Billy?' she asked again.

Grandig shrugged. 'Who's Billy?'

'Billy's my boy,' she said, in an obvious tone, like Grandig should have known. Samantha's eyes began to grow brighter as her grip on consciousness strengthened. 'Oh shit,' she said. 'Where is he – where is he?!'

Grandig tried to calm her but the girl began to sob uncontrollably: 'The woman's a fucking psycho! She's insane – she drugged me! She put something in my drink and knocked me out. Oh my God, she's taken my boy, hasn't she? Please, you got to find him! She's nuts!'

'Whoa, whoa – easy up,' Grandig said. 'He was here? In the house - with you?'

'Yes!' she said. 'He was asleep in the bedroom. Right before she drugged me, I'd just put him down to sleep.'

Samantha tried to stand but the sudden movement made her heave again. She fell back down into the seat. 'Please go check,' she said through tears. 'He was in the bedroom!'

Alec appeared at the hole where the back door used to be. 'The place is clear,' he said. 'there's no one else home. No sign of Bradley.'

Grandig looked at Alec. 'She says her baby was here…'

'The woman who lives here,' Samantha interjected, insistently, 'she's crazy! She works at the refuge – she put me up last night, but she lost the plot this morning when I told her about the guy who works there. She's gone off to find him – she's taken my baby, hasn't she!?'

'Look,' Grandig said, she took Samantha's hand again and squeezed it tight to reassure her. 'Take a deep breath and calm down. Your kid is going to be fine, okay? I know the woman who lives here – Kristen, right?'

Samantha nodded.

'She's not in a good place at the moment but she's not going to harm your baby. Trust me. She'd never do that.' Grandig fixed the kid's gaze and played her best poker-face. Inside, Grandig's mind churned – she did not have the first clue what Kristen was up to, or whether this girl's kid was safe or not. But she wanted her to calm down and not lose the plot. All Grandig could now think about was that radio call in Alec's squad car and the double-homicide over at Davis Park. And, of course, the woman seen carrying the baby.

A massive crack of lightning split overhead and instantaneously thunder boomed like a round of canon fire. The three of them ducked like a truck had fallen in the yard. Simultaneously, two paramedics appeared from the side alleyway, doing their best to cover their heads from the downpour above.

Alec crossed the deck to greet them, spoke a few inaudible words above the storm and pointed to Samantha who had just conceded to another wave of sickness. The paramedics began their work checking her over. As they did - one taking her pulse whilst the other inspected the wound to her head - Samantha looked up at Alec and Grandig. 'Please,' she asked, sniffing sicky snot from her nose. 'Find my Billy – please!'

The paramedic taking Samantha's pulse looked up from her watch. 'Hey – a car-load of your colleagues were just pulling up as we arrived. You better go meet them – I don't need anyone getting jittery with a firearm - there's been too much of that already today.'

Alec nodded, and Grandig followed him through the house.

Chapter 70

Kristen's car bumped and bounced along the Tupelo Trail and Billy looked up wide-eyed from his BiLo basket. The wipers were set to their highest speed and yet the rain still obliterated Kristen's view of the way head. The reeds, some towering nine-feet skywards bent under the weight of the falling water and they bowed down in the road ahead of Kristen - rapping the chevy as it crept onwards towards the shore.

The wheels of the car span in the mud, splattering dirt and filth up the side of the windows – this was so much more difficult than it had been the last time.

'Hey Billy,' she said, leaning back across her seat. 'Has your mom ever taken you on a boat ride down the river?'

He bounced precariously in his basket again. His face pulled a little look of shock and his arms instinctively reached out to touch the sides.

'No? That's a damn shame,' she said. 'Then you and I are going to put that right. We're going to take a trip to my favourite place, and we're going to set you off in that little make-do Moses basket of yours – and see if it floats. Are you okay with that?'

Billy blinked trustingly.

'Yeah. You'll be good with that,' Kristen said.

The car lurched into a deep, crud-filled pothole and Kristen fought hard with the steering-wheel as it jerked left and right. The engine revved loudly as the wheels lost traction. 'Jesus H Christ, we're heading to hell in a hand-cart!' she blurted. 'This is one bitch of a road, you hang on back there, Billy.'

The car stuttered and stalled, the engine spluttering in the mud. It ground to a juddering halt. 'Ah, for fuck's sake!'

The wipers continued flicking this way and that as the rain pounded the windscreen. Another crack of lightning overhead split the sky with a deafening bang. Billy whimpered.

Kristen tried the engine, but it would not fire. She turned the key again and pumped the gas with her foot. The engine spluttered but would not turn over – the car gently groaned and relaxed into the mud.

'Looks like we're doing the rest of this on foot, Billy-boy,' she said, banging the steering-wheel in frustration. 'Fucking piece of shit!'

She grabbed the gun from the passenger seat and jammed it into her front pocket. She then leaned over and grabbed a fist of the boy's babygro in her hand and heaved him out like a dog might have lifted a puppy.

Billy's neck drooped backwards, and his arms fell outwards grappling the air. He gurgled, then screamed. She man-handled him into her arms. 'Quit your bellyaching Billy, this ain't easy for me either.'

She stepped out into the storm and her feet sank six inches into the mud that had enveloped the car. Within a moment she and Billy were drenched by the hot, stifling rain. She dragged herself around the car, hanging on to the slippery, wet trunk to stop herself losing her footing. She grabbed the empty BiLo basket and staggered on down the track towards the river. Billy screamed and screamed but she barely noticed him.

Chapter 71

By the time the paramedics had sent Samantha off blue-lighting to Candler General Hospital, a dozen officers from the Savannah PD had descended onto 2310 Welyvan Street. They milled about looking busy having put up police tape all around and closed off the street. Neighbours stood at the corner, beneath umbrellas, gazing down at the fuss and excitement.

An all-points bulletin had been put out for Kristen and Bradley Engelmaier, though the general consensus amongst those officers in the know was that *he* was probably dead. Miss Chavez had positively identified a picture of Kristen Engelmaier as the individual she had seen hurrying from Andrew's house earlier that afternoon. Kristen was the prime suspect for two murders and an aggravated kidnapping this afternoon – and it was not rocket science to assume that the baby she was carrying was Samantha's missing Billy.

Inside the house the forensics team was already at work, and the lounge had been commandeered as a command post. Detectives were busy working on the assumption that Kristen had murdered her husband, and possibly three of her past foster kids – *but maybe as many as seven.* And then there was the little girl with the cornrow braids who had gone missing just over a week ago. *Probably another victim too.* A few speculated that before the night was out - this Engelmaier woman - might be Savannah's most notorious serial killer since Reginald Vance. And that irony was not lost on anyone. Overhead, the police helicopter buzzed like an annoying mosquito.

Grandig and Alec sat in the lounge and watched the furore. Everyone's focus now was tracking down the Engelmaiers. Kristen mostly. The media was in full swing and Bradley and Kristen's pictures were everywhere; every local news channel, website, radio station and newspaper carried the story live.

From within the hubbub a techie officer called over to Grandig. 'Hey, you,' he said. 'Are you the one from CPS?'

'Yeah, that's me,' she said.

'Get over here, we need you.'

Techie introduced himself as Marco. He sat at a laptop that was hooked up to a set of headphones strung around his neck. 'Do you know this Kristen woman well?'

'Yeah,' Grandig said.

'Does she know you? Will she have your number stored in her phone?'

'Undoubtedly.'

'Great,' he said. 'Give me your cell.'

Grandig rummaged through her bag and pulled out her phone. 'Here you go,' she said.

He took her phone then poked around in a canvas flip-bag full of an array of cables. He found the one he was looking for then hooked Grandig's phone to his laptop. He passed it back to her and put his headphones on. 'Call her please,' he said. 'I want to try and trace her.'

Grandig took the phone and flicked back through her 'recents'. She found Kristen's number and pressed the call button. A few officers took interest, stopping what they were doing and watched.

Chapter 72

Kristen felt her phone vibrate in her pocket. She was drenched and caked in mud. Billy screamed constantly in her ear - his little nails scratched at her neck and chest – it had taken all her willpower not to throw him into the reeds. She stopped. The rain poured down her face, neck and down her tee. She had still not reached the shore. 'Who the fuck is calling me now,' she said aloud to no one.

She ignored it and carried on a few heavy steps more. The mud squelched as her feet sank beneath her. The phone started to vibrate again. She cursed: 'Fuck off whoever you are!'

Four more steps; the mud was over her ankles and the rain ran into her eyes and over every inch of her body. The phone vibrated again. 'Christ almighty!' she exclaimed. She looked skyward into the rain. 'Fuck you, asshole! Fuck you!'

Billy shrieked so hard he seemed almost to convulse. She put him down on his back in the mud: 'Shut up, you little bastard – shut the fuck up!'

She wrestled her phone from her pocket.

Grandig – you have got to be kidding!

She put it back in her pocket, picked up the wretched child once more, and walked off towards the darkening storm clouds that refracted the setting sunlight a burning red.

Chapter 73

Grandig hung up again.

'Sorry,' she said. 'I guess she's busy.'

One of the officers behind her snorted a brief guffaw.

'Text her,' Marco said. 'It doesn't matter what you say, just text her. Say anything to get her to pick up. I just need her to connect a call so I can trace her location.'

'What the fuck am I supposed to say in a text!?' Grandig asked.

Marco replied, 'I don't give a shit – say anything to provoke a reaction.'

Grandig thought momentarily, then had her moment of clarity. She began to tap out her message – eventually clicking the send button. A few close enough to read it raised their eyebrows. Alec put his hand on her shoulder and squeezed. He had no idea. She was one tough cookie.

Chapter 74

Hey Kristen it's Grandig. how's it going girl? i'm guessing not good. bad day, huh? listen, you know this is over, right? but i wanted to say i forgive you – okay? and i'm sorry too, for my part. you don't know this – hell, i only found out earlier myself. but Vance was my dad. i'm sorry. I was a kid and there was nothing i could do. G xx

Chapter 75

Hey grandig. good to hear from you. youre full of shit. K xxx

Chapter 76

Hey girl. its the truth. you killed my sister? G xx

Chapter 77

?? K xx

Chapter 78

shit - was it Bradley or you driving? we were stood on the path and the pick-up hit her. G xx

Chapter 79

i dont believe you – you weren't there K xx

Chapter 80

Cinderella dressed in yella went upstairs to kiss a fella made a mistake kissed a snake how many doctors did it take? G xx

Chapter 81

Grandig's phone rang and she answered. A dozen officers crowded around, and Marco tapped furiously on his laptop.

Chapter 82

'Grandig – how's it going?'

'Kristen – I'm good. Where are you?'

Silence.

'I don't know what to say. That's one fucking coincidence,' Kristen said.

She looked at Marco, who shook his head *not yet.* 'Kristen, you've got to quit this now. Bring the kid back. It's all over but you can do the right thing by Billy.'

Silence again.

'Kristen? Kristen!?'

'I fucking hated you, Grandig!' she screamed down the phone, so loud Grandig had to take it away from her ear. 'And your fucking sister. Do you know that?'

Grandig pursed her lips, fighting to hold herself together, 'Yeah, I get that. But shit, girl. I had no idea. I was four years old!'

'And I was fourteen, Grandig! Your fucking dad murdered me out there – he fucking murdered me, you bitch!'

Grandig, Marco, and half the room heard the anguish in her voice. The truth of it all. And the pain.

This is the hardest conversation of my life. 'Give it up, Kristen. Let us come and get you, and the boy?'

'No – no! It's not going to happen, Grandig. It's over – I know it. I'm done. It ends tonight - on my terms.'

Marco punched the air. He was silent but he made the 'okay' sign to the room with his fingers. He knew where she was. He nodded to Grandig and waved his closed fingers to his neck - *cut the call.* He grabbed a piece of paper and scrawled down a grid reference, then handed it to an officer who took a radio and dashed from the room.

'Kristen, please. Give it up. We can sort this out.'

'Grandig – for fuck sake, smell the coffee, will you? I'm not coming in. Get your fucking head around that, you stupid bitch.'

Kristen hung up.

Chapter 83

Evening.

The police helicopter banked to the right and disappeared toward the river. Someone imposing, a precinct captain, Grandig supposed, barked orders at uniformed cops. Around her, she heard the sharp tell-tale snap of service revolvers being loaded and cops checking their body armour and radios. Blue lights flashed in through the dimming daylight from window and sirens began to wail. She stopped and watched; there was no part for her now, she realised.

Through the bustle, Alec appeared and took her arm. He was a friendly face among the throng of testosterone and shouting. 'Come on,' he said. 'We're going.'

'Going where?' Grandig asked. 'I'm CPS. This shitstorm is way out of my league now. You heard what Kristen said – this is going to end in one of two ways – either she kills herself, or we kill her. They won't take her alive.'

'Grandig, you don't know that.' He put his hand on her shoulder again. He could not begin to imagine what she felt at this moment. 'Is it true, by the way? What you wrote in that text?'

Grandig looked up. 'I've got no reason to believe it's not true,' she said. She then exhaled a rueful laugh. 'This morning I had no idea of any of this; what a difference a day makes, huh?'

Alec flashed her a brief, reassuring smile. 'Come on – there's no point hanging around here.'

I guess not,' Grandig replied. 'Beer? I know a good place out on the ocean. The Chinese food is to die for.'

'No,' he replied, then, 'Do you always think with your stomach, Grandig?'

'Pretty much,' she replied.

'I've got the co-ordinates,' he said. 'She's out by the river. She's going to try and dispose of the kid like she did with the others. You might still be able to do some good.'

'You reckon?' she asked.

'Get your stuff. You're the only one she knows here; you and she had a good relationship, right? Before all this kicked off, you and her trusted each other…'

'Uh-huh,' Grandig replied, 'I think so.'

'Well, that might be useful, don't you think?'

Alec and Grandig piled into his squad car and followed the small motorcade of sirens and flashing blue lights out of Welyvan and across the Talmadge Bridge. Daylight was weakening but the storm was not. Lightning forks danced within the heavy clouds, lighting them up like spectral jack-o-lanterns. Thunder cracked mighty booms that rumbled loud above the noise of the car. Grandig wondered what the fuck she was going to do after all this shit finally ended. She wracked the secret compartments of her deepest memories to try and draw anything about her life before Momo and the Savannah Child Protective – but they were locked tight - for the moment. She felt sure that with time and maybe with some help, she would break open the locks and chains of her past. If she wanted to. She thought she did – for the sake of her twin sister, at least. But she did not feel so resolute about unleashing the memories of her pop.

Chapter 84

Kristen could hear the police helicopter buzzing close. She scanned the horizon as best she could but could not see it for the rain or storm clouds. She supposed she was good for the time being. The thought that the police had triangulated her location using the signal from her phone and a dozen telecommunication towers had not crossed her mind – she was just relieved that the boat was where she had left it – as far as she could tell it had not been used since she disposed of Bradley.

Billy was back in his BiLo basket and Kristen had placed him at the bow of the boat. She dragged it to the river's edge, through the reeds and into the shallow waters of the shore. It felt good to kick and splash the mud off her caked pumps. As she did, another crack of thunder bellowed overhead – it was getting dark and though she knew the backwaters well - she needed to get on.

She pushed the boat out to deeper water, clambering in when the water came up above her knees. For a moment, she sat and drifted on the gentle tidal flow; catching her breath a while. In the relative peace of the rocking boat she suddenly became aware of the wailing from the basket.

She reached forward and dragged the basket between her open knees. At the bottom, Billy was sodden; this afternoon, there had been no piss-ridden jumper to act as cushion beneath his little body. 'Alright, alright,' Kristen said. 'Enough with the noise.'

She reached in and picked him up, holding him close to her chest. The boat drifted aimlessly from the shore. He was shivering, almost vibrating with cold yet he relaxed a little as the warmth from Kristen's body slowly penetrated his soaking babygro. 'You see,' she said, 'I ain't all bad, am I?'

Billy heaved a heavy, exhausted sigh and slowly stopped shrieking. The primal comfort of another human's touch comforting him.

As she held him, looking around the lush green screen of reeds that lined the meandering tributary she became aware that the two of them were being watched. The water was waveless and the rain hammered the surface of the river to a dull, leaden sheen. She glanced all around; at various points – behind, in front, to the sides - she saw them protruding from the river. Yellow, reptilian eyes – set back from dark, dinosaur-like snouts. Gators – she counted six at least, *maybe seven or more.* It was hard to tell for sure how many there were. Occasionally, there was a dull flick of a hard, scaly tail and one would drift away silently into the dark water – but then another would appear, surfacing silently like a black submarine from below.

Kristen felt a chill, despite the stifling heat of the river air. She sat Billy on the floor of the boat where brown water pooled. She leaned back and jerked the outboard motor into life.

Chapter 85

Grandig and Alec followed the squad cars until they arrived at a slipway up-river from the Talmadge Bridge. A few locals began to gather beyond the cordon that was being erected, and the boat club was being calmly evacuated to make way for the police. It had taken less that ten minutes to make the journey from the Engelmaier's and all the way Alec's car radio had been ablaze with police chatter.

Kristen's position had been pinpointed to a barren spot thought likely to be near-impossible to reach by car. Besides, it was clear she was not going to hang around for long – there was nothing there, the police knew that, apart from a small boat-storage hut and a couple of fishing huts. Nope – she was going to try and escape up the Savannah River, who knows where to, and avoid the roads all together. They would need to co-ordinate their chase by boat and air.

The helicopter had already completed one sweep of the area but had not been able to spot anything – the weather was horrendous.

Grandig and Alec got out of the car and crossed to the top of the slipway where the police were gathering again around a big, broad-shouldered guy with a greying goatee that glistened with rainwater – the precinct captain. He sported a Savannah PD jacket and had in his hand a two-way radio – he was yelling into it. Alec pushed through the throng of officers, pulling Grandig behind him.

'Captain Pagne, can I have a word please?' Alec said.

The man took the radio away from his mouth. 'Officer…?'

'Alec, sir. Officer Alec.'

He recognised him, vaguely. 'You used to work with me over on the Eastside, didn't you?' His voice was baritone deep and the rain was dripping off the brim of his hat.

'Yes, I did, sir. That's right.'

'Well, Officer Alec? We're a little busy here, this evening. What do you want?' His radio buzzed with static noises and garbled chatter.

Alec pulled Grandig forward. 'This is Officer Grandig, sir,' he said. 'Grandig works in child protective – and she knows Kristen Engelmaier well – in fact, she spoke to her a few minutes ago. It was Grandig that helped trace her location.'

Captain Pagne turned to her. 'Is that right?'

'Grandig wiped the rain off her face: 'I know Kristen very well sir, yes. If I can be of any assistance – just let me know.'

Pagne looked at Alec. 'Do you two work together?'

'No,' Alec replied. 'I've just got acquainted with Grandig these last couple of days.'

Pagne turned away and spoke briefly into his radio. Then: 'You two fancy a ride in boat?' he asked.

'Sure,' Grandig said, and Alec nodded.

'It ain't a pleasure trip,' the captain said. 'And I doubt you'll be any use. I'm guessing as soon as the SWAT team arrives this will all be over – as soon as they get a clear shot, anyway. But what the hell, nothing to lose, I suppose.'

He lifted his radio to his mouth once more and squeezed the call-button. 'Haynes, can you swing over and pick us up? I've got two people here and I want them onboard. One of them knows Engelmaier – that might be useful.'

There was a crackling return that sounded like *affirmative.*

'You see that jetty,' Pagne continued. 'Get yourself down there. The boat's coming around to pick us up. The rest of you,' he barked at the mass of officers, 'Keep the public away and seal this area off – and any sign of the FBI getting down here and trying to take over – let me know.'

Alec shook the captain's hand. 'We're happy to be of assistance, sir.'

Chapter 86

Grandig, Alec and Pagne jogged down the long jetty. The helicopter spun a low, wide loop overhead spraying rain and river water into their faces – a marksman leant out of its open side door. Pagne looked up and barked into his radio for the pilot to swing out northwards again. The reeds along the river's edge bent wildly to and fro in the churning air of the helicopter and the gusting storm.

Grandig and Alec stood at the end of the jetty and peered up the expanse of the Savannah River. In the storm and failing light it looked dark and dangerous.

Alec nudged her elbow. 'Look,' he shouted, pointing downstream.

A hundred yards out a dark grey speedboat approached. It was big and fast. Its prow sat up above the river ripping two silver wakes behind it like the whiskers of a catfish. Its twin engines roared a guttural, throaty drone. As it approached it swung around to the left, setting the jetty into a steep rise and fall on the waves. The engines cut and it sank back low in the water; it drifted in slowly.

A marine patrol officer appeared from the cabin and jumped onto the jetty – she deftly tied a rope to keep the boat close and offered her hand out. 'You three coming aboard?' she called.

'Let's get on with this shit,' said Pagne, over the thunder. 'You two – after you.'

The marine patrol officer introduced herself as Haynes - she was rugged and tanned and looked like she had been born on the water. 'The air response team have just radio-ed in. They've located the suspect about three-quarters of a mile ahead. We'll be on her in no time.'

Grandig and Alec clambered on board, and Pagne followed. Haynes untied the boat.

'Sit up front and hang on,' Haynes yelled. 'This might get bumpy!'

Momentarily the engines roared into life again and Grandig and Alec nearly fell off backwards.

Chapter 87

Kristen cut the engine to an idle as the roots and submerged branches scraped the bottom of the boat. The derelict boathouse was a just a few metres ahead of her, looming up in the half-light of dusk. The police helicopter had found her, and now circled overhead, illuminating the small craft with a searchlight that shone like a silvery disk of moonlight. It hovered lower now waiting for support to arrive. The downdraft from its propellors buffeted the river and blew a couple more shingles off the roof of the boathouse. The marksman tried to get his crosshairs on Kristen – but the buffeting weather made the shot too hard.

Kristen remained resolute. She pulled the boat around and cut the engine. She had lost count of the times she had visited this place. She had distant, childhood memories here; it had been her father who had first brought her on weekend fishing excursions when she had been a girl. They liked to watch the wildlife together. They spooked her, then, the gators. Not because she knew their danger – but because how they looked. Ancient and terrifying – like some stone-eyed monster of death. Back then, she remembered, the boathouse was stable, and they had been able to moor their boat and explore the ruined house. *How old was she? Eight? Nine, perhaps.* Years before her childhood had been stolen, certainly. And, of course, she had been here with Bradley. But those visits hadn't been quite so innocent.

She faced the boathouse. She wondered whether Bradley remained inside or whether the gators had disposed of him. She assumed they had. That shiver again; of being watched by yellow eyes. She did not bother to search them out this time – there was no need. She knew they were everywhere. Watching and waiting.

The helicopter circled low around her, tipping the boat on choppy waves.

'Leave me alone!' she screamed at it – and she pulled the gun from her pocket and aimed it at the pilot. He swung the craft backwards, pulling away. 'Give me a fucking break, will you?!'

The waves subsided as the helicopter backed off, and the boat steadied on the dark water. She stuck the gun into the waist of her denims and grabbed Billy in his BiLo basket. 'Hey little man!' she said. 'We're here. This is the place I was telling you about. You're going to be a brave little soldier, okay? Because this bit might be a little scary – but it won't take long, I promise you. It won't last long.'

Billy looked up at her with wide, innocent eyes.

She engaged the boat engine once more and put it into idle. 'We're going to go into that old boathouse over there, and we're going to take a swim together, okay? Just you and me. And I promise, it'll all be over in a moment. It won't hurt at all. You won't feel a thing.'

Billy reached up with his arms. He felt the warmth of her breath and remembered the heat of her body.

She chugged the boat forward, edging it slowly into the rotting timbers, out of sight of the police helicopter. She saw dark forms slide silently into the water in front of her; disappearing into the oil-like water of the boathouse. As she disappeared from view the helicopter rose upwards again and shone its light onto the boathouse – silvery shafts illuminated the interior, cutting through the gloom like lasers. Kristen's eyes adjusted to the dark.

Chapter 88

Bradley's head exploded in light. The little girl with the cornrow beads blinked out in an instant and was gone.

A nerve twitched and forced a tiny muscle to contract, expelling the gunk-filled mucus from the surface of his eye. A vision popped into his head - a boat! He was rescued! He imagined making a calling sound with his mouth, but nothing came out. If there was a dot of life in this ethereal place that loitered at the gate of death, it was a smudge, a shadow, and nothing more than that. The vision of the boat disappeared and darkness suffocated Bradley once more. Then something darker and more terrifying filled the vacated space of his final memory. A monster – green, leather-backed, and oh so many teeth! The light returned, illuminating its oily blackness, ensuring Bradley would remember this for the rest of eternity. The teeth closed around him and the blackness of death finally bit the life out of Bradley once and for all.

Chapter 89

Kristen looked into Bradley's eyes. She would have sworn that she saw him blink, that a glimmer of light had flickered across his face. But that was impossible. Shit – he stank like a dead fish, she thought. She was amazed the gators hadn't taken him, and she reached out and grabbed the mouldering sodden lapel of his dank shirt. The boat wobbled.

She got a good grip and tugged. At first, he would budge. But she yanked again, and something gave way beneath the damp boards on which he lay. He slid into the water and sank slowly downwards. As he disappeared, something massive swam beneath and pulled him away in giant jaws, twisting and turning and rotating in the water. Kristen held her breath and ducked back into the safety of the boat. She wondered whether this was the way she wanted to go. *Deep breaths…*

She shuffled around in the boat and pulled Billy close in his BiLo basket once more. 'Time's up,' she said, and she reached in and stroked his cheek. 'This is it, little boy. I'm sorry – but this is the only way. You won't feel a thing.'

More thunder cracked overhead, and rain pounded the boathouse in a deafening roar. She lifted the basket up and held it out over the side of the boat. She lowered it slowly onto the black water where it buoyed on the waves. Billy whimpered. She opened and closed her hand around the handle to test whether the basket would remain upright once she let go – it seemed to float okay. It would not last long, though – Billy would wriggle, or a wave would knock it – something would tip it over. Just as long as she had enough time to swim out of the boathouse into the blackness.

'Billy,' she said, softly, peering over the edge of the boat into the bobbing basket. 'You're the last one of my boys. I'm coming with you tonight – I've had enough now. You and me we'll go together. We'll go and meet the others. Timothy, Shawn and Curtis. Joe and Josh,

Christopher and Ben. They're all out here too; somewhere. Sorry, Billy. I might have got this all wrong – but you boys, you're no good. This is the best way, I promise. The best way for everyone.'

'Kristen, stop!'

The voice was familiar – and came loud over a megaphone. It cut straight through the storm and the noise of the helicopter.

A blinding light flashed into the boathouse and Kristen fell back in surprise. She hung on – just - to the handle of the BiLo basket but water splashed over its edge and soaked Billy inside. He wailed.

Kristen scrabbled up and her boat tipped from side to side. She held the basket with her left hand and held her right hand up, over her eyes, shielding them from the light that was shone into her face. She saw a boat – a big, grey marine vessel nudging just outside the boathouse. Grandig sat at the prow, Alec and Pagne at her side.

'Fuck you, Grandig!' she screamed.

The helicopter buzzed around overhead again, chopping the waters beneath.

Pagne yelled: 'Talk to her Grandig! Tell her to give this shit up – she's gonna wind up dead the second the marksman gets his shot!'

'Kristen, give it up!' Grandig cried over the wind and the rain. 'It's over, girl. Let me help you!'

'Help me – help me!? How many times have I heard that?' she screamed back.

'Kristen,' Grandig called over the megaphone. 'It doesn't have to end this way!'

'You know shit, Grandig. This is *exactly* how it needs to end!'

'Kristen – we know about the boys. We know about Joe and Christopher and Ben, and the others. We can work this out! I promise – but where's Billy, Kristen? Where's Billy?'

Kristen was suddenly alive to the elements and the howling wind and the chopping, black river. She leant back in the boat – desperately hanging on to the BiLo basket. She would end this – and end it as she planned.

'He's alive!' she shouted. 'He's in the basket! Back away and I'll set him down in the boathouse – but back away first. Else I let go and he takes his chances with the gators.'

Pagne leant in next to Grandig. 'If she let's go of that basket, he'll be dead in seconds. There's no way we're going anywhere.' He signalled to Haynes in the cabin to hold the boat still. She nodded back.

'That's not going to happen, Kristen. You know there's no way we can do that!'

Fuck!

Kristen yanked the gun from the seam of her demins. She held it to her head. 'Back away, Grandig – if you don't move that boat back, I'll shoot myself here and now and the boy dies – he'll drown in an instant!'

'For fuck's sake!' barked Pagne, grabbing his radio. He called to the marksman in the helicopter: 'Can you get a shot off?!'

There was a zing of gunshot – barely audible over the howling rain and lightning. 'That's a negative, sir,' came the crackling response from the marksman. 'I can't see jack!'

'Okay, okay – hold your fire!'

Grandig looked at Alec. Then shouted: 'Don't do it, Kristen!'

'Then back the fuck away!' Kristen called.

Haynes looked out to the three officers, but Pagne waved his hands down signalling her to hold steady.

Kristen's boat rocked on the water. She sat still and stared into the searchlight. 'I'm going to count to three,' she yelled.

'Jesus Christ!' Grandig exclaimed. 'What's the plan!?'

The rain lashed Pagne face: 'We hope to hell the marksman can get a clear shot – there's no way we can take her down with our sidearms, it's too risky.'

Kristen stood up – her boat lurched from side to side in the gloom of the boathouse. She managed to keep her fingertips round the handle of the basket in which Billy was now sobbing heavily again. She held the gun to her head. 'Three, two…'

'No Kristen!'

'One!'

Click!

Grandig's heart was in her mouth. 'A plan!' she yelled at Pagne and Alec, 'We need a damn plan!'

Kristen laughed. Momentarily, she let the gun fall to her side. The boat tipped precariously. 'I'm good at this game!' she yelled. 'The next one's a live one. Are you ready, Grandig? This one's for your dad, for you, and for your sister!' Kristen grinned, resolutely. 'I pulled the steering wheel Grandig – not Bradley. I yanked the steering wheel that wiped out your sister.'

She lifted the gun to her head, again.

Grandig turned away. She did not need to see Kristen blow her head off and the kid spill out into the gator-infested water. The marksman took another shot; and missed again.

'Three, two…'

'Wait!' Pagne yelled. 'Wait Kristen, we'll back up. Give me a minute.'

Kristen stopped. The trigger was pulled half-way, another millimetre or two and her brain would have been splashed across the boathouse. She released the pressure. She sat down in the boat and gripped the BiLo basket tight again. 'Go on then,' she screamed. 'Back up!'

'Haynes, back up,' Pagne called; then into his radio: 'Get that helicopter back outta sight!'

Lightning split the air once more as Haynes slipped the two massive engines into reverse, and the helicopter pulled away. They watched it disappear back a few hundred yards. Soon, it was nothing but a drone in the distance. Haynes pulled the boat back thirty yards – they were close enough to see the boathouse, but too far to do anything quick if it was needed. The searchlight's beam was too broad from this distance, and Kristen and her boat slipped into the darkness once more. 'Jesus, this is one hell of a gamble,' Grandig said. 'I can't see shit.'

Kristen watched the police boat reverse out. It slipped far enough away to fill her with confidence that she could end this according to her terms. She tucked the gun back into her denims. 'Are you ready for this, Billy?' she said, still holding the basket on the water by the boat.

He murmured softly.

Slowly, carefully, Kristen lay down on her back, holding the handle of the BiLo basket over the side of the boat. Water from the roof dripped down on her face and she could see the clouds breaking through the broken shingles above. She shimmied herself lengthways, then dropped her left leg over the side into the water. She felt it soak through into her pumps. Again, she shimmied further over – the boat began to tip as her weight tilted it sideways – any moment now and the boat would capsize completely. She shuffled again, bring her right leg across, then *whoosh!*

The water was deep but not cold. Kristen kicked her legs beneath her to keep herself afloat. The BiLo basket bobbed in front of her, its passenger safe, for the time being. She supported it loosely from beneath with her hands, switching back and forward so she could swim forward out of the boathouse. She kicked something below with her foot – something big.

'Keep the spotlight on the water,' Pagne said. 'Alec, Grandig - can you see anything?'

Haynes had joined the three of them on the deck and she swung the light from the boathouse to the oxbow. It was full dark now, and with the helicopter gone the water was still. They strained to see.

'I can't see jack,' Grandig replied. 'No, wait, what's that?'

She pointed out to the black water ahead of them, halfway between their boat and the boathouse.

Something was floating on the water.

'It's a gator,' Haynes said. 'The storm brings them out. He's a big one.'

Alec pointed next. 'Another one, there – do you see him?'

'Fuck,' Grandig said. 'They're everywhere.'

Kristen continued to kick. She swam forward out of the boathouse nudging Billy in the BiLo basket ahead of her. With any luck, she would have just enough time to swim out to the middle before the gators took them both. If she didn't make it that far – then shit, no biggie. If she did make it, and they didn't come, she'd tip the boy out and pull the trigger on herself. One bullet left – she knew that. It would fire well enough – it wouldn't have been submerged for long.

'Oh Christ!' Grandig exclaimed, 'Oh shit, no! Look!'

She pointed out to the boathouse and Haynes settled the searchlight. The four of them spotted the BiLo basket drifting forward on the water. It took a moment or two to realise that Kristen was swimming behind it.

'Haynes, quick!' yelled Pagne, get up there fast! We can drag her out before the gators get her.'

Haynes shook her head. 'There's no way I can do that – the boat's too big. We'll only get her out if she wants to climb in.'

'Kristen,' Grandig yelled. 'What are you doing girl!? The gators – they're everywhere!'

Kristen swam on slowly, nudging the basket ahead of her. Beneath her, within the reeds and muddy silt, large yellow eyes watched her feet kick - a swift flick of the tail next - to move in close. 'It's okay, Grandig, I know! But this is what we deserve! This is how we deserve to go – with the other boys. The other little murderers and rapists - we're all gators together! It won't…'

Then suddenly Kristen slipped silently beneath the dark water. A single, quick, toothy tug from below.

Grandig and Haynes gasped, and Alec stared in disbelief. 'Shit,' one of them said. The three gazed on as the BiLo basket bobbed on the surface still. Inside, Billy began to wriggle. Now unsupported, it began to tip gently on the water. Yellow eyes appeared all around.

Haynes made a dash down the side of the boat and returned seconds later with a long, hook-ended rescue pole. 'Here,' she said, 'Use this.'

Grandig reached over the front of the boat but was at least ten yards short of the bobbing basket. There were three gators, at least, within a few feet watching closely. Their eyes shone in the searchlight.

Haynes flicked the engines on and their roared.

'Easy!' yelled Alec. 'Minimum power – minimum power!'

Haynes pulled the engines back to idle, barely ticking over. Despite this, a small wake raced forward from the kick of the engines. Grandig leaned out, desperately reaching with the pole. They watched as the wake reached the basket and sent it tipping gently on the black water. Grandig held her breath.

The boat edged forward.

Grandig leaned out further. She reached with the pole *nearly there!*

Another little wake from the boat and the basket lurched again. Little Billy wriggled inside. A splash breached the side filling the bottom with an inch of water. Billy started to cry.

Fuck-fuck-fuckeroo! Grandig could nearly touch the basket with the end of the pole.

Haynes nudged the boat's throttle with her hand – barely stroking it. The mighty engines inched forward through the water.

'Careful, Grandig,' Alec said. 'Careful!'

Then she had it. She hooked the handle like scooping a duck at the fairground. She pulled it in across the water – more water breaching the side, but no problem. She had it fast.

The gators sunk back below the surface. But they would not be hungry tonight.

Haynes raised the engines, spinning the boat around and powered the boat away from the boathouse.

Chapter 90

Late evening.

Grandig strode into Candler General with Billy firmly in her arms, tight against her mighty bosoms. He had been lodged there since she had pulled him from his little basket on the Savannah River, as they had powered back to the jetty in the monster of the boat, and all the way here in the blue-lighting ambulance.

She had cleaned him up some, and the paramedics had checked him over. His vitals were good. He was wet and cold, and very, very hungry. But he was a resilient little fighter.

Grandig stomped down the corridors. People stepped out of her way. A young nurse tripped along beside her, trying to keep up. 'Would you like me to carry him for you,' she asked.

'Nope.' Grandig replied. 'Which way.'

The nurse skipped along. 'Down the end of the corridor – Room twenty-six.'

Grandig was still soaked. She left damp footprints down the corridor as she went. 'If you want to make yourself useful,' she said, 'go get me some food. A donut, a sub – I don't care which. Anything. And a bourbon and coke.'

The nurse nodded. Then thought better of it and went to say something, to say that she could not do that. Then she sized Grandig up again, realised this woman meant business, and figured the officer outweighed her by about sixty kilos. She also looked like she'd had the day from hell. She figured she would do her best and see what she could find in the hospital kitchen.

Billy grizzled in her arms. The fluorescent lights were bright, and he wanted to sleep, but he couldn't, not yet. There was too much light, too much noise, and something missing. He stretched – too much of everything today.

Grandig reached the end of the corridor. Room twenty-six was on the right. She knocked gently on the door.

'Come in,' came a soft, young voice from inside.

Grandig open the door. It was a quiet and peaceful room, and Samantha lay in her bed. The lights were warm and low. She looked a heap better than she did earlier today – the fluids that were dripping into her by a cannula in the back of her hand were working wonders. She was on her own – as Samantha was used to – but she looked well considering her ordeal.

'Heya honey-bun – look who I found!'

Samantha looked up, then burst into tears – her face screwed up in a ball of emotion and joy. She reached out her arms to Grandig. And Billy - sensing his mom and what was missing, turned and reached out too. Grandig handed him over, and Samantha clung to her boy – the most precious thing in her whole wide world.

Grandig looked on and smiled.

Alec appeared at the door. He saw Grandig and looked on for a moment, then coughed lightly. 'Hey,' he said. 'Samantha, right? You look great kid – you looked shit earlier – but now, you look amazing.'

Samantha smiled and grinned over the shoulder of Billy who was now nuzzling on her chest – safe with his mom once more. *Thank you* she mouthed.

Alec gestured to Grandig to come out to the corridor – to let the kid and the boy get some rest.

'Nice job,' he said outside. 'Do you reckon they're going to be okay?'

'I can guarantee it,' she said. 'Whatever that girl and little lad need from child protective, I'm going to make it my own personal business to make sure they get it. Hell, she can even move into my place, if she needs to. I figure I owe them both.'

'You don't owe them anything,' Alec replied. 'You saved his life tonight. He'll owe you that forever.'

Grandig smiled. 'You're sweet, you know that?'

Alec held out his arms and they hugged. They were both damp and cold, but it felt good anyway.

One week later.

Epilogue

Officer Grandig – big, forty-something, with her heart of gold hardened from nearly twenty years working cases in the Savannah Child Protective Unit - flipped her Rolodex round to 'E' and leafed through to the well-worn card of Kristen Engelmaier. She took it out and looked at the little girl with the frowny face and pigtails. She tore the card in half, then the pieces in half again. She dropped them in the wastebin beneath her desk.

The operation to dredge the gator pool was now in full swing. It was a difficult task – not least *because* of the gators. It had started slowly; marine conservationists had been called in to try and remove some of the bigger beasts. They had found a true record-breaker that first afternoon – a son-of-a-bitch measuring nearly fifteen feet and weighing beyond a thousand pounds. He managed to break loose before they could capture him, kill him and cut him open – they never did find Kristen or Bradley - or the kid with the cornrow braids. The dredger arrived the following day, and it spent five days pulling muck, and shit and crap from the bottom of the black water. A specialist team were currently sifting through everything that was pulled up. Grandig had it on good authority that they had already found human bones. And lots of them. Time would tell the extent of Kristen's crimes.

Grandig had been offered a week off work to recuperate but she had turned it down. She needed to keep her mind busy – not time to sit and think and stew and ponder. Christ – that would be a hell of a mistake. She knew that the police investigation into the Engelmaier's was going to take months – years, even. And that there would be an investigation into her own conduct too. But, following a brief meeting with her union rep he seemed confident that considering the time that had passed and her exemplary record since, she could expect to continue her work with CPS. They had suggested, however, a transfer – and Grandig had heard that Mount Pleasant was nice.

Her mind wandered. Her life was so much different now than it had been even a few days before. She had spent some hours a couple of night's back flicking through the paperwork that Alec had provided her. There were scant details about her sister – though more about her father. Plenty to be starting off with if she ever followed it through and sat down with a professional. She figured she should do that. And probably sometime soon. Her backwaters were clearly cold and choppy. Knowing now these few details, she knew they were going to start itching away at her curiosity sometime real soon. She just hoped it wasn't going to be like opening Pandora's box.

The one good thing to have come out of this whole shitstorm was a blossoming new friendship with Alec. Nothing romantic, *Christ no – not my type* – but a buddy to share a beer with, down on the beach. It was pleasant beginnings.

It was rocking up to five in the afternoon. The days had returned to being long and hot and boring, and Grandig liked that just fine. She had promised Momo a takeaway Chinese dinner in her hospital room, and tonight she was taking Alec along to meet the most important girl in her life. She thought the company would do Momo good – now she was on the mend.

She tossed her phone into her bag and fired down her computer. The office was clearing out and the place was beginning to fall quiet. It was time to go.

She heaved her butt out of her chair and slung her bag over her shoulder. She delved for her car keys – she remembered she still had not arranged to get the damned air-con fixed. She figured she should write herself a *Post-it* for the morning, but hell, there was never one of those around when you needed one.

She turned to leave just as her desk phone rang. *Dang!*

She toyed with leaving it, then thought better. 'Hello, this is Officer Grandig in Savannah Child Protective – can I help you?'

The voice on the other end of the line was irritated: 'Officer Grandig – this is reception. You have visitors.'

'Who is it?' she asked.

She heard the receptionist ask abruptly *who are you?* then she came back on the line. 'Apparently, you don't know them,' she said.

Christ, helpful! she thought. 'Give me a minute, I'm on my way down.'

Grandig grabbed her stuff and walked past the empty desks down to the lobby. She stepped into the elevator and took it to the ground floor. When the doors juddered open, she saw a couple of uniformed officers, one female and one male, standing in the waiting area. 'Are they for me?' Grandig asked the receptionist.

'No – they're waiting for Santa Claus,' the receptionist said, chewing her gum. 'You know the rules about visitors, right?'

Grandig ignored her and walked over to greet them. The two looked tired – they looked like they had been working an eighteen-hour shift.

'Hey, guys,' she said with a reassuring smile. 'I'm Officer Grandig. How can I help?'

The male officer shook her hand. 'Great – I'm glad we caught you,' he said. 'We were worried CPS would be shutting down for the evening.'

'Yep,' Grandig replied. 'You just caught me. I was on my way out. I hope this isn't going to take long because I have dinner plans tonight.'

The officer shifted uncomfortably on his feet, glancing back at his partner behind him. 'Well - I hope this isn't going to ruin your evening. It's just – we picked this one up half an hour ago, over on Montgomery Street – and we can't get a word out of her. We've been trying to get her to talk but she point-blank refuses.'

He stepped backwards. His partner was knelt down with a little girl, her hair braided in cornrows, sat on her knee.

'She hasn't said a word since we picked her up,' He continued. 'No one around knew who she was – they said they'd never seen her before. Are you okay if we leave her with you?'

Grandig looked on, dumfounded. She scratched her butt.

'Officer Grandig – is that okay? You'll take her right?'

You've got to be kidding me, Grandig thought. *Fuckeroo.*

Printed in Great Britain
by Amazon